The Wizard Heir

CINDA WILLIAMS CHIMA

Indigo

The right of Cinda Williams Chima to be identified as the
author of this work has been asserted by her in accordance
with the Copyright, Designs and Patents Act 1988.

First published in Great Britain in 2011 by Indigo
An imprint of the Orion Publishing Group
Orion House, 5 Upper St Martin's Lane,
London WC2H 9EA
An Hachette UK Company

A CIP catalogue record for this book
is available from the British Library

ISBN 978 1 78062 050 3

1 3 5 7 9 10 8 6 4 2

Printed in Great Britain by Clays Ltd, St Ives plc

The Orion Publishing Group's policy is to use papers
that are natural, renewable and recyclable products and
made from wood grown in sustainable forests. The logging
and manufacturing processes are expected to conform to
the environmental regulations of the country of origin.

www.cindachima.com
www.orionbooks.co.uk

For Rod, who changed everything.

❧ PROLOGUE ❧

Their target was a run-down three-story building in an area of the City of London that had not yet been gentrified. The surrounding streets had been emptied of people and traffic, and the filthy pavement perspired in the thick air. Magical barriers overlaid the soot-blackened brick, beautiful as spun glass. It might have been an ice sculpture, or a fairy castle that hid the menace within.

For once the Dragon had stayed online long enough for them to pinpoint his location. Perhaps he'd thought it safe to emerge in the small hours of the morning.

Six wizards came through the front door like wraiths, shields fixed in place, knowing the Dragon would attack when cornered. It took them less than a minute to discover there was no one in the apartment to kill.

D'Orsay followed them in. The flat was shabby and small. The furnishings looked to be castoffs accumulated over several decades. Layers of grime ground into the carpet made it impossible to guess at its original color. He passed through a front room, a kitchen, into the bedroom in the back. The keyboard and monitor were still there, a harness linked into a tangle of cables, but only a faint outline in the dust of the desk surface revealed where the laptop had been.

An inside staircase at the back of the flat led to the roof. The apartment would have been chosen for that reason, and not for the decorating. They stormed up the steps to find the roof occupied only by cats. D'Orsay scanned the grid of streets surrounding the building. There was no movement anywhere.

Something had spooked him. Perhaps the use of magic had given them away. Somehow he'd sensed they were backtracking through the Net to find him, crawling past all the online blind alleys and mail drops he'd set up to mislead them.

Or someone had tipped him off. The Dragon's spy network was legendary, his operatives astonishingly loyal. For months, D'Orsay had been searching for the flaw in it, the loose end that when pulled would unravel the web.

A loose end. Someone he could carry to the dungeon in Raven's Ghyll and torture into spilling the Dragon's secrets.

But nothing. Even worse, it was possible D'Orsay's own organization had been compromised.

The newly minted Wizard Council was struggling to overcome the centuries-old blood feud between the Wizard Houses of the Red and the White Rose so it could deal with the recent rebellion of the servant guilds. Ending the feud would be difficult under the best of circumstances, but it was nearly impossible with the Dragon fanning the flames of old rivalries, spreading rumors, and posting confidential correspondence to the Internet.

It was particularly galling to someone like D'Orsay, who had so much to hide.

Wizards were murdering each other in the backstreets of London, in castles in Scotland, and in the glittering nightspots of Hong Kong. Magical artifacts were disappearing from vaults and safe-deposit boxes and wine cellars. Traditionally submissive, sorcerers, seers, and enchanters were fleeing their wizard masters. And the Dragon's hand was in all of it.

This was the third near miss since the tournament at Raven's Ghyll. Six weeks ago, they were sure they had the Dragon cornered in a ghetto in São Paulo. Then they'd blundered into a magical quagmire, a network of diabolical traps that had decimated D'Orsay's team of assassins and left the Council empty-handed. Three wizards dead, and they were no closer to finding him than before.

D'Orsay recognized his handiwork, the elegant simplicity of the charms and devices. The wizard might as well have scrawled his signature all over it.

Most recently, the Dragon had freed a dozen sorcerers from a stronghold in Wales. That had been triply infuriating because it had been D'Orsay's own project. D'Orsay had hoped that, given enough pressure, the sorcerers might rediscover some of the secrets of the magical weapons of the past.

They found no photographs in the flat, no personal items that might have provided a clue to who the tenant had been.

D'Orsay was disappointed, though not surprised. He was confident he knew the Dragon's identity. In any case, he wasn't fussy about being right. But this was no rat to be caught in an ordinary trap. D'Orsay was uncomfortable with this kind of operation anyway. He was a strategist, not an assassin. He was present only because of the power of their adversary and the need for discretion. It was what you might call an unauthorized operation, outside of the purview of the council.

Why would a wizard involve himself in a rebellion of the lesser magical guilds? What could he possibly have to gain?

Twenty minutes later, Whitehead returned to the kitchen carrying a manila folder. "I found this between the filing cabinet and the wall." She handed it to D'Orsay. "He probably didn't realize it was back there."

D'Orsay paged through the contents of the folder—letters and copies of e-mails to and from a law firm in London, relating to the guardianship of a minor. There was also correspondence with a private school in Scotland regarding housing, tuition, and financial arrangements for the same. All of it was at least two years old.

The student's name was Joseph McCauley. D'Orsay frowned. The name didn't bring to mind any of the Dragon's known or suspected associates. He couldn't relate it to any of the Weir families, either, though it would be more reliable to check the databases. Through the centuries, genealogy had enabled the Wizard Houses to find warriors when they needed them, to hunt those who carried the gift and didn't know it. Computers only made the process more efficient.

What could be the connection between this boy and the Dragon? Possibly none, but D'Orsay's instincts told him different. What else would explain the presence of material so personal in the midst of the enemy camp? And why was a law firm handling this kind of routine correspondence? Unless the intent was to hide a relationship that might prove to be a vulnerability. D'Orsay smiled. That would be too good to be true.

This was worth spending a little time on. By now, the others were returning to the kitchen. He finished his cider and handed the folder to Whitehead.

"Find this boy for me, Nora. Contact the school mentioned in the letters and find out if he's still there. See if you can get any information from the law firm about who engaged them." He thought a moment, stroking his chin. "Check with the General Register Office also. Look for a birth registry, baptismal papers, anything at all. If you don't find any British records, try overseas. See if he's in any of the Weir databases. But be discreet."

They left the building a half hour after they had arrived, leaving a few traps behind in the unlikely event the Dragon returned. At least they may have driven the Dragon underground for a time. Any delay was to their benefit. By the time he got back into business, it might be too late for him.

Perhaps by then, they would have another card to play.

❧ CHAPTER ONE ❧
TORONTO

The August heat had persisted deep into the night. Thunder growled out over Lake Ontario, threatening a downpour. When Seph walked into the warehouse a little after 2 a.m., it felt like he had blundered into an urban rain forest. He sucked in the stink and heat of hundreds of bodies in motion and squinted his eyes against the smoke that layered the room.

It was his habit to arrive late for parties.

Seph smiled and nodded to the bouncer at the door. The man was there to intercept the underaged, but he just smiled back at Seph and waved him on. Access was never a problem.

Music throbbed from high-tech speakers wired to the struts of the warehouse ceiling. Sweat dripped onto the scarred wooden planks as the crowd thrashed across the dance floor. The black lights painted the faces of the dancers while leaving the perimeter of the room unviolated. An illegal bar was doing a brisk business in one corner, and the usual customers were already trashed.

He was stopped six times on his way across the room by people wanting to make plans for later.

Seph and his friends always held court to the right of the stage. Carson and Maia, Drew and Harper and Cecile were already there; Seph could tell that they'd been there all evening. They surrounded Seph, fizzing with excitement and the kind of euphoria that comes with hours of sensory overload. His friends were older than him, but the party never really started until he arrived.

They all started talking at once—something about a girl.

"Whoa," he said, raising his hands and grinning. "Say again?"

Harper glared around the circle until everyone else shut up. "Her name is Alicia. She just moved to Toronto, and she's totally cool."

"She reminds me of you," Cecile added. "I mean she . . . well . . . there's just something about her," she trailed off. "We told her about you, and she said she might come back later—you know—to meet you."

Prickly Maia was the only one who seemed unimpressed. "I don't think she's like you at *all*."

Maia was Asian, a part of the stew of races that was Toronto. She had an anime quality, with her spiky hair and quirky quilted cotton clothes. Plus, she could swear in three Chinese dialects.

Seph spoke into Maia's ear so he could be heard over the music. "So you don't like her?"

"I don't know. It's like, I don't trust her." Maia looked up at him, studying his face as if looking for clues, then plunged her hand into the beaded pouch she wore over her shoulder. She came up with a tissue-wrapped package. "I made you something." She thrust it toward him.

He weighed it on his palm. People were always giving him things. "What's this for? You didn't have to . . ."

"It's for your birthday. Open it."

"My birthday was two months ago." He smiled at her and tore the tissue away. It was a gold Celtic cross on a chain, centered with a flat-petaled heirloom rose, cast in Maia's distinctive, delicate style. "You can't give me this. It must've taken hours."

"It was just an art project for school." She took it from him, stretched up onto her toes, and fastened it around his neck, taking longer than was absolutely necessary. "I thought you'd like it."

"I do like it, it's beautiful. But . . ." He searched for the right words. He didn't want to start something that would ruin what they had. "I mean, you are such a cool friend, and I don't want to—"

"Just take it, okay? As . . . as a friend. No strings."

He couldn't refuse. "Well, thank you. It's brilliant." He embraced her carefully. All arms and no body, elbows down to keep a little distance. But she burrowed into him, winding her fingers into his curls, pressing her face against his shirt as if to breathe him in. Seph patted her back, soothing her with his touch. Spilling a whisper of power, but not too much.

"Here she comes!" Carson said, all excited, at his elbow. "That's Alicia."

Seph looked up to see a girl making her way across the crowded floor, dancers parting to let her through. She was small, but somehow lush, like an exotic tropical flower. She wore tight black jeans and a lace blouse that slid off her shoulders. Her blue-black curls were streaked with purple and loosely bound with a flowered scarf. She carried a gypsy bag over her shoulder. Her eyes were cat yellow.

"You must be the famous Seph McCauley." She looked him up and down like she was used to being disappointed, then extended her ringed fingers. "I'm Alicia."

"Pleased to meet you," he said, letting go of Maia and gripping her hand.

Seph felt like he had stuck his hand into an electrical outlet. For a long moment they stood frozen, the current flowing between them. Then they both dropped their hands, took a step back, and stood staring at one another. All his life, people had reacted to his touch. Now he knew what it was like.

She recovered first. "Well, well," she said, studying him with new interest, running her tongue over red-stained lips. "You *are* the powerful one, aren't you?"

"I get by," Seph said, massaging his tingling fingers, fighting down a rush of hope. Power. She had power, too. "You . . . you're . . . Where'd you say you're from again?"

"Here and there. I was just in the States, but I had to leave."

He rose to the bait. "Why did you . . . ?"

"I was totally bored." She squinted at him. "How old are you, anyway?"

"Eighteen," he said, automatically adding two years to his age. "Listen, can I . . . can I buy you a drink?" Lame. That was lame. "Maybe we could go somewhere and talk?"

"Well." Alicia surveyed Seph's friends, who were pressed around them in a tight circle. Maia scowled, swiping back her ragged fringe of hair, biting her lip and looking from Seph to Alicia.

"You." Alicia pointed at Carson. "Be a sweetheart and get us something to drink. Absolut and lime for me." She looked inquiringly at Seph.

"I don't . . ." he began, raising his hands.

"And a soda for Seph, who doesn't," she said, shaking her head.

Seph rolled his eyes at Carson, but he was already gone, hurrying to comply.

"Listen, I'll catch you all later." Seph gripped Alicia's elbow, half expecting another spasm of power, and guided her toward a table along the wall, leaving Maia and the others by the stage. "Who do you think you are, ordering my friends around?"

"And you don't?" She laughed softly. "You *should*. Who do you think *you* are?"

He'd never had a good answer to that question.

Seph chose a table in the corner between the speakers, where the din retreated enough so that they could actually hold a conversation. Carson brought their drinks and departed, giving Seph a wink.

"So why are you hanging out with them?" Alicia

asked, reaching across the table and running her finger along the rim of his glass.

"Who?"

"Your friends. The Anaweir. It must get boring, I mean, aside from being lead dog, and all."

He risked a question. "Anaweir? I'm not sure I . . ."

"The ungifted. The powerless. Even less relevant to a wizard than the servant guilds."

Seph bit back a response. They were all talented, but none of them were wizards. Nor even members of the other magical Weirguilds: the sorcerers, the seers, or the rare enchanters and warriors.

Wizards were different from the other magical guilds, because they required *charms*, words to shape the magic. His foster mother, Genevieve, had told him that much.

"I've been trying to make contact," he said. "It's hard to find other people . . . like us." There, he'd said it. "I mean, I'd like to learn more, to get some more . . . training." Implying that he'd already had some.

Alicia lifted an eyebrow. "Training comes through the Houses. What's your affiliation?"

"Affiliation?"

"Your Wizard House."

He just blinked at her, then focused on rolling up his sleeves, carefully creasing the rough-woven cotton fabric. It seemed to be getting hotter.

Alicia leaned forward, lowering her voice. "Look, I realize you can't be too careful these days. No one knows what the rules are anymore." She shook back her mane of curls. "I was at Raven's Ghyll, you know."

"Raven's Ghyll. The tournament where the rules were changed. I mean, I used to go out with Jack Swift. I can't help thinking that if I hadn't broken up with him, none of this would have happened."

She looked to him for a reaction, but he just stared at her, groping for a response that wouldn't give away his ignorance. He felt stupid, something he wasn't used to, and which he did not like.

He reached for his glass. The soda ran down his throat and exploded somewhere beneath his breastbone, leaving him breathless and dizzy. What was the matter with him? He had to keep his head.

He smiled and looked her in the eyes, a technique that had always been successful in the past. "I was hoping we could work together. You know—collaborate." Usually all he had to do was ask.

Alicia studied his face as if it were a book in a foreign language. She reached out and ran her thumb along his jawline, as if fascinated by his bone structure, then tilted his face into the light and brushed back his curls. Her touch was like tiny explosions against his skin.

"Do you know your eyes change color? Green and brown and blue."

"So I've been told." Seph shifted uneasily under her scrutiny.

She seemed to reach a decision. "Fine. I'll tell you what House I'm in. I wouldn't bother, except it's so hard to meet interesting people, and I think you're . . . you know . . . interesting." She untucked her blouse, exposing a tantalizing strip of skin, a pierced navel. There, above the waistline of her jeans, was a tattoo of a white rose. "All right," she said, rearranging her clothes, as if that explained everything. "Now you." She looked at him expectantly. "Red Rose or White?"

"I don't know what you're talking about," Seph admitted, feeling like he was playing a rigged game of Truth or Dare. He slid his hand under his collar, pulling it away from his hot skin."

Alicia looked annoyed. "Trust me, I don't care what House you're in. I leave politics to the Wizard Council. I'm a trader. I sell what people want to buy. I have to deal with everyone."

"Look, I can't tell you what I don't know." He drained his glass and slammed it down on the table. "I know I'm a wizard. I know I have power, but I don't know how to use it. I know there are others like me, but the ones I've been able to find don't know any more than I do."

He grabbed her hand and pinned it to the table. "Like I said. I need training. I have questions." He knew he was giving away too much, that it was a bad idea to let a powerful stranger know how desperate he was.

Alicia tried unsuccessfully to withdraw her hand, embarrassed by his neediness. "What about your family? What about your Weirbook? That should give you a start, at least."

Seph swallowed hard. He felt like his head was going to explode. "I don't have any family. That I know of. I don't have a Weirbook, whatever that is. My foster mother told me a little, but now she's dead. And things . . . they're out of control. If you're a trader, then find me a teacher. Find me a Weirbook, if that's what it takes. I have plenty of money. I'll pay whatever you ask."

Alicia looked across the table at him and began to laugh. "I can't believe it. You're sort of a magical virgin. You should see your expression. So serious." She brushed his cheekbone with the back of her knuckles. "You're gorgeous, you know. You have a face like a god. An angry god. And so . . . powerful," she whispered.

Seph's skin prickled and burned. Something like a heat rash spread upward from his collarbone. His lips were numb and his tongue felt thick in his mouth. He could not speak. Something sinister rippled under his skin, seeking an outlet. He felt too big for his body, as though he might split along his backbone and spill onto the floor like a snake shedding its skin.

"What . . . what's going on?" he muttered. The music clamored in his ears, and the lights intruded into their dim corner. He threw up an arm to shade his face.

She gave his hand a pat. "Believe me, it's great stuff. Like nothing you've ever had."

He gripped her hand tighter, helplessly spilling power. "What did you do to me? Is it some kind of a spell, or . . . or . . ."

Alicia fished in her gypsy bag and retrieved an iridescent glass bottle, stoppered with a crystal. "Will you relax? It's called wizard flame. The street name is 'Mind-Burner.' Sorcerers make it for the trade. Let's call this my special introductory offer."

Panic fluttered at the edge of his consciousness. "You drugged me?"

"It's an accelerator for the gifted. It strips away all the barriers and lets the power flow. You'll love it. After this, everyday life will seem like black and white."

He shook his head. "No. You don't understand. I can't control my power when I'm *sober*. Things happen."

She smiled at his distress. "Don't worry, it'll wear off in an hour or so. Here, let me show you something else." She leaned over and kissed him on the mouth. Then flinched back, fingering her seared lips. "Hey!"

His lips were no longer numb—they were burning. His skin was burning. The music assaulted him. The stench of the crowd was making him sick. He couldn't think.

Alicia struggled to withdraw her hand. "You're burning me! Let go, will you?" He released his hold on her, and she staggered backward, disappearing from his field of view. Yet he could see every person in the hall, hear a hundred conversations all at once, as if all his senses had been sandpapered.

He had to get out. He headed for the door, sliding through the crowd, twisting and turning to avoid touching anyone, leaving charred and smoking footprints in his wake. He brushed a table and it burst into flame. Incendiary sparks flew from his fingertips, igniting the curtains around the stage, the sound-deadening mats that draped the walls. All around the room, burnables ignited, vaporized, shriveled into ash. Flames licked at the walls, and molten metal dripped from the ceiling. The music still played and the black lights danced, but now a smoke alarm was clamoring as if it were the end of the world.

"Get out!" he shouted. His voice, strangely amplified, reverberated throughout the hall. Faces turned toward him, pale spots in the ruddy dark as he stood, fountaining flame like a Roman candle. His cotton clothing smoldered and smoked. People stared at him, horrified, then ran for the exit, screaming and shoving each other in an effort to get away from him.

A crowd collected at the front door, like a panicked beast trying to force itself into a narrow burrow, while embers rained down from overhead. Too many people were jammed into the opening, and no one was getting through. Those who weren't crushed stood to burn to death.

Seph charged toward the warehouse wall, arms extended, driven by nothing more than raw power and a determination not to preside over another disaster. Flame roared from his fingertips, blasting through the battered wood, leaving a charred and smoldering opening that smelled like the wood fires of winter and looked like a gateway out of hell. He stared at it, stunned for a moment, then shouted, "Through here! Go!"

The crowd poured through the new doorway. He was overtaken by the mob and carried along with the press of bodies.

Finally, he was out on the street. The storms that had threatened all day let loose, and he stood steaming in the pouring rain. Within seconds, he was soaked to the skin. Refugees who hadn't fled the scene huddled under an overhang across the street, watching him warily. Somewhere close a siren sounded.

Where were Carson and Maia and the others? Blinking water from his eyelashes, he scanned the crowd but could not find his friends. Nor Alicia, the girl who had set this train of events in motion.

He struggled back toward the entrance, against a tidal wave of humanity.

"Maia!" Maia was small, and likely to be trampled. He finally forced himself back through the opening, only to be met by a wall of flame and smoke. "Drew!"

He circled the exterior of the warehouse, desperately seeking a way in, and finding none. How could it burn like this in a deluge? Sparks gouted skyward as the roof caved in. The fire burned so hot that he had to retreat across the street again.

Pressing his back against a building, he slid to the ground and wrapped his arms around his knees. Gripping Maia's cross, feeling the gold soften under his hot fingers, he turned his face up to the downpour, letting it cool his fevered skin, wishing it could wash away the memory of what he had done.

The meeting was held in Sloane, Houghton, and Smythe's Toronto offices. When Seph arrived, they showed him to an opulent little suite lined with walnut bookcases, the carpet so thick it swallowed sound. Denis Houghton, Seph's legal guardian, had traveled all the way from London for this event. He probably wanted to make sure that Seph came nowhere near the home office.

Seph had only seen his guardian two or three times. The solicitor was a tall man with graying hair and a taste for expensive watches and elaborate pinky rings. His custom-tailored suits couldn't hide the beginnings of a paunch.

Seph couldn't help wondering how many suits and pinky rings his guardianship had paid for. His foster mother, Genevieve LeClerc, had died three years ago. It was only then that he'd learned that he had a legal guardian, a very large trust fund, and a crowd of lawyers to look after his interests.

She'd kept so many secrets. While Genevieve had taught him how to make an omelet and hang wallpaper and choose bottles of wine for their guests at the bed-and-breakfast, his feeble knowledge of magic had been acquired in fits and starts, grudgingly released, pried from her like oysters from their stubborn shells.

She had a sorcerer's mistrust of wizards and their ruthless ways, born of long service to a wizard in her native France. Her wrists had been braceleted with layered scars, evidence of the shackles she'd worn. She'd loved Seph with a fierce devotion, but seemed to hope that his wizardliness would go away if unacknowledged. Instead it had sent out long runners, climbing fences, and sprouting unexpectedly between the cobblestones.

Seph's fingers tickle, his nursery school classmates said. His teachers had loved him in those days, surrendering to the boy with the dark curls, changeable eyes, and sweet smile. The classroom guinea pig denned up under his desk and wouldn't allow anyone but Seph to handle him. The pond at the park froze in the middle of July when Seph wanted to go skating. He liked recess best of all. Sometimes it lasted all day. All he had to do was ask nicely. Until Genevieve found out and intervened.

But as he grew older, the magic grew stronger, more dangerous, more difficult to control. It had become worse since Genevieve's death. He was the ugly cowbird in the sparrow's nest, impossible to ignore.

Houghton came out from behind his huge walnut desk and motioned Seph to a table by the window. It was to be a toe-to-toe, compassionate sort of meeting, then.

Seph settled into a leather armchair and Houghton sat in the chair opposite. The lawyer regarded Seph sorrowfully for a moment, removed his glasses, polished them to a sheen, and replaced them. Then heaved a great sigh.

"So. All right now, then, are we?"

"I'm all right," Seph said, looking the lawyer in the eye, daring him to ask another question. Seph didn't want to talk about the warehouse. He was afraid he would lose control.

Houghton soldiered on relentlessly. "A bad business," the lawyer said. "A bad business, indeed. But then, with those after-hours parties, one never knows. Completely unsupervised. Often attract the wrong sort."

"Yes." One-word answers were safest.

"One hears there are drugs, drinking, and so on." Houghton paused and raised an eyebrow in inquiry, but Seph looked out the window, forcing himself to take deep, slow breaths.

"Right," Houghton said, disappointed. "Well, at any rate, we've managed to make those preposterous charges go away."

"Good."

"I mean, really. Flinging flame from your fingertips like a character from a graphic novel? Rubbish. But people become hysterical, you know."

"Yes."

"Of course, the university has some liability in this. All summer-camp students are required to be in the dormitories by ten o'clock, so it said in the brochure. And yet, there you were, sixteen years old, running the streets of Toronto at four in the morning."

Seph was finally goaded into speech. "I wasn't running the streets. I was at a party. I've gone to lots of parties, and nothing ever—"

"Then they're doubly liable. They knew, or should have known, that—"

Seph leaned forward. "You know I go to clubs. You've been paying the bills."

Houghton cleared his throat loudly. Seph half expected him to stick his fingers in his ears. "Well, then. There you are. I think we can agree that your idea of spending the summer at the university in Toronto has been . . . a disaster."

"Toronto's not the problem," Seph said. "Toronto's great. I . . ."

"No." Houghton toyed nervously with a paperweight. His forehead gleamed with sweat. "Not this time. The Metropolitan Police have required my assurance that you will leave town as soon as possible."

Seph felt a great weight descending. "I thought you said the charges had been dismissed."

"There were a number of witnesses who tied you to the fire."

Seph gripped the arms of the chair. "Really? And what do you think?"

Houghton mopped his brow with a snowy handkerchief. "What should I think? You seem to have a penchant for combustibles. There was that incident in Switzerland, the fires and explosions on the chapel roof, the . . . ah . . . demolition of the bell tower."

"I went up there with a . . . a friend. I did not go up there to blow a hole in the bell tower." Marie wanted to see the stars, Seph thought. It was after they kissed that the fireworks began.

"And that boy at St. Andrew's. That Henri Armand. Attacked by a flock of ravens, wasn't he?"

Seph shrugged. He couldn't conjure any regret about Henri. Armand was an older boarding student from Marseille, rumored to be the illegitimate son of the head of a French crime family. He was also a skilled street fighter, a talent unusual among private-school students.

Armand had considered Marie to be his personal property, like his gaudy gold jewelry and his Italian sports car. When he'd heard about the incident on the chapel roof, he'd ambushed Seph in a remote corner of the campus, pounding away at his midsection so the bruises wouldn't show.

Then the ravens had come.

"Those birds tore the boy's clothing to shreds," Houghton persisted.

Armand had been so frightened he'd wet himself.

Afterward, several of the huge black birds had settled gently onto Seph's arms and shoulders, watching naked Armand with their shiny black eyes. Never mind that Seph was just as frightened of the birds as Armand.

Well, maybe not quite as frightened.

Seph looked at Houghton and raised an eyebrow. An appeal to logic was usually effective. "So you're saying I sent a flock of ravens after Henri?"

Houghton smiled a tight little smile. "I'm saying that you've been expelled from four schools in the past three years. We are running out of options."

"But I'm going to UTS. It's all set."

"That is no longer possible."

"What about St. Michael's, then?"

"No."

Seph saw where this was going. He needed to stay in Toronto. He needed to find that girl Alicia and get some answers. She was the only lead he had.

He was reduced to begging. "Please. Let me stay here for school. There has to be someplace that'll let me in. I swear, I won't get into trouble." He extended his hand toward Houghton. If he could just make contact . . .

Houghton put up his hands and leaned away, as if to fend Seph off. "Don't . . . It won't work. Not this time. Our hands are tied. The police have made their position quite clear."

"Let me talk to them."

"You'd better leave well enough alone. Thank God they've lost interest in you. It's time you learned that you cannot talk yourself out of every situation."

"I already know that."

"Besides, it's all arranged."

"What is?"

"Your new school."

"Where?"

"Maine."

"Maine?"

"Seems a lovely place from the photographs. It's right on the ocean." Houghton thrust a brochure into Seph's face. "Luckily for us, this came in the mail right after the warehouse story broke."

Seph took it reluctantly. "I hate the ocean."

"Perhaps you'll grow to love it."

The front cover featured a sailboat. He scanned the text and shook his head. "A *boys'* school?"

Houghton shrugged. "Beggars can't be choosers. And perhaps the absence of young ladies will help you . . . focus."

"You never asked me what *I* wanted." Seph scraped the toe of his sneaker over the hand-knotted rug.

"As I said. We didn't have a lot of options this late in the day."

"Is there even a city in Maine?"

"Yes, I think so. Portland, I believe it's called." He frowned and rubbed his chin. "Or is that in New Hampshire? Well, no matter," he said briskly. "You'll need to leave immediately. The term's already begun."

Seph shrugged and slid the brochure into his pocket. Ordinarily, he would have continued to argue the matter. But just then he felt like he might deserve to go to Maine.

Or any other place with a scarcity of people.

Houghton looked at his watch, relieved that Seph hadn't put up more of a fight. "So. Well. Do you have any questions?"

"Yes. Who were my parents?"

Houghton sighed. "Not that again. You've seen the documents. The photographs. I don't know what else you—"

"I know they're fake. I've checked it out. I've been online. It's made up."

Houghton stood and fussed with his cuffs, straightened the crease in his trousers, put a little more distance between himself and his client. "I know these past three years have been trying. It is difficult to lose one's parents at a young age. And it is likely that your foster mother's death has renewed your feelings of abandonment . . ."

Seph came to his feet, and Houghton took a hasty step back. "You're a lawyer. No one's asking you to be a bloody psychiatrist." Power prickled in his hands and arms, and he struggled to damp down his anger. *It doesn't matter*, he told himself. *It's not worth it.*

". . . and now this . . . event at the warehouse. So tragic. That young girl. What was her name again?"

"Maia."

"You knew her?"

"Yes." He was back to one-word answers.

"Well, best not to noise that about. It could complicate matters just as things are settling." Houghton hesitated, then cautiously draped an arm around Seph's shoulders. He smelled of expensive tobacco, wool, and aftershave. Seph resisted the urge to flinch away.

"It may be that this is just what you need, Joseph. Go to Maine. Focus on your studies. Get away from all this for a while." The lawyer's voice was not unkind. "You've managed to come away without a police record. Your grades are good. See if you can finish strong at the Havens. Then we can begin to talk about University. Perhaps you can even come back to Toronto for school."

Two more years, Seph was thinking. Two more years, and I claim the trust fund and dismiss Sloane, Houghton, and Smythe. Two more years, and I'll have the time and money to find out who I really am.

Two years sounded like an eternity.

❧ CHAPTER TWO ❧
THE HAVENS

Seph pressed his face against the cool glass of the airplane window, watching the rugged New England coastline pass beneath him. From this altitude, the Atlantic seemed a gentle lake, a deep gray-green with a delicate frosting of lace where it broke against the beaches.

The music pounding through his headphones was not enough to occupy his relentless mind.

He thrust his hand under his sweatshirt, pulling free the half-melted cross Maia had made for him. Surprisingly old-fashioned for a free spirit like Maia. When he closed his eyes, he could still feel the ropy intensity of her embrace.

Seph didn't consider himself particularly attractive. He knew enough about art to realize he met no classical standard of beauty. His face looked like something he needed to grow into: all bony prominences and sharp angles. His hair tumbled into unruly loose curls if he didn't gel it into submission. He'd grown so recently that he still felt awkward and poorly put together. But girls still made excuses to touch him, to play with his hair. Maia had always talked about his eyes: how they changed color with the light—brown, and then green or gold.

And now she was dead. Because of him.

He stared down at his hands. Murderer's hands, though they looked like normal flesh and bone. He was . . . pathological. Was it merely a lack of knowledge, or was it some kind of fatal flaw?

He pressed his fist against his chest, imagining that he could feel the weight within. "*Vous avez un cristal sous votre coeur,*" Genevieve had said. *You have a crystal beneath your heart.* A source of power that is different for each of the guilds. For sorcerers, enchanters, warriors, and seers, the use of power is more or less hardwired.

But wizards needed training in order to use and control their power. Genevieve had told him that when magical accidents happened. So he wouldn't think he was possessed, as the Jesuits had claimed when he was still small.

But she hadn't told him the truth about his parents. And for that, he felt betrayed.

He needed a teacher. If he couldn't learn to control his gift, it was better not to have it at all. Could the stone be removed, like a diseased gallbladder?

At least Genevieve had not had to deal with the warehouse. She would have gone to church and lit a candle and prayed for him. She would tell him that in God's eyes he was perfect, though how she knew this, Seph couldn't say.

Seph's ears told him they'd begun their descent. The aircraft was a sixteen-seater, with only six other passengers—hunters and tourists, by the looks of them. Seph liked the intensity of small planes. Perhaps he'd buy a plane now that he was old enough for flying lessons. He smiled at the thought, his first smile of the day, and pulled off his headphones.

The plane banked and circled. The ground rushed toward them and bumped down on the grassy runway. Before they had rolled to a stop, he was on his feet, pulling his bag from the overhead compartment.

He closed his eyes and centered himself, as Genevieve had taught him. *You can do this. You've done it before. You're good at meeting people.* Only, this new school was small, about one hundred students, according to the brochure. He'd never done well at small schools. He made too many waves to survive in a small pond.

Somehow, he had to find a way to succeed here. Two years, and he could go back to the city and disappear.

The airport boasted one battered, sheet-metal building. Grass feathered the asphalt of the parking lot.

A man waited by the metal fence that surrounded the landing strip. He was tall—taller than Seph by at least half a foot. He was absolutely bald, but whether he was naturally so or shaved his head, Seph couldn't tell. Despite the brisk weather, he wore a white, short-sleeved golf shirt that showed off his muscular arms. He looked to be about fifty, but it was hard to tell with bald men.

Seph waited until the crew had unloaded the baggage

compartment, then pulled his other bag from the cart, swinging it over his shoulder. As he walked toward the gate, the man stepped forward to meet him.

"You must be Joseph McCauley," he said in an upper-class British accent. "I'm Dr. Gregory Leicester, headmaster of the Havens."

Up close, the headmaster's eyes were a peculiar flat gray color, like twin ball bearings. The absence of hair and the fact that his lips were the same color as the rest of his face gave him a strange, robotic quality.

Relieved that the headmaster didn't offer his hand, Seph conjured a smile and said, "Pleasure to meet you, sir." *Must be a small staff,* he thought, *if the headmaster comes to collect you at the airport.*

"Is that all you have?" Dr. Leicester asked, nodding toward the luggage.

"That's all. I shipped some books ahead, and my computer." Seph traveled light, which was convenient when you moved around as much as he did.

Of the half dozen vehicles clustered in the lot, Dr. Leicester directed Seph toward a white van with THE HAVENS and a sailboat stenciled in gold on the door. The van was unlocked. The headmaster took Seph's bags and tossed them easily into the backseat. He motioned Seph to the shotgun position, and climbed in on the driver's side.

"We're just about an hour away from school," Leicester explained. "It will give us a chance to get to know each other."

They pulled out of the gravel parking lot and turned

onto a two-lane highway. From the maps, Seph knew there was a small town south of the airport. But their destination was about fifty miles north, with nothing much in between. Why would anyone build a private school in such a remote location? A hunting lodge or a prison, he could understand.

"Did you come directly from St. Andrew's, or did you spend some time at home?" Leicester asked, keeping his gaze on the road.

"I came from Toronto. I was at a camp there all summer," Seph replied. His head ached, as if metal bands were tightening around his forehead, and he felt dizzy and disoriented. It could've been the aftereffects of the flight, though he was usually a good flyer.

They swept past two gas stations, a scattering of houses, and then plunged into a thick forest of pine and aspen. He lowered the window, hoping the fresh air would revive him, and was rewarded with the sharp scent of evergreen.

"You've had a long day, then." Dr. Leicester broke into his reverie. "I hope you were able to sleep on the plane."

"Yes. Some."

"Where are you from originally?"

"I was born in the States, but I grew up in Toronto."

"Do your parents still live in Toronto?"

"My parents are dead." Seph stared straight ahead.

"Ah. Well. We've corresponded with your guardian, Mr. Houghton. I assume you have relatives in England, then?"

"Mr. Houghton is just a solicitor. An attorney. I don't

know much about my family." *Nothing, in fact.*

What he'd been told of his parents was frail and colorless, like a line drawing, an outline of a story without the flesh and bone. His mother was a Toronto-based flight attendant; his father a software entrepreneur. They had died in a fire in their California canyon home when Seph was a year old. Genevieve LeClerc had been his childcare provider, and became his foster mother. That story had been repeated to him since he was very small.

And now he knew it was a lie.

"I think you'll like it here, Joseph, once you settle in," Leicester said. "I know you've changed schools several times. Often talented students get into difficulty when their needs are not met. Here at the Havens we rarely lose a student. In fact, we integrate high-achieving secondary students into our more specialized programs. We're believers in tailoring the curriculum to the student."

"I see," Seph said. "That sounds like a good approach."

He couldn't help being distracted by the view. He was a city creature. For the past half hour, he'd seen nothing but trees on either side of a fragile strip of pavement. Not even another car on the road. "It seems . . . um . . . isolated."

"You can wander for miles and never leave the property," Leicester said, as if that were a plus.

Many of the crossroads were now dirt roads that carried the names of beaches. Following a long stretch of unbroken trees, they reached a turnoff marked with a tasteful brick-and-stone sign that said, THE HAVENS and PRIVATE PROPERTY.

A high stone wall extended in both directions, as far as he could see. To keep the trees from wandering, no doubt. He blinked and rubbed his eyes. The wall had a smudged and fuzzy quality, as if shrouded in tendrils of mist.

Maybe he had a migraine coming on.

They turned right, through a high wrought-iron gateway onto an oiled dirt road.

Along the lane, the trees stood so close Seph could have reached out and touched them. Their leafy tops arched and met overhead, sieving the light into frail streamers that scarcely colored the ground. The air hung thick with the scent of green things long dead and half decayed. They drove through dense woodland until the trees thinned and the light grew. Glimpses of water and a freshening of the air said they'd reached their destination.

They pulled up before a large cedar-and-stone building separated from the water by a broad boardwalk. A long dock ran out into the harbor. Several sailboats bobbed alongside, sails furled and tied to the masts.

"This is the administration center," Dr. Leicester explained. "The cafeteria, gymnasium, library, commons areas, and other student services are all in here." He drove a hundred yards farther and stopped in front of another building. "This is Gareth Hall. Most classes are held here, with the exception of physical education, art, and music. We've been in session for several weeks now, so you'll have some hard work ahead of you."

Art and music shared their own building. It couldn't

really be called a campus—there wasn't enough open space for that. Each building stood isolated in its own clearing, the forest crowding in on all sides, as if struggling to hold it at bay. The tall, straight trunks of trees marched away until they collided in the gloom.

All of the buildings were of similar construction, as if the school had erupted, fully formed, out of the ground. It was a jarring contrast to St. Andrew's, with its ancient stone lecture halls, bell towers, and green lawns, the mountains framing every vista. And UTS—he shoved images of the city out of his mind.

"You must see a lot of wildlife here," Seph observed, because Dr. Leicester seemed to be expecting him to comment. Middle of nowhere, he thought.

"A little bit of everything: moose, bear, wolves, deer. The raccoons and bears can be a problem." Leicester laughed like it didn't come easy. It was hard to imagine this man presiding at a fundraising dinner or glad-handing parents.

They stopped in front of a more modest three-story structure, stone and glass and cedar, similar in design to the other buildings, but on a smaller scale. "This is your dormitory." He handed Seph a key card. "You're in suite 302. Need help with your luggage?"

"No, thanks. I'm fine." Seph climbed out and retrieved his bags from the back seat.

"I'll arrange for one of our students to give you a full tour before Monday. If you're hungry, you ought to be able to find something in the cafeteria in the admin. building."

Seph wasn't hungry. His headache was worse. He felt as if someone had been beating against his skull.

"Swimming is at four thirty," Leicester said. "Change into your swim gear and follow the signs to the cove. Everyone will be down there, and you'll have the opportunity to meet the other boys." The headmaster didn't give him a chance to argue. The van lurched forward, spitting gravel from beneath its wheels.

Seph looked around. Sunlight painted the tops of the trees, and here and there a break in the canopy overhead allowed it to penetrate all the way to the forest floor. Otherwise, the ground was bathed in a cool green twilight. Leaves shuffled overhead and branches rattled in the wind. A squirrel scolded him furiously from a nearby stump. He was already chilly, even in his hoodie. Maybe this was swimming weather in Maine, but not where he came from.

Wherever that was.

He slung his bags over his shoulder, ignored the elevator, and climbed three flights of stairs to his floor. His room was at one end of the building, rather isolated, off a short corridor. Leicester hadn't said anything about a roommate, and Seph wasn't surprised to find he had a room to himself. Students at expensive schools were used to their own space and plenty of it.

Each school he'd attended was captured by single image in his mind: the cavernous great hall at Dunham's Field School in Scotland; the view from the bell tower at St. Andrew's in Switzerland; Montreal illuminated at dusk in midwinter, where the sun seemed to set in midafternoon.

This room boasted a gas fireplace and a screened porch overlooking the woods. The furniture included a single bed with a heavy oak headboard and a thick comforter with a pine-tree pattern, a dresser, a serviceable desk and bookcase, two upholstered chairs for guests, rag rugs on the floor, and ceramic tile in the bathroom.

The walls had been left empty, a fresh canvas for someone to paint on. Only, Seph didn't do much to personalize his rooms anymore. There was no point. He'd learned to carry his sense of self around with him.

A basket of fruit and several bottles of water were arranged on a small table with a note, *Welcome, Joseph,* imprinted on cream-colored stock embossed with a sailboat.

His books had arrived and were waiting in boxes in front of the bookcase. His computer had been unpacked and left on the desk. There was no phone, however, and no data port that he could find. Pulling out his cell phone, he scanned the screen. No signal. He swore softly and returned it to his jeans pocket.

Methodically, he unpacked his bag, put away his toothbrush and paste and the rest of his washroom supplies, and took two ibuprofen. He located the electrical outlets, set his MP3 player in its cradle, and placed the speakers. He had the best sound system money could buy. He turned the music up loud, hoping it might draw visitors. It didn't.

His clothes only occupied three drawers out of six. He moved his books from the box to the bookcase, running his fingers over the familiar titles in French and English.

Maybe he didn't need to carry so many books around with him, either. How often did he read a book more than once? He'd learned to pare down, to simplify, like a business traveler trying to force his life into a carry-on.

By four o'clock his headache had eased somewhat.

He wanted more than anything to lock the door and collapse into bed. But it was his custom to get introductions over quickly.

There was no answer at any of the nearby rooms, until he knocked on the door of the room at the far end of the hall, on the other side of the staircase. A solid, athletic-looking black student answered, clad only in swimming trunks. A silver amulet hung from a chain around his neck: a stylized Hand of Fatimah.

Protection against the evil eye.

Seph smiled and stuck out his hand. "I'm Seph McCauley. I just moved in at the other end of the hall." *Good social skills*, it always said in his evaluations, along with *Excels academically*.

"I'm Trevor Hill," the boy replied, grasping Seph's hand, then flinching and letting go quickly. "Whoa, you shocked me!"

Seph shrugged, accepting no credit or blame. How often had he heard that one?

"I heard someone new was coming this week." Trevor's voice was like a slow-moving river: warm and rich with Southern silt. "Would you like to come in?"

Trevor stepped aside so Seph could enter. It was a mirror image of Seph's room, but seemed smaller, because it was crowded with extra furniture: a small refrigerator, a television, posters of sports figures. Seph's room was spartan in comparison.

"This is cool!" Seph said. "Did you do all this in the last three weeks?"

"Nah, I've had the same room for three years." Trevor glanced nervously at his watch. "I guess we have a little time. You can clear the stuff off of that chair and sit."

Seph sat in the desk chair. "Are you a senior?" he asked, trying to put the other boy at ease—knowing he could do it with a touch of his hand, but best not to try that with someone he'd just met.

"Junior," Trevor replied. "I'm from Atlanta. Buckhead area. Got no business being so far north. I about freeze to death every fall." He snatched up a heavy sweatshirt from the bed and pulled it over his head.

"I'm a junior, too," Seph volunteered.

Trevor asked the inevitable question. "Where're you from?"

"Toronto, but my last school was in Switzerland. So I'm used to the cold."

"Switzerland, huh?" Trevor stopped looking nervous and started looking impressed. "Why'd you leave?"

"It didn't work out." Seph rolled his eyes.

Trevor nodded, as if this answer wasn't unexpected. "The Havens your parents' idea?" He gestured vaguely at their surroundings.

"My parents are dead. I have a guardian. A lawyer. He set it up," Seph replied, thinking that he should buy a T-shirt that said, ORPHAN FROM TORONTO. It would save time in these situations.

"So what's the deal here? How do you get along with the staff?" Seph continued. Not that Trevor's advice was likely to be helpful in his case.

Trevor leaned forward, putting his hands on his knees. "Oh, I was in trouble a lot before I came here, too. You just need to follow the rules. Do that, and you'll be okay. They specialize in boys who've had problems at other places."

"Really?" Great, Seph thought. I've landed in some kind of upperclass reform school. Trevor seemed normal enough, though, and he'd been there three years. "Do they kick you out if you get in trouble?"

"No one gets expelled from the Havens," Trevor said. "You'll see. Their program is very—what they call—effective."

Something in the way he said *effective* sounded almost sinister. It made Seph want to change the subject. Trevor's laptop caught his eye. "I have my computer set up, but I don't see any jacks in my room. Is the cabling included or do I have to pay for wiring?"

"We don't have our own Internet access," Trevor said.

Seph stared at him. "Why not? It's so easy. They could use a campus-wide wireless network if they didn't want to lay cable."

Trevor shook his head. "No, I mean, we're not allowed. They have computers in the library. You can do searches in there if you want, but they screen the sites."

"That's crazy. They can't do that. I have friends online." Seph didn't remember *that* being mentioned in the glossy brochure.

Trevor shrugged and looked at his watch again. "Well,

it's about time for swimming. You'd better get changed if you don't want to be late."

Seph rubbed his aching temples. "I'm going to pass. It's been a long day already."

Trevor's eyes widened in surprise. "Dr. Leicester excused you?"

"Not exactly."

Trevor stood up. "Then you'd better get ready."

It seemed that the visit was over, so Seph stood also. "Oka-ay, guess I'll get ready, then," he said.

"I'll wait for you, if you hurry up."

But Seph didn't hurry fast enough, because a few minutes later he heard Trevor at his door. "I'm going ahead. I'll see you down there."

Seph changed into his trunks and pulled his sweatshirt and jeans on over them. Descending the stairs two at a time, he left the building and followed a wood-chip path back through the woods toward the waterfront. He didn't see any students around; they must've already gone down to the cove. A sign at the dock pointed him to the right, down the shoreline, to a well-worn path along the water.

A cold slither up his spine said he was being watched. Twice, he turned and scanned the path behind him, then shrugged and walked on. Finally, the path turned back into the woods.

"Hey."

He turned again, and this time a stocky boy with wire-rimmed glasses and a ruddy complexion stood in the middle of the path. He wore husky-style jeans and a sweatshirt, and blinked his eyes really fast, like he was nervous.

"Hey," Seph said. "You late for swimming, too?"

"No, I . . . ah . . . I d–don't . . ." The boy began coughing, struggling to draw breath. He groped in his pocket and produced an inhaler. He took a long pull off of it, and put it back. Then, with a determined look on his face, he extended his hand to Seph.

"I'm Seph McCauley," Seph said, thinking maybe you got excused from swimming if you had asthma. He gripped the other boy's hand, then flinched as he recognized the sting of power. "Hey! Are you . . . ?"

"Listen. I n–need to talk to you." The boy looked up and down the path, mopping sweat from his forehead with the sleeve of his sweatshirt.

"I'd really like to talk to *you*," Seph said, unable to believe he'd met two wizards in the space of a few weeks. "But I have to get to swimming. Could we meet later, maybe at dinner?"

"No. I c–can't . . . That won't . . ."

"Hello, gentlemen." Seph looked up to see a handsome young man in a tweed sport coat with leather patches on the elbows, carrying a battered leather briefcase.

"H–hello, Aar . . . M–Mr. Hanlon." The other student looked petrified, like he was about to wet himself. Or have another asthma attack.

"Joseph. Aren't you supposed to be at swimming?" Mr. Hanlon asked, smiling.

"I was just on my way."

"Good. Best be going. Dr. Leicester doesn't like it if you're late." Hanlon placed a hand on the boy's shoulder and propelled him down the path the other way.

"I didn't get your name!" Seph called after him. But the boy only hunched his shoulders and kept walking.

That guy has issues, Seph thought, continuing down the path. I don't know how much help he'll be. But I'll try to find him at dinner.

Eventually, the path broke out of the trees at a place where the ocean cut back into the shoreline, creating a protected inlet, lined with stones, out of sight of the school buildings.

There must have been sixty boys in the water, their heads sleek and dark against the gray surface. A few more were stripping off their sweatshirts on the shore. All of them looked miserably cold. Seph spotted Trevor treading water ten yards out.

Dr. Leicester stood on the shoreline, dressed in a heavy sweatshirt, jeans, and windbreaker. When he saw Seph, he blew sharply on a whistle to get everyone's attention. "Boys, meet Joseph McCauley. This is his first day at the Havens, and he is late for swimming."

The reaction to this was remarkable. The other boys all looked away or looked down, as if they wanted to avoid any connection to his transgression. Some of them peered back toward him, when they thought Leicester wasn't looking.

Seph smiled, lifting his hands in apology. "Sorry. I got confused. I was waiting for everybody at the spa."

Laughter floated across the water, then quickly dwindled under Leicester's disapproving gaze. The headmaster didn't seem susceptible to Seph's legendary charm.

Seph left his clothes on a pile of rocks some distance

from the water's edge, and hobbled over the stony beach to the water. He'd hoped that the water would be warmer than the air, but was disappointed. It was like stepping into snowmelt. His feet went numb immediately. He waded out to his knees, then to his waist, gasping.

The water was murky and unpleasant. The rocks along the bottom were slippery and invisible, so that even in the cove the waves threatened to knock him over. Something squirmed under his left foot and he thrashed backward, into unexpectedly deep water. His head went under, and he swallowed a mouthful. He came up like a sounding whale, spraying water everywhere.

He'd had enough. A few quick strokes took him back to the shallows. Shivering, teeth chattering, he hauled himself onto the shore. He'd almost made it back to his muddle of clothes when someone gripped his arm.

It was Trevor, covered in gooseflesh, lips pale with cold, water sliding off his dark body onto the rocks. "Get back in the water, Seph," he said, without meeting Seph's eyes. "Just do it. Come on." He put a cold hand on Seph's shoulder as if to urge him along.

Seph blinked at him. He looked over his shoulder at Dr. Leicester, who stood expressionless, watching. All right, he thought. If he was going to try to stay here two years, it was best not to get into a battle of wills on his first day. Gritting his teeth, he picked his way back across the beach and waded out into the water, not looking back to see if Trevor was following.

This time the water seemed more tolerable. Maybe he was getting used to it. His extremities tingled as the feeling returned, and he was no longer shivering. He strode ahead more confidently, continuing until the water lapped at his collarbone. Though the sun was gone, intercepted by the surrounding trees, he felt almost warm.

He looked around. The other boys stood as if frozen, staring down at the water in disbelief. Another minute passed, and the surface of the water began to steam in the cold air. He might have been neck deep in the warm Caribbean.

No. This can't be happening. Seph looked over at Leicester, who was in conversation with one of the boys on shore. He hadn't noticed that anything was amiss. Seph splashed toward a crowd of boys standing to one side, near the shoreline, positioning himself so that his head was just one of many pocking the gray surface. *Now, just relax*, he commanded himself, closing his eyes, trying to loosen his muscles, to empty his mind.

How long could he last? He was in trouble already, and it was just the first day.

He sorted through a litter of memories from his school career. The homicidal ravens at St. Andrew's. The explosions and fires in Scotland. The wolves that had startled the nuns in Philadelphia.

By now the water was close to spa temperature. All conversation in the cove had died. The swimmers looked down at the vapor collecting at the surface, rising up around them like morning mist on an upland lake. No one said a word, to each other or to Leicester.

Finally, the boy who had been speaking with the headmaster broke away and stepped into the water. He stumbled backward with a yelp of surprise and sat down, hard, on the rocks. Gregory Leicester swung around and stared at the boys in the water and the steam boiling up around them. Then he began searching the faces of the boys in the water until he found Seph.

Try as he might, Seph couldn't look away. The headmaster stood, studying him like a specimen on a slide. No questions, no disbelief, no challenge or confusion, only this intense and clinical scrutiny, as if he were looking into Seph's soul with full knowledge of what lay within. Then Leicester smiled like it was Christmas.

Shuddering, Seph took a step backward.

The headmaster's gaze shifted to include the whole group. "Gentlemen, perhaps it *is* a bit brisk for swimming after all. You are dismissed to your own pursuits until dinner."

For a moment, no one moved. Then the exodus began, silent as lemmings in reverse. Seph left the water on the far side of the cove, keeping as much distance between himself and Leicester as possible. He pulled his sweatshirt and jeans over his wet skin and picked up his shoes, unwilling to linger long enough to put them on. Slinging his towel about his shoulders, he followed the others toward the woods.

"Joseph."

Seph froze in midstride and stood waiting without turning around. The headmaster's gaze pressed on the back of his neck.

"Come up to my office after dinner. I think it's time I explained a bit more about our program."

Seph nodded and walked on, into the trees.

CHAPTER THREE
A MAGICAL COLLABORATIVE

Seph awoke to a loud pounding. Still groggy, he stumbled to his door and opened it. It was Trevor, dressed for the outdoors, smiling tentatively.

"Seph. Supper's at seven thirty. We have time before then, if you want to look around."

Seph rubbed his eyes and looked back at his bed. "Sure. Thanks. I'm glad you knocked. I might've slept right through." He yawned. "Do we have to dress for dinner?"

"Collared shirt or sweater. No jeans or sweats."

"Okay. Give me a minute."

Trevor hovered by the door while Seph changed his clothes and ran his fingers through his hair. They descended the stairs and pushed through the front doors.

The frail autumn daylight had already fled. It would have been pitch-black under the trees, save for the tiny lights that outlined the paths between buildings. Seph braced himself for questions or comments about the peculiar events in the cove, but none came, so Seph said, "That was pretty weird. What happened at swimming, I mean."

"You never know what's going to happen around here," Trevor said, shrugging.

"What do you mean? Are you saying weird things have happened before I—before now?"

"I mean nothing." Trevor hunched his shoulders like a turtle retreating into his shell.

"I ran into this guy in the woods. A student, I think, kind of stocky, with glasses and an inhaler. Do you know who that would've been?"

Trevor looked him in the eyes. "I don't recollect anyone like that."

Seph debated whether to force the issue. He guessed he could get what he wanted from Trevor. But decided not to push it. It's my first day, he thought. I can use all the friends I can get.

Trevor took his role as tour guide seriously, pointing out features of the campus: the tennis courts, the amphitheater.

"There's almost a hundred students here, freshmen through seniors. They come from all over, and a lot of them get scholarships. There's also a bunch of alumni living here on campus, doing research with Dr. Leicester." They passed more dormitory buildings. "All the dorms are pretty much the same. The alumni have their own dorm, cafeteria, and commons area."

"Why would alumni hang around on campus after graduation?" Seph asked. "What about college?"

Trevor looked away, focusing on the path ahead. "You'd have to ask them."

They walked through Gareth Hall, the classroom building, past empty lecture halls. "School's been going for a couple weeks, so you're going to have to catch up with your assignments," Trevor said. "Let me know if you need help with anything."

The art and music building was farther north along the shoreline. "They make us all take a musical instrument," Trevor explained. Seph nodded. Typical. He'd brought along his saxophone.

Next Trevor led him down to the waterfront and out onto the dock. "Dr. Leicester's a sailing fanatic. Our sailing team has held the Atlantic Seaboard Scholastic Cup for three years. Everyone helps."

"Mmmm," Seph replied, committing himself to nothing. He couldn't very well tell Trevor he expected to be gone by Christmas, given the start he'd made at the cove.

"This is our boathouse." Trevor pushed open the door to the small, weather-beaten building Seph had noticed when he arrived. It was a plain, square wooden structure with a rough planked floor. A narrow wooden walkway ran along the far side of the room, surrounding the boat slip. The water sucked and slapped at the pilings underneath. The building smelled of marine gasoline and what Seph assumed to be fish guts.

"They keep the motorboat in here most all the time, and sometimes the sailboats if they need to be fixed.

You'll get really good at slapping on varnish, believe me."

That was no problem. Seph was used to hard work. He'd spent every summer cleaning and changing beds and washing dishes at Genevieve's bed-and-breakfast.

"Time to eat," Trevor announced, and turned back toward shore.

The dining hall was on the first floor of the admin. building, with a full wall of glass overlooking the water. Servers circulated through the room, clearing tables and refilling water glasses.

In addition to burgers and pizza, there was hand-carved roast beef, a fish entrée, a sauté of the day, a vegetarian wrap, grilled sandwich, and a salad bar. Could be worse. Seph had been raised to appreciate good food, but he wasn't a snob.

Seph scanned the dining room, but he saw no sign of the boy with the glasses.

He and Trevor carried their trays to a large, rectangular table by the window. A half dozen boys were already seated there. Conversation died away when Trevor and Seph sat down, but then everyone took turns introducing themselves. Troy was a small, scholarly-looking black student, dressed in a white dress shirt and bow tie. Harrison had the kind of clean-cut, preppy look that is often misleading, while James was blunt and cocky with overdyed black hair and multiple piercings and tattoos.

Troy was from Philadelphia. "I've been in public school, private school, every religious school you can think of," he explained. "They said I was hyperactive." Seph found that hard to believe, given his buttoned-down appearance. Troy was a senior, and said he hoped to attend Yale the following year.

Harrison and James were juniors, Harrison from San Diego and James from Houston. Both readily admitted to a history of heavy partying.

"I had a trust fund, you know?" Harrison said, stuffing down the last bite of a burger and chasing it with soda. "So I didn't see much point in school. I got high a lot, cut class a lot. Meanwhile, my parents were spending all their time getting a divorce. Then my grandfather said I had to come here, or there would be no more money. I guess I forgot that a trust fund has a trustee." He laughed loudly and punched Seph playfully in the shoulder.

This place is full of misfits, Seph thought, rubbing his shoulder. Just like me.

Well, not exactly like me.

Once again, he waited for mention of the incident of the cove, but it didn't come up. It might as well have never happened.

"What about you?" James asked Seph. "How'd you end up here?"

"I had to leave my last school." Seph tilted back a bit from the table, resting his palms on the edge of the hardwood, rocking back in his chair. "I had a difference of opinion with the administration."

"About what?" Troy leaned forward.

"They thought I should come to class," Seph replied, making eye contact with each of them. "I had other priorities."

"Like what?" Harrison grinned in anticipation.

"You know. Hanging out with girls. Hacking into the school computer." He rocked forward, so all four legs of the chair struck the floor with a bang. "Skinny-dipping in the faculty pool."

This brought hoots of laughter from Harrison, smiles all around. An end to the inquisition.

Time to change the subject, he thought. Seph never had any difficulty directing a conversation. "How do I get my schedule? I guess I should've asked Dr. Leicester about it."

"They'll deliver it to your room before Sunday night, with the books you'll need," Trevor replied.

Seph went through the rest of his usual list of questions. All the students had mailboxes in the administration building. He could get money at the cashier's office, but there wasn't much to spend it on. He could use his student card to rent movies and order pizza through the bookstore.

"So what do you do for fun around here?" Seph asked, pushing a last bite of fish around his plate.

"Not much," Troy replied. "Watch movies, hang out. And hey, you can go see the bears and raccoons at the Dumpster."

Harrison added, "There's lots of sports, like cross-country skiing and snowboarding. Sailing's over, but it'll start up again in the spring. Over at the rec. center you can do tennis and racquetball." He shrugged. "That's about it."

"Don't worry about having nothing to do," Trevor said, rolling his eyes. "They work us pretty hard."

"What about girls?" Seph had attended boys' schools

before, but mostly in cities, where there was ample opportunity for socializing.

"You'll have to wait until summer," Harrison said regretfully. "Or winter recess, anyway."

Seph took this news philosophically. *N'exigez pas beaucoup et vous ne serez pas déçu.* Don't expect much, and you won't be disappointed.

One thing he *did* expect was Internet access. "What's this deal about not being able to go online?"

"It's weird," Harrison said. "They're up-to-date in a lot of other ways."

"Let's go ask Dr. Leicester about it," Seph suggested. This was greeted by a notable lack of enthusiasm. Which was surprising, because people always liked his ideas. He tried again. "We could get up a petition. Have a demonstration."

Troy cleared his throat. "Um . . . I don't think that's such a good idea."

"Don't you even care?" Seph demanded, exasperated. Being online was like having access to oxygen.

"*You* could ask Dr. Leicester about it," James ventured, making it clear Seph was on his own. "But I wouldn't get your hopes up. I think the alumni go online, but that's it."

"That's another thing," Seph said. "The alumni. What's up with them? What are they doing out here in the middle of nowhere?" He looked around the table, but nobody met his eye. "I mean, aren't you curious?" There was some shrugging of shoulders and clearing of throats. But no real response.

"Okay. So you're not curious." Seph pulled out his cell

phone, wondering if the change in location would make any difference. It didn't. "My cell phone isn't getting a signal. Should I change providers?"

"I guess there's no transmission towers around here," Trevor said. "Nobody's phone works. You'll have to use a land line."

This was the most passive group of students he'd ever met. It was as if something had taken the rowdy right out of them.

"Is there a Catholic church near here?"

"There are no churches of any kind that you can get to," James said. "You'll have to make it up to God in the summertime."

"There's nothing?" Seph looked around the table. "I can't believe that."

"They have an outdoor chapel here, though I can't tell you why, in this climate," Trevor said. "There are ecumenical services once a week, either there or in the admin. building."

Genevieve had been a devout Catholic, so Seph had attended Jesuit schools until she and the Fathers had disagreed on how to deal with his magical extravagances. The Jesuits had proposed an exorcism. Genevieve had declined.

Church had always been a sanctuary. The Latin Masses relaxed him. He liked the reassuring cadence of the old language, like ancient charms against the darkness, the perfumed smoke rising from the censers, the cavernous architecture within which his problems seemed small and manageable. He seemed to have an affinity for ritual.

No Masses. Well, he didn't expect to stay long.

"Which one of you is Joseph McCauley?"

Seph looked up, startled, realizing that the table conversation had died away. Two young men, perhaps college age, stood at the head of the table. One was tall and whippet thin, with hair and lashes so pale as to be almost transparent. The other was dark haired, broad shouldered, and bulked-up. The kind of guy who had creases in the back of his neck and needed two-a-day shaves.

"That's me," Seph said, raising his hand and waggling his fingers. "What's up?"

"Dr. Leicester would like to see you in his office."

Seph noticed that everyone else at the table was focused on the floor. Like in class, when you hadn't read the chapter and were afraid the teacher would call on you. "Oka-ay. And you are . . . ?"

"I'm Warren Barber," the blond one said. "This is Bruce Hays." As if that explained anything.

Seph glanced at his watch. Almost eight o'clock, and, despite his nap, he was bone tired. Best to get this meeting over with so he could go to bed. He pushed back his chair and smiled around the table. "Hey. Good to meet you. Thanks for all the inside. Guess I'll see you later."

They all studied him as if they were trying to fix his image in their minds, like they might forget what he looked like after he was gone.

"Good luck, Seph," Trevor said softly.

"Welcome to the Havens," Hays said as they climbed the stairs from the cafeteria level to the administrative offices on the third floor.

"Thanks. Ah—are you faculty members?" Seph asked, while trying to imagine what these two could possibly teach.

"Nah. We're alumni," Barber replied. "We're the alpha wolves in this organization. Hate to tell you, but you've been dining with the sheep."

"I . . . um . . ." Seph had no clue how to respond to this.

"Dude, you're going to like it here," Hays said, clapping him on the back. "We promise."

Dr. Leicester's office occupied the choice position at the front of the building, with the best view of the ocean. It was like no headmaster's office Seph had ever seen: sleekly modern, with a fax, computer, printer, and scanner. He saw none of the usual diplomas, awards, and other detritus of interschool competitions, save several large sailing trophies.

Seph looked longingly at the array of cutting-edge hardware, then leaned his hip against a table by the window. "So. What exactly do you do here?" he asked Hays and Barber. "Are you like, teaching assistants?"

Hays and Barber looked at each other. "I guess you could say we're more like, you know, research assistants," Barber said, grinning.

Seph thought they looked more like, you know, *thugs*. If you saw Hays and Barber walking down the street, you'd cross to the other side.

Well, maybe good help was hard to find. "What's your research about?" Seph asked. "Do you have a grant, or what?"

"Dr. Leicester will tell you more about the—ah—research," Hays said. "The thing to remember about us is that we *rule* on this campus. We answer only to Dr. Leicester."

Well, if so, it's kind of a remote kingdom, Seph thought. I'd rather rule a few square blocks of Toronto than—

"Hello, Joseph."

Seph swung around. Dr. Leicester stood in the doorway.

"Thank you for coming up. Have a seat." Leicester pointed to one of two chairs drawn up to a table in the corner. Seph sat. Leicester took the other seat. "You've met Mr. Hays and Mr. Barber? Good."

A file folder lay on the table. Leicester pulled it toward him and began leafing through the contents. "Joseph, I told you earlier today that here at the Havens we pride ourselves in tailoring the curriculum to the student. Based on your record and the difficulties you've been having, I suspect that you may require special attention."

Seph peered at the pages between Leicester's hands, trying to read upside down. "I'm not sure what you mean. What difficulties?" Muddled by fatigue, his mind was not as nimble as usual. "I've been doing really well. If you look at my transcripts, you'll see that . . ."

"I'm talking about the episode down at the cove this afternoon."

Admit nothing—that was his first rule. "I'm sorry I was late. I'll make sure it won't happen again."

Leicester waved away his answer impatiently. "The

ocean very nearly came to a boil. Most unusual, even in midsummer. In fact, it's never happened before."

Appeal to logic—second rule. "What's that got to do with me?" Seph looked from Leicester to the two alumni and back again.

"We believe you were the cause—intentional or not."

Delay the inevitable—third rule. "Look, I'm really tired, and none of this is making sense. Could we talk about this tomorrow?"

Leicester riffled through his papers. "You've changed schools four times in three years."

"Sometimes it takes a while to find a good fit."

"I understand there have been other incidents. Fires. Explosions. Flying sheep?" Leicester raised an eyebrow.

Seph was baffled. If Leicester knew his history, then why had he been admitted in the first place? He shoved back his chair and stood. "Flying sheep? Sorry. I don't know what you're talking about. I've really got to go." He turned toward the door, but Hays and Barber blocked the way.

"Sit down, Joseph," Leicester said calmly. "Please. Trust me, it's in your best interest to hear me out."

Hays and Barber weren't moving. Seph returned to the table and sat.

"That's better." Leicester sighed and thought a moment, as if unsure how to begin. Finally, he reached out and closed his hand on Seph's forearm. Seph flinched, expecting the crushing grip characteristic of men who make a religion of working out. What was surprising was not the strength, but the raw power that roared through.

Seph sucked in his breath, struggling to keep a stunned, stupid look off his face and not sure he succeeded. After a moment, Leicester released his arm. The print of his hand remained.

Dr. Leicester was a wizard, too.

Leicester's voice trickled into his brain, exploding with a heat like Genevieve's brandy. "None of what's happened is your fault, Joseph. Wizards need training, and I expect you've had none. You are very powerful, from what I've seen. And power will find its . . . outlets." He paused, then spoke aloud. "So. Am I right so far?"

Wordlessly, Seph nodded, still trying to grapple with this sudden twist of events.

Leicester patted him on the shoulder. "I know this must be a bit . . . jarring." The wizard settled back in his chair. "Once, Mr. Hays and Mr. Barber were just like you—gifted but unschooled. Now they are well on their way to becoming masters."

Hays and Barber smiled modestly.

If I were a master of magic I would work on my appearance, Seph thought.

"What about everyone else?" he began. "Are they all . . . ?"

"Most are not. Most are only what you would call wayward." Leicester shrugged dismissively. "We recruit students who've had difficulty elsewhere because often that includes persons like yourself. The untrained gifted." The headmaster toyed with an elaborate ring he wore on the middle finger of his left hand. "How much do you know about the guilds and the elements of power?"

"A little."

"Tell me."

Seph searched his memory. "Um. The gifted are born with Weirstones, a crystalline source of power that sits behind the heart," he recited. "The power runs in families. The . . . ah . . . kind of Weirstone you have determines the nature and extent of your power and which of the guilds you belong to."

When Seph paused, Leicester nodded, encouraging him to go on.

"The magical guilds include sorcerers, seers, warriors, enchanters and wizards. In the specialty guilds, the magic is more elemental, more direct. Wizards are the most powerful, because they shape magic with words."

"And who told you all this?"

"My foster mother. She was a sorcerer."

Genevieve claimed she'd promised his parents not to involve him in the dangerous world of wizardry. So she'd left him with a thousand questions and a power he couldn't control.

"And where is your foster mother?"

"She died three years ago."

"Pity." Leicester mustered up the familiar, sympathetic look. "So you don't have any family."

"Not really."

"What is your House affiliation?"

The same question Alicia had asked. Maybe now he could finally get some information. "I guess I don't know much about the Houses."

Leicester studied him with his ball-bearing eyes, as if

trying to decide if he was telling the truth. "As the ruling guild, wizards have been required to develop systems for the allocation of power. Else we would have had Armageddon on our hands."

Seph sensed that Leicester had delivered this speech many times before.

"There are two major Houses of wizards, the Red Rose and the White. Wizard families align themselves with one or the other, and many of those allegiances go back to the War of the Roses in fifteenth-century Britain. Interactions between the Houses have been governed by a document called the Rules of Engagement, the treaty that ended the war.

"For centuries, power has been allocated between the Houses by a series of tournaments. Members of the Warrior Guild fight as proxies for the Roses. The winning house rules the Weir—the magical guilds—until the next tournament is held. It's a system that has worked well."

Seph leaned forward. His weariness seemed to have disappeared. "Why haven't I heard of this?"

"Here in the States, many of the Weir don't know they are gifted. Old connections have been broken. Some who came here made a conscious decision to leave their Houses behind." Leicester sighed. "I suppose the under-guilds saw it as an opportunity to escape from service. But for wizards, the result is that young people like yourself have no guidance or instruction. And that can be disastrous. Our purpose here at the Havens is to remedy that."

"So you're saying you can train me in wizardry?"

Leicester smiled. "I am saying that, yes."

"And I'll learn how to control magic, and how to avoid . . . accidents."

"Yes."

After the warehouse, Seph had wanted to have nothing to do with magic, ever again. But he had no choice. In his case, power had a way of surfacing in uncontrollable ways. To be able to control magic, to use it properly . . . that would be a miracle.

But he knew enough to question wizards bearing gifts.

"What's in it for you?" Seph asked.

Leicester stood and walked to the window. He gazed out at the harbor, hands clasped behind his back. Then turned back to face Seph.

"These are troubled times for the Houses, a time of great danger. Back in the summer, a tournament in Britain went wrong. The Rules of Engagement were broken. A group of mostly servant-guild rebels has taken sanctuary in Ohio. An anarchist who calls himself the Dragon is fomenting rebellion and attacking wizards of both houses all over the world. Alliances are shifting. If war breaks out between the Houses again, we are all at risk."

He paused, as if expecting a reaction, but Seph said nothing. He'd always found that he learned more if he kept quiet.

"To answer your question, I am still nominally affiliated with the White Rose. But it is my hope that through our work here at the Havens we can create a new path, a new order that ends the bloodshed and eliminates the constant warfare between the Houses. Think of what we could accomplish if we were not focused on murdering each other."

That made sense.

"Are there students from other guilds here?" Seph asked. "Like warriors and . . . and sorcerers?"

"They hardly need the kind of instruction I can provide. After all, they are bred to a purpose." Leicester's expression was faintly disdainful. "No, we focus on wizards. Our graduates become the most powerful users of magic in the world."

"How long have you been doing this?"

"We graduated our first class five years ago."

"How do people find out about the Havens? I've been looking for help for three years, and I've never heard of it."

Leicester smiled thinly. "The nature of wizard politics requires that we be discreet. You may have heard that we closely control communications in and out of here. There is a reason."

"But I don't understand why . . ."

"When you know more, you'll understand," Leicester said sharply. "We can't risk discovery by those who would destroy our only real hope for peace. There are those who have a strong vested interest in maintaining the status quo. For that reason, it's important that no whisper of this reach the Roses."

From what he knew of wizards, Seph wasn't surprised to learn that Leicester had a political agenda. Genevieve had infused into him a deep suspicion of wizard politics, which often seemed to involve bloodying the under-guilds. No doubt the headmaster would try to get him involved sooner or later. But he'd deal with it, if he could get the help he needed. "How does it work? Who does the teaching? How long does it take?"

"Shall we assume, then, that you are interested in joining our magical collaborative?" Leicester's eyes glittered.

"Yes. Absolutely." The precision of the wizard's language was a warning, but he could not afford to say no.

"Good," Leicester said. "I thought that would be your answer."

"When do we get started?" Seph persisted.

"Take a few days to settle in and get caught up with your other classes. Then we'll talk again. We have techniques that streamline the process."

"Isn't there something I could be reading in the meantime, some way to prepare?"

Leicester studied him a moment. "Perhaps. Do you have a Weirbook?"

"I don't know what that is." Alicia Middleton had mentioned Weirbooks at the party.

"Each member of the Weirguilds has a Weirbook, created at birth. Even those in the servant guilds. It summarizes the member's magical lineage and family history. Wizard Weirbooks include charms and incantations that have been handed down through families over the centuries." He paused, raising his eyebrows in inquiry.

"I don't have one," Seph admitted.

"Actually, you do have one," Dr. Leicester said. "It's a matter of locating it. What is really key is what I told you earlier: we require total commitment from our wizardry students. Are you capable of that?"

"Yes, sir," Seph replied. "You won't be disappointed." He'd lived precariously for years, like someone with a terminal disease, never able to plan more than a few months ahead. Whatever the consequences of this decision, he'd risk it.

"Good," Leicester said. "Oh, and it would be best for you not to discuss any of this with the Anaweir." At Seph's blank look, he added, "The ungifted students. It only causes resentment, and we don't want them spreading rumors once they leave the Havens. In fact, it would be best for you to keep your distance from them outside of class."

Seph thought of Trevor and Harris and Troy and the others. "I don't understand. Why do we . . ."

Leicester waved his hand impatiently. "Oh, be polite, of course. But you'll find you'll have little in common with them as your training progresses. Once you are properly enrolled, we'll move you into the Alumni House with the others."

Seph remembered how Trevor and the others had responded when he mentioned the alumni. "The wizard students live in the Alumni House?"

Leicester nodded. "All of the alumni are gifted."

Seph glanced at Hays and Barber. "Are they . . . have they all graduated? I mean . . . is there anyone else my age? Will I still be in class with the others?" He felt connected to Trevor and the others now that he'd met them.

"We'll get into that once your training is underway." The wizard stood, signaling that the interview was at an end. "Now, you'd better get on to bed. You've had a long day."

And Seph realized he had been dismissed.

❧ Chapter Four ❧
A Visit to the Alumni House

As promised, Seph's books and class schedule were delivered to his door early Sunday morning. He found the locations of the classroom buildings on the campus map, reviewed the syllabi, and started in on his reading. He'd always been a good student, so he didn't think he'd have any trouble catching up. He wanted to get as much work as possible out of the way before his classes in wizardry began.

By late afternoon, however, he was having trouble concentrating on eighteenth-century European history. He tried it with and without headphones. He moved from his bed to his desk, hoping sitting upright would enforce some discipline. But he found himself punching randomly at his keyboard, wishing he could go online. He was used to spending hours every day online with his friends, a stimulating blend of media, music, IMing, and homework.

He thought about Leicester and the alumni. Wondered how long it would take to gain control over his gift, as Leicester called it. How would the lessons work? Would Leicester tutor him one-on-one so he could catch up with the others? Would they recite incantations in class? Practice spell-casting on the soccer field? Would his not having a Weirbook be a handicap? He'd always been popular among the Anaweir. Would he have trouble making friends among the gifted?

Leicester had said that Seph had a Weirbook somewhere. If so, he could find the answers to his questions between the covers.

Some of them, anyway.

Maybe he should try and get to know some of the alumni right away. Organize a study group. Make some allies who could help him along.

Preferably someone other than Hays and Barber.

He finally gave up and set his textbook aside. Shoving his feet into his shoes, he walked down the hall to Trevor's room. Trevor's door was open, and Seph heard the throb of a heavy bass line halfway down the corridor.

Trevor was sprawled on the sheepskin rug in front of his fireplace, two-finger typing into a notebook. Papers and books lay scattered all around him. He looked up at Seph, blinking, as if surprised to see him.

"Let's do something," Seph said.

Trevor hit the mute button on his player and squinted at Seph. "Such as . . . ?"

"Anything," Seph said expansively. "Let's go."

"I don't know. I've got a lot of homework." Trevor

hesitated, studying Seph warily. "By the way, you okay? How'd it go with Leicester last night?"

"Fine. Great. We talked things out, and we're okay."

"You're kidding, right?"

Trevor looked so solemn that Seph had to smile. "Yeah, I'm kidding. Sort of. You coming? It's going to be dinnertime pretty soon, anyway."

They walked out into the dusk. Seph breathed in the complex, burnt-toast scent of the autumn woods.

Trevor became more animated once they'd left the dorm and his homework behind. "Maybe we can get a racquetball court and play before dinner," he said.

Seph looked down at his jeans and sweatshirt. "What about dressing for dinner?"

Trevor grinned. "It's Sunday. Weekend rules. Dr. Leicester's usually not around."

They were passing the Alumni House. "Hey, hang on a sec. Let's take a look inside."

"No, Seph, come on." Trevor grabbed for his arm, but Seph was already through the doorway.

The foyer opened into a common room with a large stone fireplace at one end framed by bookshelves. Leather sofas crouched like stranded bovines along the perimeter of a Persian rug. It was similar in style to the other buildings Seph had seen, but more opulent, more expensively decorated, aggressively masculine. No one was in there, but Seph could hear the murmur of conversation and clatter of silverware from a nearby room.

Trevor gripped his arm hard. "We're not supposed to be in here," he whispered.

"I just want to look around a little," Seph whispered back. "Don't worry. It's cool."

"I mean it," Trevor persisted. "Let's go."

Seph scanned the directory next to the stairwell. "Hey, there's a library on the second floor. Have you ever been up there?"

"No. I said. We're not allowed."

"I bet they have Internet access."

"Seph. I'm leaving. Come on." Trevor took two steps toward the door.

"Be right back." Seph took the steps by twos, paused on the landing, and turned left along the gallery, passing rows of unmarked doors. A door at the end of the hallway stood partly open. Peering in, he saw rows of shelves loaded with dusty, leather-bound books. A flicker of movement to the right startled him. He jerked back, flattening himself against the corridor wall. Then he heard an explosion of voices from the first floor.

"What are you doing in here?" someone demanded. The voice was familiar. Then something or someone was slammed hard against the wall.

Seph leaned over the gallery railing. Bruce Hays had Trevor shoved up against the wall. Seph heard a scraping of chairs, and then a half dozen others poured in from the dining room, forming a jostling semicircle around Bruce and his captive. Warren Barber was among them.

Trevor said something back, so faintly that Seph couldn't make out the words. Whatever it was, it must have been unsatisfactory, because Bruce did something and Trevor screamed.

"Hey!" Seph charged back along the gallery and vaulted down the stairs. He shoved his way through the circle of wizards and gripped Bruce's arm. "Let him go!"

Bruce flinched, released Trevor, and swung around, hands raised as if to fight. His eyes widened when he saw Seph. "What? You're with him?"

Warren Barber turned on Trevor. "You know you're not allowed in here," he said in a soft voice. Barber extended a hand, and Trevor pressed himself back against the wall, closing his eyes, sweat pebbling his forehead despite the chill in the air.

"Ease up. It was my idea," Seph said, stepping between them. He smiled and shrugged, turning on the charm. "I just wanted to look around."

Warren wasn't impressed. "This one should know better." Warren's breath stank of beer, and he spoke with the deliberation of the profoundly wasted. He reached around Seph, grabbing at Trevor, and Trevor jumped backward.

Seph pushed Warren's hand away. "I don't see why it's such a big deal. What are you hiding in here?"

"Well, it is," Warren said, rubbing his stubbled chin with the palm of his hand. "It is a big deal."

"Warren . . ." Bruce cleared his throat.

"Didn't Dr. Leicester tell you to be careful who you hang out with?" Warren said to Seph, nodding at Trevor.

Seph lifted his chin defiantly. "Come *on*. Do you do everything Leicester tells you to?"

Warren's smile faded, leaving resentment in its wake. "What do you mean by that?"

Seph looked around the circle of wizards, his gaze

lingering for a moment on each face. "I mean that my friends are my business."

Nobody said anything for a long moment. Then Warren shrugged and smiled, as if trying to disclaim all the threats and innuendos that had gone before. But the smile never made it into his eyes. "All right then," he said. "It's just a—you know—misunderstanding."

"It's cool, Joseph," Bruce said reassuringly. "Wait till you move in here. It'll be great. The other dorms suck in comparison. The food's a lot better, too. Hey, why don't you come on in and have dinner with us? We can fill you in on some things."

It was an invitation that clearly did not include Trevor.

Seph was tempted. He could definitely use some filling in. But he felt the need to establish a boundary, to make a statement about who he was and what he would tolerate. "I've already got plans tonight," he said, smiling. "Maybe another day?"

"Sure," Bruce said. "Come to dinner tomorrow. We start around seven."

Trevor looked from Bruce to Seph to Warren. "Don't tell Dr. Leicester I was here," he whispered. "Please."

Warren smiled wolfishly. "What's the matter? Afraid you'll get a demerit?"

"Please," Trevor repeated. "I'm really sorry. Just don't tell Leicester."

"Maybe you'd like to be my personal servant for a month. Hmmm?" Warren said. He grinned at the other wizards. "Trevor is very good at doing laundry. Much better than the service. Gets those colors sparkling."

"Hey, Warren," Seph said, keeping his tone light. "Enough already. What don't you understand about *leave him alone?*"

Warren raised a hand, grinning. "Sure. No problem. See you tomorrow."

Seph touched Trevor on the shoulder. "Come on, Trevor. We got places to be."

Once outside, Trevor didn't speak, but turned and headed back toward the dormitory, head down, scuffling hard through the leaves.

Seph had to trot to catch up. "Hey! Trevor! Look, I'm sorry. You were right. I should've listened to you."

Trevor didn't look up, and his pace didn't falter. Finally, Seph grabbed his arm, spinning him around. "Talk to me, will you?"

Seph half expected Trevor to rip free, or punch him, or something, but he just stood, gazing down at the ground, a muscle working in his jaw.

"I said I should've listened to you," Seph repeated. "That was totally bizarre. But no harm done, right?"

Trevor looked up at Seph like he'd told the sickest kind of joke. "Right. Sure. No harm done."

He went to turn away, but Seph tightened his grip on his arm to keep him in place.

"Let. Go. Of. Me." Trevor kept his eyes averted, as if it might be dangerous to look at him.

Seph kept hold. "What? What is it?"

Trevor just shook his head.

Seph carefully released a trace of power into Trevor. Feeling bad about it, but needing to know.

He could tell Trevor didn't want to answer, but the words poured out just the same. "You never said you were one of them."

"One of who?" Seph asked, though he already knew.

Trevor cut his eyes toward Alumni House.

"I'm not an alumnus," Seph said, lamely. "I'm a junior. It's just that I'm enrolling in a special program." Trevor said nothing. "Ah . . . why? What do you know about them?"

Trevor shuddered. "I don't want to know anything about them—you." Now he did try and wrench free, and Seph let him. "You don't care what happens to any of us. Some of us listened to Jason, and . . ."

"Who's Jason?"

"He told us we should fight back, and we tried, and now Sam is dead and Peter and Jason are living at the Alumni House."

Trevor may as well have been speaking in Japanese. He'd left Seph back at the first sentence. "Fight back against what? Who's dead? I don't know what you're talking about."

Trevor had his hands over his ears, speaking loudly enough to drown Seph out. As if afraid Seph would seduce him with words. "I've gone six months without a disciplinary, and now . . ."

"I'll go to Dr. Leicester," Seph offered, still bewildered by the emotion in play. "I'll explain. Whatever it takes."

"No," Trevor said. "Don't do me any favors. You'll make things worse. Just stay away from me." He wheeled and walked away, back toward the dorm. Seph stood and watched him until he was lost in the shadows of the trees.

❧ CHAPTER FIVE ❧
TOTAL COMMITMENT

The next evening, Seph dressed carefully in a cotton shirt, khakis, and a jacket (no tie), and gelled his hair, reasoning that there was a chance Dr. Leicester would be at dinner. He made his way to Alumni House at the appointed time, hoping that the evening would go better than the encounter of the day before.

To be honest, he didn't really care for any of the wizards he'd met so far.

Mr. Hanlon, whom he'd met in the woods, greeted him at the door to the dining room.

"Call me Aaron," Hanlon said.

Although Seph had been careful to arrive on time, service was already underway. The room was reminiscent of the dining hall in a very expensive ski lodge: soaring beamed ceilings, flagstone floors, a mammoth fireplace, and a wall of windows overlooking a waterfall.

The alumni were gathered around a long table. There were fifteen in all, not counting Seph, a mixture of faculty members and "researchers" like Warren and Bruce. Leicester wasn't there. Servers circulated un-obtrusively, pouring beverages, passing platters of appe-tizers, clearing dishes, and taking orders from an upscale menu. To Seph's surprise, beer, wine, and liquor flowed freely, but then, he guessed most of the alumni were of age.

Aaron placed Seph in a position of honor, at the table center, then sat beside him, with Kenyon King, a phys. ed. teacher, on his other side, and Bruce and Warren across the table. Someone set a platter of spiced shrimp in front of him, a glass of wine by his right hand. The alumni up and down the table introduced themselves.

At the far end of the table was a rumpled kid with glasses and a twitch, who introduced himself as Peter Conroy. It was the boy Seph had met in the woods two days before, on the way to swimming. He tried to catch Peter's eye, but the other boy wouldn't look at him. Seph shrugged. It seemed less important here, surrounded by wizards, than it had been the other day.

Seph sipped cautiously at his wine, meaning to keep his wits about him. It had a distinct Gewurz nose. He smiled to himself. Genevieve had taken a typical French attitude toward wine, considering it less risky than water. So he'd had his share at her table and in Europe.

"So tell us about yourself, Joseph," Aaron suggested. Everyone leaned forward.

The question he despised. "Um . . . I was born in

Toronto, but I've moved around a lot. I was raised by a foster mother. A sorcerer."

"That must've been fun," Bruce said, making a face. "Raised by a sorcerer. Did she have you hunting toadstools and grinding up frog's tongues and like that?"

Seph blinked at him. "Well, no. Can't say that I ever did that." He thought of saying, *We used to go to markets in Chinatown and pick exotic roots and vegetables.*

But he didn't.

"Anyway, I haven't had much training in wizardry. I was hoping you could tell me something about the program here."

"We have a great library, reserved for the use of the alumni," Aaron said. "Thousands of volumes on charms, incantations, attack spells, and shields. Plus Weirbooks from famous families."

"So. Is it mostly independent study?" Seph asked.

"Well. Kind of," Bruce said. "Dr. Leicester has a magical shortcut system that allows all of us to share knowledge and power. So you'll be in business in no time."

"Shortcut?" Leicester had mentioned something about that at their meeting. Seph looked down the table, and it seemed that there was a lot of foot shuffling and seat shifting going on.

"Plus we're involved in a lot of off-campus assignments," Warren said. "Special operations."

"Like what?"

"Well, you know." Warren looked uncomfortable. "I think Dr. Leicester told you something about his dream of uniting the wizard houses. So we work on that."

"It's really cool. Getting out on our own," Bruce said. "We've traveled all over the world. Thailand. London. Brazil."

Seph felt that somehow he still wasn't getting it. It's was like sex, the way people talked all around it but you could still end up not knowing the basics. "Who pays for all this?" he asked.

"Dr. Leicester has backers," Aaron said. "Trust me, money's not a problem. We don't pay a penny for tuition, clothing, room and board, or anything else." He picked up a shrimp. "As you can see, everything's top shelf."

"How long does the program last?" Seph asked, handing his plate to the server. "How long do most people stay?"

Everyone just kind of stared at him as though it were a really hard question.

He tried again. "I mean, by the time I graduate next year, will I know everything I need to know?"

Aaron was the first to recover. "Yes," he said, smiling. "By next year, you'll know all you need to know."

Over the next two weeks, Seph settled into the cadence of life at the Havens. Schools were totally different; they were totally the same. The course work wasn't as rigorous as he'd feared. In fact, it was rather superficial. It seemed that the administration at the Havens wasn't focused on the Anaweir students who filled most of the seats.

It was a small school, and because Seph and Trevor were both juniors, they had several classes together: algebra II/trig and physics, social studies, and English literature. But Trevor's warm friendliness had morphed to a sullen and twitchy mistrust.

Trevor must have told the others about what happened at Alumni House. Harrison and Troy and James were still chatty and cheerful, but it was the spun-sugar kind of speech about nothing, usually reserved for snitches and the rich, insufferable cousins you see once a year. Seph knew he could win them back if he tried, but he reined in his powers of persuasion. Friendship didn't mean much if it was inflicted. Once or twice a week he ate dinner at the Alumni House. He wondered what they said when he was gone.

At first glance the faculty seemed to be a mixed lot, from the charming Aaron Hanlon to gruff Elliott Richardson to the buff physical education teacher Kenyon King, to tiny, blue-blooded Ashton Rice. They were diverse, but there was something the same about them, too, some shared experience.

Like Harvard men. They all have the mark of the Havens upon them.

One evening, Seph received a note at dinner, on the sailboat stationery. PLEASE BE AT THE ALUMNI HOUSE AT 9 P.M. G. LEICESTER.

Nine o'clock was a funny time for a meeting, but maybe this meant his magical training was about to begin. Seph felt a rising excitement, mixed with apprehension. So far, he didn't much care for Leicester *or* the alumni. But he would take what he needed from them and move on.

That night, the fog rolled in off the Atlantic and condensed into rain—the cold, relentless drizzle that

Genevieve called *larmes d'ange*. Angel's tears. Seph pulled on a bulky sweater she'd knit for him, jeans, and a leather jacket. Thus armored, he walked through sopping leaves and dripping trees to his rendezvous.

When he arrived at Alumni House, he was surprised to find the common room empty, except for Warren Barber, who leaned against the mantel, smoking and flicking ashes into the fireplace.

Warren tossed his cigarette into the hearth and scooped up an armload of clothing from the nearest chair. "Everyone else is meeting us at the chapel," he said. "Let's go."

Seph hesitated. "We're meeting outside?" *Was this some kind of hazing event?*

"Brilliant, ain't it?"

Seph had no choice but to follow. Warren led the way into the woods, following a wood-chip path that bridged a little stream in several places. Mist clung to the ground, waist-deep in places, beaten down by the rain. Seph swiped water from his face, looking from side to side, wary of an ambush.

About a mile into the woods, the trees thinned into a clearing, revealing a rude amphitheater. Rows of stone benches faced a raised platform with an altar in the center, framed by standing stones and lit by torches, the light smeared by the mist.

It reminded Seph of places he'd seen in Britain— Celtic temples of druidic magic. "What's this all about?" he muttered, shivering.

Warren led the way up the center aisle toward the

platform. When they reached the front, he tossed Seph a wad of cloth. "Put this on," he said.

It was a rough-woven wool cowled robe, bleached white. Seph pulled it on over his damp clothes. Warren shrugged his way into a robe of his own, his a deep gray color. The gloom under the trees eddied and shifted, and other gray-robed persons appeared, moving silently onto the platform, behind the altar.

"You. Stand here." Warren tugged Seph to a spot in front of the benches, facing the platform, then joined the others on the stage.

And then, finally, a black-robed figure, tall and spare, materialized on the platform. His face was hidden in shadow, backlit by the torches along the perimeter, but Seph knew beyond a doubt that this was Gregory Leicester.

Leicester carried a staff, a tall column of metal—bronze and gold layered together, topped by a faceted crystal. Embedded in the crystal was something dark, like a shadow or a flaw. An amulet. Seph's eyes were drawn to it; he had to force himself to look away.

It was, perhaps, a show—some kind of initiation ceremony meant to establish solidarity. Like joining a lodge. It should have been amusing, what with all the pageantry and costume, but Leicester didn't come off as much of a showman. Seph didn't like being singled out, placed before the altar, dressed like a sacrifice. His skin prickled and his mouth went dust dry.

"Joseph McCauley has come before us, with a request to join our order of wizards," Leicester intoned, his voice emerging from his black hood. "Is this, indeed, your intention, Joseph?"

Seph cleared his throat, feeling an intense pressure to respond. "I . . . ah . . . guess so," he replied.

Seemingly undeterred by this lukewarm reply, Leicester continued. "We have agreed to consider this request. Does the petitioner understand what is required of him?"

Again, the feeling of focused pressure, the pressure to say yes. Instinctively, Seph pushed back. "No, not really," he said. "Can you tell me?"

Leicester paused, as if this answer were unexpected, then responded awkwardly. "You are required to link your Weirstone to mine."

Reflexively, Seph pressed his fingers into the skin of his chest, through the folds of the robe. His eyes fastened on a shallow stone bowl that sat atop the altar. And the knife that lay next to it. He licked his lips and swallowed. "What?"

Leicester shoved back the hood of his robe. "Through the speaking of charms, and the letting of blood."

"Is that necessary?" Seph asked, struggling to maintain an expression of polite inquiry. "I just want to be trained in wizardry."

Leicester rolled back the sleeves of his robe like a surgeon preparing for a procedure. "Wizardry manifests early," he replied. "Most begin their training very young. You are far behind your peers. This system is a shortcut. It allows your powers to be used safely without extensive remedial training. We haven't the time for that."

Seph had the sense that Leicester was choosing his words carefully. As if what he said might be technically true, but intentionally misleading. Seph felt a more subtle pressure, like an undercurrent of magic at work. His muscles loosened and his head swirled with inarticulate thought.

He mounted a faint protest. "So you're saying that if I don't go through with this . . . um . . . ceremony, you won't train me in wizardry?"

"I'm saying it takes years to develop skills enough to practice wizardry safely. I'm saying you are getting a very late start. I'm saying this is the way we do things at the Havens." Leicester picked up the knife and nodded to someone behind Seph. "Bring the supplicant."

Bruce Hays and Warren Barber materialized behind Seph and gripped his elbows. They dragged him forward, half lifting him up the steps and then pushing him to his knees in front of the altar. They stripped back his sleeve and pressed his arm against the cold, rough stone, exposing the inside of his wrist.

It was like a dream. Almost as if he were watching it happen to someone else. He barely felt the blade as it bit into his flesh, and his blood flowed into the stone bowl. He should have been horrified as Leicester spoke words over the bowl in some language of magic, dipped the crystalline head of the staff into the blood, and then lifted it to drink.

This is wrong, Seph thought. But he felt muddled and lethargic, limp and passive, carried along through the ceremony like a leaf in the current.

"Now, rise," Leicester said to Seph, "and speak the words after me." Barber and Hays lifted Seph to his feet and held him upright. Their hands burned through the rough fabric of his robe as a thought burned itself into his mind.

This was clearly some kind of pagan ritual. What, exactly, was he being asked to deliver into Leicester's hands?

He pressed his bleeding arm into his side. The crystalline head of the staff blazed, casting a greenish light over the participants. Something fluttered at the edge of his vision, like a scrap of black fabric. And again, and more, blotting out the torchlight. Bats. Clouds of bats, swooping about the heads of the alumni, silently dive-bombing the proceedings. Several of the celebrants covered their heads with their arms.

A sign.

Seph looked across the altar, to where one of the alumni stood watching. Peter Conroy. His face was a mask of dismay. When he saw Seph looking, his eyes widened behind his glasses. He shook his head, ever so slightly.

A warning.

Leicester spoke his magical phrase, then paused expectantly, waiting for him to echo it, like a vow in a devilish wedding ceremony. The hooded figures leaned forward in anticipation.

"No," Seph said. "I can't."

"Would you like me to repeat it, Joseph?" Leicester asked softly, encouragingly.

"No. I mean I changed my mind."

For a moment, Leicester seemed too astonished to speak. "What?" The word seemed to spatter out into the mist.

"I refuse."

A rumble of surprise rolled through the alumni, quickly stifled. Peter closed his eyes and breathed out, as if relieved.

Leicester's voice was calm and reassuring. "What's bothering you, Joseph? The painful part is over. When we're finished, we'll go back to the Alumni House and dress that scratch and make arrangements to move you in. Your training will begin immediately."

"What's bothering me?" Seph shivered. It was raining harder now, plastering his hair against his forehead and soaking him nearly through. Somehow, it seemed to clear his head.

His arm still streamed blood, and he pressed it tight against his side. "You're drinking my blood. Asking me to swear some kind of oath I don't really understand. I can't be involved in a ritual like this. It's like, out of a screamer movie. To be honest, this is really freaking me out."

Leicester's breath hissed out impatiently. "You said you wanted to learn about wizardry."

"I do." Seph looked around the circle of robed wizards, hoping someone would speak up in his defense.

"That can't happen unless we finish."

Seph took a breath. "Then it can't happen."

"Two weeks ago, I asked if you were willing to make a total commitment. You assured me that you were."

Seph jerked free of Hays and Barber. "I think you

need to tell me exactly what I'd be committing myself to."

A muscle twitched in the headmaster's jaw. Leicester's voice was still soft, but there was a thread of steel in it. "You'd do better to ask about the consequences if you refuse."

It sounded very much like a threat. "What consequences?"

"There's a reason wizardry training starts early," Leicester said. "When untrained wizards reach adolescence, they . . . self-destruct."

"What do you mean?"

"Perhaps it's hormonal," Leicester said delicately. "Perhaps developmental. It begins with uncontrolled releases of power. Then the magic turns inward and destroys the mind, resulting in depression and hallucinations. It's not unusual for untrained wizards to go insane."

Seph thought of the warehouse. The destruction of the bell tower. It seemed that he'd had uncontrolled spasms of power all his life. And they seemed to be getting worse—more frequent. He scanned himself for symptoms. Since the warehouse fire, he'd been depressed. He'd found it difficult to concentrate. But wasn't that normal for a person with innocent blood on his hands?

"Joseph," Leceister said, in the manner of a man who is trying hard to be reasonable. "Everyone else here has agreed."

Seph looked around the circle of faces. Hays and Barber were openly smirking, eyes slitted against the rain. Some of the celebrants looked back at him stoically.

Others, including Peter, looked down at their feet or off into the distance. It was not especially reassuring.

"I'm sorry," Seph said. "I just can't."

"Fine," Leicester said venomously. "Then *suffer* the consequences." The wizard took a step toward Seph, extending the staff. Seph retreated, but came up against someone—Hays or Barber—who held him in place. Leicester pressed the blood-smeared head of the staff against Seph's chest, over his wildly beating heart. Power pulsed through it like some kind of magical CPR machine.

"It won't be long before you'll beg for another chance." He motioned to the rest of the alumni. "Come along. We're wasting time here."

The alumni disappeared into the trees, leaving Seph to pick his way back through the wet forest on his own.

❧ CHAPTER SIX ❧
CONSEQUENCES

Seph woke in the pitch black, freezing and soaking wet. He pushed himself upright, his palms sliding against sodden, splintering wood. Moonlight intruded through two windows, high on the wall. He sat hip deep in frigid water, and more poured in through a great square hole in the floor. Still disoriented, he staggered to his feet.

He was in the boathouse. He recognized it from his visit with Trevor during the campus tour. He could make out the vague shapes of equipment hanging on the wall, see small objects already bobbing against the dark surface of the water.

He'd returned to his room after the aborted ceremony in the woods. How had he ended up here? And where was the flood coming from?

The water slapped against the walls, higher than before, almost to Seph's knees. His mind was slow to process. Was the tide coming in? Surely they would build a boathouse to withstand the tide. People who knew about oceans would know better than that.

His wet khakis clung unpleasantly to his legs. The water had reached his thighs. With difficulty, he waded to the door and pulled the handle. It didn't budge. He yanked again, bracing a foot against the doorframe. Stuck. Or locked. Panic fluttered under his breastbone. The water was rising, and he couldn't get out.

It didn't make sense. Surely this old building wasn't watertight. It ought to leak water like a sieve. Had he been drugged, spelled, carried here by the alumni on Leicester's orders? For what?

He squinted into the darkness, teeth chattering with fear and cold, looking for a way out.

He could swim out through the boat well, though he didn't like the idea of diving into that black water. By now it was so deep, only a disturbance on the surface told him where the opening began and the floor ended. He moved cautiously forward, feeling for the edge of the floor with feet that felt clumsy and numb with the cold. Blundering off the edge, he plunged feet-first into freezing water. He shot back to the surface, propelled by the current, and raked his wet hair out of his face. Folding himself at the waist, he tried to dive deep, but was thrust back to the surface each time, gasping for air. There was no escape that way.

Coughing and spitting out salt water, he found the edge of the floor again. When he stood up, the water lapped at his collarbone. He needed to get to higher ground. He bumped into the fish-cleaning table, pulled himself up, and managed to plant his feet on it. Now he was immersed only to his waist, but he hit his head on the ceiling, and the water was still rising.

"Help!" he screamed, his shouts faint and ineffective. "I'm locked in the boathouse! Help! I'm drowning!"

While standing on the table, he could just reach one of the small windows if he stretched far to one side. Grabbing a large landing net that hung on the wall, he slammed it against the glass. The net was lightweight, and he was working at such an angle that he couldn't produce much force against it. Finally he lost his footing, flailed wildly for a moment, and went under again.

He surfaced, spluttering, treading water. Then he gasped as something slid past him, roiling the surface of the black water like a great serpent, its rough hide scraping him as it went by.

Seph sucked in a breath and went absolutely still, save the rough pounding of his pulse. For a moment, the water was quiet. Then a thick, muscular tentacle searched along his leg, slid upward, and tightened around his waist.

He pushed at the creature, pounded on it, tried to push himself out of its grasp using both hands, getting a mouthful of water as he did so. His fists made no impression on its leathery hide. His flailing foot encountered something soft and yielding, and the monster's grip relaxed fractionally. Launching himself upward, Seph wrapped his arms around one of the rough wooden beams that supported the roof.

He clung there, gasping for breath, but he could not lift himself completely out of the water. Ripples spread from the far corner as the creature surfaced, its pale, dispassionate eyes and razor teeth revealed in the light from the window. A squid? An octopus? Some unknown monster that had lain hidden in the ocean's depths until now?

Once again, a tentacle quested forward, sliding beneath the

water like a great snake. It explored along his thigh, then wrapped about his hips.

Slowly, inexorably, it dragged at him. Desperate, he tightened his hold on the ceiling beam, turning his face upward so he could gulp some air. He no longer tried to dislodge his attacker, but held on for dear life. His joints cracked as a relentless strength threatened to pull him apart.

Suddenly, the monster rocketed forward in an explosion of spray and fastened its teeth into his right leg. Seph screamed and tried to pull it off, losing his grip on the beam. He managed one last breath, sucking in a mixture of seawater and air, before he was pulled beneath the water and into black despair.

Light awoke Seph a second time, painful light that caused him to roll onto his face to exclude it. He was in bed. Something terrible lurked in memory, a beast kept leashed in the back room of his mind.

He swallowed; his throat was so raw it brought tears to his eyes. He felt like he'd been beaten. Every muscle in his body ached. He struggled to his knees, and then the full recollection of the night before flooded back. He vomited over the side of the bed and onto the floor. His throat felt worse than ever.

He rolled over onto his back and stared at the ceiling. It gradually came to him that he was in a bed, back in his room in the dormitory. He was soaked in sweat, not in seawater, and he was alive. He ran his hand tentatively down his right leg, then his left, and could find no evidence of injury. He checked twice, to make sure. Hot tears of relief filled his eyes, slid from the corners and onto his pillow.

The monster had ripped him apart. He'd gazed hopelessly up at the undersurface of the ocean as his own blood clouded the water, had tasted it in his mouth, had felt the great jaws close on his flesh, tearing it away in pieces. His struggles had grown weaker as he succumbed to oxygen starvation and loss of blood.

Still, it had taken a long time to die.

He sat up, drew his knees up into a protective position, and leaned his chin on his hands, shivering. Had it been a dream, then? If so, it was like no dream he'd ever had before. It was the three-dimensional, surround-sound, full-color mother-of-all dreams.

His bedding was completely mangled, evidence of a struggle that had lasted most of the night. The ceiling and walls were pocked with scorch marks, as if he'd been flinging out sparks. Good thing they hadn't caught or he'd have burned to death.

He slid out of bed, avoiding the mess on the floor, went into the bathroom and rinsed out his mouth. His face stared back at him from the mirror, pale and haggard. Gingerly, he fingered the broken blood vessels around his eyes. Half-moon welts marched across his palms, the prints of his nails.

Grabbing a towel, he mopped up the floor as best he could. He carried it into the hall and threw it into a laundry bag, then helped himself to fresh towels from the linen cart, working automatically. He lay back down in bed and turned his face to the wall, afraid to sleep, too tired and heartsick to do anything else.

Leicester's words came back to him.

It's not unusual for untrained wizards to go insane.

The next morning was Monday. Seph didn't go to breakfast, or attend his first class in the morning. Around 10 a.m., when Dr. Leicester returned to his office, Seph was waiting outside, seated on the floor, arms clasped around his knees.

"Joseph," the headmaster said, looking down at him. "Aren't you supposed to be in class?"

"I need to talk to you," Seph said. It was more of a whisper. It hurt to speak.

"Why don't you come back this afternoon, after classes are over? You don't want to get off on the wrong foot."

"I'm already off on the wrong foot. I need to talk to you now."

"Of course. Come in." He stood aside so Seph could enter his office. Seph moved carefully, because every part of him hurt, body and soul.

For his part, the headmaster looked almost cheerful.

"Sit down," Leicester said, closing the door behind him and gesturing toward the table by the window.

"I'll stand. This won't take long." Seph gathered his thoughts. "I came to tell you that this isn't working out, this placement, I mean. Since I can't be trained in wizardry here, I'm going to contact my guardian and make arrangements for a transfer."

Leicester raised his hands to stop the speech. "Joseph, sit down." When Seph didn't respond, he added, "Sit *down*, I said."

Seph sat. Leicester sat across from him, steepling his hands and resting his chin on his fingertips. "I'd hoped perhaps you'd come to tell me you'd changed your mind."

"I have. I've realized that coming here was a mistake."

"Are you so sure of that? Where else are you going to get the help you need?"

"I'll find someone else to teach me."

"Really? Who? You told me yourself you've been looking for a teacher for two years. I believe you're running out of time."

"I've done all right so far."

"Have you?" The headmaster studied him. "You're having symptoms, aren't you?"

Seph looked him in the eyes. "No." He'd been lying for a lifetime and was really good at it.

Leicester wasn't impressed. "What is it? Hallucinations? Voices? Dreams? Paranoia?"

"Nothing."

"If you are hallucinating, it is your own fault. You have to give us the chance to help you." Leicester leaned back and folded his arms. "Cooperate with us, Joseph. That's all we ask." He smiled.

Seph remembered the scene at the chapel: the flickering torchlight, the altar, his blood flowing into the stone cup, the staff blazing up.

The warning on Peter's face.

Seph leaned forward. "If you want to help me, then teach me. But I'm not joining your cult or club or whatever."

The smile froze on Leicester's face. Then withered. "Let me be plain. Our enemies are gathering. My House—the White Rose—is the current holder of the

Hoard. That is the collection of magical artifacts handed down over the centuries through the tournament system.

"Last week, operatives believed to be working for the Dragon launched an attack against a magical repository in the southwest of Britain. They carried off weapons of unimaginable power.

"However, some believe the thieves were actually working for the Red Rose. There is talk of retaliatory action. As you can see, the stakes are incredibly high. The tiniest spark could set off a conflagration like the world has never known. I believe my initiative may be the last great hope for peace. Can you understand why I can't risk training someone as powerful as you whose loyalty is questionable?"

It made sense. It made total sense. And yet Seph had been on his own long enough to learn to trust his instincts. And his instincts said that Leicester and Barber and Hays were not peacemakers. Maybe he was crazy, but he had nothing else.

He smiled his best smile. "Dr. Leicester. I wish you and the alumni the best of luck in preventing a Wizard World War." *If that's what you're really about.* "But I'm really—you know—apolitical. I have a lot of personal issues to work through. I can't be joining a *movement.* I'll find someone to train me on the outside. And maybe when I'm older I'll feel differently." It was a pretty speech.

Seph stood. "I'm going to call Sloane's in London. They'll get me a flight, but I'll need a way to the airport. I tried my calling card on the phone in my dorm, but couldn't get through. I need to call this morning, during business hours."

"I'm afraid that won't be possible," said Gregory Leicester.

Seph was sure he'd misheard. "You're not going to let me make a phone call?"

Leicester stood and leaned his hips back against the table. "It's time to grow up, Joseph, and understand a few facts. Your guardian committed you. You are a minor, and he signed papers. Do you know what that means?"

"Committed me? Like I'm mentally incompetent or something?"

The headmaster sighed. "It looks like Mr. Houghton has not been completely straightforward with you. This is, in fact, a school for wayward and emotionally disturbed adolescents. I am, in fact, a psychologist."

"What?" Seph thought of the glossy brochure with the sailboat on the front. "Houghton never said anything about psychiatric treatment."

"The fact is, Mr. Houghton doesn't want any more catastrophes. He only wants to know that you're in recovery."

The headmaster returned to the table and sat down, dropping the file onto the polished wood in front of him. Retrieving a pen from his pocket, he pulled a fresh sheet of paper from the folder and scratched out a few notes.

"I don't believe you," Seph said. Leicester kept scratching away. "I don't drink or use drugs. No one ever said that I am a danger to myself or anyone else."

Leicester glanced down at his folder. "Didn't a student in Switzerland file assault charges against you?"

Perspiration trickled between Seph's shoulder blades.

He wiped his damp palms on his jeans. "It was a misunderstanding. They dropped the charges."

The headmaster tapped his pen on the papers in front of him. "There was also an . . . incident in Philadelphia."

Seph stared at him wordlessly. How could Leicester possibly know about Philadelphia?

Unless Denis Houghton had told him.

After Genevieve died, Seph had been determined to find out more about his parents. Sloane's had stonewalled him, so Seph had begun a search online, using the resources of adoptive children's networks, the genealogy Web sites and mail lists, and electronic vital records. He'd finally found his birth record, showing he'd been born in Toronto to Helen Jacoby and Jared McCauley. When he'd tried to dig further, he'd found no birth records for them, no grandparents, aunts or uncles, no listings in city directories in California or Toronto, no news stories about the fire, no real estate records, nothing.

It was all just a pretty construct with no truth behind it.

He'd broken into the administrative offices of the school he'd attended at the time, in Philadelphia. He'd hoped there would be some record of his parents, or a money trail that might lead to some answers. All he'd found in his file was copies of tuition payments and vouchers for living expenses from Sloane's. He had trashed the office in frustration. For that, he'd been expelled once again.

"Then there was the warehouse fire, of course." Leicester opened the folder again and scanned a document inside. "You've quite a record with the police. Pity about that girl."

A prickly heat collected in Seph's hands and arms, symptoms that often portended a release. He struggled to control his anger. "Houghton doesn't know anything about . . . about magic. Why would he blame me?"

"Mr. Houghton doesn't think you're a wizard. Mr. Houghton thinks you're a violent young hoodlum who likes to set fires and blow things up."

Seph recalled that last meeting in Toronto, Houghton's tweeded arm about his shoulders. But who knew what Houghton might do? Sloane's had been devoting some very expensive partner time to Seph McCauley's problems.

"If Houghton had me committed, I want to hear it from him," Seph said finally. His face was hot, his arms heavy, as if laden with power. And just then, he didn't care to restrain it.

Leicester shrugged. "Write to him, if you like. You will not be allowed phone calls in your current . . . unstable condition."

"Let me e-mail him, then."

"Joseph. You must understand. I can't risk having the Havens come to the attention of our enemies. And given your history, I cannot safely teach you wizardry without some element of control. It would be like putting a gun into the hand of a lunatic."

As if to underscore the headmaster's words, the fax machine exploded, sending shards of metal flying and clouds of toner rolling toward them.

Leicester looked a little rattled. "Joseph . . ."

A row of Chinese vases lined a shelf over Leicester's desk. They began to vibrate—then, one by one, imploded like targets in a shooting gallery.

The headmaster spoke in his psychiatrist voice. "Joseph. You're out of control."

The track light flickered, and the fixtures exploded. The front window bowed outward, then shattered, bits of glass glittering in the sunlight as they fell into the harbor.

"I'll go to the Roses," Seph said. "They'll give me the training I need."

Leicester extended his hand and spoke a charm. Something slammed into Seph, like a missile from a compressed air weapon, and he was down on his back on the floor, unable to move.

Leicester spoke from above him. "We call that a *subduen* charm."

Seph said nothing.

"Given the current political situation, I can't risk your alerting the Roses to what's going on here. They would murder us all." Leicester paused. Seph still didn't respond. "I'll let you up when you can control yourself."

Seph lay there a moment, breathing hard, then said, "Okay." Leicester muttered a few Latinesque words and Seph was able to sit up and drag himself to his feet. "So you're going to hold me prisoner here."

Leicester twisted the ring on his right hand. "Write a letter, Joseph, if you must, and we will mail it. And carefully consider the choice before you. If you don't learn to manage your power, it will destroy you. I will not waste time on anyone who is unwilling to commit to our cause and submit to my leadership. It's unfortunate, but that's the way it is. Until you complete the ceremony, nothing happens."

"There are plenty of lawyers in the world. If Denis Houghton committed me without a proper evaluation, I'll sue both your asses." Seph stalked out, slamming the door and clattering down the stairs.

When he was sure the boy had gone. Gregory Leicester picked up the phone and pressed an extension. "Joseph McCauley may attempt to call off-property," he said. "See that he's unsuccessful." He thought a moment, then added, "Meet me in my office in ten minutes. All of you." When he replaced the receiver in its cradle, he was smiling again.

He walked to the window. It was a beautiful autumn day. The sun glinted off the waves in the harbor, and the trees on the point were all in high color, the reds and golds that brought the tourists out. He sighed, flexing his hands. He must find the time to go sailing again before the weather turned.

Joseph was incredibly powerful. As soon as Leicester had reviewed the boy's carefully worded recommendations, he'd known. He had an instinct, after all these years. But he'd been overeager. He'd tried to move too fast, and the boy had balked. He should have laid the groundwork, should have softened him up before he asked him to commit.

Still, Leicester thought he could be managed, untrained as he was. Right now he was more angry than frightened. But that would change. Leicester would break him, he would rein in that wild power and put it to use. He closed his eyes, and his breath came a little faster.

It would have been easier if McCauley were younger. Twelve was ideal, but sixteen would work. He'd never known his system to fail, save once. Last year, he'd accepted an older student who had received some training elsewhere. It had been a mistake. The boy was still at the Havens, but perhaps not for much longer.

There was a knock at the door. "Come!" Leicester said. The alumni filed in, fifteen of them, all talented wizards. But none so powerful as Joseph McCauley. Leicester surveyed them, sorting through his mental notes. Being linked to them, he knew more about them than they ever suspected.

Warren Barber hated serving anyone. That, and the fact that he was the most powerful of this lot, made him dangerous. But his cruelty and his lack of a moral compass made him useful.

Bruce Hays loved having power over others. He would serve, if in turn, others served him.

Aaron Hanlon was smooth and articulate, a master of mind magic. Kenyon King was reasonably powerful, physically strong, and skilled at covert operations. John Hughes was invaluable as a systems expert. They were the core.

Wayne Eggars had accepted his role as physician. Ashton Rice and Elliott Richardson would serve, if reluctantly. They were reasonable men. They had accomplished much already.

Martin Hall and Peter Conroy were weaklings. It was not a matter of lack of power, but a reluctance to take ruthless action when required. Conroy in particular was a loose cannon, but they both contributed power to the mix.

"Good morning, gentlemen," he said. "Joseph McCauley still declines to link to us."

A mutter of surprise rolled through the alumni, but was quickly stifled.

"He has threatened to go to the Roses. This is unacceptable. I believe a peer-to-peer approach may be effective. I make it your charge to convince him to join us, through whatever means necessary.

"When he links with us, you will be richly rewarded. If he continues to resist, well, I think you all understand that there will be consequences." Now they all looked down at their feet, afraid he'd use one of them as an example. He'd done it before.

"Give him to me," Warren suggested. "I'll turn him around in a day."

Leicester sighed. "If it were a matter of brute force, Warren, I'd have settled the matter already. This requires subtlety. Creativity. Seduction. Not your long suit, I'm afraid." He rubbed his palms together. "We'll meet again on the subject in two weeks. Are there any questions?"

There were none.

The next day, after another night of excruciating dreams, Seph walked over to the art and music building and found a house phone back in the vending area in the basement. He picked it up and dialed 0. When the secretary in the admin. building answered, he said, "I'd like to place an outside call, using a calling card." He gave her the calling card information and the phone number, including the country code.

There was a brief pause. "Your name, please?"

"Joseph McCauley," Seph replied, hope evaporating.

"You'll need to get administrative approval," she said briskly. "Shall I put you through to Dr. Leicester?"

"No, thank you," Seph said, and hung up the phone.

The classroom routine was soothingly familiar, a little eddy in the madness of life at the Havens. Lecture, discussion, homework, examinations. All of the usual tools were in evidence: wood-and-metal desks lined up in rows, chalkboards, sinks and burners and hoods in chemistry lab. New textbooks that smelled of ink, with spines that crackled when you opened them. Like students everywhere, the students at the Havens whined about homework.

Seph sat in math class, chin propped on his fist, watching Mr. Richardson scribble equations on the board. Richardson would have been at the outdoor chapel, garbed in long gray robes, helping preside over that magical sacrifice. In retrospect, it seemed like a bad dream. What had spooked him? Rain and mist and bats and mummery.

And the fact that it seemed so important to Leicester.

In music, Mr. Rice told Seph he could schedule private lessons outside of class to work on piano or saxophone or another instrument. He encouraged Seph to consider joining the wind ensemble.

The bloody wind ensemble. It was so *normal*. So hard to reconcile with his fear of sleep, his dread of getting into bed.

After his last class, and before dinner, Seph went back to his room and booted up his computer. He'd decided to go ahead and write his letter.

TO: Denis Houghton, Esq., Guardian of Joseph McCauley
FROM: Joseph McCauley
RE: School placement at the Havens

When I arrived at the Havens, I was told that I'd been committed here for psychiatric treatment. I'm not sure what your intentions were, but the staff is unqualified and the methods used are cruel, arbitrary, and inconsistent, thus unlikely to prove effective.

This placement is not meeting my needs. I would like to request an immediate move so that I miss as little school as possible. I would consider a public school placement with private therapy if that is easier, in any geographic location. I will do everything I can to make it work out.

It is critical that this request be acted on right away. At the very least we need to meet to discuss my situation and arrange to get a second opinion. If you believe I would benefit from therapy, I have to think that there are better options.

He read it over again and bolded the part about doing everything to make it work out. He thought it sounded, well, *sane*. And non-accusing. He got it ready to mail and dropped it in the mail chute at the admin. building when he went in for supper.

The dreams came like heat lightning in summer, terrible dreams that illuminated those places in Seph's soul that were better left in the dark. The violence was sometimes physical, sometimes emotional, or both. All of his fears and insecurities surfaced and became weapons against him. The worst of it was that he never knew what to expect. Sometimes he would struggle to stay awake, then fall asleep in the early hours and sleep untroubled until his alarm sounded. Sometimes he dreamed three nights in a row, then nothing for three days.

The bizarre occurrences that had always dogged Seph seemed to intensify. He touched a light switch in his room and the electrical power in three buildings went out. Cakes fell and milk went sour in his presence. Hawks and ospreys collected on the roof of his dormitory and escorted him to his classes, swooping down on faculty along the way. The water froze in the pipes of the administration building, and trees bloomed out of season. A pack of wolves haunted the campus for a time, gray shadows lurking among the trees.

Seph constantly second-guessed his decision. He knew there was no guarantee he could find help outside of the Havens. Maybe Leicester's offer was his only option. Maybe his magical outbursts would increase until he had to be shot like a rabid beast.

The leaves on the aspens had been turning when Seph mailed his first letter to Sloane's. They lay like gold dust on the ground when he posted his second. He began to write several times a week so he could feel that he was really doing something. He gave up on sane and nonaccusing and resorted to desperate and threatening. There was never any response.

He tried to phone off-campus a half dozen times, from various phones and under assumed names. He was always intercepted by polite staff members who referred him to Dr. Leicester.

He continued to eat dinner at the Alumni House. They were his only potential sources of information, his only avenue of hope. They'd been trained in wizardry; they already knew how to manage their power. He reasoned that if he could win some of them over, they might share the secret that would prevent the dreams.

He focused especially on Peter Conroy. That first day, Peter had been eager to talk with him, obviously had information he wanted to share. But now Peter practically ran the other way when Seph approached. If he managed to corner him, some of the other alumni would intervene. Something had happened to frighten him away.

Others of the alumni worked hard to win him over. They shared no useful magical secrets with him, but plied him with offers of food, liquor, and illicit drugs. Faculty and alumni mingled at parties where he seemed to be the unwilling guest of honor. Maybe, he thought, drugs and alcohol would help.

But something told him they wouldn't.

Bruce Hays whispered to Seph about the unlimited power that lay within his grasp. "Maybe you report to Dr.

Leicester," Hays explained. "But when you think about it, the rest of the world reports to you."

Aaron Hanlon advised him that, given the current unsettled political situation, it was best to shelter under the protection of a powerful wizard. "There's going to be bloodshed," he warned. "Though Dr. Leicester is doing his best to prevent it. Just like during medieval times, it wouldn't hurt to have a patron."

It was like being rushed by a desperate and diabolical fraternity. But, given the fact that Trevor and the other Anaweir were avoiding him, Seph found himself spending more and more time in their company.

Seph was in the warehouse, stumbling through darkness, his wet shirt pressed to his face to defend against the oily smoke. His throat was raw from shouting and from breathing in the toxic air. He could see nothing, could hear nothing, save the roar of flames and the groaning of the old building as the timbers burned through.

"Maia! Maia, can you hear me?"

The fire crews had arrived, and were pouring water on to the roof. He was sloshing through knee-deep water while the skin on his upper body blistered and burned. He reached down, wet the shirt again, and pressed it to his face. He breathed in the stench of burning hair, and realized it was his own.

He was in a corridor now. When he extended his arms, he could feel walls to either side. He must be in the office areas to the back. Perhaps she'd taken refuge here when the way out was blocked. He passed through several doorways, carefully closing the doors behind him to keep the flames at bay a little longer.

Then he heard it, a faint cry from somewhere ahead. "Help!"

He stumbled on, touching the walls now and then to guide him. The walls were hot, the paint sticky under his hand. "Maia!"

He pushed through another doorway.

"Seph!"

The voice was weak and thready, but close, now, only a few feet ahead and to the right.

"Keep talking, Maia. I'm here to get you out." He crawled along the floor, groping with his hands, until he felt fabric under his fingers. She was huddled in a corner, where she'd retreated to try to keep her face beneath the smoke.

He tried to gather her up in his arms, but at his touch, her skin charred and burned and turned to ash, spiraling to the floor. He tried again, and her flesh crumbled in his hands, revealing bone. He screamed and let go, and she fell.

"Maia," he breathed, sliding to the floor, gathering her lifeless body into his lap, rocking her as gently as he could. "Maia, I'm so sorry." The heat was blistering. His tears evaporated, hissing, as soon as they emerged.

He was aroused by an incessant pounding. Firefighters. He didn't answer. He'd resolved to stay and burn. Somewhere, a door opened and closed.

"Seph?"

How did they know his name?

Everyone knew. Everyone knew he was guilty.

"Go away," he whispered, holding fiercely to Maia's body. "You're too late."

Someone had hold of his arm, shaking him. "Seph! Come on! Snap out of it."

Seph opened his eyes to a view of Trevor's worried

face. He looked over Trevor's shoulder. He was in his room. Sunlight dappled the hardwood floor. He had no idea what time it was. "Sorry." He forced the word out painfully, groaned, and wound his fingers into the bedclothes. "I'm okay now. Please. Leave me alone."

Wood scraped against wood as Trevor pulled a chair up next to the bed. It creaked as he dropped into it. "I don't get it," he said.

Seph turned his face away. There was no point in pretending. He felt like crap and knew he looked it. The room still reeked of vomit and terror.

When he was younger, they'd said he was possessed. He supposed he preferred crazy. But he knew what happened when the only people who care about you are on retainer. You end up in places like this. He needed to plan, to strategize. But first, he needed to get rid of Trevor.

"Look, I was up barfing all night, all right?"

Trevor cleared his throat and looked away. "I heard you."

"So I don't want company."

Trevor didn't move, but sat, biting at his lower lip. "I don't get it," he repeated. "You're one of them."

Seph blinked, brushed the back of his hand across his eyes, refocused on Trevor's face. "What?"

"You're one of them. You've been hanging out at Alumni House. So why are you up screaming every single night? I have to wear my headphones to get any sleep."

"Oh. Well. Sorry. I get nightmares when I'm sick. That's all."

"What did you do? You must've really messed up."

"What are you talking about?" Seph rolled onto his back, staring up at the ceiling.

Trevor leaned in close, breathing the words into Seph's ear, as if afraid of being overheard. "He calls it therapy." Trevor looked down at his hands. "The dreams, I mean."

Seph's battered mind grappled with this, teasing out a revelation. "You're telling me Leicester has something to do with . . . with . . ."

The look on Trevor's face was a *yes*. "It's like, whatever you're scared of, that's what he uses."

Seph shoved himself into a half-sitting position, leaning back against the carved headboard. "You're saying he makes people hallucinate. Dream. Have nightmares."

"That's what I'm saying."

"*This* happened to *you*?" Seph gestured weakly, taking in the trashed room.

Trevor swallowed hard. His dark face was nearly gray, the brown eyes muddy with remembered pain, his hands clasped tightly together. "I acted out a lot when I first got here."

"He uses this . . . as punishment?"

"He calls it therapy," Trevor repeated. "If you don't cooperate, I guess he thinks you need more therapy. So . . . in a way . . ."

"And other people have dreams? The Ana . . . other students? Not just us?"

"Everybody has dreams, at least at first. He says they're working through their hostility. Only, I figured you were different. I mean, you're like him. You and the alumni. Y'all have . . . some kind of power. Elsewise, why would the alumni stay? I'd leave, quick as I could."

Seph was only half listening. He wasn't crazy. It wasn't his own power that was destroying his mind. It was a spell. It must be. Leicester was spelling him, making him think he was crazy, make him desperate enough to agree to . . . to . . . what?

"Just do what he says," Trevor said, as if reading his mind. "Whatever he asks. I can tell you from experience what will happen if you try to fight him. It's up to you, but my advice is to sit up and speak and roll over, whatever it takes. Sucking up ain't that hard, once you get the hang of it."

"Doesn't anybody complain?" Seph asked.

"What're you going to say?" Trevor lifted his hands, palms up. "You had a nightmare at school and Dr. Leicester did it? Who would believe a story like that from someone with a track record like mine?"

"Leicester says this is a place for . . . for psychiatric cases. He told me we're hallucinating."

"I guess it's possible. I was a little rough before I got here, but nobody ever said I was crazy. Before I came to the Havens, all I dreamed about was girls."

"Couldn't your parents get you out of here, if you asked them?"

Trevor laughed bitterly. "Look. My parents love the Havens. This is the first school that didn't expel me inside of six months. All of my bad behaviors have been—what's the word—*extinguished*. I'm getting good grades. I'm probably going to college. I'm not a problem anymore. How'm I going to convince them to bring me home?"

"A few times, since I've been here, parents have come to campus all fired up about something they've heard. Leicester meets with them, and they go away satisfied. Or, at least they go away. He can be very persuasive, I guess. Anyone who complains really pays for it later." He cleared his throat. "Besides, it ain't so bad if you don't give him a reason to mess with you."

Seph remembered their visit to the Alumni House, Trevor begging Warren not to tell Dr. Leicester. "So what are Leicester and the alumni up to?"

Trevor shook his head. "I don't know, and I don't want to. Tell you the truth, he don't seem interested in the other students. I'm not sure he could pick me out of a lineup. But I'm not stupid. I figured out that if I cut class and messed with the teachers and smoked in the locker room, I'd pay for it. So I stopped. And since then he's left me alone."

Seph pushed back his sweat-matted hair. "Listen, how can I call out of here?"

"You can use any of the campus phones," Trevor said. "If you have a calling card, the office makes the call for you."

"No, I need a phone I can use myself."

"There's some kind of code to call direct. The office makes the calls." Trevor hesitated. "Who you going to call?"

"I need to reach my guardian. I've got to get out of here. Leicester won't put the calls through."

"Just be careful, Seph. Leicester knows everything. What he doesn't know, he'll get out of you somehow."

"So if he asked you about this conversation, you'd tell him?"

Trevor raised his hands, palms up. "Look, man, don't blame me. It's like you can't help it. He's a hypnotist or something."

Or something. Of course. Which meant Seph couldn't confide in anyone, or ask anyone for help.

"You mentioned someone named Jason. What'd he do? What happened to him?"

"Look, forget I ever said anything about him."

Seph rested a hand lightly on Trevor's shoulder, looked him in the eyes. "Tell me."

Trevor swallowed hard, as if trying to stop the words. "He was stirring things up. Wanted people to fight back against Dr. Leicester. Him and Sam and Peter. Then Sam drowned, and Peter and Jason are with the alumni now."

"Sam drowned?" Seph repeated. "Do you think . . ."

"I don't think anything." Trevor gave Seph a look. "And don't you push, because that's all I know."

Seph had to find a way to escape. Leicester had made it clear he wasn't going to let him go until he got what he wanted. With Leicester torturing him every night, Seph didn't know how long he could keep saying no.

After the conversation with Trevor, Seph began waging a very small, very unequal war against the Havens. He tried to run away three times in October, but they seemed to have an uncanny ability to track his movements. He hid in a delivery truck, but was intercepted at the gate. He tried to steal the school van, but the electrical system shorted out when he put the key into the ignition.

His class attendance deteriorated. He took a case of

beer from the Alumni House, and drank until he passed out, hoping to anesthetize himself. The first part of November, he set a fire in the art and music building after hours. When they dragged him into Leicester's office, he said, "Expel me." Instead, they confined him to his room and the dreams intensified.

Night and day began to merge into a long and painful continuum. If he stayed up all night, he hallucinated during the day. Several times, hopelessly confused, he begged Trevor to tell him whether he was awake or asleep.

Trevor seemed to have forgiven Seph for the sin of being gifted. He tried to help by cooperating with all of Seph's experiments. On the theory that his dreams were being triggered by something in his room, Seph spent the night on Trevor's floor. The dreams followed him. Trevor stayed over in Seph's room, so he could wake him when the dreams began. But it was impossible to wake Seph from his nightmares, and Trevor couldn't bear to be anywhere near while they were going on.

Meanwhile, Leicester and the alumni watched him, like predators stalking wounded prey, waiting for him to falter so they could close in for the kill.

Gregory Leicester sat in his favorite chair and gazed moodily out to sea. It was unnaturally dark for that time of day, and the lights were already ablaze out on the dock. They were predicting a northeaster, one of the first of the season. Leicester could always detect the drop in pressure when a storm was on the way.

Joseph McCauley was both extraordinarily powerful

and amazingly resistant. He'd been at the Havens for more than three months under intensive pressure. Save the one previous failure, no one had ever held out so long. Could Joseph have had some contact with Jason? No. He'd been careful to keep the two apart.

As always, Leicester was impatient with the process, more so in this case, given the prize that lay within his grasp. Recruitment was messy and uncontrolled, and there was always the chance that the intended would escape by taking his own life. This his continuing rebellion was a warning. He resolved to have the staff keep a closer eye on Joseph.

He was sure the matter could be handled more efficiently. He had no doubt he could quickly get what he wanted, given a free hand with the boy. It was D'Orsay who had insisted on this tender approach, the dreams that marked the soul and not the body. D'Orsay believed it would be difficult for the Wizard Council to trace this kind of slow poison to them, if it came to that. It was splitting hairs, but then that was a politician's job.

Leicester wished he had Joseph's Weirbook. It would help to know a little more about him, his strengths and weaknesses. That might bring some insight, provide a strategy. He hungered for the opportunity to put that remarkable power into play.

He drained his glass, feeling a little better. The boy knew there was a way out; he couldn't help but be tempted to take it eventually. It might take a little research, a little more pressure, but Leicester was confident he would be successful in the end.

❧ CHAPTER SEVEN ❧
JASON

You don't have to understand. You just have to survive, Seph told himself.

He dreamed every night now, and the nightmares were longer and more intense than before. He felt wasted mentally and physically, yet he forced himself to get up out of bed and walk over to the cafeteria and eat breakfast. Sometimes he went to class, sometimes he just returned to his room and lay staring at the ceiling.

They were coming in the daytime too, striking out of nowhere, splitting him cleanly from reality in an instant. He would awaken screaming in math class, crying out in the middle of government, muttering and twitching in chemistry class. He nearly blew up the building when he ignited the chemicals in the lab.

Everyone pretended not to notice. It was as if he traveled around campus with a dreadful disfigurement, and those around him had been told not to stare and point. It was impossible to learn anything. He no longer fought back, no longer spun any plots against them. The spark of resistance was extinguished in him, save his refusal to give them the one thing they wanted. He was like a prisoner under torture who refuses to surrender the password long after he's forgotten why. It was all he could do just to be in the world.

The only thing that helped was walking. As long as he kept moving, the demons couldn't catch him. At first he walked restlessly from building to building. Later, he put on snowshoes and walked for miles through the woods. Once he made it as far as the wall that bordered the property. But he couldn't find the gate and he couldn't seem to get a grip on it to climb before they came and took him back.

Or maybe that was just a dream.

Christmas was coming, but Seph wasn't looking forward to it. Trevor had invited Seph to spend Christmas in Atlanta, but Leicester vetoed the idea. Seph's condition was too delicate, he said. Seph had to admit that anyone who saw him would have to agree. He looked terrible. He continued to lose weight despite eating all he could.

He had begun to think of ways to kill himself: clever, foolproof ways that wouldn't land him in the infirmary. He imagined he was locked in a room with two doors. Death lay behind one of them, Gregory Leicester and his offer behind another. There was no other way out, as far as he could see.

★ ★ ★

Trevor Hill was worried about Seph. He knew from experience that one night of "therapy" was life changing. From what he'd seen and heard, Seph had suffered through forty or fifty of them. Yet there seemed to be something iron-hard in Seph, some stubborn instinct for survival that kept him going.

Still, Trevor could tell that Seph was failing. He looked frail, insubstantial, like someone whose spirit is devouring his flesh. By now, he might actually be mentally ill, his brain damaged by days and nights of torture. Trevor felt guilty because he hadn't been able to offer any help. Guilty because he was glad it was Seph and not him. Confused because he couldn't figure out why Seph was being targeted. He wasn't like the other alumni, who treated Trevor and the others like dirt when they noticed them at all.

On the day the term ended, Trevor invited Seph to his room to keep him company while he packed. Trevor had ordered Christmas presents through the mail to take home with him. He'd wrapped up some books for Seph, and insisted that he open them.

Seph sprawled on his back on Trevor's bed in a kind of persistent twilight. He clenched and unclenched his hands, twitching and shivering by turns, staring out at the world with his changeable eyes as if he could see things no one else could see. Sometimes he touched the cross he always wore around his neck and muttered to himself in French.

"Look," Trevor said finally. "Give me the name of that law firm in London. I'll call them from my folks' house while I'm home."

For a moment, Trevor thought he hadn't heard. Then Seph stirred. "Won't do any good. I've written to them a hundred times. They've never responded."

"Well, maybe it would help if they heard it from someone else," Trevor insisted.

"All right. I'll get you the number."

Trevor studied him. "Hey," he said softly. "You going to be all right?"

Seph didn't answer for a moment, and that hesitation worried Trevor even more. "I'll be okay," he said finally. "I don't know what else they can do to me."

The campus was eerily quiet after the departure of the other students. The regular meal service was discontinued over break, but the dining room in the Alumni House continued to operate. Seph took his meals there with the faculty and other alumni who remained on campus.

It made no sense. Didn't they have families? Didn't they have anywhere better to go for the holidays?

Seph shuffled through Trevor's books with the idea of losing himself in fiction, but couldn't seem to concentrate. Entire days vanished from memory. He continued to walk when he felt up to it.

Sloane's sent a large gift basket and a generous gift certificate, a card printed with his name. Back in September, Seph had been convinced he'd be expelled from the Havens by Christmas. Now all he could think about was escape.

Christmas Eve dinner was served by candlelight in the elegant, two-story alumni-staff dining hall. Bruce Hays and Warren Barber, the two enforcers, sat on either side of

Seph. The other thirteen alumni were ranged around the table. He grappled with the names, was pleased when he remembered most of them. He hadn't dreamed for several days, and his head was clearer than usual.

Martin Hall was functioning as sommelier, circling the table, opening wine and pouring. Liquor flowed at the open bar, and a different wine was paired with each course. Leicester wasn't there.

Tension crouched in the room like a snappish dog, and Seph couldn't help but think that he was the source of it. The others watched him when they thought he wasn't looking and whispered together at the far ends of the table.

"Where's Dr. Leicester?" he asked Bruce, as the fish course was taken away.

Hays wiped his mouth with the back of his hand. "He left two days ago. Went back home to England, I guess. Be gone a week."

"So, drink up, Joseph." Barber put the wine glass into his hand. "Cat's away."

Seph had, in fact, been pacing himself, making a show of sipping at his wine, and ignoring the whisky Barber set by his right hand. The others drank with desperate intensity, like mourners at a wake.

After dessert, Ashton Rice sat down at the piano and began banging out carols. Their voices rose in a drunken, off-key chorus. Hays and Barber didn't sing. They set a whisky bottle between them and took turns pouring.

"Doesn't anyone go home for Christmas?" Seph asked, oppressed by the forced gaiety, yet hoping he might learn something useful.

"Home is no longer . . . relevant," Hays mumbled, looking surprised to have come up with the word. He blinked at Seph owlishly. "You'll find out. You'll see. We're like . . . blood brothers. Bloody . . . Siamese twins." He groped for the bottle.

Barber slammed his glass down on the table, rattling the crockery. "Only, Joseph's too good to join, remember?"

The singing dwindled away, and Seph was once again the reluctant center of attention. He cleared his throat. "Maybe if you tell me what's going on . . ."

"He'd rather go crazy." Barber clutched at Seph's shirt-front and dragged him to his feet. "The rest of us have to answer to Leicester. But Seph's got his *principles.*"

Seph found himself nose to nose with Barber's stubbled face. "Hey, let go!" Seph tried to wrench himself free, and heard fabric tearing. "What's wrong with you?"

Hays pawed ineffectually at Barber's shoulder. "C'mon, Warren. Joseph'll be all right. Give him time."

"In the meantime, we're paying for it." Barber shoved Seph up against the wall. "Maybe we haven't properly explained . . . the benefits of membership. We're your only friends now, do you hear me? Other than us, you got nobody."

Seph felt the burn of power building at his core. "Let go. I'm warning you."

"Warren . . ." Hays sounded worried. Eggars rose to his feet like he wanted to intervene, but was unsure how to proceed. The others clustered unhappily around them.

"Leicester's been . . . on our backs . . . since September," Barber gasped, punctuating his speech by slamming Seph against the wall. "What's it going to take?"

"Leave . . . me . . . alone!" Seph shoved out with both hands. Months of fear and frustration seemed to detonate in his fingers and a percussion like a gunshot sent Barber flying backward onto the table. He slid across it on his back and off the other side, sending wineglasses and dessert plates crashing. Seph charged after him, vaulted over the table, and leaped on top of Barber as he lay on the floor. They wrestled briefly, Seph smashing his fist into Barber's face, Barber too drunk to evade him. And then they dragged Seph back, several of them together, pinning his arms, their hands hot and electrical against his skin.

Barber staggered to his feet and stumbled toward Seph, murder on his face. But help came from an unexpected quarter. Martin Hall stepped between them, holding the butcher knife that had been used on the crown roast. The blade wavered in his hand, but it was very large. "Get back, Warren. You're not yourself."

"Get out of the way!" Barber said, coming on.

"And if Dr. Leicester comes back and finds you've beaten him to death, what then?"

Barber's forward progress slowed, then stopped.

"Stop it, Warren! Hasn't there been enough bloodshed already?" Martin waved the knife wildly, and Barber stepped back. Martin turned toward Seph, and Seph was surprised to see that his face was streaked with tears. He gestured with the knife. "Let him go. You know as well as I do that he's not the enemy."

After a moment, the grip on Seph's arms relaxed. The hot hands dropped away.

"What's the matter with you?" Seph pivoted so he could look into all their faces, hidden and revealed in the candlelight. "Why do you stay here? What kind of hold does he have on you?"

Barber clenched his fists. "Who the hell do you think you are, lecturing *us*?"

Seph was beyond caring. "He's gone! He's in England. This is our chance. Let's get out of here. Or, if *you* like it here so much, then let me go."

Martin spoke with great dignity and sorrow. "We can't do what you ask, Joseph. Now, go on back to your room and lock the door until my colleagues have sobered up."

They all stood watching as Seph backed out of the dining hall, leaving with more questions than answers.

Despite the episode in Alumni House, Seph slept peacefully on Christmas Eve and Christmas Day, nearly twenty-four hours in all. He assumed that it was because Leicester was away. As a result, his head was clearer than it had been for a long time, and being in the Alumni House gave him an idea.

He knew his letters to Sloane's were being intercepted. After all, Seph was a valuable client with a large trust fund who would gain control of it one day.

Which made him think of e-mail again.

Surely the alumni were online. That must be why they had their own library. If there was no access in the library, he'd break into someone's room. Maybe Trevor had called Sloane's, but Seph decided he couldn't afford to wait until classes resumed to find out. By then, Leicester would have returned and he would no longer have easy access to the Alumni House.

He waited until the day after Christmas, after his third good night's sleep in a month. He ate a late breakfast with Martin and Peter in the dining room at the Alumni House. He made it a point to sit with them, and tried to question them, but got nowhere at all.

Barber slouched in just as they were finishing, wearing what looked like a major hangover. Seph jumped when Barber patted him on the shoulder, but Barber acted like he didn't remember the confrontation at dinner. And perhaps he didn't. He'd been pretty wasted.

When the dining room began to empty, Seph went to the washroom and took his time. Finally, he slipped through the hallway and into the back stairwell beyond. The door into the stairwell bore a sign, FACULTY AND ALUMNI ONLY. He took a deep breath. What could they do, kick him out of school? Send him another nightmare?

The door at the top of the stairs opened onto a small circular landing, with hallways spoking off to either side, the stairway to the third floor directly ahead. The corridors were lined with gleaming wood molding, shaded wall sconces, rows of closed doors. No one seemed to be around.

He'd try the library first. His presence there would be easier to explain.

The hallway to the left was lined with classrooms, with the library at the far end. Fortunately, the heavy wooden door was unlocked. He glanced over his shoulder, stepped inside, and pulled it shut behind him.

The library smelled like Genevieve's attic: of dust and mildew and disintegrating paper. He stifled a sneeze. The books on the first set of shelves appeared to be quite old, with dark leather covers and stamped gold lettering. Curious, Seph pulled a volume from the shelf, tilting it so the title caught the light. It seemed to be in Latin. *Transformare.* The next one was entitled, *Extracten Poysoun 1291.* Not Latin, exactly. He'd studied Latin with the Jesuits. But close. Middle English? He moved on into the room, hoping to find what he was looking for at the rear.

He worked his way toward the back wall. More old books and some new ones. He pulled out one of the newer ones. *Spellbinding: The Art of Influencing Others.* Here was the reading he should have been doing. Rows and rows of large volumes were shelved together, books that looked somewhat alike. Their titles were similar, too. *Weir Smythe John Artur. Weir Thompson Harold Franklin. Weir Huntingdon Bru Amfeld.*

Weirbooks. They must be. Seph lifted one down and leafed through it. The first part was taken up with a family tree, all handwritten, going back centuries, illuminated in bright colors. Another section of the book was entitled "Charms and Incantations." Something about the books struck a chord with Seph, stirring up a memory he couldn't quite capture. Reluctantly, he returned the book to its place on the shelf.

He finally found what he was looking for under the windows at the back of the room. There were six computers lined up on tables and networked to a cable plugged into the wall. They shared a common printer.

Seph couldn't shake the feeling that he was being watched. The hair on the back of his neck stood up, and his arms prickled with gooseflesh. The building creaked and complained under the assault of the wind. He peered over his shoulder, seeing only books and dust and narrow aisleways. Shrugging, he hit the power button on one of the PCs. It sounded jarringly loud in the stillness as it booted up.

The computer hadn't even made it through its startup routine when he heard running feet. Swearing softly, Seph hit the power button again and the screen went dark. The door slammed open, and the lights overhead flickered, then kindled into brilliance.

"I saw someone moving around in here," someone said breathlessly.

"You stay by the door," the other replied. "I'll check it out."

Seph slipped between the rows of shelves and cat-footed up the aisle along the wall toward the exit. Peter Conroy waited by the door, nervously scanning the aisles, forehead gleaming in the overhead light.

"You sure you're not seeing things again?" The other voice was familiar and startlingly close at hand. "You'd better not have dragged me up here for nothing." Seph could hear the sound of feet moving toward him. He was trapped.

Someone clapped a hand over his mouth and grabbed him by the arm, pulling him back against the wall. "Be quiet!" a voice hissed in his ear. It said something else Seph couldn't make out.

At that moment, Warren Barber came around the corner and walked toward them. He still looked a bit green from last night's drinking. Seph didn't struggle. He stood quietly, wondering what the penalty for breaking into the alumni library would be.

To his amazement, Barber walked right past them toward the front of the library. "Nobody's back here now."

"I swear I saw someone on the monitor."

"Yeah? Well, maybe he flew out the window. As if someone would break into a freaking library."

"Keep still!" the voice whispered again. Seph turned his head slightly so he could see who had hold of him. To his shock, he saw nothing but the shelves of books behind him. There was no one there. The hand over his mouth tightened, smothering his exclamation of surprise.

He felt sick. He was hallucinating again. He must be. His palms went clammy with sweat, and he wiped them on his jeans.

Barber and Conroy met up at the front of the room, then walked up and down the stacks again, passing within inches of Seph and his invisible captor. Barber still reeked of beer.

"You're delirious, Conroy," Barber said, shaking his head. "You must've blundered onto the Sci-Fi Channel." Conroy was still protesting as they walked out and closed the door behind them.

"Just be cool a minute," Seph's captor instructed him. "Make sure they're really gone." Seph stood as still as he could, although he was beginning to tremble, his heart pounding wildly. After a minute, the hand was removed from his mouth.

"Come on," the disembodied voice said. Someone shoved Seph up the aisle to the front of the room, then to the right, toward a door marked AV Storage. "In there," the voice said, and Seph pushed the door open. It was a large closet, lined with projection equipment, AV carts, and a couple of old computers. Seph stepped inside and the door was pulled shut behind him.

"No cameras in here," the voice explained, following with something that sounded like Latin. Suddenly, as if assembled out of the air, he could see the body that went with the voice.

He looked to be seventeen or eighteen, slightly built, dressed in a black T-shirt and jeans. His hair was dark, but had been bleached out at the tips and spiked, an amateur job. He had two earrings in one ear and one in the other. He was grinning as if delighted.

"So you're the newbie," he said. "I heard you were here. Not that anyone offered to *introduce* us, of course." He swept an arm toward an audiovisual cart. "Welcome to the catacombs," he said gravely. "Have a seat."

Seph sat down on the cart with a bump and put his head in his hands. He'd thought he was clearheaded after two nights of sleep. Apparently he'd thought wrong.

"Are you all right?"

Seph looked up to find the stranger staring at him. "I . . . I'm not sure," Seph replied cautiously. "I . . . ah . . . I haven't been well."

The boy leaned against the wall. "Allow me to offer you a belated welcome to the Havens—where all your dreams turn into nightmares."

Seph laughed in spite of himself. It struck him that it had been forever since he'd laughed, forever since he'd actually heard anyone make a joke. "I'm Seph McCauley." He hesitated. "How'd you do that? Are you one of the alumni? I don't remember you from Christmas dinner."

The stranger rolled his eyes. "No, I'm not planning to join that particular club. I'm just the poltergeist in this haunted house. I'm Jason Haley."

Jason. According to Trevor, he was the one who'd instigated the ill-fated rebellion. Who'd gotten Sam killed.

"You're gifted, but you're not one of them?"

"Nope."

"That's not what I heard."

"Well, you heard wrong. By the way, if you're going to be sneaking around in here, you ought to know that they have cameras just about everywhere. Matter of fact, I wouldn't do or say anything in your room that you don't want to share."

"Then you're a student?" Seph persisted.

"So to speak," Jason said dryly. "I'm not supposed to be up here, either, but I'm doing a little independent research."

"So what'd you *do* in there? It was like we were invisible."

"Oh, we were better than invisible," Jason replied. "We were *unnoticeable*." He laughed as if this were a fine joke. "How long have you been here, Seph?"

"Since September."

"You've been here almost four months, and you haven't given in?" A note of respect crept into Jason's voice. "And they've been doing you?" He touched his head with his fingertips.

"Almost every night now." Seph laced his fingers together and stared at the floor.

"You must be damn tough," Jason said. "But they're getting to you, aren't they?"

Seph nodded, without looking up.

"And you're clueless about what's going on." It was not a question.

"It's like they're trying to make me crazy."

"If you think they're trying to make you crazy, it's because they are. Crazy enough to join them." Jason pushed away from the wall and came and sat next to Seph on the cart. He stared at him for a long minute at close range. "Can't your family get you out?"

Seph shook his head. "I don't really have any family. Only a guardian. A lawyer in London."

"What were you doing in the library?"

"I'm trying to reach my guardian. Dr. Leicester won't let me call him. I've been sending letters, but no response. So I thought I'd email him from the computers out there."

Jason shook his head. "Won't work. They batch everything and go through all the messages before they go out, even in the Alumni House. You'd need to use one of the machines in administration. And you can forget about your letters. If they didn't go straight to the shredder, Leicester's been reading them in bed."

Seph blinked. Jason Haley was matter-of-fact, author-itative, convincing. "What about you? Why haven't *you* joined?"

Jason stood. "Look, I've been warned against having any contact with you. If they find out we've been together, there'll be hell to pay."

"You're saying I might end up like Sam?"

Jason nodded, rubbing the bridge of his nose as if it hurt. "Yeah. Or I might." He cleared his throat. "Anyway. Nice meeting you, Seph. Good luck." He turned away.

Seph slid between Jason and the door and put his back against it. "No. Tell me what's going on. I can't fight them if I don't know what I'm fighting. If I stay here much longer, I *will* be crazy." He cast about for a weapon. "If you don't help me, I'll tell them about the invisibility thing. I've got nothing to lose."

Jason stood, hands in his pockets, lips pressed together, looking off to the side as if he might find his answer writ-ten on the wall. "Listen," he said after a long pause. "Let me think about it. Meet me in the woods by the outdoor chapel tomorrow at six. And you'd better not let anyone follow you."

Seph nodded, and stepped aside. Jason brushed past him and was gone.

The next evening, Seph left the dorm, avoiding the paths and cutting through the woods. The air was cold and clear, prickling his nose, and his breath emerged in clouds of vapor. The winter sun had already set and the moon hadn't risen, but the snow reflected back what light there was and made it easy to pick his way through the trees.

Trevor had said Jason was with the alumni now. But Jason said he wasn't, and Seph hadn't seen him at the ceremony in the woods or at dinner. It was as if Jason had been hidden away from Seph, and perhaps from everyone. Why had Jason been told to stay away from him?

Now Jason wanted Seph to meet him at the outdoor chapel. He couldn't help wondering if it was a trap.

He approached the chapel from the woods on the right side. Surrounded by soaring pines, it had the look of a primitive cathedral. Someone had been there before him. Snow had drifted over the seats to the rear, but several rows of stones at the front had been brushed clean. The clearing was quilted with tracks, and the snow around the seats was beaten down, as if by many feet. The notion of a trap returned.

He climbed onto the stone platform. There were signs of recent activity there as well. Someone had constructed a ring of weathered gray stones in the center, and left blackened remnants of a fire within. Had there been another ceremony? The bonfire must have happened within the past week, because it had snowed a few days before Christmas.

Seph shivered, and not from the cold. The wind sighed through the trees.

He grabbed up a fallen branch and poked it through the ashes and chunks of charred wood on the makeshift hearth. Something glinted in the pale moonlight that filtered through the trees. He caught it on the branch and lifted it. It was a gold chain with a pendant, blackened from the heat of the fire. It looked familiar, but he couldn't place it. He put it in his pocket.

"Someone was celebrating the solstice." Seph spun around to see Jason standing a few feet away. The moon was behind him, his face hidden, his shadow tall and angular as it stretched across the stone toward Seph. His gelled hair stood up a bit from his head like a crown. He looked like a shaman from an ancient tribe, in a leather jacket and blue jeans.

"Solstice?"

Jason nodded. "It's the best time to conjure old magic. Leicester'd better be careful or he might get burned." Stooping, he picked up a piece of the wood from the fire and put it into his jacket pocket. "I'm surprised they didn't clean this up."

He sat on one of the stone benches, his shadow compressing itself, and motioned for Seph to sit next to him. Warily, Seph complied.

Jason stared into the cold hearth for a long moment, a muscle working in his jaw. But when he began to speak, the words poured out in a rush, as if he had already made his decision, and just wanted to get it done.

"Look. I'm going to tell you some things. But you'd better know now that I'm dead if Leicester ever gets a whiff of this. God knows what he'll do to you. After what happened with Sam and Peter, I swore I'd work alone." He paused again. "So what I'm saying is, if I help you, and Leicester twists your arm and you spill your guts, I'll kill you." He opened his eyes and looked directly at Seph, and Seph believed Jason Haley when he said it.

"So the question is, are you strong enough to say no to him?" Jason's eyes were like bright blue crystals.

Seph nodded. He had already said no to Leicester, and he was paying for it, every night.

"Good," Jason said. He sat thinking for a moment, as if he weren't sure how to begin. "How much do you know about the magical guilds?"

"A little. Nobody's trained me, if that's what you mean."

Jason grinned. "Truly. I've seen your work. Nice job on the chemistry lab."

"You said you had something to tell me."

Jason's smile faded. "All right. Leicester is trying to get control of young, ignorant wizards like yourself." Jason threw him a sideways look. "Wizards born into Anaweir families. Mostly he gets your common hoodlum. A lot are referred from the courts. The program up here works well for them. Leicester shows them a few of his nighttime videos, and they settle right down. So his success rate is very high." Jason pushed himself up and off his stone seat, pacing back and forth in front of the dais. "But every so often he turns up a pearl in his oyster. That's you, Seph."

Seph nodded toward the stone platform. "He brought me up here right after I came. I was the guest of honor at some kind of . . . of ritual."

Jason rested his hand on the altar. "It's Old Magic. He wants you to link to him. You've seen the faculty and the alumni. All former students, all wizards, all under Leicester's control. I guess it's an easy sell for most of them. You're a teenager, you've been in trouble all your life, and he promises to make you 'one of the most powerful magical practitioners of the age.' I mean, why would you read the fine print?"

Jason had totally nailed Leicester's stuffy private-school British accent, and Seph couldn't help laughing. "What's he want with them?"

"I don't know, exactly," Jason admitted. "But if you have even two or three wizards, you have an army. He trains some of them, anyway. That's what the library is for. All magic and poisons and incantations. Huge section on attack spells. Some of the alumni have spent years studying here. Leicester's in no hurry, because wizards live a long time. He hits pay dirt probably only once every two or three years. I came last year as a kind of bonus, but I haven't worked out very well. But, you—" Jason smiled crookedly. "Powerful as you are? He's never going to let you go."

"What makes you think I'm powerful?" Seph was absurdly flattered.

"Trust me. That's why you've been having so much trouble. When you don't know how to use it or dissipate it, magic builds up and eventually explodes. It's like shaking a bottle of soda."

"But what's he going to do with an army of wizards?" Seph persisted.

"Did you hear what happened at Raven's Ghyll?"

Raven's Ghyll. That girl Alicia had mentioned it at the warehouse. "Some kind of tournament?"

Jason settled back on the bench. "I hate to break this to you, but as a rule, wizards are nasty people. They're powerful, capricious, ruthless, egotistical, used to getting their own way. That's being kind. There are two great wizard Houses, the Red Rose and the White. They started fighting back during the War of the Roses, if you know your British history. After a couple centuries of bloodshed, they adopted a document called the *Rules of Engagement*. Without it, they might have wiped themselves out years ago.

"For hundreds of years, the only sanctioned fighting they've done is through the Game. Even in the tournaments, the fighting is done by warriors, not wizards. It's a fight to the death. They use medieval weapons, and it's all really structured under the rules. The winning house controls the Hoard: a crapload of property, magical artifacts, and like that. Still, there's a lot of *unofficial* bloodshed and intrigue that goes on behind the scenes. They call that *wizard politics*.

"There was this tournament at Raven's Ghyll last spring. An army of ghosts showed up, the players revolted, and the rules were changed. They established a sanctuary—in Ohio, of all places. Some little town called Trinity.

"Since then, the Roses have been conspiring, trying to figure out how to retain control of the Hoard and regain control of the other guilds." He paused. "You know about the other guilds?"

Seph nodded. "Sorcerers, seers, warriors, and enchanters. I know a lot about sorcerers. Less about the others."

"They've been dominated by wizards, because wizards can shape magic with charms. But they each have their own special talent. Sorcerers are good with materials, magical objects, potions, plants, and like that. Seers have the gift of prophecy. Warriors kick butt in a fight. Enchanters . . ." Here he smiled dreamily. "Enchanters have the gift of charisma. They cloud the mind and stimulate the—ah—senses."

"Okay." Seph had never heard the guilds described in just that way before.

"I've never met an enchanter," Jason said, rather wistfully. "So. The Roses have established something called The Council of Wizards, supposedly to facilitate planning of the Interguild Council required by the new rules.

"There's also an underground interguild network led by someone called the Dragon. They've managed to keep the Roses occupied fighting among themselves. They intercept messages, plant false ones, blow things up. After the council refused to give up the Hoard, the Dragon's operatives began raiding weapons caches all over the world. When I get out, I'm joining up with him. Or her. I figure any enemy of Leicester is an ally of mine."

"So is Leicester working for the Roses?" Seph asked. "I got the impression he's not."

"Leicester's in league with another powerful wizard, name of D'Orsay, who is Gamemaster of the Council. They have meetings up here sometimes. They're planning something, and you know it has to involve the alumni. It may be the wizard wars, all over again."

"How did you end up here?" Seph asked.

Jason hunched his shoulders and looked away. "I'm the product of a mixed marriage. My mother was a hedge wizard—an expert in spirituality and Old Magic. My father was Anaweir. He wasn't exactly okay with the occult, so she downplayed her gift. When I came along, she taught me some easy charms, how to use talismans, kids' stuff, mostly. It took me a long time to understand that the magic was in us and not in the tools and incantations.

"She died when I was thirteen. Really young for a wizard." He seemed to be picking his way carefully. "Anyway, my father remarried, this time to an Anaweir woman. They were happy, but I was pissed off. My mom had dropped this big load on me and there was no one I could talk to, no one to teach me. I didn't get along with my stepmother."

His face twisted, a recollection of old pain. "They both acted like I was crazy or dangerous or something. They were probably right. I knew how to stay out of trouble, but I didn't. The courts got involved. So they sent me here. I actually thought it might be . . . better. To get away, I mean." He laughed bitterly. "I was wrong."

"How long have you been here?"

"I'm a senior. I came midway though my junior year."

"Why'd you come back?" Seph demanded. "I'd do anything to get out of here."

"I never left. He kept me here all summer, some bull about making up work in summer school." Jason rolled his eyes. "That was a treat. Me and Leicester and the zombies in the Alumni Club. He got to me too late. I know too much about Old Magic to agree to any kind of linkage." He fumbled in his jacket pocket, pulled out a pack of cigarettes. His hands shook, and it took him three tries to strike a match. The flame threw the angular bones of his face into sharp relief. "See, I'm like you, Seph. Nobody's got the frickin' porch light on for me."

There was nothing to say to that, so Seph didn't say anything.

Jason waved away the smoke and the sentiment. "Whoa. Didn't mean to get maudlin. Anyway. I'm not staying much longer. I'm here for two reasons. For one, I'm teaching myself wizardry, and their library is amazing. Secondly, I'm trying to find out what D'Orsay and Leicester are planning. If I want to join the Dragon, I figure I'd better bring something to the table."

Seph studied him skeptically. "How are you going to get away? I've been trying to leave since September. Even when I make it to the edge of the campus, I can't get past the wall."

"It's a wizard wall. A magical barrier. You'll never get near enough to climb it, and forget about finding the gate." Jason seemed to relish the role of expert.

"So how are you going to get out?"

"That's one of the things I'm researching. That bastard won't keep me here when I'm ready to go." Jason had a reckless confidence that Seph envied.

Seph sorted through his mental list of questions. "If your mother was a wizard, that is, if women can be wizards, then why would Leicester start a boys' school?"

Jason snorted. "Probably has more to do with Leicester's attitude toward women than anything else. Not exactly collegial, if you know what I mean."

"How'd you do that thing in the library? The invisibility thing."

"Unnoticeable. It's a charm that acts on the observer. A subtle difference. What's *invisible*? You? Your clothes? The stuff you're carrying around? The unnoticeable charm requires a talisman. An artifact of magic. Barber and Conroy didn't *notice* us, but we were unchanged. The only thing is, you can't cast spells while you're unnoticeable. Because charms are noticeable, of course."

Of course. "How does Leicester do it? The nightmares, I mean?"

Jason shrugged. "He's a wizard. It's a charm of some kind, probably a spoken one. It wouldn't be too hard, I guess, since it's used against people with no training."

"I don't get it. He's a trained wizard. There's got to be another way he can get what he wants."

"He can use High Magic to make you crazy, but not to make you submit. Linkages are tricky. They have to be voluntary. Plus, linkages go both ways. So there's always the chance that he'll encounter a wizard more powerful than he is, and then he'd be toast." At Seph's blank look, he added impatiently, "This is Old Magic. He uses it because other wizards aren't familiar with it, but he's not an expert, either."

"What's the difference between Old Magic and High Magic?"

"Old Magic is more basic, hedge wizards and backstreet conjurors use it. There's a lot of blood sacrifice and whatnot."

"He has this staff he uses in the ceremony."

"Yup. Probably has a magical element in it. You know, a dragon scale or something." Seph couldn't tell if he was joking or not.

Seph stuffed his frozen hands into his pockets. "What happened with Sam and Peter?"

"Sam and Peter." Jason looked away and kicked at an icicle on the underside of the bench. It exploded into shards of glittering ice. "I had this idea for a coup. I mean, you could tell the alumni were miserable and the Anaweir were scared. I figured if we all joined together, we could win.

"Peter was the only other gifted student who hadn't joined. Sam was Peter's best friend. Anaweir, but fearless. They were up for it." Jason fell silent for a moment, staring bleakly out into the seats.

"It was doomed from the start. The alumni are totally under Leicester's control. Magically, at least. Worse than useless. Someone told Leicester. He threatened to kill Sam, and Peter caved and agreed to link." Jason smiled bitterly. "Afterward, Peter needed to be taught a lesson and Sam was expendable, so they killed him." He looked up at Seph. "And, no, I can't prove it. But it's true."

"What'd he do to you?" It seemed like a personal question, but Seph had to ask.

"Well. He didn't kill me. I'm too valuable an asset, potentially, at least. And he and his buddies are leery about physical punishment that leaves evidence. But as you know, he can be very creative." Jason swallowed hard and stared down at the snow.

Seph shuddered, looking about the chapel. "How do you do it? How've you lasted so long? He's been at me night and day with dreams and hallucinations. I'm literally going crazy. I don't know how much longer I can take it."

It didn't make him feel any better to know that Leicester would be back in a few days.

"You promised you wouldn't give in, remember? We'll both be screwed if you do."

"I'm doing the best I can."

Jason smoked in silence for a few minutes, flicking ash onto the snow. He seemed to be grappling with an important decision. Finally, he shrugged. "Okay. I'm already halfway in, I might as well go all the way." He stared up at the sky. "Look, Seph, I can teach you how to deal with the dreams. But if Leicester finds out I'm helping you, we'll both end up in his zombie army."

Seph straightened, suddenly hopeful. "If I could just get some sleep, I think I could hold out indefinitely," he said.

Jason took a long drag on the cigarette, released a spiral of smoke. "How do I know you're not a spy for Leicester?"

Seph shrugged. "I was thinking the same thing about you."

Jason put his hand on Seph's shoulder and stared into his eyes.

"I'm guessing you're for real," Jason said finally. "You don't have that dopey look I'm used to seeing. All right." He stood, grinning crookedly, and stubbed out the cigarette. "Now I'll take you to my lair."

They walked back through the woods toward the Alumni House, following the path Seph had broken through the snow on his way out. When the wind caught the tops of the pines, snow cascaded down around them, some of it finding its way under the collar of Seph's jacket. Under the clear sky, the heat of his body bled away, leaving him shivering. Jason's light jacket hung open, and he didn't react to the cold at all. He stopped just inside the edge of the trees.

"Hold on to my arm, and be quiet." Jason muttered his words of magic and disappeared, but Seph could still feel his arm under his fingers. "No one will notice you, either," the voice said. The invisible, or rather, unnoticeable Jason led Seph out of the woods and across the lawn to the Alumni House. They entered the front hallway and passed through the common room. Martin and Peter were sprawled in front of the TV, playing cards, but they didn't acknowledge their passage. Jason led Seph to the staircase at the back of the building, and then down the steps to the basement.

There were workout rooms at the base of the stairs, then more offices and storage rooms. Jason went on past them down two intersecting corridors to a door at the end. The door opened, and he was propelled inside. The door slammed shut behind them, and a bolt slid home on the inside. There was more scrambled Latin, and then Jason reappeared, laughing at the startled expression on Seph's face.

"If they have cameras everywhere, aren't you afraid we'll be spotted in here?" Seph asked, looking around the room.

"Oh, I handled that. I've provided them with an alternate sound and video. Wizards call that a *glamour*. It's a sensory charm that works whether you're there or not." Jason hit a button on his CD player and music erupted from the speakers. Despite being in the basement, his room was comfortable. He had his own refrigerator and private bath. Ceramic tile covered the floor, and rows of bookshelves, mostly empty, lined the walls. A computer desk stood against the far wall. The open walls were papered with music posters. Jason pointed to an upholstered chair. "Have a seat."

Seph dropped into the chair. "Why are you staying over here if you're not one of the alumni?"

"Leicester needs to keep me away from newbies like yourself. They think they can keep track of me better. As far as they know, I spend most of my time sulking in my room." He opened the refrigerator and rummaged inside. "Want something to drink?"

"Soda's good." Seph accepted a can of orange.

Jason sat down on the bed and gestured toward a CD rack next to the sound system. "Pick out something else if you don't like Irish punk." There was an eagerness about his hospitality that suggested Jason had been lonely, too.

"This is fine." Seph gestured at his surroundings. "Nice place."

"For a prison." Jason leaned forward. "Now, about your dreams. If I teach you how to block them, there can't be any change in your behavior. Do you understand? You've got to convince him that you're still at the end of your rope and beginning to swing. If you start bopping around campus, chipper and carefree, he'll know something's up."

"I don't think there's much chance of that."

"The thing is, you have to follow directions, or you may

end up dead." Jason slipped his hand into the neck of his shirt and pulled out an object attached to a chain around his neck. He lifted it over his head and handed it to Seph.

It was a stone circle, heavier than Seph expected from the size of it, in a flat black color. It was covered with faint markings scratched into the surface. There was a sense of depth to it, as if he were looking through a window. But when he peered through the center, he was looking into . . . nothing. When he passed his hand behind it, there was still nothing.

"What is it?" he asked, trying to hand it back to Jason.

The other boy shook his head. "The general term is *dyrne sefa*, meaning heartstone, or secret heart. They are objects that act as assist devices to the gifted," he said. "They were made by sorcerers a long time ago. They're the experts when it comes to materials. But no one knows how to make them anymore."

He sailed on, warming to his topic. "This one is called a portal. It's a piece from my mother's collection. It's very old magic. Not well known today. I don't even know all the things it can do. And I can guarantee you there's nothing in the alumni library about it. Dr. Leicester thinks of himself as a scholar, but he dabbles in things he doesn't understand." Jason snorted in disgust.

"Really?" Seph touched the talisman with his forefinger as if it might bite.

"Portals are used for illusion and spiritual travel. I use it to cast the unnoticeable charm. Dreams are just a kind of brain chemistry. You're going to use this to step away from your body so you can escape Leicester's enchantments. I'll go over the charm with you until you get it right. Put the portal on the table while you practice. We don't want any screwups."

Seph hastily set the piece down on the table, resisting the urge to wipe his hands on his jeans.

In terrenus sanctum. The charm was a kind of bastard Latin. It wasn't too difficult. He had always had a facility with languages, anyway. It didn't take him long to master the incantation. He had to say it five times correctly before Jason was satisfied.

"What does it mean?" Seph asked.

"Into the sanctuary," Jason replied. "The way I understand it, you're retreating into your Weirstone. Where Leicester can't intrude. The talisman allows you to go and return. Before you go, you need to decide when you want to return. If you don't, well, you never come back. Okay, put it on under your shirt," he said, gesturing toward the *dyrne sefa.*

Seph scooped the portal from the table and dropped the chain over his head. He shoved the stone into the neckline of his sweatshirt so it rested against his chest. He expected it to be cold, but it felt warm and heavy against his skin.

Jason pointed to the bed. "Now lie down here and tell me how long you want to sleep."

"Do we have to do this now?" Seph assumed the position anyway.

"No worries," Jason whispered. "Trust me."

"An hour, then."

"An hour." Jason ran his finger over the runes on the

dyrne sefa. "These can be read as numbers, if you know how to read them. For example, this is a one. You can choose one, two, three hours and so on. I can do it in the dark, but I don't recommend you try." He grinned. "Wizardry is a kind of anti-tech thing. Meaning it's not that exact. But time passes quickly.

"Now say the charm. You don't have to say it out loud."

All right, Seph thought. Choose an hour and say the charm. He touched the stone circle as Jason had done, found the symbol for one hour, spoke the charm carefully, moving his lips but not speaking aloud.

Seph felt as though he had plunged into an icy pool. The shock of it drove the breath and blood from his body. Then the cold was gone and he was light, very light, a vapor, an idea in the void, a glimmer in the darkness. Free. He was conscious of a boundary, an enclosure, no more than a thickness of the air.

He was aware of a spreading warmth, a tingling in his extremities, inrushing sensation. He opened his eyes to find Jason sprawled in the chair, headphones on, fingers steepled together, studying him.

"It didn't work," Seph said.

Jason laughed and pulled off the headphones. "You've been out for an hour. Check your watch."

Seph did. It was after nine o'clock. He blinked, opened his mouth, closed it again.

Jason looked gratified at Seph's reaction. "Not exactly like sleeping, but close enough. You get some rest. Your mind is safe from Leicester."

"And you can do this for eight hours?"

"Or ten," Jason said. "Here, I'll show you." He pointed out the relevant symbols on the portal. "Only, best if no one finds you've checked out, since you'll look like you're dead. So you'll want to lock up before you use the charm, and don't plan on sleeping too long."

Jason was right, Seph thought. Sleeping without dreaming. It was a miracle. Only, he wouldn't be sure until he tried it overnight. His hand found the stone, traced the shape of it under his sweatshirt. "Do you have any more of these?" he asked, feeling hopeful for the first time in a long while.

"Keep that one. I have something else I can use. Just don't lose it. Like I said, they don't make them anymore." He frowned, biting his lower lip. "We'll need to build a glamour so Leicester's convinced you're still dreaming."

Seph straightened. "I thought you didn't know much about wizardry."

"My mother specialized in illusions, glamours, spirituality, traveling around outside the body using talismans," Jason replied. "I grew up on this stuff. Unfortunately, she never taught me much about how to kill people." Seph looked up, startled, but Jason was staring down at his hands, and Seph couldn't see his expression.

"What else can you teach me?" Seph asked.

Jason shrugged. "Like I told you, I don't know a lot. I'll be glad to teach you what I know. But you can't go showing off all around the campus. Remember what I said: as far as Leicester and everyone else is concerned, you need to stay scared and stay stupid."

"No problem," Seph replied.

ℜ Chapter Eight ℠
Through the Portal

Jason spent an hour or more in Seph's room, prowling around, weaving his "glamour," as he called it. First he blocked the cameras, then constructed a complicated multilayered charm, parts of it triggered by the assault of the dream spell. When he was finished, Seph's room was a fortress against prying eyes, and his dreams were his own.

Seph used the portal when he went to bed. He would lie down, choose the duration of his absence, and spin out the charm in his head. Sometimes he woke up when the charm wore off, and lay quietly in the dark. Sometimes he kept right on sleeping. Jason warned him not to use the charm twice in one night. "You know how sometimes you go to hit the snooze alarm and hit the wrong button? If you blow this one, you'll never wake up."

Whether it was the magic in the stone or the charm Jason taught him, or both, it worked. The portal was the talisman that kept the dreams at bay and kept Gregory Leicester out of his head for as long as the charm was in force. Sometimes the dreams came on toward morning, after his return. Sometimes they caught him during the day. But the fact that he could sleep peacefully for six or eight hours, could keep the nightmares away when he chose, that made all the difference. Before the encounter in the library, Seph had felt himself dissolving, as if he would eventually cease to exist. Now he slowly reassembled himself, and his head was clearer than it had been since Thanksgiving.

Jason had a second stone pendant, hexagonal in shape, and good for some of the same purposes. He used the unnoticeable charm to roam all over campus, lurking, as he called it, while his glamours convinced the school administrators he was holed up in his room. He spent much of his time in the library, studying the attack charms and sorceries Leicester had collected for the alumni.

Seph never knew when Jason would be waiting outside his door in the morning, or touch him on the shoulder as he crossed the campus. "Unnoticeable is better than invisible," Jason pointed out. "It acts on the observer and not the observed. Ergo, unnoticeable doesn't leave footprints."

And so, the unnoticeable charm was the second charm Jason taught him, so they could sneak back to his basement room. Jason cautioned Seph to speak the charm out of sight of the ubiquitous cameras. Seph was already known to have a habit of walking in the woods. He would walk a distance into the forest, in a different direction every time, speak the charm, and then walk back to the Alumni House.

They generally met in Jason's room where he kept notes and papers on his research as well as books of charms. Jason seemed almost as hungry for companionship as Seph, since he didn't go to classes and didn't interact with either the alumni or the Anaweir. He lived life in the shadows—studying wizardry as best he could out of books, and spying on Leicester and his coconspirators.

Seph had no interest in going to war against anyone. He knew that once the distractions of the holidays were over, Leicester would turn his full attention back to Seph. Although he felt stronger after only a week of uninterrupted sleep, he worried about his ability to hide it from the headmaster.

Students trickled back during the last weekend of winter break. At the end of fall term, Seph had felt himself sliding into the abyss. Now he was eager to see Trevor, wondering if his friend had contacted Sloane's and what the response had been. Though he checked his room several times, Trevor still hadn't arrived by late Sunday night.

A message had gone out over the intranet that there would be a student assembly in the auditorium of the art and music building early in the morning on the first day of the term. So Monday morning, Seph knocked at Trevor's door just before eight o'clock to see if he wanted to walk over to the assembly together. Still no answer. Probably already gone, afraid he'll be late, Seph thought as he slogged through the snow to the art building.

The auditorium was nearly full when Seph arrived, so he sat in the back. The hall reverberated with voices grumbling about being back at school, exchanging stories about the winter holidays. Seph nodded to Troy and Harrison, who were sitting toward the middle. Even Jason slipped into the room at the last minute, taking a seat close to the door.

Gregory Leicester mounted the stage at the front and called for quiet. He looked out over the students, as if mapping the faces in the crowd. Seph thought the headmaster had picked him out before he started speaking. He wondered if he'd noticed Jason in the back.

"This morning I must welcome you back to the Havens on a sad note. I regret to inform you that we've lost one of our students in a tragic episode over winter break."

Seph knew who it was before the words were spoken. He wanted to run from the room before he heard, but it was as if he were bolted to his chair.

"Trevor Hill took his own life while he was home for the holidays." Leicester paused. "Trevor was a boy with a great future ahead of him. He was a junior, an honor student, and a Havens success story. He was especially known for his generosity of spirit, for his willingness to help others without regard for his own safety." Leicester's gaze settled on Seph.

"We cannot know what was in his mind at the time of his death. But his passing represents a great loss to the school and to all of his many friends. Let's all observe a moment of silence in memory of Trevor Hill."

A hush fell over the auditorium. Some of the students

closed their eyes; others stared at each other, stunned. Seph slumped in his seat, eyes wide open, watching the man in the front of the room.

After a moment, Leicester spoke again. "We sent a floral arrangement on behalf of the faculty and students. We also have contact information for those who would like to send a card or letter to the family. Thank you for coming." And then Leicester was gone out the side door.

Seph sat without moving as the rest of the students shuffled out. A series of disconnected scenes ran through his head like an endlessly repeating video. He half hoped he would wake up to find that it was all a dream.

He recalled the last time he saw Trevor in his room, before he left for the holidays: Trevor offering to contact Sloane's from his parents' house, and Seph agreeing. Then Jason telling him that all the student rooms were wired by the administration. Finally, the night at the amphitheater, pulling the gold chain and pendant from the remains of the fire. Now Seph knew where he had seen it before.

He pushed himself up out of his seat and forced his way through the small knots of students who still lingered in the back of the auditorium, buzzing with scandal and voyeuristic grief. He went outside and headed for the administration building at a trot, his boots crunching in the snow, his breath pluming in the clear air.

He was just passing the Alumni House when someone reached out and grabbed his arm, pulling him into a doorway.

"Where do you think you're going?" It was Jason, of course—unnoticeable Jason.

"Leave me alone." Seph tried to rip his arm free.

"Where are you going?"

"To see Leicester." Seph struck out at the air, but it seemed that Jason had more than his share of arms and legs. It was like fighting an invisible octopus.

"No, you're not, and you'd better chill out or I'll spell you."

Seph stopped struggling.

"Now come downstairs where we can talk." Jason kept a tight grip on Seph's arm, maneuvering him into the stairwell.

Once in his room, Jason rematerialized. "Sit down," he commanded. Seph subsided into a chair, gauging the distance to the door, trying to figure out how he could get past Jason.

"Now tell me," Jason said, planting himself in the way.

"Leicester killed Trevor Hill because he was going to try to reach my guardian. It's all my fault." Seph trembled with rage and remorse.

Jason tilted his head to one side. "Why would your headmaster kill someone for contacting your guardian?"

"You of all people should know why."

Jason leaned forward and put both hands on Seph's shoulders, his blue eyes blazing. "You go into Leicester's office with a bunch of accusations, and the first thing he's going to think is, 'What's happened to Clueless? Who's he been talking to? Couldn't be Jason Haley, could it?'"

Seph tried to look away, but Jason kept his grip on him. "And let's say you confront Leicester, and you find out your theory is true? What exactly are you going to do about it?" Seph said nothing. "Don't you see? Every piece of information you give him is a weapon. And there's nothing you can do to him. Nothing." Jason released Seph and stepped back.

"You don't understand. Trevor tried to help me, and now he's dead." Images came back to him: Maia's flesh disintegrating under his touch. Trevor's scorched amulet amid the ashes at the amphitheater.

Jason dropped into a chair and closed his eyes. "If you're asking me if I think Leicester would do it, I'd say yes, in a heartbeat. And for less of a reason, too. He'd do it because Trevor was your friend and supported you while Leicester was trying to make you crazy." Jason shook himself, as if trying to dislodge a memory. "Haven't you wondered why I don't hang out with the other students? Don't you think I'm tired of being alone all the time?"

He released a breath, a long, wounded sound. "It's because Leicester can get to you through them. I talked Sam and Peter into going up against him. Now Sam is dead, and Peter . . ." His voice trailed off.

"You're scared of him."

"You're damn right I am, and you should be, too. The Anaweir are so damned fragile." He gripped the arms of the chair as if holding himself in his seat.

"Last spring I complained to my father about this place. I bitched so much he decided to investigate. He called Dr. Leicester, asking questions, even came out for a visit, but didn't learn much. Everyone here was happy except me, blah, blah, blah. Still, Dad promised he would talk to a couple of psychotherapists, figure out if what was going on here was legitimate. Within a month, and before he could get very far with it, he died of a heart attack."

"You think Leicester had something to do with it?"

Jason waved his hand impatiently. "Leicester has never taken any pains to deceive me about what he is, because I already knew too much when I got here. On the day my father died, Leicester called me into his office, and told me when and how and where it would happen. Then he made me sit there until the call came."

"My God." Seph swallowed down the sick that rose in his throat.

"He thought he'd found the way to break me. And it almost did, because I knew it was my fault." Jason closed his eyes again, and Seph could see tears collecting at the corners. "If I hadn't been such a jerk when my dad remarried, I wouldn't have ended up here. If I hadn't complained about it to my father, he'd be alive today."

"How can you think it was your fault?" Seph whispered. "Leicester is a monster."

"If I don't get to blame myself, then you don't, either. But I think you can see that if anyone has a reason to go after Leicester, it's me."

"I didn't know," Seph said quietly. "How can you stand it?"

"I can stand it because I know I'll find a way to get Leicester and D'Orsay in the end. I'll do it or die trying. I've stayed here because I need to learn enough to do it. And then I'll join up with someone powerful enough and organized enough to help me. Right now, that looks like the Dragon, if I can find him."

He looked up at Seph. "Leicester enjoys inflicting pain on people. I've been a source of entertainment for him. He thinks he'll have me in the end. He can take his time. I'm an orphan like you. Nobody cares what happens to me.

"Just stay away from him. At least, you can tell yourself you're not sure about Trevor, because you aren't. If you can't do anything about it, it's better not to know."

Jason unfolded from his chair and began pacing, a cat in the small cage of the room. He could never stay still for long. "If Trevor was killed because he was going to talk to your guardian, then Leicester didn't want that to happen. I bet the whole story about them committing you is bogus, and Leicester is worried about what might happen if you contact Sloane's. So maybe Sloane's is your key to getting out."

With the death of Trevor Hill, the old guilt returned. Trevor had found a way to survive at the Havens until Seph had come along. Even though he was Anaweir, he'd risked everything for Seph. Now Seph's nightmares were mostly about Trevor.

Along with the guilt came a hatred for Leicester that smoked and smoldered under his breastbone like a deep mine fire. He began wearing Trevor's pendant, along with the portal stone and Maia's cross. Images of revenge alternated with dreams of escape.

Seph took his lead from Jason and kept his distance

from the other students. Sometimes he ate lunch with Troy, Harrison, James, and some of the others, but he never accepted their invitations to play racquetball, or tennis, or to go up to the movies in the auditorium. He spent his free time in his room, reading, or roaming the campus by himself.

Seph did his best to project the image of one whose hold on reality is tenuous. He let his appearance go. His hair grew long and curly for lack of cutting, and he rarely combed it. He still hallucinated during the day, checking in and out without warning. Sometimes whole chunks of time went missing.

He mumbled to himself in the hallways, flinched away from phantoms, and sat through classes as if in a trance. Some of the other students seemed to regard him as they might a fly caught in a dangerous web. Get too close and you might become entangled yourself. So they left him strictly alone.

On the other hand, the alumni continued to take an unwelcome interest in Seph. Now it seemed that everywhere he went, Warren Barber turned up, offering help with homework, music downloads, pills and peppermint schnapps and potent South American weed that might settle Seph's nerves. Bruce Hays and Aaron Hanlon invited him to eat with them in the alumni dining room, and to work out in the fitness center in the basement. On Leicester's orders, no doubt.

Seph went, hoping to glean information that might prove useful. But the alumni were more resistant to mind magic than the Anaweir.

Now that he knew the stakes in the game they were playing, Seph was extraordinarily careful about using magic in the open. He kept his distance from Leicester for fear the headmaster would see the truth in his eyes. He and Jason spent as much time as possible in the alumni library. Jason tapped volumes of notes into a tiny electronic organizer, while Seph used his knowledge of Latin to decipher the Middle English manuscripts.

They spent hours trying out incantations in the hidden corners of campus, mostly attack charms and charms of protection and influence. As Seph became more self-aware, he emitted fewer "sparks," as Jason called them, that is, unintentional releases of power. When Seph noticed the magical tension building up in his body, he found ways to use or dissipate it.

Jason proved to be reckless, a risk taker when it came to magical experiments. He would launch powerful combinations of charms without a clear notion of the consequences. Sometimes Seph wondered if he had a death wish.

Seph tried to fit the concept of magic into math and physics: the teleology that he had always taken as the truth. As far as he could tell, physical magic was most useful in generating energy: light and heat and air currents, the movement of molecules that were loosely packed to begin with.

The other important role of magic was in influencing others. As Jason said: the Anaweir had little protection against wizards in that regard.

"Anaweir women can't resist wizards," he said. "All

that barely controlled power. They can sense it, you know. The touch of a wizard drives women wild. That kind of direct physical magic is called *persuasion*." He grinned and laced his fingers behind his head. "It can get very complicated." Jason apparently thrived on those kinds of complications.

Seph thought of the way girls responded to his touch, the power that spilled from his fingers. He hadn't used it inappropriately—had he?

He was more comfortable with spoken charms, because he could better control the outcome. Seph loved the cadence of magical language. He rolled the ancient charms off his tongue, conjuring words from the ancient magi. Sometimes the words came from within, like a spring bubbling up from a deeper pool. He had never been more convinced of the power of language, the leap from symbol to reality.

He noticed Jason watching him as he drew the spells off the page and spun them out, like shimmering flames in the air. "You really have a gift, Seph," Jason said once. "You're more powerful than I'll ever be. If you could find a teacher, I bet you could blow Leicester away."

Jason's strength lay in the area of glamours: deceptive images and visions that carried no firepower, save their ability to confuse, distract, startle, and scare. And that was enough. Sometimes, out in the woods, Seph would walk into one of Jason Haley's fever dreams. He'd encounter a gryphon grazing on ferns or a satyr or a phoenix perched in the branches of an oak, or a great ship sailing through the trees crewed by impossibly beautiful mermaids.

Seph asked about Weirbooks.

"You have one somewhere," Jason said. "It was created by the Sorcerers' Guild when you were born, and it can't be destroyed. If you could find it, it would tell you all you want to know about your family.

Jason showed Seph his own Weirbook. Jason's name was recorded on the last page, along with his parents and grandparents. The genealogy went back to the tenth century. He kept it locked up, protected by a series of complicated charms. "You don't want your Weirbook to fall into your enemies' hands. Then they have your history, and they know your weaknesses and strengths."

Seph was fascinated by the idea that, somewhere out there, his history lay between the covers of a book, if he could only lay his hands on it.

By the end of April, spring was visiting the Havens in frustrating fits and starts. The snow melted away to patches where the heavy drifts had been, and daffodils glittered among the trees. Gregory Leicester had visitors, also. Rental cars and cars with out-of-state plates appeared in the parking lot, feeding what appeared to be a series of small meetings. One morning, Jason intercepted Seph on his way to class, pulling him into a stairwell.

"D'Orsay's here," he whispered. "Gamemaster of the Council. Let's go." Within seconds, they were both unnoticeable, loping across the grounds, heading for the administration building.

This was a very private meeting, just Leicester and D'Orsay, held in Leicester's office on the third floor, with Hays and Barber stationed in front of the door like bouncers at an exclusive club. Seph and Jason had to wait in the hallway for two hours until Martin Hall arrived with lunch. They managed to slip through the doorway behind him when he rolled the cart in.

D'Orsay and Leicester sat at the table by the window, bodies rigid, faces stony, like a quarreling couple interrupted midspat. Papers were spread out across the table and a notebook computer sat between them.

Claude D'Orsay was a tall wizard with close-cropped gray hair and custom-tailored clothes. He wore a heavy gold chain around his neck, the emblem of his wizardly office.

When the door closed behind Martin, Leicester hissed, "I can't believe the Dragon's that difficult to find. He puts up new messages every day. Listen to this." Leicester pulled his laptop toward him and read from the screen. "'One wonders what games the Gamemaster is playing. Sources tell the Dragon that D'Orsay has scheduled a series of secret meetings leading up to the Interguild Conference. If you've not received an invitation, I suggest you watch your back.' Where the hell does he get his information?"

"Guesswork and speculation," D'Orsay suggested, sipping at his wine.

"Really? He goes on to list the dates, participants, and locations of three of the meetings."

"Let me see that." D'Orsay turned the screen so it faced him. Then swore softly and pulled out a cell phone. He punched in a number and spoke into it, low and urgently. Jason nudged Seph with his elbow.

When D'Orsay put the phone away, Leicester said, "We're running out of time, Claude. He's got the Roses murdering each other in the streets. How long before they come after us? He knows we're meeting outside of the usual channels. You promised you'd run him in to ground before the conference."

"We almost had him in London. We'll get him the next time. Nora Whitehead's working on it."

Leicester frowned. "Nora? This is too important to hand off to her. Why aren't you handling it yourself?"

"I *am* handling it. Nora's working for me."

"She doesn't stand a chance, if it comes to a duel. If it's who we think it is, he'll cut her to pieces and then where will we be?" Leicester didn't seem to be as concerned about Nora as worried his quarry might get away.

D'Orsay flicked imaginary lint off his trousers. "Don't be theatrical. I'm not planning on a duel. There's no one we could send against him, one on one."

"Doesn't the man have a family? Someone we could use to draw him out of hiding?"

"I was told they were all murdered back in the day," D'Orsay said, frowning, as if this was most inconvenient. "Apparently that's the source of his fanaticism. But we think we may have found a vulnerability."

"A vulnerability?" Leicester raised an eyebrow skeptically. "What?"

D'Orsay glanced about, as if there might be spies behind the stonework. The outing of his meeting had clearly rattled him. "Ah . . . let's see what comes of it. We should know, fairly soon."

"Fairly soon?" Leicester rolled his eyes. "We've spent years on this project. They're too close to you as it stands. If they trace us back here . . ."

D'Orsay's expression morphed from disappointed to annoyed. "Unlike you, I have other responsibilities. While you're playing schoolmaster, I'm courting seven different sides, trying to keep this whole scheme from unraveling. Keep in mind that there are advantages to having the Dragon at large. When items disappear from the Hoard, he always gets the blame."

He stood and dropped his napkin on the table. "No one wants to catch the Dragon more than I do. But just now I have to go and reschedule three meetings before our colleagues walk into a trap."

The two wizards glared at each other, emitting faint showers of sparks.

"I'll call you when the roster is finalized," D'Orsay said, stuffing a sheaf of papers into a briefcase.

Seph and Jason managed to slide out after him when he went out the door.

Back in Jason's room, Jason fizzed with excitement and worry, pacing back and forth. "Did you hear that? 'If you've not received your invitation, watch your back.' And did you hear D'Orsay? They don't know who they'd send against him—he's that powerful. The Dragon's got this network of spies all over the world that he works constantly . . ."

"Do you think they really know who it is?" Seph asked. "They seemed pretty confident."

"I've heard rumors." Jason shrugged. "Seems to me the Dragon would be dead by now if they did know."

"So Leicester's online," Seph muttered to himself, sorting through a pile of CDs. "He must have a wireless network in his office, at least."

"But they think they've got something on him," Jason leaned against the doorframe. "I wish there was some way to warn him."

Seph chose a CD and slid it into the player. "If I could just get into Leicester's office, I bet I could break into his system."

"To warn the Dragon?"

"No. To e-mail Sloane's. So I can get out of here. And don't give me that look. I don't really want to get involved with the, um, wizard politics, as you call it. You don't have enough information to warn the Dragon, anyway. What are you going to say? 'Be careful, they're on your trail? Watch your back?'"

Jason wasn't really listening. "Maybe it *is* time to leave. Maybe I should get out and try and find him. Tell him about the meeting here, the alumni, and all that. See what he makes of it." He tugged at his earlobe. "Then again, I could hang around, see what else I can find out. I wish I knew when this Interguild Conference they're talking about is."

Seph fastened on the notion of leaving. "How would you deal with the wall?"

Jason grinned. "I think I've finally got that nailed. Barber's the architect, you know. I heard him bragging about it when I was lurking in the alumni dining room. So I tossed his room and found some books on the subject."

"So how does it work?"

"It's a real, physical wall overlaid with confusion charms. So you can't stay focused enough to get over or around it. I've put together some countercharms that should work."

"*Should* work," Seph said skeptically. "Then let's try it."

Jason shook his head. "I don't want to tip Leicester off before I'm ready to leave."

"If you *can* leave, you *should*. Before something happens."

"I really don't care what happens to me. As long as I get Leicester."

In the end, Jason decided to stay a little longer to see if he could gather more news to take to the Dragon. But Leicester and D'Orsay didn't meet again.

A few weeks later, in mid-May, Seph brought his workout gear to the Alumni House one evening, intending to meet Jason to go over some books they'd taken from the library. He ate dinner with Martin and Peter, then walked through the common room and into the stairwell. He took a quick look around, then spoke the unnoticeable charm. Just then, the door flew open behind him.

It was Warren Barber. He must have followed Seph out of the common room. He looked around the landing, puzzled. Seph had just stepped through the door, and now he was gone. Seph wondered if Barber had even heard him say the end of the charm.

Barber stood frozen for a moment, listening, then loped down the stairs with Seph ghosting along behind him. When Barber reached the basement, he looked up and down the empty hallway. Seph slipped into the workout room. A moment later, when Barber opened the door, Seph had disabled the charm and was adjusting the weights on the rowing machine. Fortunately, there was no one else in there.

"What are you doing in here?" Barber demanded, scanning the room, his pale brows drawn together suspiciously.

Seph locked the weights in place and looked up at Barber, lifting an eyebrow. "I'm . . . um . . . working out?"

Barber leaned against the doorframe and lit a cigarette. "Yeah? Well, it ain't helping. You look like a bag of bones."

Seph shrugged. "It helps me sleep."

"I've got stuff that'll help you sleep. What do you need?"

"No, thanks."

Barber blew out a stream of smoke. "What are you trying to prove?"

Seph stopped wrestling with the machine and turned and faced Barber. "I don't get it. Why does it matter to you so much? Do you get a bonus if I link with Leicester?"

"More like, he'll make us miserable until you do."

Careful. You don't know anything. "Why does he want this so much?" Seph asked. When Barber rolled his eyes, he added, "No, really. I want to know."

"You're just a blue-blood rich kid. You think you can just decline Dr. Leicester's invitation like he asked you to a fricking soiree. He won't take no for an answer. If he can't use you, he'll destroy you." Barber stubbed out his cigarette, turned on his heel, and walked out.

Seph waited half an hour. When he peered out into the corridor, there was no sign of Barber or anyone else. He slipped down the hallway to Jason's room.

"Sorry I'm late," Seph said after Jason shut the door behind him. "Barber almost caught me." He explained what had happened, as Jason cleared books and papers off a chair so Seph could sit.

"He believed you?" Jason asked, frowning. He pulled two cans of soda from the refrigerator and handed one to Seph.

"I think so. I mean, he left a half hour ago."

Jason started to say something else, but then his head snapped up and the blood drained from his face. "We're screwed!" He flung an arm out toward Seph, casting an unnoticeable spell. At the same instant, the door banged open, the bolt dropping to the tile with a hollow ping. Gregory Leicester stood in the doorway.

"Dr. Leicester," Jason said, almost choking on the words. "I didn't hear you knock."

"Hello, Jason," the headmaster said, his gaze drifting around the room, settling on the two cans of soda still sitting on the table, the piles of books and papers on the desk. He remained where he was, filling the doorway, as if to prevent any attempt at escape.

Jason and Gregory Leicester faced each other. The air shimmered with the tension between them. Jason was deathly pale.

"Jason, what do you know about Joseph McCauley?"

The voice was complex, full of fire and ice, sorcery and menace.

Jason toyed with his earring, frowning, as if struggling to remember. "He's the one you told me about, right? He spent a lot of time in this building over winter break. I think I've seen him in the workout rooms."

"We've been working with him all year, but we aren't making the kind of progress we would like. He's hallucinating. Delusional. Dangerously symptomatic. But refuses our help. And now there's been a change in his behavior that makes me think perhaps he's been spending time with you." The voice was gentle on the surface, but there was steel underneath. "Do you remember our discussion about your negative influence on the other boys?"

"I'm not stupid."

"I hope you haven't been filling his head with a lot of talk about conspiracies," Leicester continued. "He's extremely vulnerable right now."

Jason stared at the floor. He didn't say anything.

"Have you forgotten the consequences we had talked about, both to you and to him?"

"I haven't forgotten," Jason replied, He looked up at Leicester in the eyes. "Believe me."

"Good," Leicester said softly. He took another look around the room. And then he was gone.

Seph breathed. "Thank God," he said, half aloud. He waited a count of five, then disabled the charm. Jason did *not* look relieved. He still sat on the edge of the bed, staring out at nothing. His face was the color of putty, and he was shaking.

"Well, that was too close," Seph said.

Jason looked up as if startled out of his reverie. "That's wasn't close, Seph. That was dead on." He stood and went to his closet, rummaged through it, and produced a backpack. He unzipped it and spread it out on the bed.

"What are you doing?"

"I've got to get out of here."

"What?"

"He knew you were in the room, Seph. Barber must have gone to get him as soon as he left the fitness center. All that stuff about your delicate condition—that was for your benefit." Jason shoved his Weirbook into the daypack, followed by his organizer and notes from the library.

"How do you know?" Seph watched as his friend continued to pack. He took very little: a photograph of a woman in a frame, a sweatshirt.

"Trust me. We've never had a conversation like that—ever." Jason zipped up the pack. "If you hadn't been here, I'd probably be dead by now. He's not sure how much you know. He's hoping I haven't ruined you. As it is, they'll probably come for me tonight. They'll wait until you're back in your room."

"I'll stay here, then." Seph sat back in his chair.

Jason laughed. "You're really something, you know that? Believe me, you don't want to do that. Besides, I'm leaving."

"Then I'm going with you."

Jason shook his head. "No. You're safer here than you would be with me. They may be waiting for me, but they won't kill you as long as they think they can get to you. Make sure they keep thinking that."

Seph cast about for an alternative. "We've been study-ing attack magic for months. We can take him if we work together."

"Look, man, I'm flattered. You're the one with the tal-ent. I'm cagy as hell, but I'm just not that powerful. It'd be two against sixteen, and they've been training for years. Leicester channels them, somehow. There's no way we win. I'm not getting anyone else killed."

"I'd rather be dead than stay here."

Jason shook his head. "Listen to me. You're tough. You made it on your own for four months, remember? I still don't know how you did it. And now you have the *dyrne sefa*." He paused. "Look, if I get out of here, I'll get you out. I promise. I'll contact Sloane's, whatever it takes."

Seph swallowed hard. "I'm sorry, Jason. I'm the one who got you busted. First Trevor, and now you."

"Seph, I'm afraid I haven't appropriately oriented you to your new role."

"What do you mean?"

Jason grinned. "Wizards never say they're sorry—not about anything." Jason embraced, then released him quickly. "Whatever happens, it's been cool knowing you, Seph. Never think any different."

Seph was speechless for a moment, his throat congested with grief. Then he said, "Where will you go? How can I find you?"

"If you get out, look for the Dragon. If you can't get out, I'll come after Leicester, sooner or later." He pulled on his jacket, slung his pack across his back, spoke his charm, and was gone.

❧ CHAPTER NINE ❧
DESPERATE MEASURES

The normal cadence of life at the Havens continued after Jason's departure for everyone but Seph. For most of the students, Jason had never existed so no one noticed his absence.

Days passed, and there was no word from Jason and no indication from Sloane's that he had contacted them. Seph was increasingly worried. Had Jason even made it past the wall? There was no clue from Leicester or the alumni. They asked him no questions about Jason's disappearance, which Seph took as a bad sign.

Seph continued to visit the alumni library, but it was an empty gesture. There seemed to be no future in it, no outlet for the magic he copied into his memory. Seph felt more alone than before. Jason had been his first teacher of magic.

His only teacher.

The weather continued to warm. Students clustered under the pavilions between classes, eagerly exchanging summer plans. Frisbees soared over tiny patches of lawn and the school dress code was challenged on a daily basis. Seph checked the mail regularly, hoping he might at least hear something from Sloane's about arrangements for summer. Then Gregory Leicester called Seph into his office one afternoon after class.

Seph went reluctantly. He assumed an audience with Leicester could not bring good news. He was right.

The headmaster rose from his computer when Seph arrived. "Come in, Joseph," he said. "Sit down." He gestured toward the same table where they had sat the night of Seph's arrival. Seph perched on the edge of the seat, bracing his palms on the arms as if ready to launch. Leicester sat down across the table.

"We're concerned, Joseph," he said. "I had hoped that your continued deterioration might convince you to cooperate, to submit to treatment."

Seph fixed his gaze over Leicester's shoulder, looking out at the horizon. "I don't need treatment. I need training."

Leicester shook his head, as if this notion was preposterous. "I cannot risk training a wizard who is so totally out of control. It would be like handing a flamethrower to a child. You require limits and close guidance in order to develop your powers safely."

"Let me go, then. I'll find someone else."

Leicester sighed. "I think it's time we change our approach. I'm going to ask your guardian to let us keep you with us this summer. I'll have more free time, then, and you won't be in class. We'll work on your issues together, Joseph. We'll do some intensive one-on-one therapy, some guided imagery. How does that sound?"

Seph could imagine what kind of images Leicester would share with him. And with the wizard present, he wouldn't be able to use the talisman.

No doubt Houghton would agree to Leicester's proposal. The lawyers would be glad they didn't have to find a summer placement.

Unless Jason got to them first. He cultivated that fading hope.

Two weeks before the end of the term, Seph decided he couldn't wait for Jason any longer, but had to try again to contact Sloane's on his own. For that, he'd need to break into Gregory Leicester's office. If any computer on campus had unrestricted access to the outside world, it would be his.

Seph began monitoring the headmaster's movements. Leicester sometimes worked in his office until late into the night. Fairly consistently, however, he walked over to the alumni building for dinner around eight. For several nights running, Seph marked his departure from the admin. building, his arrival at the Alumni House, the walk back to his office. He was always gone for at least an hour, sometimes an hour and a half. That would be long enough.

At his previous schools, Seph had been known as something of a hacker. He thought he could probably break into the school's e-mail system, depending on the service provider, operating system, and level of security. He might even be able to come in through the front door without breaking code, if Leicester was sloppy about passwords. Which he might be. This kind of attack might not be anticipated at a place like the Havens, where magic and wizardry were the weapons of choice.

He chose a Sunday night in late May. Sitting at the end of the dock, facing to the side, he could monitor activity at the admin. building. The office was illuminated and he could see Gregory Leicester at his desk overlooking the harbor.

About 7:45, Leicester threw on a jacket and cut the lights in his office. Seph left the dock and walked around to the front of the building, speaking an unnoticeable charm when he reached the shadows along the side. Leicester exited through the front door, his boots crunching on the gravel of the parking lot. He was heading for the Alumni House.

Seph turned the corner and entered the admin building. Unnoticeable, he walked past the cafeteria where students lingered over dessert and climbed the steps to the third floor. Passing through the darkened hall, he tried the door to Leicester's office. It was unlocked. He listened for a long moment and, hearing nothing, slipped inside and closed the door behind him.

Now he just wanted to be in and out as quickly as possible. He crossed to the computer and sat in the chair. He touched a key and the screen illuminated. Leicester had signed off but left the computer on. *gleicester* was the user name.

Seph plugged his jump drive into the USB port and ran the script he'd written earlier on the computer in his room. It crunched away, trying passwords. While he waited, he searched the desk drawers, which were nearly empty. He eyed the phone on the desk, but decided against chancing an outside call. Sloane's would be closed at this hour, anyway. He was rooting through the filing cabinets when he heard the computer cycling through its startup routine. He was in.

Seph opened the browser, then typed in the URL for a search-engine company that offered free e-mail service. In a few minutes, he had set up a new account and user name. It wouldn't fool anyone if he were caught, he realized. All Leicester would have to do was look at the mail's destination. But at least it might prevent any bounce-back mail from going to the headmaster. He logged back in under his new name, *Dragon*.

His fingers flew across the keys. He typed in Sloane's gateway e-mail address and accessed the firm's online address book. He selected every personal e-mail box on the list, Sloane, Smythe, Houghton, and all the rest of the associates.

MR. HOUGHTON AND COLLEAGUES: I am being held prisoner here at the Havens School in Maine. I was told that your firm had me legally committed for mental health treatment, but I have not been allowed to confirm that with you. Although I have written to you via the post numerous times, there has been no response. I am not allowed telephone or e-mail access.

I have been subjected to severe emotional abuse and mental torture since my arrival in September, which I can no longer endure. If there is no response to this e-mail within three days I will kill myself. I am perfectly serious. JOSEPH MCCAULEY

BTW: Do not reply to this e-mail. Do not call. Come in person and don't leave without seeing me.

He looked the e-mail over and was satisfied. No lawyer could fail to respond to such a message. He drew a shaky breath and hit the SEND button. A message came up. YOUR MESSAGE HAS BEEN SENT. It was done.

He knew he should leave, but Leicester's mail program beckoned. Perhaps he'd find some mention of Jason, or the Dragon, or the other parties to the conspiracy Jason had described. He opened the mail program and scrolled down through the inbox. Here was something: RE: RECORDS FOUND AT THE DRAGON'S LONDON HEADQUARTERS from D'Orsay.

Just then, Seph heard a door slam and footsteps approaching. The lights kindled in the outer office. Heart pounding, he exited out of the mail program and signed off, leaving the desktop as he'd found it. He jumped up and crossed to the door, flattening himself against the wall next to it.

It was Leicester, of course, back from dinner. The headmaster tossed a folder onto his desk and sat down at his workstation. Seph edged around the corner and out the door. He was halfway across the outer office when he remembered he'd left his jump drive plugged into the port of Leicester's computer. He considered retrieving it later, but decided against it. There was nothing to link it to Seph specifically. It would be less risky to leave it than to try and retrieve it, unnoticeable or not.

He walked through the suite of offices and down the stairs. A few minutes later he was on his way back to his dorm, one shadow among many in the gloom under the trees.

It was a little after 6 a.m. on Tuesday morning when they came for him. Seph was still in bed, but he was a light sleeper now, whenever he wasn't using the portal, and he woke when he heard the key turn in the lock. He had the deadbolt thrown, so it gave him time to make sure the portal stone was inside his shirt before the door flew open. It was Warren Barber and Bruce Hays.

Seph propped himself on his elbows. "What's going on?"

"Get up, Joseph," Warren said. "You need to come with us."

"Am I late for something?" Seph looked from one to the other for a clue. They had their stone faces on. He swung his legs around and put his feet on the floor. "Is it okay if I get dressed?"

They stepped back to allow him to get out of bed and stood waiting while he pulled his jeans on and found his shoes and yesterday's socks under his bed. Since they were wearing jackets, he pulled on a sweatshirt. Something told him they wouldn't wait for him to brush his teeth. He ran a hand through his ragged hair and said, "Okay." They pushed him out the door ahead of them and descended the stairs, Warren and Bruce on either side, each gripping an arm. Once outside, they steered him toward the administration building.

Seph decided to try again. "What's this all about?"

"I tried to warn you, Joseph," Warren said.

It must be the e-mail, Seph thought. Unless it was Jason. The critical question was whether Sloane's had responded or not. It occurred to him that the day could bring either a major improvement or a dramatic deterioration in his prospects.

There weren't many students on the campus at that hour, except for a few hardy souls headed for the gym. The air was soft, the sky was pale, and the light was growing. A light mist lay on the harbor. It was going to be a beautiful day. For someone.

Seph and his escorts entered the admin. building and climbed the open staircase to the third floor. They took him directly to Gregory Leicester's office and pushed him forward.

Leicester was standing at his magnificent window, his hands clasped behind him, watching the sun come up over the water. John Hughes was seated at Leicester's PC, frantically typing in commands. Hughes was one of the alumni, a stocky man in his twenties with a receding hairline. He functioned as the systems administrator for the school.

It was the e-mail, then.

Warren cleared his throat nervously. "Here's Joseph."

Leicester did not look back at them, but turned instead to Hughes. "Well?"

Hughes half turned around in his chair and shook his head. "A number of them have already been opened. They were sent out on Sunday night. No response." He glanced at Seph, then looked away.

"I see." Leicester sighed, and stared out to sea again for a moment, then turned to face the trio in the doorway. "So, Joseph. It appears you have made a mistake."

Seph remembered Jason's advice. Be stupid and be scared. He tried to play stupid. "Already?" He lifted his shoulders slightly. "I just got out of bed."

Leicester's hand came up and forward. The blow came so quickly, Seph had no time to react. A fistlike concussion of air struck him full in the face and threw him back against the door, his feet literally leaving the ground. His head slammed hard against the doorframe before he slid to the floor. His right eye swam with tears and he tasted blood in his mouth where his lip was cut. He wiped his nose with the back of his hand, and it came away covered in blood.

He looked up to see that Leicester hadn't moved from his position by the window. Warren and Bruce had split off to either side, out of the target area.

Leicester thrust his hand toward him again. The next blow caught Seph just under the ribcage, throwing him back into the wall and driving all the breath out of him. He rolled over, trying to scramble out of the way, but the third hit him square in the back. Each felt like a sledgehammer against flesh and bone. Seph doubled up on the floor, making as small a target as possible. After two more blows, he wondered if Leicester intended to beat him to death.

He struggled to pull the air back into his lungs. It hurt to breathe, and he suspected his ribs might be broken. Leicester crossed the space between them and spoke to Seph on the floor from his terrible height.

"Who do you think I am? A high school principal?" he spat the words out derisively. "Did you think you were going to get a bloody detention?" His voice grew louder with each sentence.

Despite the pain, Seph managed to push himself into a half-sitting position, leaning against the wall. He shook his head, trying to clear it, flinging blood in a small arc. His lip was swelling, and the entire right side of his face felt numb, which was probably a blessing. His legs tingled, and he wondered if his spinal cord had been bruised by the blow to his back. "Why can't you just let me go?" he whispered.

"No one leaves the Havens until I'm ready. You should know that by now."

Seph knew he should just keep quiet, but he couldn't help himself. "Jason Haley left," he said.

"Ah, yes. Jason Haley has indeed left the Havens." Havens smiled. "Did you think I'd let him out alive?"

It was one of those times when the body seems to act without the counsel or approval of the conscious mind. Seph McCauley bunched his quivering legs under him and launched himself at Gregory Leicester. He hit him hard, in the midsection. It was very much like hitting a concrete wall, but Seph was able to land at least two good punches before Leicester pinned his arms to his side with one massive arm and wrapped the other around his neck, cutting off his air supply. He increased the pressure until black spots appeared before Seph's eyes, then relaxed it enough to keep Seph from passing out completely.

As soon as Seph had enough air to do so, he launched into one of the attack charms he and Jason had memorized in the library. But he was cut off mid sentence by blinding pain like a current that flamed through his body and left him limp and trembling when it was finally over.

"Don't be a fool," said Leicester.

But Seph was reckless with anger. "You'd better kill me," he gasped, "because if you don't, I swear I'll kill you."

Leicester was speaking into his ear. "Why would I kill you, Joseph, when I have so many other options?" He laughed softly. "You think you've had dreams? I can give you a nightmare that will last a week. Why, I can give you a nightmare that will last the rest of your life. We call it going insane.

"Now, the question is whether we need to keep you around in case someone responds to your message. I think not. You won't be in any condition to talk to them anyway. You threatened to kill yourself, Joseph, and I think you're going to succeed. You'll cease to exist as far as Sloane's is concerned. Think of it. We'll have you all to ourselves. A wizard's lifetime. No more paperwork, no pesky correspondence going back and forth." He touched Seph's damaged face, running his thumb down his chinline. "No need to keep you pretty in case someone comes to call."

Leicester tightened his grip and spoke a charm. The flames raked through Seph again, and he screamed, all of his muscles seizing with the pain of it. He couldn't say how long it went on, but Leicester suddenly released his hold on him, and Seph dropped to the floor like a rag doll, whimpering, desperately sucking in air.

"At last, perhaps, you begin to understand. You see how restrained I've been. Now the gloves come off. I won't make the same mistake I made with Jason. You're going to beg for the chance to give me what I want. I promise to take my time. We'll learn so much, you and I, about your capabilities. You've been a tough little bastard. Now we'll find out just how tough you are."

Seph lay with his face against the varnished hardwood, his breath coming in ragged gasps, his heart pounding in his ears. His skin was slick with sweat, and he was shivering. He could think of only one way out of his predicament. He had to find a way to make Leicester kill him.

Gradually, he became aware of a commotion in the outer suite of offices. Raised voices, like an argument. Seph turned his head slightly so he could see. Leicester turned toward the door. Peter Conroy slipped into the office and spoke, quietly and urgently, to Leicester. Leicester listened, with his eyes on Seph. He nodded, said a few words, and Conroy left again.

Leicester lifted an upholstered chair like it weighed nothing and set it in front of the door. Then he slid his hands under Seph's arms and hauled him into it. Seph bit his lip to keep from crying out. He tried to retreat into the chair, to curl himself around his many hurts like an injured animal. But the headmaster gripped his chin hard and lifted his head so Seph had no choice but to look him in the eyes.

"It appears there's been a response to your message. Sloane's has sent someone to inquire after you." Leicester dropped his hot hands onto Seph's shoulders. Power roared into him again, different from before, power that drove the strength from his muscles and bones, leaving him totally conscious but helpless—too weak to hold up his head. An immobilization charm. He couldn't speak or move a muscle.

Leicester arranged Seph's body in the chair, making no attempt to be gentle. He raked Seph's curls back out of his eyes and looked down at him, apparently satisfied. "Now you can listen while I send her away." He paused. "And when I return, I promise I will make you wish you'd never been born." Then he was gone, the three alumni following him.

So Sloane's had sent a woman. Seph had hoped they would send someone he knew, Denis Houghton, even. He didn't know any female associates of the firm. Seph swallowed down his despair. These wizards could outfox or overpower any lawyer. He didn't want to have to hear it.

The group outside must have moved closer to the door, or perhaps Leicester engineered it so, because suddenly the voices came through clearly. First a woman's voice. "We received his message at our offices

Sunday night. I'm not leaving without talking to him."

"I'm afraid that won't be possible just now," Leicester replied.

"What do you mean?" the woman demanded.

"Joseph has disappeared. No one has seen him since supper last night. He left this in his room." There was a brief silence, as if the woman were reading something.

"This doesn't sound like him. How do you know he wrote it?"

"It was in his room, Miss . . ."

"Downey," the woman said.

"Are you a relative?" Leicester asked, like a coroner seeking the next of kin.

"I am the boy's legal guardian," the woman said. "That's all you need to know. I fail to understand how you could lose my ward overnight."

"One of the boats is missing," Leicester said. "He might have taken it out last night."

"I find that hard to believe," the woman replied. "Seph has never been fond of the ocean."

There was something oddly compelling about her voice. It was like a song that you can't let go of. Seph was struck by the use of his private name, her confidence in her knowledge of him. She claimed to be his guardian. But Denis Houghton was his guardian. Downey? He'd never even heard her name before.

"Why haven't you called the police?" she demanded. "Why didn't you call us before now?"

"We've only just discovered he was missing," Leicester said. "We're conducting a search ourselves. It wasn't unusual for him to disappear for hours at a time. He liked to walk alone in the woods." He was already speaking in the past tense.

"First you imply he's gone boating in the dark, now you tell me he's been walking in the woods all night. Do your students never stay in their beds?"

The woman was persistent, but it wouldn't matter. She couldn't force them to produce him if they claimed he was missing. And Seph knew he would never be found.

"Why don't you come down to the cafeteria and have some coffee," Leicester said. "The search parties will be reporting back here. As soon as there's any news—"

"Seph said you wouldn't allow him to call us. He said you were holding him prisoner here."

Seph could almost see Leicester shrugging his shoulders. "I don't know where he gets these ideas," the headmaster said. "Frankly, Miss Downey, we've done our best to work with Joseph. You can tell by the note he left that he's unstable. In fact, we've come to believe that he's psychotic. Yet we were told none of this when we admitted him."

"You make it sound like he's been a problem since September," she said. Papers rustled. "I have all his progress reports here, and they suggest nothing of the kind."

Soon enough, the dance would be over. They would maneuver the woman out of the office and down to the cafeteria. Then they could tuck him somewhere out of the way, and his chance would be gone. He'd sacrificed so much, perhaps everything, to get Sloane's to send someone to rescue him.

I can't let her leave without seeing me, he told himself. He tried to move, to twitch a finger, but nothing happened. Frustration built up in him, and then something else, more familiar. He focused his attention on the door, concentrating, pushing energy into his extremities. And then it happened. A cascade of blue flame erupted from his fingertips and blew down the door between the offices with a bang like a gunshot.

There was a brief, stunned silence. "What the bloody hell was that?" the woman cried.

A clamor of voices erupted. Explanations and protests. Someone appeared in the doorway.

She was small, with short, layered hair, like silver and gold spun together. She wore a tailored black suit with a very short skirt, and had amazingly long legs for such a small person. When she moved, Seph found it impossible to look away. She seemed to shimmer, sending sparks in every direction. She looked like no lawyer Seph had ever seen.

"Thank God," the woman said. He could tell she recognized him immediately. She shook off Leicester and came toward him, the others trailing behind her like the tail of a comet. Warren and Bruce blundered into each other in their eagerness to get near her.

It was an exquisitely awkward moment, the wizards, the woman, the briefly lost and suddenly found Seph. For his part, Gregory Leicester looked like he might just murder Seph, right then and there, regardless of witnesses and the representative from Sloane's.

The woman's eyes never left Seph's face. Now that she was closer, he could see that they were deep-blue violet flecked with gold. "Dear God, what have they done to you?" Seph was desperate to reply, but all he could do was stare at her helplessly.

Gregory Leicester found his voice. "We . . . ah . . . didn't want you to see him like this. He's heavily medicated. He's been uncontrollably self-destructive these past few days." Leicester looked *disconcerted*, something Seph had never expected to see.

She was finally within arm's length of Seph, but now she looked back at Leicester for the first time. "I see what you mean. He's given himself a brutal beating. Most unusual."

She looked upset, distressed, angry, yet she was not making as much fuss over his appearance as he might have expected. She's not shocked, he thought. Not even surprised. Like she knows what's up. And with that came a fragment of hope.

"Hello, Seph. I'm Linda Downey."

Seph kept staring at her, spinning out silent pleas. *Find a way to get me out of here.* And then the tears washed over the great dam of his eyes and streaked down his face.

Linda Downey nodded, almost imperceptibly, as if she'd heard, and understood. She leaned in and gave him a light kiss on his forehead and whispered, so only he could hear, "Courage, Seph." Then she turned back to Leicester and the others.

"Clearly, this placement has been nothing short of a disaster. I'm taking him back to see his regular therapist. I'm hoping he won't require hospitalization."

She gestured to Hays and Barber. "You two. Help me get him into my car."

They stepped forward obediently. But Leicester shook his head. "The boy stays here," he said. "As you can see, he's in no condition to travel."

The woman sighed and changed tactics. "Dr. Leicester, I think it's time we were frank with each other. I do believe you all are wizards and you have this boy under a spell."

She might as well have said the law firm of Sloane, Houghton, and Smythe believed in fairies. Seph squinted at her in disbelief. The alumni stirred and muttered, but Leicester seemed unimpressed. "So?" he said, letting the word drop between them like a gauntlet. He was making it clear that what Linda Downey knew, or didn't know, was irrelevant.

She shook her head and regarded Leicester with a look of pity. "Do you have any idea who this boy is?"

Leicester frowned, opened his mouth, and then closed it again, looking from Linda to Seph.

"Obviously, you don't." She put her fingertips under Seph's chin and tilted his face upward. "Look at him! Look at his eyes, the shape of his nose."

Leicester studied Seph, but his scowl said he was clueless as before.

"I find it hard to believe you can't spot it." She cleared her throat. "Joseph McCauley is the natural child of one of your colleagues on the Council of Wizards. A delicate matter, as he is married to someone other than the boy's mother." She paused again. "His wife is a powerful wizard and has been unforgiving of such transgressions in the past. The boy has been kept ignorant of his background, for fear the story would come out. But Seph's father takes a strong interest in his welfare and upbringing. Seph is his only son."

She knows who my father is. Despite Leicester and the Alumni, despite his desperate situation, despite everything, Seph waited breathlessly for Linda Downey to say his name.

Leicester seemed to be rummaging through some kind of mental list. "Who is it?" he demanded. "Tell me. Who's his father?"

Linda said nothing.

"You don't mean . . . Ravenstock?" The wizard's face transitioned from incredulity to cunning conviction. "It is, isn't it?"

She hesitated, then said, "It's really none of your business. But you'll find out soon enough if you don't unbind the boy and let him go. His father flew into Portland yesterday. You can imagine his reaction when I forwarded Seph's message. If I don't show up with his son in Portland by this afternoon, his father will take this place apart, stone by stone, until he finds him. No excuse will be good enough to satisfy him. And you can be sure he'll bring the matter to the Council next week."

Leicester clenched and unclenched his fists. "Why didn't Ravenstock come himself, if he's so concerned?"

Ravenstock. Joseph Ravenstock. Hey, I'm Seph Ravenstock. Seph tried out the name in his mind.

"Considering his position, he wishes to keep the matter private. So he sent me as his representative. If he'd expected a problem, I'm sure he would have come himself."

"How do I know you're telling the truth?" Seph could tell Leicester didn't want to believe her.

"I'm the boy's guardian. I can show you papers, if you like." She dug in her briefcase, pulled out a wad of papers and handed them to Leicester. He scanned them unhappily and handed them back.

But Houghton's my guardian. Isn't he?

"Look," the woman said. "We're counting on your discretion. Seph's father doesn't care about whatever it is you're doing up here. But his tolerance does not extend to his own son. The boy has been badly beaten, starved, and tortured. If this comes out, it would be natural for the Council to assume that you were targeting his son for a reason. A political reason."

"And why should we allow you to leave here, carrying tales?" Leicester asked. He took a step toward her, reaching out to take her wrist. She stepped back, deftly avoiding his hand.

"I'm expected back with Joseph tonight," she said calmly. "How would you propose to explain our disappearance?"

Leicester looked bereft, like his birthday had been canceled. Clearly, he was trying to devise some alternative to letting Seph go. But it was also obvious that the woman's threats had been effective. He wouldn't want the Council involved, wouldn't want to draw any unnecessary attention to the Havens. He had to weigh the potential risk of releasing Seph against the damage of certain exposure.

Finally, he shrugged, not at all gracious in defeat. "Very well. Wait in the outer office a moment. I need to speak to Joseph in private."

She didn't want to go. Seph could tell. And he didn't want her to go, either. But she went, looking back over her shoulder as if it might be the last time she saw him.

Leicester pointed at Seph and muttered the counter-charm. Seph stirred in his chair and tried unsuccessfully to get to his feet. The headmaster grasped him by the front of his sweatshirt and dragged him upright so their faces were inches apart.

"So, Joseph, you're going back to your father. I hope you'll have a wonderful reunion. Just remember one thing—if even a whisper of what's going on here reaches any member of the Council, whether it's traceable back to you or not, I will make it my mission in life to track down every member of your miserable family and every friend you ever had down to the most ephemeral romantic *fling*, and I will kill them in the most excruciating way possible. And when I'm done with them, I will come after you, and we will resume where we left off."

Seph looked back at him and said, "Can I go now?" And thought, *You come after me and I'll be ready next time.*

Leicester let go of him and took a step back. Keeping his back straight, feeling Leicester's hostile glare on the back of his neck, Seph limped into the outer office, where Linda Downey was waiting. Though he towered over her, she slid her hand under his elbow to support him. Magic flowed into him, powerful stuff that made his head spin, though somehow different from what he was used to.

Leicester and the alumni had followed him out. He seemed to be trying to place Linda within his scheme of things. "I assume that you are Ravenstock's latest . . . lover?"

"Assistant," she said, steering Seph toward the door.

Seph looked back at Leicester, burning an image for later use. Somehow, I'll make you pay, he thought. For Sam, whoever he was and might have been. For Trevor. And for Jason, most of all.

He shuffled painfully to the door, with Linda's hand at his elbow, and then out the door and to the stairs. They managed to navigate the stairs, and hobbled out the front door.

The BMW waited in the parking lot. Linda opened the passenger door for Seph, helped him in, closed it behind him, and climbed in behind the wheel. Though she seemed calm, her hand was shaking and it took two tries to fit the key into the ignition.

Seph pressed himself back into the seat. Linda Downey drove fast and aggressively, ramming through the gears, jouncing down the dirt road at a reckless speed, remind-ing Seph of each and every injury. He looked over at her. There were spots of high color on her cheeks, and her eyes were alternately revealed and concealed in the shift-ing light under the trees. This was his father's girlfriend?

Seph tried to get comfortable, still unable to believe that he was finally leaving the Havens. "So we're heading for Portland?" He could hardly force the words between his swollen lips. His tongue explored a jagged spot where a tooth had broken off.

She nodded. "It's the fastest way out of Maine. But first we need to find you a doctor." She looked over at him, biting her lip. "The nearest hospital is probably in Portland."

Linda's scrutiny made Seph uncomfortable. "I'm all right. Really. It looks worse than it is. I'd rather not have to answer any questions."

"Seph, I'm so sorry. I had no idea what was going on." Her voice broke. "And when we received your e-mail, I . . ."

"Who is Ravenstock?"

"Never mind him. He's no one you're related to."

He wasn't surprised, somehow, but he was a little disappointed. He erased Ravenstock from his mental file, the place where he kept the clues to who he was. "Weren't you taking a chance in there?"

"I didn't have much choice. I had to hope you looked like someone on the Council."

"Thank you . . . for coming . . . when you did," he said. "They were going to kill me. Or worse."

She glanced over at him. "Why?"

"I think he likes it. Hurting people, I mean." Leicester's threat was fresh in his mind. He wasn't going to say much until he found out who and what she was.

Linda cleared her throat. "I don't really know how much you know . . . about the magical guilds." She looked straight ahead, as if embarrassed. As if she were about to deliver "The Talk."

"I know all about it," he said, rechecking the rearview mirror for the fifteenth time. "Weir, Anaweir, wizards and spells. If that's what you mean."

He'd surprised her. "Who told you? Was it Leicester?"

He shook his head. "My foster mother told me a little. The rest, I learned here." He thought of Jason, and his breath came ragged when he drew it in. He closed his eyes, trying to remember how it had felt when he'd smashed into Leicester. Wishing he'd managed to get off a charm.

"Are you sure you're all right?"

"I'm fine," Seph said. "Perfect." He looked sideways at her. "So you're a wizard?"

She shook her head. "No. Enchanter." She delivered the word quickly, as if unsure of his reaction.

An enchanter! Jason had been fascinated by enchanters, but said he'd never met one. Seph remembered something Jason had said, and before he could think, he had blurted it out. "Is it true an enchanter can bewitch any wizard, no matter how powerful?" Then he clapped his mouth shut. Not a question to be asking someone he'd just met.

"Well. I suppose that depends on the enchanter, and the wizard, and how careful he or she is about being bewitched. Of course, as a general rule, wizards are more powerful than enchanters. But if I come on a wizard unawares . . ." She let go of the wheel and flexed her fingers like a cat unsheathing its claws.

"But who are you? Do you really work for Sloane's?"

"No. They work for me. What I said in there was true. I'm your guardian."

Something told him she wasn't being completely honest. It was as if she were translucent, and every so often the light would shine through, illuminating her, revealing shards of the truth, like gold glittering in the sand.

"Did . . . do you know my parents?" He wasn't sure what tense to use.

"I knew them. Years ago," she said.

Another lie. He sat up straighter. Linda Downey knew the truth about him, he was sure of it. He would find a way to get it from her, no matter how awful it was.

"If you're my guardian, how come I've never heard of you?"

"I became your guardian after your parents died. I . . . I travel a lot and I wanted something stable for you. So Genevieve LeClerc agreed to foster you."

"But who were my parents?" Seph persisted. "What were their names? Where did they live? How did they die? Do I have other family?" It was a cascade of questions, the questions of a lifetime.

She ran her tongue over her lips. "Surely Genevieve told you all that. Your father . . . was a software engineer. There was a fire."

"Don't give me that fairy tale. I'm just a made-up person. My birth record is a fake. There is no news story about a fire. No Social Security death records. I'm not stupid."

"No one ever said you were." She kept her eyes on the road, as if it would be dangerous to look at him. "The truth is, I can't tell you what you want to know. So don't ask me any more." Her tone was sharp, her knuckles white against the steering wheel. There was a brief, strained silence. Then she went on.

"I placed you with Genevieve when you were a baby, because I knew she would take good care of you. You liked it there, didn't you?" The question came in a rush, a plea for reassurance.

"I liked it there." Seph looked out the window. "I loved Genevieve."

"I guess I haven't done so well the past two years. You see . . . my nephew was in trouble, and . . . well . . . I got distracted. There's been a lot going on. Houghton assured me that you were doing well. Until he called me about the e-mail." Her voice trailed away.

"Where are we headed, anyway?"

"A town called Trinity. It's in Ohio, on Lake Erie. A college town."

"Trinity, Ohio." Jason had mentioned that name. An image surfaced. Barns and silos. From the forest primeval to the Midwestern farm. He tried not to make a face. It hurt to make a face.

Anywhere is better than where I came from, he told himself. Just then he wanted to burrow into the Midwest, to pull the farmland of Ohio over himself like a blanket.

"Why Trinity?" he asked. "Is there another school there?"

"My sister lives there. Plus, it was designated as a sanctuary after the tournament at Raven's Ghyll."

Right. Jason had said something about a sanctuary, "in Ohio, of all places."

"Why a sanctuary?"

"There's a lot going on," she said again, as if that explained anything.

"Are there any wizards in Trinity?" he asked.

She nodded. "Yes, I know of at least two, and there are probably more. Why do you ask?"

"I need more training."

She nodded. "I suppose your lack of training is my fault. Genevieve was . . . was wonderful, but not very approving of wizards." She nodded again, as if confirming some unspoken thought. "Yes, I imagine we can find someone in Trinity to train you."

"Good." He leaned back and closed his eyes, but he could still feel the pressure of her gaze.

"If you feel up to it, why don't you tell me what happened at the Havens."

He kept his eyes closed. "I really don't feel up to it."

She fell silent. She had secrets, so did he. Gregory Leicester's threat lingered in the back of his mind. It might be that the only person to tell this story to would be the Dragon. Someone powerful enough to put it to use.

Linda Downey had saved his life, and for that he was grateful. If she wanted more than that, she'd have to earn his trust.

Late that evening, Gregory Leicester sat at the end of the dock, leaning against the cold metal of the boatlift. Not even the loveliness of the spring evening could soothe him. He was drinking Courvoisier again, and more than usual.

The boy had made a fool of him. First he'd broken into his office and sent the e-mails. Then he had actually dared to attack him. And he'd walked away with hardly a scratch. Not a good lesson for the alumni who were there to see it.

He consoled himself with the anticipation of the summer to come. There would be a meeting of the Council the next week. He wondered if he could use the information about Ravenstock's bastard to direct his vote on the constitutional issue.

Once the other students were gone, he'd need time to work with the alumni. In truth, he could do without the distraction of trying to break the boy, and then train him. Even with the loss of his two latest prospects, he had fifteen wizards linked to him. That should be plenty, assuming the Dragon and the others could be kept in the dark a little longer.

He swirled the amber liquid in his glass, feeling better. The cell phone at his belt buzzed and he considered ignoring it. But the number had been given only to a chosen few. So he pulled it from its clip. "Leicester."

It was Claude D'Orsay. His voice was tight with excitement, unusual for the reserved Master of the Games. "You have a student by the name of Joseph McCauley." It wasn't a question.

Joseph McCauley again. "What about him?" Leicester drained his glass.

"I'm coming to Maine tomorrow. Confine him until I arrive."

"What are you talking about?"

"Do you know who the boy is?"

Oh, that. Leicester snorted. "I heard about it today. He's Jeremy Ravenstock's bastard. Apparently, Ravenstock's trying to keep it a secret. Not very successfully, I'm afraid."

"Ravenstock? Not unless Ravenstock is the Dragon, which is absurd. We both know the Dragon's true identity. We think the boy's his son."

For a long moment, Leicester could say nothing at all. "Are you sure?"

"We found his name in some files at the Dragon's hideout in London when we raided it a few months ago. We searched all of our databases, Social Security records, and so on, but it took a while to find him. The boy was born in Canada. The birth certificate is a phony. His parents never existed. Someone has gone to a lot of trouble to hide who he really is."

It had definitely not been a good day for Gregory Leicester, and now the cognac was no longer working. Joseph McCauley's face was before him again, and he saw the resemblance immediately. It was unmistakable. The imprint of the devil was clearly on his offspring. It confirmed both the father as the Dragon and the son as his blood. "He's gone, Claude," he whispered, unable to believe it himself.

"What do you mean, he's gone?"

"He left this morning. His guardian picked him up."

"His guardian? Who?"

"A lawyer named Linda Downey. She said she was representing Ravenstock. The boy acted like he'd never laid eyes on her before."

"Linda Downey," D'Orsay repeated. "I remember her. She was at the tournament last summer. An enchanter."

"An enchanter!" The glass shattered in Leicester's hand and he stared down at the blood that ran across his palm. It was suddenly clear to him why she had been so hard to resist.

D'Orsay was still going on about Linda Downey. "She was unforgettable. Bewitching, really. I wonder what her connection is to the Dragon." He was quiet for a moment. "So she charmed you into giving up the boy?"

"Never mind how she did it. How was I supposed to know who he was?" But looking back, he had trouble remembering how she'd persuaded him to relinquish something he wanted to keep so badly.

So young. So powerful. So resistant to persuasion. He should have suspected from the beginning that the boy was a spy. But why would the Dragon have risked his son in such a scheme when he had gone to so much trouble to hide his identity?

"I think we can assume that by now the Dragon knows all about the Havens," D'Orsay said. "You're going to have to vacate."

"I'll reinforce the perimeter. We were leaving soon, anyway. There's no reason to change our plans. The boy declined to link to me, so he doesn't know much. And if we can find him, we can use him to lure the Dragon out of hiding."

"Did they say where they were going?" D'Orsay asked.

"No." Probably not Portland, Maine. "Where is she from?"

"I don't know where she lives, but I could find out. She has some connection with the Sanctuary that was established after that disaster at the tournament last spring. Some little town in the Midwest. It might be a place to start."

"Let me look for them. I'll try to intercept them before they get into the Sanctuary." Leicester had his own, personal reasons for doing so. "I have video of Joseph, and I may have some still pictures. I'll e-mail them to you."

And so it was agreed.

ᚼ Chapter Ten ᚼ
The Weirweb

Seph alternately watched the scenery and dozed in the brief, intensive catnaps that had become his custom at the Havens. He was like an animal for whom a moment of inattention could be the difference between life and death.

Linda watched him when she thought he wasn't looking.

They followed the long circle of I-95 around Boston before taking the turnpike west across Massachusetts.

They stopped at one of the plazas on the turnpike where the restless traveling public can buy whatever they need. He picked out two Toronto Maple Leafs T-shirts and a Blue Jays sweatshirt, two pairs of sweatpants, underwear, and a toothbrush. The sum total of his possessions at the moment. He changed his ruined shirt and carefully cleaned the blood from his face in the washroom, his skin stinging from the nasty dispenser soap.

They left the highway at Stockbridge, Massachusetts, just across the border from New York. Linda drove into the hills, high above the town to an inn she knew. They ate dinner in a small dining room overlooking a tumbling stream, and took two rooms under the name of O'Herron, because she happened to have identification in that name. He didn't question that, nor did he bother to call Denis Houghton to verify Linda Downey's story. There didn't seem to be any point.

Seph didn't use the portal stone when he climbed between the sheets that night. He was apprehensive, though, wondering if Gregory Leicester could still reach out to him over the distance between them. He slept restlessly, but his dreams were the natural kind.

The next morning, they left before the sun rose, while the inn was still clothed in the shadows of the mountains. They struck out across the state line into the long corridor of New York State, crossed the Hudson, and joined the New York Thruway near Albany.

Linda could tell from the way Seph moved that he was stiff and sore. He kept his elbows down, close to his sides, as if guarding his midsection. His lip was cracked and swollen, and the entire right side of his face was bruised. He didn't complain, though, and shook off Linda's questions.

Linda liked being able to look over at him after so many years of watching him from a distance. She studied the dark curls, which were longer than usual, and ungelled; the eyebrows that would be heavy when he grew to be a man, the bones of his face as the light changed. He needed healing, she knew, but she didn't know the remedy for what ailed him. She would ask Nick Snowbeard about it when they reached Trinity.

She wondered how she could keep the gathering darkness away from him. The Sanctuary would be safer than anywhere else, but it might also bring him to the attention of those who had overlooked him up to now.

Hastings would know the news from the Wizard Council, but she would have to be careful with him, what she asked and how she asked it.

Leander Hastings didn't need to know about Seph McCauley.

They left I-90 west of Cleveland. By now it was after seven, and Seph's stomach was reminding him that they hadn't eaten lunch. Linda glanced over at him. "We're close," she said. "Do you want to stop and eat, or wait till we get to town?"

Seph shrugged. "Let's just get there."

They were driving close to the lakeshore now. Seph saw signs for wineries, bed and breakfasts, and Trinity College. When they rounded a curve, he saw the town itself, across a small bay, like a scene from a post-card. Quaint storefronts and Victorian houses clustered along the water, the stark white steeples of churches rising behind, a picturesque harbor and marina lined with boats. More sailboats were anchored just off shore.

The town shimmered in the slanting sunlight, as if there were an iridescent veil draped across it, some peculiar trick of the light. The car slowed, and Seph glanced over at Linda. She was frowning, head tilted, as if seeing something she didn't like. She removed her sunglasses and leaned forward, squinting through the windshield, then took a quick left at the next intersection and headed south.

"What's wrong?" Seph asked.

"I don't know."

They detoured south for a few miles, then cut west and back north so that they approached the town from the south. They came over a ridge, perhaps an ancient shoreline of the lake, and once again, the town lay glowing before them with the lake beyond. Indistinct, purple-pink, like a poorly printed illustration in a pulp magazine. Linda shook her head, muttering to herself, made a sudden right turn into the parking lot of a small diner, and jerked to a stop.

"Let's eat here," she said. "Go in and get us a table. Get whatever you want, and order me a salad. I need to make a phone call." She pulled out a cell phone and waved him off.

Baffled, Seph went on into the restaurant. It was nearly empty, maybe because it was a weeknight. The only employee in evidence was wiping off glasses behind the bar. He motioned Seph to a back table, staring at his bruised face with frank curiosity, as if hoping his guest would pay for his dinner with a story about his recent beating.

By the time Linda came in, the food had already arrived. "Who'd you call?" he asked.

"My nephew. Jack," Linda explained. "He's going to meet us here. My sister, Becka, is a lawyer. She also teaches literature at Trinity College. Jack's her son, a little older than you."

Seph shrugged, puzzled by the change in plans. "Okay."

"He's a warrior," Linda went on. "One of the Weirlind."

Seph stopped chewing and looked up. Jason had said warriors were exceedingly rare. Like an endangered species. "A warrior? Are you expecting trouble?"

Linda shrugged. "I don't know. I hope not. He might bring some other people along."

"What's wrong?" Seph asked.

"There's a magical barrier around the town—a Weirweb. I want to know how long it's been there and who put it up."

A Weirweb. A cold finger ran down his spine. Seph recalled the barrier around the Havens, with its smudgy, iridescent appearance. The veil over Trinity was similar. Could it be a coincidence?

They finished their food, and Seph ordered a piece of apple pie à la mode. He was dissecting it, consuming it in a hundred small bites, when the door opened and three people walked in.

One was an old man, very thin, with a trimmed white beard and bright black eyes. He leaned on a staff with an intricately carved bear's head on it. Although wizards couldn't readily recognize their own kind, he seemed to be a prototype.

He was unlike the other wizards Seph had met. There was something kind and reassuring about his face, in the laugh lines around his eyes.

The other two were about Seph's age. One was a tall, athletic-looking teenager with bright red-gold hair and blue eyes that reminded Seph of Linda's. He was dressed in jeans and a T-shirt that revealed his broad chest and shoulders and muscular arms. He grinned when he spotted them in the corner and crossed the space between the door and the table in a few long strides.

I've never seen a seventeen-year-old built like that, Seph thought. This must be Jack, the warrior. He glanced down at himself, ashamed at how gaunt he looked.

"Aunt Linda!" The red-haired boy put his hands on her shoulders, leaned down and kissed her cheek.

The third member of the trio was a girl, almost as tall as the boy, though her hair was chestnut brown. There was a certain physical grace and confidence about them. Their raw physical power seemed to push everyone else to the periphery. If Jack's a warrior, Seph thought, then so is she.

"Hullo, Aunt Linda." The girl embraced Linda Downey also, a little more shyly. Seph was beginning to feel left out amid all the meeting and greeting. But he felt the wizard's eyes upon him, and in a moment, the warriors noticed him too. Jack rocked back on his heels, and the girl's right hand crept to her belt as if she might find a weapon there.

Seph stood up. "I'm Seph," he said, sticking out his hand to the wizard. Seph sensed well-controlled but elaborate power behind the grip. He had the feeling the old man already knew exactly who he was.

Linda nodded toward the wizard. "I'm sorry, Seph. This is Nicodemus Snowbeard," she said. "And my nephew, Jack Swift, and a friend, Ellen Stephenson." She put her hand on Seph's shoulder. "This is Seph McCauley." She didn't qualify him in any way.

Jack Swift, Seph thought. Where have I heard that name before?

"You never said he was a wizard," Jack said, not bothering to hide his surprise. They were all three looking curiously at Seph's cut and swollen lip, his battered face. "Since when does a wizard need sanctuary?" There was a degree of challenge behind the question.

Seph lifted his chin and looked Jack in the eyes. He was almost of a height with the warrior, though Jack probably outweighed him by half. "Why? You the gate-keeper?"

"Jack, you of all people should know it's not difficult to make enemies, no matter who you are," Linda said quickly.

That was it. Jack Swift was the warrior who'd played in the famous tournament at Raven's Ghyll. The rebel behind the change in the rules. And he was Linda Downey's nephew.

Seph remembered what she'd said in the car. *My nephew was in trouble, and . . . well . . . I got distracted.* Seph studied Jack with new interest, like he'd suddenly discovered a celebrity sitting next to him in a movie theater.

The newcomers pulled more chairs around the table.

"How did you get through the barrier, Nicodemus?" Linda asked.

Snowbeard nodded at the two warriors. "Jack and Ellen brought their blades. They were able to cut a path for us."

"And before we were through, we had company." Jack stretched his long legs into the aisle. "Four wizards showed up, all excited at first, but they lost interest when they saw who we were."

"The wizards who put up the web can detect any disturbance in it. Rather like a spider waiting for its prey," Snowbeard said. "Whoever did it has a real talent and an excess of power. It's incredible that it went up that fast."

"What did the wizards look like?" Seph pushed aside the remains of his pie, no longer interested.

"They were all pretty young, maybe a few years older than us," Ellen said.

"They asked about an enchanter and a young wizard, matching your descriptions," Jack added, fixing Seph with a gaze that conceded nothing. "They were typical wizards—arrogant and pushy—but I guess they decided they didn't want to get into it." The warrior flexed his hands and rested them on his knees, as if he wouldn't have minded getting into it.

"They ordered us to leave the web alone," Ellen added.

"How does a Weirweb work?" Seph asked.

The old man stroked his beard. "It's a soft barrier that

selects for Weir, for people carrying a stone. Anaweir can pass through it without even noticing. For us, it's a very sticky trap. It will hold you fast if you touch any part of it. Given enough time, I could force an opening. But it's made to be resistant to spellcasting."

Barber had put up the wizard wall at the Havens. But how could they have tracked them here so quickly? And why let him go, only to come after him here?

"The Weirweb is an interesting choice of weapons," Snowbeard said thoughtfully. "It was commonly used in the wizard wars back in the sixteenth century. Wizards would trap Weir from the opposing houses in the web and then pick them off at their leisure, or take them prisoner. It's fine work. I haven't seen anything like it in several hundred years."

Seph blinked at the wizard. How old could he be, anyway? Jason had said wizards lived almost forever, but Seph had thought he was exaggerating.

"Well," Snowbeard continued. "We're going to have to assume that someone wants to keep you from reaching the sanctuary. Their use of the web suggests they want to take you alive. Otherwise they would have set a different kind of trap."

"So," Jack said, leaning across the table, speaking directly to Seph. "Did you piss somebody off, or what?"

"Will you relax?" Ellen said, frowning at Jack. "Can't you see he's had a hard time?"

Seph shoved his chair back. "Hey, if we can't get in, I'll just go somewhere else. I don't want to inconvenience anyone."

Linda put her hand on his arm. "No. I want you in the sanctuary." She glared around the table, daring anyone to disagree.

"What's so special about the sanctuary?" Seph asked

"Attack magic is not allowed within its boundaries," Snowbeard replied. He covered Linda's hand with his, and murmured something to her. "Now, then. It will take some time to get through the web, and I don't think we want to have to entertain four wizards while we are doing it. So I suggest we create a distraction."

He leaned forward. "We'll spread out. Jack and Ellen will cut a path through for Seph. They're familiar with your car, Linda, yes? So you and I will create a diversion with the car. With any luck, they'll come after us. By the time they discover their mistake, you're in." He paused. "Hopefully. At least it will split them up. I can create a rather spectacular diversion, if I do say so. I'm the most likely to succeed and come out alive, and if I don't, I'm nearly four hundred and ninety-two years old." He turned to Linda. "Is there anything you would like to get from the car?"

Linda paid the check, and they walked out to the parking lot together. A black Subaru stood in a secluded spot in back of the restaurant. Jack opened the trunk and lifted out two ornate swords, handing one hiltfirst to Ellen.

The weapons illuminated the parking lot, bright sparks in the gathering dusk. Jack's was the larger of the two, and it had a large red ruby set into the hilt. Jack handled it as though it weighed nothing. He buckled on a leather harness with a scabbard that slanted across his back.

Maybe those are magic pieces from the golden age of sorcery, like the *dyrne sefa*, Seph thought.

"Let's synchronize our watches. It's seven forty-five," Snowbeard said. "Linda and I will break into the web at eight fifteen. Wait a few minutes, then cut through yourselves."

Snowbeard slid behind the wheel of the BMW, with Linda on the passenger side. Jack and Ellen and Seph climbed into the Subaru, laying the swords down between the seats.

They drove in tandem, with Snowbeard leading the way along country roads, turning as often as necessary to keep close to the shimmering border. It seemed to stretch as far as the eye could see, even arching over top of the town. It would be easy to walk into, if you weren't paying attention.

About a mile to the west, Jack pulled well off the road, into the edge of a field. The three of them climbed out, Jack and Ellen carrying their swords. Snowbeard drove on, disappearing over the next ridge.

They'd chosen a spot where the barrier cut across a field. A battered farmhouse crouched next to the road, its paint gone gray with weather. The foundation of the house was overgrown with wild roses, sprays of red and white flowers with yellow centers. In the pasture, cattle wandered back and forth through the barrier, oblivious to it. The late day sun slanted across the barnyard.

They slipped past the house, moving behind the barn

where they would be less likely to be seen from the road. Here, between the barn and the fenced pasture, the grass was nearly knee-high and concealed hidden hazards: rusty pieces of old farm machinery and piles of cow manure.

Up close, the barrier was revealed as an intricate network of nearly translucent cords, as thick as Seph's little finger. There was hardly an inch of space between them anywhere. There was something mathematical about the pattern, like the spokes of a spiderweb. It had a kind of malevolent presence, as if it were alive and watching them. He couldn't tell how thick it was.

Jack paced up and down impatiently, swinging his sword like a scythe, clipping off the tops of weeds. Seph and Ellen sat down in the grass and waited. Biting insects buzzed around their faces.

At 8:15, they queued up at the wall, Jack first, then Ellen, followed by Seph. "We'll only be able to hack a narrow path," Jack warned Seph. "This stuff is tough to get through and it kind of fills in behind. So be careful not to touch any part of it."

In the distance, they heard a *boom* and saw flames fountaining into the air like a series of gigantic Roman candles. The diversion had begun.

They'll be lucky if they don't draw the local police, too, Seph thought.

Jack's blue-edged blade bit into the web, sending bits of cording flying. The net responded immediately, shrinking back before them. A muttering arose from the Weirweb, like the sound of an angry crowd. It grew until it became a great wailing clamor.

Jack looked over his shoulder, making a face. "Hard to take, isn't it?" He turned back to his work. He flowed from stance to stance like a fencer, the sword a bright blur, singing as the web keened. The warrior's swordplay was poetry in flesh, although it wasn't long before his T-shirt was stuck to him, and sweat poured down his face. Ellen followed behind, clearing loose tendrils and widening the path behind Jack. They swapped places every few minutes. Seph watched to the rear, looking for any sign of pursuit.

They had cut a path about thirty feet into the net when it happened. One of the tendrils Jack had broken whipped back, and Ellen sidestepped to avoid it. Her arm brushed one of the loose tendrils at the side of the path. The web reacted swiftly, throwing three new cords around her waist.

"Jack!" She hacked at the cords with her sword, but a line tangled around her legs, and she fell. More strands wrapped around her sword arm, seemingly attracted by her violent efforts to free herself.

"Will you hold still?" Jack plunged into the growth around her, slicing away at the bonds that held her whole body prisoner. He used his blade like a surgeon, slicing through the web, miraculously never drawing blood. Ellen sat stone still, unflinching, though swearing creatively. But the net responded by throwing out more cords. Jack had to be careful not to become entangled himself. He was making no visible progress. He yanked a blade out of a sheath at his belt and looked over at Seph. "Listen, are you any good with a knife?"

Seph was no good with a knife at all, but he accepted

the blade and began hacking at the thick tendrils, conscious of time passing, working as quickly as he could while trying to stay away from vital organs. All around them, the web seemed to be chuckling triumphantly.

After five minutes, Ellen was wrapped up as securely as before. She looked up at Jack and Seph. "Go on," she said. "You've wasted too much time already."

"No," Jack said stubbornly, slashing at the cords at her waist. His hair was plastered down with sweat.

"Linda told us to get Seph to the Sanctuary. Take him and come back for me. I can take care of myself."

"Right," Jack growled. "Against wizards. When you're trussed up like a . . ."

"Whose fault is that? I mean, if you were a little less clumsy with that sword of yours . . ."

"Don't think you can make me mad enough to leave you here."

"I know these people," Seph said, chopping at the cord that bound her ankles. "We're not leaving you here."

"That's brilliant. Let's all three get captured." When they didn't respond, she added, "You know I'm right."

"Fine!" Jack swiped at the sweat that streamed down his face. "*You* come on!" he said to Seph. "The sooner we get through, the sooner I can be back." Jack pivoted away from Ellen and began hacking away again with a vengeance, sending tendrils flying. The keening wail started up again. They moved forward rapidly. It was probably another twenty yards to the inner wall of the barrier and half a mile beyond that to the edge of the town.

When they broke through, Seph turned and looked

back at Ellen. She was sitting quietly, no longer struggling. She scowled and waved him off when she saw him look-ing at her.

"Go back for her," Seph said. "I'll go the rest of the way on my own."

Jack shook his head. They would be in the open from the edge of the barrier to the city limits. "Let's go." He started across the field at a run, his long legs covering the distance in great leaping strides. Seph followed, deter-mined to keep pace despite the complaints of his tortured muscles and bruised body.

Once they passed the edge of the barrier, Ellen could no longer see Seph and Jack, or hear the sounds of their progress, only the gloating whisper of the web around her. She tried to ignore it. She was uncomfortable, but she kept still, because the web around her tightened every time she moved. A cow passed through the barrier and stopped a few feet away, staring at her curiously. The cow lifted her head and looked back down the pathway. Ellen heard something, too. Someone was coming.

It was one of the four young wizards they'd encoun-tered on their way out of town. He had backcombed, white-blond hair, and a stubble of beard so pale as to be almost translucent. His eyes were a diluted color, like whitewash spread too thin over blue.

He looked surprised to see Ellen, as though it was inconceivable that she would disobey his orders. "You again. I told you not to touch this." The tendrils making up the wall responded to his presence like snakes to a charmer, curling over his shoulders and sliding between his feet, murmuring excitedly.

"I was just trying to get back to town, and I got tangled up." Ellen assumed what she hoped was a blank, stupid expression. She'd spent a lifetime lying to wizards. Their arrogance made it a lot easier.

"What's this?" The wizard gently freed Ellen's sword from the tangle of vines and examined it, turning it to catch the light. He took a few practice swings, handling it like a golf club. "This is awesome. Where'd you get this?"

"I bought it off a dealer."

"Do you have any more pieces like this?"

Ellen shook her head, watching the wizard brandish the sword and wishing she could get her hands on it.

"What are you, a sorcerer?"

"I don't know what you're talking about."

The wizard rolled his eyes. "Right. What's your name?"

Not a good idea to give a wizard identifying information. "Nikki. With two k's and an i. What's yours?"

"Warren Barber." He eyed her suspiciously. "Look, sweetheart. I know something's going on. Fires. Explosions. People running around with magical swords. Old men in sports cars."

"It's been like this ever since they set up the Sanctuary. It attracts all kinds of riff-raff. It used to be a nice little town." She looked up at him. "Now. Could you get me out of this web?"

Barber carefully set the sword down out of Ellen's

reach, then began crooning charms, coaxing the cords away from Ellen's body until her legs were freed. He left her hands securely tied. She extended her bound wrists. "What's with this?"

"I have a feeling you know more than you're saying. I think with a little persuasion you'll tell me what it is." He smiled and extended his hands.

Ellen knew well how painful a wizard's touch could be. So much for peaceful coexistence. She bunched her legs under her and rammed her head into Barber's face, feeling his nose crunch at the impact. She landed, rolling, and gripped the sword hilt with her bound hands. Swinging the blade upright, she thrust it at the wizard's midsection, flames dancing eagerly at the tip. But he leaped back out of range, spinning additional cords from his hands that snaked around her body, despite her efforts to cut them to pieces. They constricted until she was totally immobile, and then Barber yanked the sword from her hands and set it aside.

He knelt and leaned over her, blood streaming from his broken nose, pale face spotted purple with rage. He wrapped his hot wizard hands around her throat and squeezed. She twisted and turned under his weight, but couldn't free herself. Spots danced before her eyes, then coalesced into darkness.

Something thudded into them, and then the wizard's weight was gone and her airway was miraculously open. Ellen sucked in great lungfuls of air until her vision cleared. She looked up to see Jack and Barber circling like fighters being paid by the round.

"You all right, Ellen?" Jack asked, without taking his eyes off Barber.

"I'm fine," she croaked, feeling stupid, lying on the ground, tied up like a holiday ham. "Cut me loose when you get a minute?"

Jack reached over his shoulder and drew his sword, Shadowslayer, with a delicious hissing sound. He stood with his feet spread apart a little, the sword pointed at the wizard.

Barber took a step back, outside of the immediate reach of the blade, and swept his hand toward Jack. Flames sprayed at Jack's face, but he parried them with his sword.

Barber cast an immobilization charm, but before it was out of his mouth, Jack spoke the counter spell, stumbling over the words a bit. Barber licked his lips. "You're a wizard?"

"Maybe." Jack stood in a ready position, his blue eyes hard and cold.

Barber feinted toward Jack, then launched a gout of flame at Ellen. Jack threw himself into the path of the attack, shoving Ellen aside. Tongues of flame engulfed his sword arm. Shadowslayer slipped from his grasp, landing with a thud in the tall grass. Swearing, Jack leaped after his blade, but Barber spun out long cords that tangled in his legs and wrapped themselves around his body.

Almost lazily, Barber raised his hands to deliver a killing blow. Suddenly a peculiar expression spread across his face. He swayed, then toppled forward into the grass and lay still.

Finally free, Jack retrieved his sword and stood over

the wizard, both hands wrapped around the hilt, the tip of the blade pressed into the back of Barber's neck. But Barber was out cold.

Seph McCauley materialized before their eyes, as if out of the air, holding a large branch like a baseball bat. When he saw that Barber was truly down, he tossed the branch aside. "Best I could do," he said apologetically. "I can't cast charms while I'm unnoticeable. Anyway, I don't know a lot of magic."

"Well, obviously you've learned something," Ellen said, extending her wrists so Jack could cut them free.

"Not that I'm ungrateful, but what the hell are you doing here?" Jack demanded of Seph. "I told you to stay where you were."

Seph swept his hair out of his eyes. "Did you? I must've misunderstood." He nudged Barber with his foot. No response. He looked around. "Hey, the wall's down."

Ellen looked up. The wall was disintegrating, dissolving into tattered wisps of mist.

"I guess it needs some sort of conscious attention from Barber to keep it intact." Seph shrugged. "The other wizards will know he's down. Now would probably be a good time to get going."

Reluctantly, Jack lifted his blade away from Warren Barber's neck and shoved it back into his baldric. He was pale and sweating and obviously in pain. His forearm was blistered from wrist to elbow where Barber had flamed him.

"That arm looks bad," Ellen said. "Maybe Nick can take a look at it before your mom sees it."

They began walking toward town, this time crossing the fields and orchards unimpeded.

Jack swiped sweat from his brow with the back of his good hand. "Who was that guy?" he asked Seph.

"I went to school with him," Seph said. "At the Havens."

"Must be a great place, the Havens," Jack said sarcastically. He seemed to be in a foul temper, probably not improved by the pain in his arm. He glanced sideways at Seph. "I can't understand why we're getting involved in a fight between wizards."

"We're going to be involved, whether we like it or not," Ellen said. "You know that."

Seph scowled. "I don't expect any of you to get involved. If I have my way, I won't impose on you any longer."

It was full dark by now. They began walking along the highway toward the town center. They had walked perhaps a mile when they saw a car slow down and pull onto the shoulder. It was the black Subaru, with Nick Snowbeard behind the wheel and Linda next to him.

"Hey!" Jack said, pulling a set of car keys from his back pocket. "How'd you start my car?" he demanded in mock amazement. "Do you even have a driver's license?"

"If I did, they would probably take it away after tonight," Snowbeard replied.

They drove to a pavilion in a park along the lakefront and gathered around a battered picnic table for the debriefing. Snowbeard kindled a wizard light in the center, casting a soft illumination over all of the participants.

Linda leaned forward and squinted across the table, then reached out and gently touched Jack's hand. "What happened to your arm?"

They told Snowbeard and Linda about the encounter with Warren Barber.

"Can you do anything for him, Nick?" Linda asked.

Snowbeard studied the injury, then leaned toward Jack and gripped him at the wrist and shoulder, careful not to touch the blistered area. Power rippled between the old wizard's hands, like a cool stream flowing over Jack's skin. The blisters subsided, though the area was still angry red.

Jack released a long breath and managed a grin. "Thanks, Nick. That feels a lot better."

"Less chance of infection now, Jack, but the area will be very tender for the next few days," Snowbeard said. He looked at Ellen. "What about you, my dear?"

Ellen had a necklace of purpling bruises around her neck, but she brushed off Snowbeard's question. Seph was getting the impression that she was not the kind of person who enjoyed being rescued.

Jack turned to Snowbeard. "What happened with the other wizards? Where's the Beamer?"

Snowbeard smiled, rolling his staff between his hands. "I managed to bore quite a way into the web with wizard flame and what-not. Then I set off some spectacular fireworks. When the wizards arrived, we raced off in the car. They, of course, assumed it was Linda and Seph.

"They were young and quite enthusiastic. We led them on a merry chase, but we never actually made it into the Sanctuary. So I parked at the mall out by the highway interchange. We went in and lost ourselves among the shoppers. Your car's still there."

"How'd you get back to town?" Ellen asked.

"We found a kind family willing to drive us," Snowbeard said blandly. "We told them we'd missed the last bus."

"We thought we'd have trouble getting through the Weirweb, but it was already down," Linda added.

"So," Seph said. "What do you think is going on?"

Linda cleared her throat. "Leicester wants you back. For some reason. Barber is working for a wizard named Gregory Leicester," she explained to the others. "He was Seph's headmaster at a private school up in Maine." She slid a glance at Seph and he looked away.

"Leicester is also on the Council of Wizards," Snowbeard added thoughtfully.

"They can't be sure that Seph is here," Linda suggested.

"They've seen the Beamer," Ellen said. "And they've seen you."

"They haven't seen Seph, though," Linda pointed out.

Snowbeard said, "It occurs to me that there's nothing to keep them from coming into town for a look around. And, depending on how you read the Rules of Engagement, they might be able to find a way to get you or Seph out of town by trickery or force as long as they don't use magic."

"But I can use wizardry to defend myself, right? Assuming I can find someone to train me." Seph shrugged.

"I can teach you," Snowbeard said, looking from Seph

to Linda and back again. "Depending on what you want to learn."

"Great. Thank you." Seph turned to Jack. "Um . . . where did you learn to use a sword like that?"

"My teacher was a wizard named Leander Hastings," Jack replied. "He specializes in training warriors. He taught me how to fight."

Hastings. "Does he live in Trinity?" Seph asked.

"No." Linda answered for Jack.

"I'd love to learn how to fight like that," Seph said.

Linda put a hand on his arm. "Seph, you're not a warrior, you know."

"Most wizards can get what they want without fighting anybody," Jack said. He looked at his watch and shoved back from the table. "I'd better get home. I've got exams tomorrow."

"What are you two going to do?" Ellen asked.

"We'll stay at Jack's," Linda said.

"Shouldn't we call first or something?" Seph looked from Linda to Jack.

Jack shook his head. "My mom's used to Aunt Linda showing up unexpectedly. If she didn't show up unannounced, she'd never show up at all."

"Don't worry, Seph," Linda said. "Believe me, she won't have a problem."

When they returned to the car, Jack slid behind the wheel this time, shoving the seat back to accommodate his long legs. Snowbeard sat next to him, and the others climbed in back.

"Snowbeard lives in an apartment over Jack's garage,"

Linda explained. "He's kind of a part-time caretaker. He was Jack's wizardry teacher, too. He's been with Jack since he was a baby."

"If wizards don't need to learn how to fight, what does a warrior need with a wizardry teacher?" Seph asked.

"I guess you could say I'm kind of a mongrel," Jack said, rolling his eyes. "A wizard with a warrior's stone. Or a warrior with a wizard's body."

Another long story, apparently.

Jack and Ellen lived two doors apart on Jefferson, a brick street lined with tall shade trees and huge old homes set back on big, informal lawns. They dropped Ellen off first. The Subaru coasted to the curb, and Ellen climbed out and retrieved her sword from the trunk. A shadow detached itself from the darkness on the front porch of the house and came toward them.

"Hey, Will," Jack called. "Waiting up for Ellen?"

"Hey, Jack." Will leaned into the passenger window. "When I see Ellen charging out of the house with a big smile on her face, carrying her sword, I know it means trouble." He was built like a football player, maybe a lineman. He had close-cropped dark hair and wore cutoffs and a tank top.

"Aunt Linda!" Will had spotted her in the backseat. "I should've known. There must be sorcery afoot!"

"Hi, Will," Linda said.

"This is Seph McCauley," Linda went on, resting a hand on Seph's shoulder. "He's going to be staying at Jack's this summer." She said it as if it were a done deal. "Seph, this is Will Childers, a friend of Jack's. I'm not really his aunt. Jack's friends just call me that. Ellen moved in with him and his parents last year after Raven's Ghyll."

Okay, Seph thought. Maybe that's the way it is in small towns, everyone related to everyone else, living in each other's houses. Maybe Trinity is just one big commune. He would try to relax and go with it.

"Good to meet you, Seph," Will was saying. "See you tomorrow, Jack. I'll be by around seven." Will and Ellen walked back toward the house.

They drove past two more houses and pulled into a gravel driveway. Circling around to the back of a hulking Victorian house, they jolted to a stop in front of an old, detached garage. Jack shut off the ignition. Linda turned to Seph.

"Jack's mom—my sister—is Anaweir. She doesn't know anything about this wizard and warrior business. Okay?"

Seph nodded. "Got it."

Jack retrieved his sword from the trunk. Snowbeard said good night and slowly mounted a staircase to the second floor of the garage. A moment later, a light kindled in the upstairs window. Linda and Seph followed Jack up the wooden steps to the back door of the house, sliding between two overgrown hydrangea bushes.

We must look pretty scary, Seph realized, suddenly self-conscious. Though his arm looked much better than it had, Jack was all muddy and grass stained, and Seph looked like he'd been on the losing side of a fight. His change of clothes was still in the BMW.

A narrow back staircase ascended into darkness

just inside the back door. Jack put his finger to his lips and disappeared up the steps, returning empty-handed and without the baldric. Then he called, "Mom! Are you presentable? I brought guests!"

"I'm in the study," a woman replied. "Is it anyone I know?"

"Yes and no." Linda and Seph followed Jack into the kitchen. It was huge, with a ceramic tile floor and a large farm-style dining table. Takeout containers crowded the counter next to the sink, unwashed dishes stacked next to them.

A tall, strawberry-blond woman entered the room carrying a coffee mug. It was clear where Jack got his coloring. She wore faded blue jeans and sturdy, hippie sandals, a sweatshirt carrying the slogan BREAD AND ROSES. Hers was the kind of beauty that pretty turns into: fresh-scrubbed and straightforward.

"Hi, Becka," Linda said.

"Linda! When did you get to town?" Becka embraced the enchanter, leaning down to deliver a quick, fierce hug. "How long can you stay?"

Linda looked over at Seph. "I'm not sure."

"Why do I bother asking? That's always your answer." She turned to Jack. "Jack, where have you been? You know you have exams tomorrow."

"He was with me," Linda said. "Sorry."

Becka finally noticed Seph, still hesitating in the kitchen doorway. "Oh!" she said, her hand flying to her mouth as she took in the evidence of his recent beating. Then she smiled and came toward him, extending her hands. "Hello. I'm Becka Downey."

"I'm Seph McCauley," he said. "Pleased to meet you." He extended his hand, and she took it in both of hers and held on to it for a minute. There was something reassuring about the gesture, as if she were already on his side. And blessedly, she did not ask questions. About his face, at least.

"Have you eaten?" Becka looked over her shoulder at the debris on the counter.

"Oh, yes, plenty," Seph said, feeling awkward again.

"Then I'll get you something to drink, at least. I have some soda down cellar."

"I'll go with you," Linda offered. Both sisters disappeared down the stairs.

"You might as well sit down," Jack said wryly, pointing to the chairs gathered around the table. Seph sat. Jack pulled four glasses down out of the cabinet and filled them with ice, then carried them carefully to the table. He turned a chair around and straddled it, resting his arms on the back and gazing at Seph. There was an awkward silence.

"Is it just you and your mom?" Seph asked.

Jack nodded. "My dad lives in Boston. They're divorced. I think when they bought the house they thought they'd be here forever." He rubbed his chin. "Where are you from?"

"Mostly Toronto," Seph said automatically. "But I've moved around a lot." He was suddenly very tired.

"What are you, a junior?"

Seph nodded.

"Aunt Linda said your parents are dead?"

"She did." Seph ignored the implied question, which he couldn't answer, anyway. But fortunately, just at that moment, Becka and Linda emerged from the cellar with bottles of old-fashioned root beer, glistening with condensation. They lined them up on the counter and opened them. As Becka set a soda in front of Seph, she smiled at him and rested a hand on his shoulder. Seph wondered what they'd been talking about downstairs. He didn't have to wait long to find out.

"Seph, Linda says you could use a place to stay this summer. Jack and I would love to have you here. It'll give us an excuse to finish the wallpapering in the third-floor room."

Seph felt blood rush to his face. "Really, I——"

Becka plowed on undeterred. "It'll be great. We'll get to see more of Linda, since I know she wants to spend some time with you. And Jack can introduce you to his friends."

Seph glanced at Jack, who probably knew better than to object. "I don't really want to impose. . . ."

"If it would make you feel better, you can help Nick with the wallpapering. There's always plenty of work to do around here. Please say you'll stay."

Wordless, Seph nodded. Jack's mother was hard to refuse.

"Then it's all settled." She smiled at Seph. "Why don't you bring in your things?"

Seph looked at Linda for help. She jumped in quickly. "We don't have much, because we . . . ah . . .

were in a hurry. We'll get you some clothes tomorrow, Seph."

"I bet some of Jack's old clothes will fit him," Becka suggested. "The ones from before that growth spurt last year." She laughed. "We have clothes in three sizes upstairs. They're scarcely broken in."

They changed the subject. Linda asked about Becka's work, and people Seph had never heard of. Their voices gradually faded to a kind of buzzing sound. Seph opened his eyes to find everyone staring at him. He'd actually fallen asleep at the table. "Sorry," he whispered, mortified. "It's not that you're boring. Really."

They all laughed. "Jack, why don't you show Seph upstairs and help him make up his bed?" Becka suggested. "And you need to get to bed also. I hope you found time to study before your aunt came."

Jack carried his glass to the sink, then nodded toward the back staircase. They climbed the narrow stairway to a landing on the second floor. Jack scooped up an armload of sheets and towels from a linen closet in the hall, and they ascended another flight of stairs to the third floor.

There were four rooms on the third floor, three of which were crammed floor to ceiling with old furniture, filing cabinets, and boxes of books. The largest room was sparsely furnished with a double bed, bookcase, and dresser. One and a half walls were papered in a William Morris print. More rolls of paper and a wetting tray leaned against the wall. There was a bathroom off to one side. The bed was stripped, and everything was covered with a fine layer of dust. It was suffocatingly hot and stuffy.

"I planned to move up here if it ever got finished," Jack explained. "Maybe now it'll finally happen. I hope you're not allergic to dust." He dropped the linens on the bed and muscled one of the windows open while Seph went to work on the other, which seemed to be painted shut. With the windows open, a cool breeze carried in the soft sounds of the summer night.

Jack and Seph rolled back the comforter and laid the sheet over the pad. Seph worked quickly and efficiently, despite being half asleep. He'd made a thousand beds in his lifetime.

"Look," he said to Jack as he crafted a perfect corner. "I'm sorry about moving in on you like this." He couldn't seem to remember that wizards never say they are sorry.

Jack finished up his side too, less expertly. "It's okay. Really. I don't mean to be rude. I just need to get used to the idea. I guess you'd say I've had a lot of trouble with wizards." He straightened and looked across the bed at Seph. "So you and Aunt Linda have known each other for a long time." There was a question hidden in the statement.

"I met her for the first time yesterday," Seph replied. "She said she's been my guardian for years, but it was news to me."

Jack frowned. "Yeah, well . . ." his voice trailed off. "I'm sure there's a good explanation."

"I guess." Seph shrugged. "Is it true you used to go out with Alicia Middleton?"

"What?" Jack straightened, almost bumping his head against the ceiling.

"Nothing. I ran into her in Toronto is all. She mentioned your name." He raised an eyebrow. "She seemed like bad news to me."

Jack stared at Seph. Then shook his head. "Look, I don't know what's going on, either. But I'll tell you this: I had the year from hell two years ago. It started with Leesha and ended with the tournament at Raven's Ghyll. Ellen was the only good thing that came out of it. That and the establishment of the Sanctuary."

He leaned on the bedframe, and the muscles stood out along his arms. "This past year has been nice and quiet. In Trinity, at least. I don't know how long it'll last, but I just hope you're not the one to mess it up." He smiled, as if to take the edge off, but his blue eyes were cold and direct. "I'll get you some shorts to sleep in."

When Jack came back up the stairs with an armload of clothes, Seph was already fast asleep on top of the comforter.

❧ CHAPTER ELEVEN ❧
THE SANCTUARY

When Seph awoke, the sun was sliding through the branches, dappling everything in the room. It took him a moment to remember where he was. It had been a long time since he'd slept so long or so soundly. He was still lying on top of the comforter.

A pile of clothes lay heaped at the foot of the bed. He found a toothbrush and towels and soap in his bathroom, and it was obvious that someone had cleaned in there. He washed his face carefully. The swelling in his lip had gone down, but the rest still looked pretty bad, having gone from red and purple to purple and yellow. What he really wanted to do was take a long, hot bath. Instead, he tried on clothes until he found a workable pair of jeans. He pulled on a T-shirt that said TRINITY SOCCER and walked downstairs.

The house had emptied out while he was asleep. Dirty

coffee cups and glasses sat in the sink, boxes of cereal on the counter, and a newspaper lay spread out on the table. He poured himself some juice.

"Seph, is that you?" Linda appeared in the doorway, barefoot, wearing jeans and a tank top. She didn't look much older than Seph. "We're on the porch."

Seph walked out onto the screened porch. The stone floor was cool under Seph's bare feet. Linda and Nick Snowbeard were sitting in two wicker chairs. Linda had a mug of tea in front of her on the glass table.

"Hi." Seph paused. He still hadn't figured out what he should call Linda Downey. She noticed his hesitation.

"Why don't you call me Aunt Linda," she suggested. "Everybody else does. I guess I'm a pretty good aunt," she added, as if reassuring herself.

Seph set his juice on the table, and drew up a chair.

"Where is everybody?" he asked.

"Jack's at school. Becka's at the university." Linda drew her feet up under her and settled the mug of tea onto her lap. "So it's just us."

Seph took a sip of juice. His lips and tongue still felt swollen and clumsy. "What did you tell your sister about me?"

"I told her you were hiding from an abusive family. Your parents beat you, and I was unable to get you removed from the home, so I spirited you away."

"Isn't that illegal?" Seth asked.

"Becka doesn't always play by the rules. She has a soft heart for children in trouble. I knew she would take you in."

"I finally get a family, and they beat me up." Seph looked at Linda out of the corner of his eye. "Well. If I'm going to be here all summer, I'd like to find some kind of part-time job."

She frowned. "If you need money, I'll . . ."

"I'm used to working. I'd like to earn my spending money, at least." Seph wanted a source of income that didn't go through Linda Downey. That wouldn't involve questions and explanations and contacting Sloane's.

"Maybe he could work for Harold Fry," Nick suggested. "Jack's crewing for him this summer, so he might need someone at dockside and in the office."

"Who's Harold Fry?" Seph asked.

"He runs fishing charters to the western basin of Lake Erie," Nick explained. "He's one of my chess partners. I could put in a word."

"Could you? I don't know much about fishing, but I'm willing to learn. Thanks." Seph was pleased the old wizard was willing to help him. He turned back to Linda and continued his gentle interrogation. "So Jack was the warrior who fought in the famous tournament at Raven's Ghyll."

"It was Jack and Ellen Stephenson."

"Jack and Ellen fought each other? Aren't those tournaments to the death?"

"Well, they refused to go along with killing each other. That started it all." She smiled wryly at the expression on Seph's face, then went on, "The Judges of the Field made the mistake of trying to amend the rules during the tournament, the first time they'd been opened in nearly a thousand years. They didn't realize that breaking the Covenant made them vulnerable. They were forced to make other changes as well. The old rules codified the rule of wizards over the Weir. Warriors, enchanters, and sorcerers may be powerful relative to the Anaweir, but we have always been at the mercy of wizards, treated as playthings, gladiators, and slaves.

"The new rules do away with the old hierarchy and require the participation of all of the guilds in decision making." She shrugged. "That's why there's so much turmoil. No one's sure how to implement that. There's considerable mistrust among the guilds. The other Weir aren't eager to sit down in a room with a bunch of wizards. They would be in fear of their lives."

"Not all wizards are like that," Seph pointed out.

Linda nodded. "Particularly here in America, families are mixed. Jack is a warrior; I'm an enchanter. Leander Hastings is a wizard; his sister was a warrior. There are many wizards like Hastings who hate the old system. They would like to make the new system work."

Seph pushed his cereal bowl away and settled back in the wicker chair. "How do Jack and Ellen get along now?"

"Oh, they fight all the time. On and off the field." Linda laughed. "Warriors in love."

Seph digested that for a moment, then decided to change the subject. He turned to Snowbeard. "When can I start training? I've already done a lot of reading." He thought of the library at the Havens, all those rows of ancient books.

Snowbeard's eyes flicked briefly to Linda. She nodded reluctantly.

"Is there a Weirbook we could use?" the wizard asked. Another exchange of meaningful glances between Linda and Snowbeard.

He's in on the secret, too, whatever it is.

"You could use Jack's," Linda suggested.

"Would a warrior's Weirbook do me any good?" Seph asked. Jason's wizard Weirbook had included pages of spells and incantations. "Warriors don't use charms, do they?"

Linda studied her hands. "It's actually a wizard's book. Remember, Jack was a wizard born without a stone. A wizard implanted a warrior stone in him. That's why he can do some wizardry. Nick taught him, too."

Seph shook his head. "I don't get it."

"Jack was dying, so I found him a doctor, a wizard named Jessamine Longbranch," Linda said, a little defensively. "She tricked me and implanted the wrong stone, hoping it wouldn't kill him. She planned to play Jack in the Game if it worked out. That's how he ended up in the tournament last summer."

Seph was beginning to understand Jack a little better. But just then he was in no mood to be cooperative.

"What if I want to use my own Weirbook?" The question was intentionally abrupt. He held her gaze, experimentally flexing his mind a bit, exerting some pressure. She looked startled, then angry, and then pushed back fiercely. She was a master of mind magic, no doubt about it.

"Don't try that with me," she snapped. "You'll have to work with what we have."

She knows where the book is, Seph thought. He was sure of it.

"We can start today, if you like." Snowbeard looked at Linda for direction.

"Seph, why don't I show you around town a little first. Then the three of us can get my car. You and Nick can start after lunch. Can you wait that long?" she asked sarcastically.

"No problem," said Seph. "I'll get my shoes." He carried his dishes into the kitchen.

"We should be back in an hour or so." Linda slid her feet into her sandals and stood. "Let's go."

It was a beautiful late spring day. Now that it was daylight, Seph could see that Jefferson Street was lined with painted ladies: lovely old Victorian houses in authentic colors, iced with gingerbread, lovingly restored. Many of them were flanked by gardens planted with old-fashioned flowers: peonies, irises, bleeding hearts, and delphinium. Blue and purple spires of lupine lined the walk of the house across the street. There must have been money in this town a hundred years ago, he thought, to have founded a neighborhood like this. It reminded him of Toronto's Cabbagetown.

Jack had left the Subaru for their use. As they drove down the street, Linda nodded to a man with close-cropped white hair and layers of silver jewelry who was retrieving his paper from his driveway. Across the street, an older woman with clouds of gray hair was working in her garden. She wore loose trousers and a short, Oriental-looking jacket. She waved at Linda as if she recognized her, but seemed to be studying Seph.

Seph twisted around to look at them after they had passed by.

"Do you know them?" he asked, turning forward again.

Linda nodded. "Mercedes Foster is a sorcerer and a weaver. Blaise Highbourne is a seer and silversmith. We have quite a compound on Jefferson Street. Wizards. Sorcerers. Seers. Warriors. There are more Weir in town than ever before. The establishment of the Sanctuary has made Trinity attractive to Anawizard Weir, the nonwizard guilds that used to be controlled by wizards." She braked to allow a fat gray tabby cat to saunter across the street. "Trinity has always been a refuge for artists and counter-culturists associated with the university. So the Weir fit in quite well."

She showed him the high school, a relatively new building at the western end of town. Because it was exam week, groups of students hung out in the parking lot, talking or waiting for rides.

Seph thought of the Havens. School would be in session for another week, and then the Anaweir would disperse to wherever they came from, leaving the wizards behind. He wondered what story, if any, had been concocted to explain his disappearance.

The town center had a familiar, European look. It was anchored by a large town commons surrounded by the nineteenth-century stone buildings of Trinity College. Small businesses crouched along the edges of the campus: art stores and bookshops, galleries and restaurants. Linda explained that both Blaise and Mercedes had shops in the area. They parked in an angle space along the green.

The air was cool under the trees, and Seph's shoes were soon soaked from the dewy grass. A crowd of people was gathered around a brick-and-stone pavilion at the center of the commons, focused on an elaborate marble structure that extended above their heads. Their excited voices floated over the lawn.

"It's just a fountain," Linda said, looking puzzled. "Kind of a Greek Revival piece. I can't imagine what everyone is so interested in. Maybe somebody's giving a speech." Curious, they changed directions and headed for the fountain. They had nearly made it there when they were intercepted.

"Ms. Downey?"

He was a large, bulky man with sandy hair and a graying mustache, wearing a brown sport coat that was worn at the elbows. The fabric strained across his shoulders and back.

"Ms. Downey," he repeated. "I thought that was you. I don't know if you remember me. Ross Childers. My brother Bill's boy, Will, is good friends with your nephew, Jack. We . . . uh . . . met after that episode at the high school last year."

Linda smiled. "Of course. It's good to see you again, Sergeant."

"Please. Call me Ross."

"Ross." She nodded.

"Here for a visit, I guess?" He squinted at Seph. "Good Lord! What happened to your face, son?"

Seph had almost forgotten about his appearance, and the question caught him off guard. He blinked at the officer, then said, "I was hit by a fast pitch."

"Forgive me," Linda said hastily. "I should introduce you. Seph, this is Ross Childers. He's a sergeant with the Trinity police."

"Detective now, actually." He stuffed his hands into his trouser pockets.

"A detective," she amended. "Ross is Will's uncle. Remember, Jack's friend? You met him when we dropped Ellen off last night. Ross, this is Seph McCauley. He's going to be staying at Becka's this summer."

"McCauley?" The detective frowned and glanced over his shoulder at the crowd around the fountain, then back at Seph.

"What's going on over there?" Linda inquired, following his gaze.

"There was some vandalism there overnight," Ross replied. "Kind of bizarre. Come take a look." To Seph's surprise, the detective dropped a hand on his shoulder and propelled him quickly toward the fountain. Linda had to hurry to keep up.

The crowd parted sufficiently to let them through. Everyone seemed to know the police detective, but they looked curiously at Seph and Linda.

The fountain was made of white marble, a collection of scenes of Greek mythology. At the center of the pool stood a statue of Perseus holding aloft the Medusa's head. The decapitated Medusa lay crumpled at his feet, and alongside her lay another headless body, this one dressed in a Toronto Blue Jays shirt and jeans. Blood was spattered everywhere over the white marble, draining from the body as the water hit it. Blood sprayed out of the fountain and fell into the bloody pool below with a soft sound, like rain.

In case the point was missed, a message in large, violent letters was scrawled in blood across the back of the marble bench that ringed the fountain. *McCauley.*

Seph tried to take a step back from the carnage but Ross Childers's arm was holding him in place.

"Kind of a mess, wouldn't you say?" The detective studied him shrewdly.

"Do . . . do you know who it is?" Somehow, Seph managed to choke the words out.

Ross let him dangle a minute longer, then said, "It's a mannequin. They dressed it up and chopped its head off. Then they killed some kind of an animal, a pig we think, let the blood drip into the fountain. Pretty sick." He paused. "You sign your work, Seph?"

"I never took you for an idiot, *Detective*, but I guess I was wrong," Linda snapped.

Ross nodded grudgingly. "Okay. If I'm any judge, this was a complete surprise to him." He blew out his breath as if unhappy with this assignment. "But that doesn't mean he can't help us find who did it. He comes to town, and suddenly there's a crazy stunt in the park with his name on it. Must be someone he knows." He moved to one side, in hopes of addressing Seph directly, but Linda sidestepped into his path, so he had to speak over her head. "Blue Jays. That your team, Seph?" Seph just stared down at his hands. "You know anyone who might do something like this? You ever play around with black magic?"

"I'm Catholic," Seph replied in a whisper. "I don't do that."

Linda glanced at Seph, changed tactics. "Look. Those are Seph's clothes. We left my car at West Market Mall last night while Nick and Jack and I were showing Seph around. The clothes were in there. We planned to go back and get the car today.

"Someone must have broken in and taken them. How would we know who it was? Seph just came from school in New England. He's never been here before, and he doesn't know anyone around here, right?" She looked at Seph, and he nodded. He was more than happy to let her make up a story.

Ross massaged his temples. "Maybe the three of us should go take a look at the car," he suggested.

Linda shook her head. "You and I can go. I'm taking Seph back home."

"I said I was sorry, didn't I?" He looked sorry, too. "Listen, I'll pick you up at Becka's around two."

Seph didn't have much to say on the way back to Jefferson Street. Anything, in fact.

"What is it?" Linda said finally.

Seph cleared his throat. He didn't mean to sound ungrateful. After all, Linda Downey had rescued him from the Havens only two days before. "I thought this was a sanctuary."

Linda looked over at him. "It is. This is the safest place for you."

"Then why don't I feel safe?" Seph fingered the *dyrne sefa* and rested his forehead against the side window. "They were already waiting for us when we got here. They went after Ellen. Then this. It doesn't make sense. Leicester let me go, didn't he? Or did you just put a spell on him, and now it's worn off?"

"Think about it. Why do you think they tried to keep you from reaching Trinity? As long as the rules are in force, he can't really attack you here. Unfortunately, the rules don't forbid them from trying to scare you to death."

The other possibility was that Gregory Leicester was reinforcing his warning to Seph to say nothing about his experiences at the Havens.

"Well, they know exactly where I am. I don't like waiting around to be ambushed. Maybe I should just go. Find me a summer camp in Canada, maybe. I'm used to being on my own."

"That's just what they're hoping you'll do. Promise me you'll stay in town."

Seph shrugged. He wasn't making any promises. But he did need training in wizardry, and right now, Nick Snowbeard was his only option.

It was almost one by the time they pulled in next to the garage.

Snowbeard was waiting for them on the porch. Linda told the old man about the bizarre display at the fountain. He asked a few careful questions, but offered little comment. Linda went upstairs and returned with a leatherbound book.

"This is Jack's Weirbook," she explained, opening it to the last page and pointing to his name inscribed at the end of a family tree. She handed it to Seph. He scanned the genealogy, and then quickly turned to the section on spells and incantations.

There was a knock at the front door. Linda stood up and picked up her purse. "Ross Childers and I are going to pick up the car and probably go back to the police station to make a report. That should give you two time for your lesson." And then she was gone, out of the deep shade of the porch and into the bright sunlight.

Seph thought Snowbeard might ask for a demonstration of what wizardry he already knew, but he didn't. Instead, the old wizard steepled his fingers together and spoke in a soft voice, quite formally. "You may call me Nick. Shall I call you Seph?" Seph nodded. "Let's start at the beginning, Seph, and lay the foundation. You may know some of this already, but it bears repeating. This is not the kind of education that should come to you piecemeal, as it has."

He paused a moment, as if sorting through a myriad of mental files. "Wizards can call upon magic in three ways: corporeal, through the body, incorporeal, through the mind, and *langue d'charme*, through words of power, incantations.

"Wizards have long dominated the other magical guilds, by virtue of a covenant forced on them by deception at Raven's Ghyll in Britain centuries ago. With the exception of wizards, each guild operates in a selective realm of magic, and each is supreme in its own realm. For example, warriors like Jack and Ellen dominate in the physical, corporeal world of warfare. Their magic depends on physical proximity and strength. There is no mind magic about it. In a fair, physical fight, a warrior will over-come a wizard every time." He smiled ruefully. "Naturally, a wizard wouldn't confront a warrior in a fair fight. We have other ways to dominate.

"Enchanters like Linda specialize in magic of the mind and emotions. Again, they are supreme in their own realm. Even wizards have difficulty resisting an enchanter, and the Anaweir are particularly vulnerable to them.

"Sorcerers specialize in material magic. They create tools, compounds, materials that can do magical tasks, or enhance the magic of others. They used to be much more powerful than they are now. Many secrets of the sorcerers have been lost over time. That is why talismans of ancient times are so highly prized."

Seph was acutely aware of the weight of the *dyrne sefa* under his shirt.

"Seers are probably the least powerful of the Weir. They see the future, but often cannot interpret their visions in time to do any good. Some of them use talis-mans—mirrors, crystals, and the like—to focus and con-centrate their power, to make it more effective, their visions easier to read.

"If a wizard comes after you, he may use any of the three realms. For example, he may use mind magic to influence you to do something foolish. It's a subtle trick in the hands of wizards, most effective on the Anaweir. Or he may use physical power. Wizards can inflict pain with a touch."

Seph lifted his hand to his face, thinking of Gregory Leicester.

"You can be trained to resist a physical attack, and you are powerful enough to do it, I believe. That leaves the use of charms. You told me you had received some training in that regard." The wizard raised his eyebrows.

And so Seph went through his meager repertory, demonstrating those charms he knew he could perform flawlessly—small, rough magics that could be practiced in a dormitory room.

Nick nodded in approval when he was done. "There are two components to a wizard's power when it comes to charms: the strength of the stone he carries and the power of the articulated word. Have you had any training in countercharms?"

Seph shook his head.

"Then we'll start with that. A wizard's charm is like any other weapon. You must be alert for it at all times. And when the attack comes, you need to counter it before he draws blood, so to speak. If he completes it, it may be too late." Nick marked a few passages in the Weirbook. "Spend some time studying those charms. We'll review the charms and the countercharms tomorrow."

"You mean we're done?"

Nick smiled. "It's nearly five o'clock. I'm surprised Jack isn't home already."

"I have a question." Seph had been leafing through Jack's Weirbook, and it still lay open on his lap.

"What is it?"

"Everyone says the same things about wizards. We take advantage of the Anaweir. We treat the other guilds like dirt. We're always plotting against each other. What I want to know is: is it some kind of inborn trait? If it is, why aren't you like that? I had a friend at school, and he wasn't like that either."

Nick sat back in his chair and thought a moment. "The problem with wizards is that their power manifests while they are still young. Young people shouldn't have so much power, because they lack wisdom and discipline. They grow up spoiled, used to having their own way." He paused. "You can compare wizards to wine. The best quality wines are harsh and strong when they are young. But good wines improve with age. A poor quality wine never improves. Sometimes it gets worse. Wizards are the same." He leaned forward. "Sometimes I think it would be better if all wizards were raised as you were, by Anaweir, ignorant of their powers until they are grown. They might be more tolerant of others."

There are drawbacks to that, Seph thought. The Anaweir are not always tolerant of wizards.

Somehow it was easy to talk to Nick. He was like the earth, wise and ancient and nonjudgmental.

"Do you know Gregory Leicester?" Seph asked. He looked down at the Weirbook to avoid the old wizard's eyes.

Nick nodded. "I know him. He's one who hasn't improved with age. But he's very powerful."

"He murdered two of my friends. It was my fault," Seph added, recalling his months of torture at Leicester's hands, Trevor's death, and the final capstone tragedy of Jason.

"Why do you think it was your fault?" Nick asked gently.

"They were trying to help me. If it hadn't been for me, they would still be alive."

"Perhaps that was their choice, not yours."

"They didn't choose to be murdered." Seph traced the names in Jack's genealogy with his forefinger, envious of his links to family.

Nick studied him. "And now you mean to take revenge on Dr. Leicester."

Seph didn't respond, but embedded himself deeper into the chair.

"A high-risk enterprise, certainly." Nick smoothed down his mustache with his thumb and forefinger. To Seph's surprise, the old wizard appeared to take him seriously, but he didn't lecture him or try to talk him out of it.

"What about the Dragon? Do you know where to find him?" Seth asked.

"A risky admission to make, these days," Nick said.

Seph noticed he didn't really answer the question. "I have information that might be helpful to him."

Nick cleared his throat. "Perhaps you should think of the Dragon as more of an icon representing a movement than as an individual."

"Fine. I'd like to talk to the icon who's been ripping off magical weapons from the Roses, freeing members of the underguilds, and posting Leicester's secrets on the Internet."

Just then they heard a door slam elsewhere in the house, and someone's noisy progress through the kitchen. "Hello?" came the familiar voice. It was Jack.

"We're on the porch," Seph called back.

A moment later, Jack joined them. "Hey, Nick. Hey, Seph. I think I aced my government exam, even though I didn't get to study." He sprawled into one of the Adirondack chairs, seeming to fill up the porch with his raw physical presence.

"Hey," Jack said. "Did you hear there was some kind of Satanic sacrifice on the commons?"

They filled Jack in on the news. "So Will's Uncle Ross thinks you're a practitioner of the Old Religion?"

"Old Religion?" Seph looked from one to the other for explanation. "Is that like Old Magic?"

"No. This is a kind of blood magic that predates wizardry," Nick explained. "It goes back to the polytheism that existed before the Anglo Saxons came to Britain. Their ceremonies focused on animal sacrifice, sometimes human sacrifice." Seph shuddered, and the old man smiled reassuringly. "Don't worry, Seph. Like the other gifts of the Weir, wizardry is not a religion. It's a gift, and a talent and a calling. It's compatible with Catholicism, or any other faith. You would be surprised how many well-known defenders of the faith have been Weir."

Maybe. But when Seph thought of the display on the commons, it reminded him of the ritual at the amphitheater at the Havens, Trevor's neck chain in the ashes.

It didn't help when Ross Childers brought Linda

home in late afternoon to report that the BMW was a total loss.

"I've never seen anything like it," he said, shaking his head, watching Seph for a reaction. "They slashed the seats to ribbons and then they set the thing on fire. How they got it to burn, I have no idea. It burned so hot the tires were melted to four puddles on the asphalt. It would've been hard to even tell what make it was, but they wrote your name on the pavement, just like they did at the fountain." He whistled, like he was glad it wasn't him. "You got any enemies Seph?"

Once school ended, Jack and Ellen and their friends Will Childers and Harmon Fitch were in and out of the house all day long. Fitch was tall and lanky, with bleached-blond hair, glasses, and an uncanny ability to speak to computers in their own language. He spent several days helping Seph build a new computer system to replace the one he'd left at the Havens.

Fitch had his own computer consulting and Web page development business, counting among his customers the school board, Trinity College, the town government, and chamber of commerce. He also had several major corporate customers in Cleveland.

Seph began working for Fitch part time, writing basic HTML code, taking digital photos for the sites, and calling on clients, since Fitch's edgy thrift-shop attire freaked some of the corporate customers.

They worked for several weeks installing the hardware for the first citywide wireless network. Fitch danced on rooftops like some kind of manic digital maestro in a Wi-Fi headset, waving his arms and crying, "More power! Need more power!"

Fitch rented space on the second floor of Blaise's shop, since his four younger brothers and sisters made it impossible to work at home. The room was lined with servers and flat screens. On Monday nights he hosted a Multimedia Monday Monster Movie Megafest (5M).

While Fitch wasn't a member of any of the magical guilds, Seph was reminded that there are many kinds of gifts. Fitch had the ability to turn out the lights on the entire county or change any grade at Trinity High School.

Seph also worked part time for Harold Fry down at the docks, helping in the charter office and filling in dockside. He found he enjoyed the physical labor at the harbor. His skin resisted the sun, as always, but his body filled out, morphing from gaunt to lean and muscular.

One night, Jack and Ellen invited Seph to something called a *plaisance* at heavily wooded Perry Park. Jack parked the Subaru in a secluded spot, and he and Ellen retrieved their swords from the trunk. The three of them hiked more than a mile through the woods to a hidden meadow. Jack paced the perimeter, throwing up a kind of magical barrier with quick, impatient gestures, while Seph trailed behind, making mental notes on the charms he used.

Ellen stood, relaxed, waiting at the center of the field, the late-day sun glinting off her blade. When Jack was finished, he strode toward her, stopping a short distance away, facing her. They both inclined their heads, grinning like they were about to be married. Seph had his instructions, and when he saw they were ready, he said, "Go to."

It was the remarkable dance of two gifted athletes, evenly matched. They covered the meadow, moving furiously forward and back, thrust and parry, attack and then retreat, calling challenges to each other, trading insults and promises. The forest rang with the clash of their blades, and flames spun and sparkled among the trees. Seph called time every fifteen minutes, and they battled to a draw after four bouts.

Although the heat of the day had gone, they were both soaked in sweat, practically steaming. Ellen drank long and deep from her water bottle and wiped her mouth with her gauntleted arm. "Are you feeling all right, Jack? Your play's flat, all in all. I was hoping to give Seph more of a show."

Jack tested the edge of his blade with his thumb. "Actually, Ellen, I wondered if you were coming down with something. You were downright lethargic. I nearly dozed off once or twice."

"Well, that explains it. You looked like you were asleep."

With that, they threw down their weapons and it dissolved into a wrestling match. In the end they were kissing each other.

It was certainly a different kind of courtship, but there was a chemistry, an understanding, a kinship between Jack and Ellen that Seph envied.

★ ★ ★

The Weir colony of Jefferson Street embraced him, and he made the most of the opportunity, marshaling weapons for a battle that might never take place.

Mercedes Foster, weaver and sorcerer, invited him into her garden, being careful to warn him away from the poisonous plants that grew there. In the kitchen of her cottage, she made dyes and love potions and memory cures. Soon Seph was helping her with potions and extractions, scanning through her recipes for poisons and hypnotics, committing them to memory. He asked questions about talismans like the *dyrne sefa* and borrowed her books on the subject.

She was less cooperative when he asked about Flame, the drug Alicia had used on him in Toronto. They were in her kitchen, drying trays of plants in her oven.

"I hear sorcerers make it for the trade," Seph said. "It's also called Mind-Burner."

Mercedes fixed him with her sharp, birdlike gaze and put her hands on her bony hips. "I don't know how to make it, and I wouldn't tell you if I did. I don't believe in trading away your future for a little extra power in the present."

She wouldn't say anything more about it, but he found several recipes for it in old texts, written in Latin.

Blaise Highbourne, seer and silversmith, demonstrated the art of lost wax casting and showed Seph how to make silver wire jewelry. He also explained the irony of prophecy: the fact that it is always true, but often misleading. Iris Bolingame, wizard and glass artist, showed him how to capture space with blown glass, to wrap bits of glass with copper foil, and solder them together. She also shared charms and incantations from her own Weirbook. While Nick carefully edited the information he shared with Seph, Iris did not.

It wasn't long before a walk down Jefferson Street was like running a gauntlet. Mercedes had a new plant to show him, or berries to send back to Becka. Blaise wanted to share a book with him, and Iris had another trick of wizardry for him to try. He couldn't make a move out of the house without reports flowing back to Becka and Linda.

"Welcome to life in a small town," Jack said dryly. "Where everybody makes it their business to put their noses in yours."

The perpetrators of the sacrifice on the commons were never apprehended. Ross Childers dropped by occasionally to update Linda and Seph about it, but the investigation went nowhere. Seph saw no more signs of the alumni.

Seph joined St. Catherine's, the Catholic church by the university. He usually attended on Friday nights, when the masses were in Latin.

Though Jack had said that Linda never lingered very long in Trinity, she seemed in no hurry to leave. Seph helped Nick finish wallpapering the room upstairs, and Jack helped him pick out a new sound system.

Linda still refused to allow Seph to leave the sanctuary. When Becka invited Seph to go to Niagara on the Lake with her and Jack for the Shaw festival, Linda kept Seph in Trinity with her.

He argued with her to let him go to Canada. "Don't

you think it's safe now? I can't stay locked up in here forever." It had been more than a month since their encounter with the alumni, and there was no sign of invasion of the sanctuary. But Linda was unmoved.

When he wasn't working, Seph spent long days at the public beach with Jack and his friends once the weather turned hot. It was lorded over by cliffs, with clear, cold water and pebbled sand that sparkled with quartz when the water retreated. Jack taught Seph to windsurf, and he found he had a talent for keeping the frail board upright and driving forward in long slaloms, parallel to the shore.

Best of all, after his long dry season at the Havens, there were girls.

"Anaweir women can't resist wizards," Jason had said. Once, the notion had made Seph feel uneasy. Now he flexed his wizard muscles in every way he could.

He flirted with the year-round residents and summer girls, ate their chocolate-chip cookies and fruit salad, and smoothed sunblock into their sun-warmed skin. He danced with them at the beach pavilion on Friday and Saturday nights and stole kisses under the pier. He stayed out late, since Linda was unaccustomed to enforcing curfews.

Despite his late hours, most mornings he rose early and walked to the lake, grappling with memories that kept him from sleep. Jason, Jason's father, and Trevor were dead, but Gregory Leicester still lived, spinning his intrigues, effectively imprisoning Seph within the Sanctuary. Seph was building his arsenal of magic, but he had no way to use it against his enemy—and no way to connect with the

Dragon, who might be able to use the information Seph had.

When he walked in the mornings, he often saw the same girl sitting on the rocks at the water's edge, her fair head bent over her sketchbook, one knee up, the other straight, her bare feet braced against stone. Her hand danced over the page, laying down shape and color. She frowned as she concentrated, her lower lip caught behind her teeth. Sometimes she swiped at her face with the back of her hand, leaving a smear of color.

He began to look for her, and she was there most days. She usually brought her sketchbook, but sometimes she sat and read, the book tilted to catch the slanting light, drinking coffee from an insulated travel cup. Some days she wore jeans and a T-shirt; on others she wore long tiered flowered skirts and sheer cotton blouses that slipped off her shoulders.

He thought she noticed him, but she was careful not to look at him, and something in her expression and body language kept him at bay. He began bringing books along, an excuse to linger, sharing the same stretch of beach. Finally, after a long, frustrating afternoon in the hot sun, he decided to introduce himself.

As soon as his shadow fell over her, she clutched the sketchbook to her body as if to protect it.

"You're in my light," she said, without facing around. Her accent reminded him of Trevor's, with its soft southern vowels.

"Sorry." He circled around, squatting next to her. She'd hitched her skirts up to mid thigh, exposing her legs to the sun. The wind had torn locks of her hair free from the elastic, and she tucked them behind her ears. Up close, he saw that her hair was all different colors, like butter and sugar and caramel, painted by the sun. "I see you here all the time," he said. "I was wondering what you were drawing."

"Your being curious don't make it your business, now does it?" Her eyes were watercolor blue in her sun-gilded face.

Seph blinked and sat back on his heels. "Well, no, I guess not. . . ."

She laughed. "You should see your face. You aren't used to girls saying no to you, are you?"

He shrugged and rested his arms on his knees. "We haven't even come to the hard questions yet."

"Save them for someone else. I come up here to sketch, not to flirt with the summertime boys."

"You're not from around here, are you?" No. He couldn't believe he'd said that.

"No. I'm not." Sand adhered to her long legs, to the tops of her feet. Following his gaze, she scowled at him, then redistributed the fabric of her skirt, covering herself to the ankle. She wore a ribbon with a familiar cameo around her neck, and he suddenly realized where he'd seen it before.

"You work at the Legends?" The Legends was an inn and restaurant in a Victorian mansion overlooking the lake. Linda and Becka liked to go there for brunch.

"I'm waitressing there, okay? I'm from Coalton County, a place I'm sure you never heard of." She snatched up the case of pastels and snapped it shut, shoving it into her tote bag, following with her sketch pad.

Seph watched this, unsure what he'd done wrong. "Look, I'm sorry. I didn't mean to run you off." Why was he always apologizing?

"Never mind. The light has changed, my mood is ruined, and my shift is about to start." She stood, brushing sand off the back of her skirt.

A pile of drawings sat nearby, anchored by a large rock. Seph reached for them.

"No! Leave them alone!" She shoved him, hard, and the pages went flying, caught by the shore breeze.

Bewildered, he scrambled after them, snatching some of them practically out of the waves. When he had them all, he turned and found she hadn't waited for him. In fact, she was already a good distance away, striding down the beach, shoulders hunched, head thrust forward. "What the . . . ?" He looked down at the wad of paper in his hand. The drawing on top was a face in charcoal, a three-quarter profile, long, curling dark hair, high cheekbones, a Romanesque nose, half smile, eyes set under a smudge of dark brows.

His own face.

He pawed through the others. Seph McCauley sprawled on his back in the sun in his bathing trunks, muscles picked out under the skin of his chest, one arm flung over his eyes. Seph walking along the shore, a tall, angular figure silhouetted against the bright water. Seph sprawled on the rocks at the water's edge, looking toward Canada. Studies of his back and shoulders, his arms and hands, tendons and muscles faithfully rendered.

In each, he was surrounded by a nimbus of light, as if illuminated from within. Like images of the saints in the old manuscripts. They were all of him, save a few still lifes of shells and rock at the bottom. Thoughts surfaced, as from a dark pool.

Why is she drawing pictures of me?

She knows I'm a wizard.

And then he was running, pounding down the beach after her, leaping over boulders and half-submerged driftwood. He was perhaps a hundred feet away from her when she heard him coming. She didn't look back, but increased her speed until she was running herself. Her hair escaped from its elastic and streamed out behind her as she dodged around tree stumps and late-day beach strollers.

He ran faster.

He'd almost caught up with her when she tripped over a tree root and went sprawling, sliding forward in the sand.

He fell to his knees next to her. He put his hand on her shoulder and she flinched at his touch. "You okay?" She didn't reply, but folded into herself as if she wanted to disappear. He rolled her over onto her back and wiped the sand from her face with the hem of his T-shirt. She squinched her eyes shut, like she could pretend he wasn't there. Her white lace blouse was smeared with wet sand, her chest heaving as she fought for breath.

"Who are you, really?" he demanded.

"I . . . told . . . you. I'm a waitress."

"What's your name?"

"Madison Moss."

"Did Leicester send you?"

Now she opened her eyes and squinted at him. "I don't know what you're talking about."

"How did you know that I'm . . . a wizard?"

She said nothing.

He dropped his hands onto her collarbone on either side, fingertips pressing lightly against her skin. Her stealing of his image somehow gave him permission. "Now you're going to tell me the truth," he muttered. He released power into her—gentle persuasion. At first it felt good, like a long breath exhaled. A trickle at first, and then a flood, and then he tried to pull away and couldn't. And more, and more, until he was drained and nauseous and dizzy, like his very essence was being pulled out through his fingertips.

Finally she reached up and pulled his hands away, then rolled him over on his back, folding his hands across his chest like a corpse laid out on a bier. Black spots circled through his vision like vultures, blotting out the sun.

She leaned over him. Touched his cheek gently and kissed him on the forehead. "Good-bye, Witch Boy," she whispered. She stood, retrieved her bag, slung it over her shoulder, and walked away, not in any hurry this time, as if she knew he couldn't follow.

He wasn't sure how long he lay there, unable to move. Like a drunk on the sidewalk. Or a creature that had washed up in a storm. Finally, he propped up on his elbows. His head swam, and he thought for a moment he might be sick, but it passed. He rolled to his hands and knees. Several of the drawings had been trapped under his body. He folded them carefully and stuffed them into his back pockets, then stood, listing a little, shaking the sand out of his hair. He felt empty. He looked up and down the beach. The sun had passed midday, and the beach was crowded. No sign of Madison Moss.

He hauled himself up the wooden stairway from the beach, laboring like an old man. He found Jack, Ellen, Fitch, and Fitch's girlfriend, Miriam, sitting at the picnic tables under the trees, slurping down frozen-custard cones.

Miriam was from Cleveland, and her family owned a cottage at Trinity Lakeside. She wore black crushed velvet, kohl eyeliner, and fishnets to the beach. Seph thought it was cool, in an impractical sort of way.

"Hey, Seph. Want to play tennis later?" Ellen asked when she spotted him. Then she frowned, shading her eyes. "Are you all right? You look like you've got sunstroke or something."

Seph dropped onto the bench next to her, exhausted by the climb from the beach. "I'm okay."

"Here. Have some." She handed him her cone. He licked off half and handed it back.

"Who was that girl you were dancing with at the pavilion last night?" Fitch asked.

"Christy Laraway. She's taking classes at the Institute." He closed his eyes, trying to remember her face.

"Dude. I thought you were going out with Julie Steadman."

"I've hung out with Julie a few times," Seph said, without opening his eyes. "I'm not *going out* with her."

Jack finished his cone and licked his fingers. "The local girls are just thrilled to meet someone they didn't hate in second grade."

"C'mon, Jack, it's more than that," Ellen said. She switched to a ditsy high falsetto. "He's so *hot*. He's practically *European*. I mean, he's lived all over the world. And he speaks *French*." She nudged Seph with her shoulder. "And have you seen his *eyes*? They change colors, and he has these long, dark *lashes*. And the way he *kisses*." She rolled her eyes.

"Shut up, Ellen," Seph said. Their conversation was necessarily edited because of the presence of Miriam, who knew nothing of the magical subtext.

"So. What's the secret of great kissing, Seph?" Jack asked. "Is it technique, duration, intensity, or *power*?"

Seph sighed theatrically. "Oh, all right, Jack. I'll kiss you. But just this once." He rolled sideways to dodge Jack's half-hearted swipe at him. Somehow, Jack always came off sounding critical. Like he thought Seph was taking advantage of Persuasion.

"Guys are grumbling about the out-of-town competition," Jack went on. He stripped off his T-shirt and mopped his face with it.

Seph shrugged. "Don't you think everyone brings something to the game?"

"What do you mean?"

"We all use our assets. For instance, some people are really buff." Seph glanced sideways at Jack. "Or they're great conversationalists. They play football or they're in a blues band. They write poetry or they paint or they're good listeners. They have great hair, great legs, a boatload of money *and* a boat. Or they have that je ne sais quois . . ."

"Or that je definitely *sais* quois, as the case may be," Jack replied.

"Shut up, Jack," Seph said, grinding the heel of his hand into his forehead. His head was pounding.

"Some people would say love isn't a game," Ellen mused. "I never bought that all's-fair-in-love-and-war bit."

Seph shrugged in surrender. "Anyway, I can't do tennis tonight. I'm working for Harold this afternoon, and tonight I'm meeting someone at the Legends."

"Another date?" Miriam asked.

Seph stood to go. "Not exactly. She doesn't know I'm coming."

The manager at the Legends Inn was happy to tell Seph what time Madison Moss got off work. He was even willing to let her off early, but Seph said no, he would just wait. He bought coffee at the carryout counter and found a bench in the park across the street that afforded a good view of the entrance. She came out of the front door right on time, looking up and down the street as if she hadn't decided what to do next. She jumped and let out a squeak of fright when he stepped out of the shadows and touched her shoulder.

"Oh, it's you," she said, when he turned toward the light. "You about scared me to death." She'd rebraided her hair, but was still wearing the beach-stained blouse and skirt.

"I need to talk to you."

"Oh. Well. Sorry. I . . . um . . . have plans. I have to go."
She made no effort to be convincing.

"It won't take long. Promise." He took her elbow,
careful not to let the slightest dribble of magic escape. He
wasn't sure he had any to spare, anyway. "Do you want to
talk here or somewhere else?"

"I'm not going anywhere with you."

"Okay." He towed her back into the coffeehouse and
out onto the terrace overlooking the lake. He chose a
remote table overlooking the gardens. The waitress drifted
over, grinning and raising her eyebrows at Madison. "May
I help you?"

Madison just stared straight ahead, scowling and tapping her fingers on the edge of the table. Her nails were
painted purple.

"Two coffees and biscotti," Seph said.

"I wanted tea," Madison said when the waitress had
departed.

"You were drinking coffee on the beach."

"Right now, I feel like tea."

"Next time, speak up."

"What makes you think there'll be a next time?"

Seph pulled her drawings from his jeans pocket and
flattened them out on the tabletop.

Madison pursed her lips and looked out at the lake.
"Do you know I got chastised for the state of my uni-
form, Witch Boy?"

"My name is Seph."

"What kind of name is that?"

"Short for Joseph."

"Is that a family name?"

"I have no idea." The scent of jasmine wafted up from the gardens and fireflies sparkled in the lawn. "I don't really know my family."

She wrinkled her nose. "Sometimes that's not a bad thing. Who do you stay with?"

"Rebecca Downey. She's my guardian's sister."

"Oh, I know her. She comes into the inn a lot." She gave him an appraising look. "*She's* very nice." The subtext being, *Unlike you.*

"What about Madison? Where's that from?"

"I'm named after a county in Kentucky. Where my parents first—ah—met."

The waitress set down coffee cups and plates of biscotti. "Hey, those are good!" she said, pointing from the sketches to Seph.

"Will you put those away?" Madison gestured at the crumpled pages.

Seph said nothing.

"Look," she said, wrapping her fingers around her cup. "I'm sorry I sketched you without asking permission."

Seph waited. "That's it?"

"What do you want?"

"Well, to start, what did you do to me on the beach today?"

"You mean after you attacked me?"

He nodded grudgingly, conceding the point. "I'm sorry about that. It's just that I thought you might . . . have a hidden agenda." He couldn't very well say, *There are wizards after me and I thought you might be conspiring with them.*

"Well, you came up to me, you know. I was minding my own business."

"I know. But what did you do to me?" he persisted.

"I kissed you." The corners of her mouth twitched.

"Before that. You left me on my back."

Now she grinned flat out. "Sounds improper."

"This isn't a joke. I want to know what . . . who you are and what you're up to." Seph waved a hand at the drawings. "What's with the aura? Why do you call me Witch Boy?"

"Because that's what you are."

"What makes you think so?"

She gave him a look that said he wasn't fooling her one bit. "There are people in this world who can get whatever they want, who can talk the money right out of your hand and make you glad you gave it up. Some have the knowin' or the second sight. Where I come from, we call them witches or conjure men."

I call them wizards. "Why would you think I'm . . . a witch? I never even spoke to you until today."

"You didn't have to. I've always been able to spot it. You shine like a house lit up for a party." She reached a hand toward him, stopping an inch from his face, as one might hesitate to touch a hot stove.

"What happened on the beach today?" Seph persisted.

"I don't really know." She shrugged. "I just don't seem to be susceptible to spelling."

Seph leaned forward. "It was more than that. It's like

you wrung me out or something."

Madison took a bite of her biscotti. "This is a totally weird conversation, Seth, or Seph, or whatever your name is."

"So can you use it? The power, I mean. After you drain it out of a person?" He reached out and gripped her hand.

She snatched her hand back. "You're the witch, not me." She looked at her watch. "Listen, I'm working breakfast tomorrow. I need to get some sleep."

Seph ignored the hint. "Why do you sound like you're from the South?"

"Because I am. Coalton County's down by the river. Southern Ohio."

"Why are you working here, then?"

"My cousin Rachel owns the Legends. She needed a waitress, I needed the money, and I thought I could add some beach landscapes to my portfolio."

Seph laid some bills on top of the check. "But you're not sketching landscapes. You're sketching me."

She turned a deep red and looked away. "I . . . I thought you'd make a good subject. You have an interesting face. And challenging. I mean, you actually make your own light." She stood, signaling that the conversation was over.

Seph followed Madison back through the coffeehouse. In the entryway, she turned and stuck out her hand to him. "Well, good to meet you, Seph McCauley. And thanks for the coffee."

He took her hand, but she didn't react to his touch the way other girls did. "Where are you staying?" he asked.

"Me?" She nodded toward the stairs. "Right here, at the inn."

"If you work breakfast tomorrow, does that mean you get off early?"

She pulled her hand back. "No. I'm working a double shift."

"When's your day off? Maybe we could hang out."

"I've seen you at the pavilion. Seems to me you're pretty booked."

Small towns. "I'm trying to cut back."

She lifted her chin. "What am I, a challenge to you, or something?"

He shrugged. "You're the one who kissed me." He knew he'd said the wrong thing when she pivoted away from him and headed for the stairs. "Hey! Madison! I'm sorry, okay? Can't we just hang out? You don't have to sign anything. We'll do whatever you want."

"Well . . ." She paused, one foot on the first step, her hand on the railing. She turned back toward him, considering. "It's been a long time since I've been on a picnic."

Chapter Twelve
Hastings

The next day was miserably hot. Seph left the beach early and stopped at the market on his way home. Madison had agreed to a picnic, and Seph had agreed to provide the food. He meant to keep it simple: focaccia, cheese, antipasti, fruit. That and a burnt-sugar pecan tart that would steal anybody's soul.

At first he thought no one was home, but as he pulled a bottle of iced tea from the refrigerator, he heard voices on the porch. He wandered out, expecting to see Linda and Becka, perhaps. Becka was there, but she was sitting across from a stranger.

He was tall and lean, yet muscular, and had strong features—that other-side-of-ugly look that women seemed to favor. He had green eyes and dark, unruly hair. He was dressed for the weather in a cotton shirt and khakis, and there was a bottle of beer on the table in front of him.

There was something compelling about him, a tightly coiled power that drew the eye.

"Oh hi, Seph. Is Jack with you?" Becka asked, looking over his shoulder.

Seph shook his head. "I came back from the beach by myself." He stared at the man, who was looking back at him curiously.

Becka noticed. "Seph, this is Leander Hastings, a friend of the family. He's visiting from out of town. Leander, this is Seph McCauley. He's been staying with us this summer."

Seph stuck out his hand to Hastings, and there was that usual electrical exchange between wizards. "I've been looking forward to meeting you," Seph said. "I've heard a lot about you."

Hastings smiled. "Don't believe everything you hear." His eyes were fixed on Seph, taking his measure. There was something about him that reminded Seph of Gregory Leicester. He had the same ability to intimidate, to overwhelm. But just now he looked a little puzzled. "Are you a friend of Jack's?"

"No," Becka explained quickly. "He was Linda's guest, originally, though we've managed to steal him from her. He comes from a complicated family situation."

"I see."

Seph needed to find a way to talk to the wizard, to ask questions in private. This was likely to be someone who could lead him to the Dragon. "Are you going to be staying in Trinity long, Mr. Hastings?" Seph asked, hoping for a yes.

Hastings shook his head. "Only a few days, I'm afraid. And a few days in Trinity is never enough." He paused. "Where do you come from, Seph?" The wizard had a trace of accent, as if he were British, or had learned English overseas.

"I was born in Canada," Seph replied. "But I moved around a lot."

Becka looked at her watch. "Oh my, I'm sorry, Leander. I need to be down at school in half an hour. Jack should be home soon, though, and I hope you'll stay for supper. Will you and Seph be okay for a little while?" She seemed flustered, her face rosier than could be accounted for by the heat.

"I'm fine on my own, Becka, you know that. It's my fault for dropping in. I'll stay for supper, if you'll have me, but I'm sure Seph has other things to do besides entertaining me. I can do some reading." He rested his hand on a stack of books on the table.

"Oh, it's no problem, really," Seph said hastily.

Becka gathered up her laptop and papers, kissed Seph on top of his head, and then she was gone, banging the screen door behind her.

Hastings looked after her for a moment and then turned his attention to Seph. He looked like someone who had forgotten something important and was trying to remember.

"So you came here with Linda?"

Seph set his tea on the table and settled into the chair across from Hastings. He decided to answer the next three questions all at once, before they were asked. "She's my guardian. I'm told my parents are dead. And I don't know where I'm from. Not really."

Hastings looked surprised. "Linda never—"

"I know, she never mentioned me," Seph cut in. "I only met her a few weeks ago. But she's been . . . great. So's everyone else here in Trinity."

"Who were your parents?" Hastings asked, leaning back in his chair. An unusual ring on his right hand caught the light as he did so.

Seph hesitated, unsure whether to pass along the lie. "I never really knew much about them. I was raised by a foster mother. A sorcerer," he added.

"Perhaps your foster mother would tell you about them, if you asked." His meaning was clear. No sorcerer could resist a wizard asking questions.

"She's gone now, too," he said. *There is something deadly about this man*, Seph thought. In the world of wizards, it was sometimes difficult to tell the good guys from the bad.

Seph decided it was time to ask a few questions before they were interrupted. He leaned forward. "Jack told me you taught him how to fight."

Hastings nodded. "I did."

"Can you teach me, too?"

"Jack is a warrior. That's his gift. You're a wizard. You're not allowed to fight under the rules."

"But not everybody plays by the rules, do they?" Seph said quietly.

Hastings picked up his beer and drained it. "Why do

you want to learn to fight?" he asked, rolling the bottle between his hands.

"I have enemies."

"Who?"

"Gregory Leicester," Seph said, watching Hastings for any reaction to the name. There was none, not even a flicker, though the wizard paused a moment before he spoke again.

"What do you have against Gregory Leicester?" he asked, as if they were talking about the weather.

"He murdered two of my friends."

Hastings didn't seem surprised by this news. "I'm sorry to hear that," he said. "Were they wizards?"

"One was a wizard. One was Anaweir."

"Can you prove that he killed them?"

Seph thought about it. "Probably not."

Hastings sighed and ran a hand through his hair, leaving it more tumbled than before. "Does Dr. Leicester know you are gunning for him?"

He's making fun of me, Seph thought, although there was no trace of humor in Hastings's voice or manner. "I told him I'd kill him," Seph admitted.

Hastings shook his head and leaned forward. "Let me give you some advice, Seph. If you really want to kill a man, don't tell him what you're about. And don't tell everyone else, either. It sounds too much like you are trying to convince yourself." He smiled, and it was not unkind. "For all you know, Gregory Leicester and I are old friends," he said.

"But you're not," Seph said. "Are you?"

"We're not," Hastings agreed, without stopping to think about it. "But I know him well enough to suggest you reconsider tangling with him."

"It's not my choice." Seph moved on to his primary question. "Do you know where I can find the Dragon?" he asked.

"The Dragon?"

"The leader of the wizard faction opposing Gregory Leicester. Leicester is in league with someone named Claude D'Orsay."

"And how do you know all this?" Seph realized suddenly that he was still the one who was answering most of the questions. And despite spending the day at the beach, he was already sticky with sweat again, while Hastings appeared cool and relaxed. *How does he do that?*

"I was at a school called the Havens all last year, up until June," Seph said, irritated. "The friends he killed were students there. Leicester was the headmaster. So do you know the Dragon or not?"

Now Hastings studied him with more interest than before. "I've heard of the Dragon, of course, although I'm new to the Wizard Council. The Dragon's not actually on the council. He keeps his identity hidden, but has considerable influence. Why do you ask?"

"I want to find him. I have some information that could help him." Seph meant to make Jason's mission his own. Only, he was even younger than Jason, as Hastings immediately pointed out.

"You're too young to get involved in wizard politics. It's not a game for children. I already have the reputation of being careless with the lives of children," Hastings added, rubbing his chin.

"I'm not a child," Seph said hotly.

"I'm sure you are not. Not after a year at the Havens." Hastings was about to say more, when there was a choking sound, like a gasp, from the doorway, and Seph realized they were no longer alone. They both looked up to see Linda Downey standing there.

"Lee! What are you doing here?" she demanded. She was looking from Seph to Hastings and back again.

Hastings rose easily to his feet. "It's good to see you too, Linda." He stepped forward, extending both hands, but she stepped back, so he let them drop after a moment. He towered over the enchanter, and the air shimmered between them like two weather fronts meeting. Seph filed the information away.

"I hadn't heard you were coming," Linda said finally. "What a surprise." Her voice was flat.

Hastings nodded. "I didn't know you would be here, either. I showed up unannounced, but Becka was kind enough to invite me to dinner. I was just getting to know Seph, here."

"I thought you were at the beach," she said to Seph, in a tone that made him wish he were.

"I came back early," he explained hastily. "Jack should be home pretty soon." As he spoke, they heard someone at the back door.

"Seph? You hiding out in here? I have five messages for you." Jack was laughing as he came onto the porch. He stopped short when he saw Hastings. "Mr. Hastings! I didn't realize you were here. I would have come home sooner." This was one wizard he seemed pleased to see. "Does Mom know you're here?"

"I already saw her," Hastings said. "I brought her some old books from the UK that I thought she might enjoy."

Seph looked from Jack to Hastings to Linda Downey. He was already sure that dinner would be interesting.

Dinner *was* interesting. Becka put salmon into the smoker and there were grilled vegetables, warm bread from the bakery, and fresh sweet corn. She had bought raspberries and whipping cream, so Seph made crepes for dessert.

Aside from the food, dinner was a feast of secrets. And all of them revolved around Leander Hastings. Linda was brooding about something and had little to say to anyone. Seph realized quickly that Jack and Hastings had a history Becka knew nothing about. She and Hastings got into a spirited discussion about Celtic archaeology that lasted through most of the meal. Yet Becka seemed tentative, unsure of herself where the wizard was concerned. And Seph noticed Hastings looking at him intently several times.

If he was hoping for more private time with Hastings after dinner, he was disappointed. The adults sat on the porch, talking and drinking wine until late. Finally, Hastings thanked Becka for hosting him and said goodbye to Jack and Seph. When he came to Linda, he took both her hands firmly and lifted her to her feet. "Can you walk me out, Linda?" It was more a command than a request. Seph wondered what the wizard was up to.

Maybe he was going to tell Linda about Seph's plans to find the Dragon.

He felt disappointed. He was convinced that Hastings knew where to find the Dragon, but obviously he wasn't going to share that information with Seph.

The air outside was soft with the exhalation of the lake. When Linda and Hastings reached Hastings's car, he opened the passenger-side door. "Get in," he said, and walked around to the other side without waiting for a response.

Fine, she thought. It would give her a chance to speak her mind to Hastings. She got in.

Hastings climbed in the driver's side, but he didn't put the key into the ignition. "I want to talk to you about the boy," he said.

"If you mean Seph, I have something to say to you, too." She looked him in the eyes. "Stay away from him, Leander. Don't get him involved in any of your schemes. Even if he wants to be. He's already been hurt, and I don't want to see him hurt any more."

"*My* schemes?" Hastings raised an eyebrow. Linda glared at him, so he sighed and sat back in his seat, draping his arms across the steering wheel. "How well do you know him?" he asked.

"I've known Seph all his life," Linda replied. "Why?"

"He says he just met you this summer," Hastings said mildly. "And I'm wondering why I've never heard of him before."

Linda hesitated. "Well, maybe our relationship has been a bit . . . one-sided."

"So you know him but you'd never actually *spoken* to him?" Hastings rubbed his hand along his jaw.

"I've been his guardian since he was a baby," Linda said sharply. "Why? What are you getting at?"

"If you're his guardian, then how in bloody hell did the boy end up at the Havens?"

Linda shifted uncomfortably on the seat. "I . . . I didn't arrange the placement. I never . . . I never made the connection. I didn't realize he was in trouble until the end of the school year." Guilt swept over her.

Hastings was blunt. "I don't believe in coincidences. I know Gregory Leicester, and I know what he does to his students. If Seph McCauley spent a year there, then you have to assume Leicester has control of him now."

"That's impossible," Linda said flatly. "He was a mess when I found him. It was all I could do to get him out of there. Leicester was ready to kill him. And then they tried to keep us from getting to Trinity."

"How did you happen to take him out of school?" Hastings asked. He'd turned away from the light, and she couldn't read his expression in the darkness.

"He sent out an e-mail asking for help." Hastings was silent. "Come on, Leander. You don't think this is some kind of trick, do you?"

"This might be just where Leicester wants him to be, right in the middle of the Sanctuary, right next to you, Nick, Jack, and Ellen: all the people who ruined their tournament last year and engineered the change in the rules."

"How would they know he'd end up here? It's like I told you. Seph didn't even know about me until I showed up at school."

"What did he tell you about school?"

"He . . . well . . . he wouldn't tell me much. But you could tell from the way he looked that—"

"Don't be naïve. Look, as soon as he met me, he was asking about the Dragon and where he could find him. Said he wanted to help him. The boy's just a child, but he's powerful. Powerful enough to overwhelm you. Don't you see? It's too risky to leave him here."

Linda made an irritated sound. "You're right about one thing. He is a child. He's just an untrained boy who's been through hell this past year. And now he needs to heal."

Hastings turned and took Linda's hands. She flinched and tried to withdraw them, but he held tight, exerting pressure of his own. "Let me take him with me. I promise I won't hurt him. Given a little time, perhaps I can undo the damage. It might help us learn more about what Leicester is up to, and how to help his victims."

"That's what it's all about, isn't it?" she said bitterly. "You're hoping to use Seph to help you win."

"We have to win, Linda," Hastings said softly, urgently, searching her eyes. "You know that as well as I do."

She withdrew her hands. "Yes, we do," she agreed. "But not over the body of this boy. I'm not letting him leave the Sanctuary." When she saw his expression, she squared her shoulders and her chin came up. "*Don't* try to bully me. And don't try to go behind my back, either. If you lay a finger on him, or talk him into anything, there will be a war between us, I promise you."

She pushed open the car door and slipped out into the darkness.

The next morning, Seph was awakened by a tapping at his bedroom door. He pulled on his shorts and went to open it. It was Linda. "Let's go get some breakfast," she suggested.

Seph shrugged. "Okay." She had dark circles under her eyes, as though she hadn't slept well. He wondered why. He'd been sleeping better and better as the summer progressed and memories of the Havens faded.

He pulled his T-shirt over his head and picked up his flip-flops, padding downstairs barefoot. They slipped out of the back door, and he sat down on the stoop to put on his shoes. He could tell it was going to be another hot day, but the morning was still and cool and fragrant with the scent of the hydrangeas that crowded the foundation of the house.

They stopped at a coffee shop down by the university and picked up bagels, juice, and coffee, and then drove to the beach. It was nearly deserted, save a few early-morning walkers, and the snack bar sat silent at the top of the cliff. They picked their way down the ancient stairway to the sand and walked out to the end of the pier. There they sat down, took off their shoes, and dangled their feet over the water. Sea gulls wheeled over their heads, hoping for a handout. Way off to their right, the sun gleamed over the horizon, turning the tops of the waves to gold. The air carried with it the scent of Canada, fresh and clean, across the water.

He thought about Toronto, far to the north and east. He wondered who was living in his old house now, if they still took in guests, if they'd kept the big commercial range and the tiny-print wallpaper.

"How do you like it here in Trinity?" Linda said finally.

"Well," Seph said. "I never thought I'd like living in a small town, but I do. Mercedes and Blaise and the other neighbors mind your business too much, but I like them. Jack and Ellen are really cool. They take me with them when they go out with their friends, and I've been meeting a lot of people. At the beach," he added, thinking of Madison. "Nick is awesome."

Linda gave a quick nod, as if satisfied. "I'm wondering about school in the fall." She gazed down at the water percolating around the rocks.

"I'm sure I'll be okay, wherever I go," Seph said. "Now that I have more training."

"Do you always have to be so damn agreeable about everything?"

Seph said nothing. He couldn't recall anyone applying that particular term to him before.

"What would you think about going to school here in Trinity?"

He looked up, startled. "That'd be okay. Sure." His only contacts with the Wizard Guild were Leander Hastings and Gregory Leicester. And his connection with Hastings ran right through Trinity. "But . . . how could I? I can't stay with Becka forever."

"You probably could. Becka is absolutely taken with you, Seph." She paused. "I could get a house here, too. I can't promise to spend all my time in Trinity, but you could stay with me when I'm here and with Becka when I'm not."

Seph couldn't hide his surprise. He'd had the impression Linda never stayed in one place for long, never even wanted to say how long she would stay when she visited. He'd been thinking she might be ready to get back to London, that only her concern for him was keeping her in Trinity.

"That'd work. Only . . ." He paused, and then rushed ahead. "I'm going to have to leave the Sanctuary one of these days. I like it here, but I don't want to be a prisoner. I'm used to big cities, and I haven't been anywhere all summer. Don't you think it's safe now?"

"I don't know," she said, looking out at the water as if she might find answers in the waves. "I'll feel better when the year is over. Maybe you could go to school here this year, and then we'll see." She brushed bagel crumbs off her lap and clasped her hands together. "I've been wondering how you're doing. I mean, if you've been able to . . . come to grips with what happened at school last year. If . . . you'd like to talk about it."

He looked straight at Linda and said, "I'm doing the best I can." And that was God's truth.

She backed off. "Okay. I'll register you at the high school and we'll see how it goes."

Seph smiled. He had never had the chance to

participate in this kind of decision making before, and he liked it. "Fine with me," he said.

"And, Seph, one more thing." He looked up. "Be careful with Leander Hastings."

"What do you mean?" He remembered Linda and Hastings walking out together the night before, and wondered what they'd talked about.

"He and his allies have done a lot to keep people like Gregory Leicester in check. He's always focused on the big picture. But sometimes he runs over innocent people on his way."

"He said he has the reputation of being careless with the lives of children," Seph said. "What did he mean?"

"Oh, he told you that? But he didn't explain it, of course. Last year, in the tournament, he was Jack's sponsor in the Game." Linda sipped at her coffee. "Leander talked him into fighting. In the end, it turned out well. But he's a gambler. He takes chances with other people's lives." Linda put her hand under Seph's chin and turned his face so she could look him in the eyes. "You could be next."

"Oh, I don't think so," Seph said. "He didn't seem too interested in me."

Linda shook her head. "You're wrong. You don't know him like I do. Just remember what I said."

Later, during his wizardry lesson, Seph had a question for Nick. "Why does Linda Downey dislike Leander Hastings so much?"

The wizard glanced up at him sharply. "What gives you that idea?" They were sitting in the kitchen of Nick's apartment. A large floor fan whirred at their feet.

"She warned me to watch out for him. She doesn't trust him."

Nick sighed. "Linda's feelings for Leander are complex. She doesn't entirely trust him, that is true." He paused, as if considering how much to share. "Linda and Leander were—ah—*involved* years ago."

"What?" Seph looked up at his teacher in surprise. "You wouldn't know it."

"Well, yes, Seph, you would know it, if you were older and just a bit wiser. Their past makes it difficult for them to deal with each other in the present."

Seph remembered the tension between the wizard and the enchanter, the spark and energy. He thought about Linda's warning. "Is Hastings a bad man?"

"No, I wouldn't say he's a bad man. He is one of those wizards who has improved with age. He was quite dangerous and impulsive when he was young. Still dangerous, I suppose." Nick fell silent for a moment, frowning at some old memory. "Leander's father was a wizard and his mother Anaweir. His older sister, Carrie, was a warrior. The family did its best to keep her out of the tournaments, but the Roses eventually tracked her down and she was killed. His father died defending her. His mother was never the same. Leander was ten at the time.

"By the time he was your age, he was already fighting a personal war against the wizard-dominated hierarchy and the tournament system. He has never been afraid of a fight. Never afraid of dying, either."

"But . . . if Aunt Linda and Mr. Hastings agree about

the tournaments and all?" Seph persisted, wanting to understand.

Nick smiled. "These are difficult times. Linda and Leander may agree about the ends, but often disagree about the means." He put his hand on Seph's shoulder. "They are both very powerful people in their own way. They will pull you, Seph, whether you like it or not. Eventually, you'll have to decide for yourself."

Chapter Thirteen
A Picnic on the River

Seph saw no more of Leander Hastings, reinforcing his belief that the wizard had no particular interest in him. The next day was Thursday, Madison's day off; the day of the picnic. She said she knew of a good place, and she was the one with the car. She suggested he bring his swimming gear, so he assumed it would be somewhere up on the lake.

The house had emptied out early. Jack had gone to play soccer with Will and Harmon, trying to beat the heat of the day. Becka was in court, and Linda was actually out looking at real estate.

Seph was just loading the cooler when Madison tapped on the screen door. "Come on in," he said. "I'm just about ready."

She wore a green tie-dyed sundress over her bathing suit, a wide-brimmed hat, and sandals. Her glittering hair was partly braided and beaded, partly hanging free, like rivulets down her back.

"This is a great neighborhood," she said. "I'd like to paint this entire street. It's like a whole shelf of wedding cakes, each fancier than the last." She looked around the kitchen, at Seph's bags and parcels. "Who else did you invite?" she asked in amazement.

She helped him carry it all out to her old pickup. They loaded the food into the back, under a tarp.

"Do you come from a big family, that you live in such a big house?" she asked.

He shook his head, sliding into the passenger side and buckling his seat belt. "There's just me. Like I told you, that's Becka's house. I'm staying here for the summer, at least."

She turned left on Jefferson, toward downtown, ramming up through the manual gears. Seph liked that she drove stick shift. "What are you, a senior?" she asked.

He nodded. "Will be. What about you?"

"I'll be a senior, too. But I'm going to be taking classes at Trinity in the fall. At the Art Institute." She ducked her head away as she said it, as if he might question her right to be there.

"Wow. Congratulations. I hear it's hard to get in. But how do you take classes at the college if you're still in high school?"

"I'll be there as a post-secondary student. Here in Ohio, you can take college classes for free while you're still in high school. The school district pays for it." Madison's cheeks went pink as she warmed to her subject. "My art teacher at Coal Grove High School set it up. She said I'd really improve with the right teacher, and I can get college credit without having to pay for it. I'm going to be living with my cousin and working at the inn, so . . ." She shrugged self-consciously, and Seph realized she must be nervous about fitting in as a high school student at an elite private school like Trinity College.

"Becka teaches English lit at Trinity. I've sat in on a few of her lectures. The students seem really laid back. I bet you'll like it there." After his years of attending prep schools, Seph had been surprised at the way the students dressed at Trinity: flannel shirts and sweatshirts and jeans in cool weather, T-shirts and shorts in the summer.

He was so engaged in the conversation with Madison that he didn't realize they were heading south instead of north, until they reached the highway interchange. As they accelerated onto the highway, Seph sat up straighter, looking out the window, fighting off a sense of foreboding. "I didn't realize we were going out of town," he said.

Madison nodded. "Uh-huh. There's this really cool nature preserve on the Vermilion River. In Huron County. It's not far." She was looking at him a little strangely.

"Oh." *It's all right*, he told himself. *No need to make a scene.* He hadn't seen a strange wizard all summer. There was no way the alumni could be waiting at the city limits to intercept him, watching all the routes out of town. Besides, he was unlikely to be spotted riding in an unfamiliar car.

They passed the city limits without incident. The park

was about a half hour away. It was remote, thickly wooded, embraced by a great loop of the river gorge, and embroidered by rocky streams that flowed into the river. The parking lot was empty.

"How'd you find this place?" Seph asked, hoisting the cooler onto his shoulder.

"I've been here fishing a couple of times." She grinned. "Fishing's an excuse to sit by the water and do nothing. Perfect." They hiked upstream a short distance to a little meadow, shaded by tall trees and bordered by little umbrella plants that Madison called May apples. They spread a quilt and Seph laid out the food.

It was a hot day, but it was cool under the trees along the water. *This is fine*, Seph told himself when he'd finally eaten enough. He looked over at Madison and smiled. *More than fine.*

Madison took off her hat and set it aside, groped in her tote and pulled out her sketchbook and charcoals. "You ruined my other drawings, so you have to sit again."

Seph scooted closer to her. "I already cooked for you. You mean I have to sit for you, too?" He cupped her chin in his hands, pulled her toward him, and kissed her. She tasted of brown sugar and butter, and her hair smelled of citrus and lavender. Sunlight rippled over the quilt while the trees moved overhead, as if they were underwater.

"Madison," he whispered.

"My friends call me Maddie." She extricated herself from his embrace. Pulling her sketchbook onto her lap, she pointed with her chin to the riverbank.

"You. Sit over there."

Grumbling under his breath, Seph rose and took his place among the rocks at the river's edge while Madison issued orders. "Half turn. Tilt your head to the left. Right leg straight. Stop scowling."

Seph thought she'd done fine in the past, sketching him without his cooperation. He posed for an hour in the dappled shade, with the Vermilion River sluicing about his feet, before she relented and suggested they go wading in the river.

They loaded the picnic gear back in the truck, then walked about a mile and a half downstream to the gorge. Seph stripped off his shirt and Madison her sundress, and they left them high on the riverbank. The water was cold, but refreshing in the afternoon heat. It was very clear, unlike the cove at the Havens. Seph turned over rocks, disturbing salamanders and crayfish, catching them in his cupped hands. He hadn't realized there were tiny lobsters in Ohio. Then the two of them sat in the shallows, letting the river roll over them.

"Do you have brothers and sisters?" Seph asked.

"I have a little brother, John Robert. And a younger sister, Grace." She spoke about them with a fierce affection, as if they needed defending.

"Your parents were okay with you coming up here on your own?"

"There's just Carlene. My mom. She wasn't too thrilled about it, mainly since I'm the babysitter. But I can make more money working for Rachel than anywhere in Coalton County. And Rachel watches me closer than Carlene ever has."

"So," Seph said, trying to understand. "At home. Do you live on a . . . a farm?"

"I live on Booker Mountain. My family's been there since before Ohio was a state. It's a beautiful place, but I'm afraid it's not much of a farm unless you want to grow rocks." She skipped a stone across the river so it landed on the opposite bank. "I guess you've lived all over."

"I guess."

"What's Europe like?" She rolled her eyes. "I suppose that's like asking *what's the ocean like.*"

"Yeah." He thought a moment. "There's less room in Europe. It seems like everything's packed together compared to Canada or the U.S. But you have to pay closer attention. It's layered. Like a tapestry woven with lots of colors and very small stitches. Or . . . or an Impressionist painting," he added, pleased to have come up with examples from art.

"Have you been to the Musée d'Orsay? In Paris?" She studied him like he was an exotic species.

He nodded. "It's a feast, if you like the Impressionists."

"I'm going there some day," she said with conviction. "I'm going to visit every gallery in Paris and every church in Florence. And eat gelato every day."

When they were numb and shivering, they climbed out onto the rocks and sunned themselves like turtles. Madison ran her fingers over the *dyrne sefa* that hung around Seph's neck. "What's this?"

"A friend at school gave it to me," Seph replied. "I guess you could say it enhances magic. It lets the gifted do things they couldn't otherwise." The memory of Jason brought pain, as it always did, but just then the Havens seemed far away. "You mentioned that you'd met . . . witches at home."

"Well, there's a strong tradition of magic around there. The folks that settled that area came from Ireland, England, and Wales. My grandmother was a reader and adviser. People used to come to her to have their fortunes read." She fell silent for a moment, as if lost in a memory.

A seer, Seph thought. "Were there also wizards in Coalton County?"

She considered this a moment. "There are people with auras. Like you. People with power. Trinity's full of them. What kind of power, I couldn't tell you. And I'd guess most of them don't know they have it."

"Were there others like you?"

She laughed. "It'd be pretty hard to tell. I don't have an aura and I don't have magic. I just kind of swallow it up."

When they were sunbaked and drowsy, they pulled their dry clothes on.

The shadows were deeper than before when they headed back. They followed a path upstream along the riverbank until they reached a place where the sides of the ravine swept steeply up on either side, forcing them back into the river. Seph had just taken Maddie's hand to help her across some slippery stones, when he looked up and saw someone standing in the riverbed ahead, between them and the sun. The contrast between light and shadow made it difficult to see, but there was something familiar about the silhouette. When Seph shaded his eyes against the light he saw that it was Warren Barber. And behind him, Kenyon King, from the Havens.

Madison stepped up even with Seph, and looked curiously at Barber, who was standing, smiling, right in their path.

"Hello, Joseph," Barber said. His voice was marbled with sorcery, meant to sedate and cloud the mind.

Seph looked around. On either side, the banks were too steep to climb. Behind them, two more wizards were picking their way down the riverbed. Bruce Hays, and Aaron Hanlon, who taught social studies.

"Who's that?" Madison began, but when she saw Seph's face, the words died away. She looked over her shoulder, at Hays and Hanlon, and back at Seph.

"We thought you'd never leave your little nest," Barber said. There must have been an unspoken question on Seph's face, because he added, "I used a different kind of web this time. Something to let you out, but tie a line to you. Something that made you easy to track."

Seph brushed at himself as if trying to dislodge the invisible tether.

Barber flexed his fingers, readying them for use. "We've come to take you back, Joseph," he said. "It hasn't been the same since you left."

Seph spoke to Maddie without taking his eyes off Barber, acutely aware of the wizards behind him. "It's okay. I went to school with these people. Go on back to the truck."

"What's going on?" Madison looked over her shoulder. Hays and Hanlon had stopped a short distance away, as if waiting for a signal.

"Just go. If I'm not there in half an hour, go on without me." When she didn't move, he pushed her hard, and she stumbled a few steps forward. She looked back at him, her face still full of questions. Then she turned and walked away from him, up the riverbed, her fists clenched at her sides. But as she tried to slip past Barber and King, King reached out a long arm and caught her by the hair, pulling her to him and wrapping one arm around her. She struggled for a moment, all knees and elbows, then stood still, eyes wide with surprise and fright.

"Let her go," Seph said, trying to keep his voice calm and even. "She's not involved in this."

Barber smiled. "But you're involved with her, right? You wouldn't run off and leave her with the likes of us, would you? Just cooperate and maybe we'll let her go."

Seph knew that his primary advantage was surprise and the overconfidence of the alumni. If not for that, he would have been immobilized already. If he didn't do something soon, he wouldn't get the chance.

But Madison took that issue out of his hands. She twisted like an eel and kneed King in the groin. He screeched and doubled over. He must have released power into her, because after a few seconds he went down like he'd been clubbed in the head.

Seph pointed at Barber and cast an immobilization charm. He spun around and launched charms at the other two wizards, but they were already throwing up shields and muttering counters. Barber stood frozen, an incredulous look on his face.

"Go! Now!" Seph shouted to Madison, who had extricated herself from King's grip. "Get out of here!"

"But I can help you!"

"I don't want your help!" Seph said, keeping his eyes on the three wizards. He didn't want anything from the Havens to contaminate Maddie Moss. Didn't want Warren bloody Barber asking questions about her.

Didn't want her to get hurt.

She turned and splashed up the riverbed, in the direction of the parking lot, leaping over obstacles like a deer. She'd lost her hat, and it floated down the river toward them, spinning in the current.

Then Hays disabled the immobilization charm Seph had used on Warren Barber. That was the problem. Unless Seph could take down all three at once, they would help each other.

"What's this?" Barber said, looking more amused than worried. "I believe the boy's been studying out of school." He looked after Madison, as if debating whether to go after her, then shrugged. "Pity," he said. "I was taking a liking to her." He nudged King with his foot, frowning. "What's up, Ken? You going to be singing soprano from now on?" King lay on his back, still stunned.

Barber signaled to the others, and the remaining wizards separated, advancing toward Seph from three different directions.

Seph climbed partway up the side of the rocky gorge and turned to face them. The way to the parking lot was blocked, and he had no hope of climbing the rest of the way without being overtaken or disabled.

It was eerily silent in the gorge. The birds were quiet, and he couldn't even hear the sound of water cascading over the rocks. All he could hear was the harsh breathing of the three wizards as they advanced on him.

"You may think you're a wizard now, Joseph," Warren said. "But we think you have a lot to learn. And we can teach you, back at school." His voice turned soothing. "Tell you what. You won't have to mingle with the other students anymore. We'll let you stay in the Alumni House. We'll be best friends."

Seph extended his hands. "Back off. I don't want to hurt you, but I won't let you take me."

"Please don't hurt us, Joseph," Barber mocked. As he spoke, he gestured and a lattice of shadows slid over Seph. He looked up to see the net descending on him and threw up his hands, speaking the countercharm. He had been spending considerable time on Weirweb counters. The net dissolved into gleaming shards of silver that fell harmlessly about his shoulders. Then he swept his arm out in a broad arc, sending a wall of blue fame roaring downhill. The alumni threw themselves on their faces in the river as the flames raked over them.

Seph teased earth out of the side of the hill, releasing a landslide of boulders, then drove a flash flood of water down the gorge. He was desperately flinging charms he'd never tried before. Some worked and some didn't. He had to keep the alumni busy. If he took even one hit, he was done.

His only advantage was that Leicester wanted him alive. He was under no such restriction, although he really had no desire to harm them. They were victims as much as he was.

Except for Warren Barber. Seph was beginning to think Barber was bad to the bone. *Should've killed you when I had the chance*, he thought.

Seph inched up the riverbed toward the parking lot, fighting the alumni for every foot of ground. He sensed rather than heard the *subduen* charm Barber cast, and threw back the countercharm. Warren spun out more spider cords from his hands—looping, iridescent cords that threatened to ensnare Seph—but they dissolved under the same counter he'd used on the web.

They pressed against the barricades he put up, seeking weaknesses, and toppled small trees on the slope above, sending branches crashing down around him. They sent clouds of vapors toward him, and birds tumbled out of the sky, stupefied. He was already getting tired. He wondered how long it would take them to devise something he'd never heard of, or to simply overwhelm him.

The wizards were soaked, plastered with mud, and bleeding. They'd obviously expected an easy catch.

"Does Dr. Leicester mind if he's damaged or broken?" Hanlon gasped.

"I think we might have to damage him. I think it might be unavoidable." As if to reinforce his words, Barber swung his fist, sweeping stones from the river bed into a deadly cloud that flew at Seph. Seph fashioned a shield and managed to deflect most of them, but a fist-size stone struck him above the right eyebrow, stunning him momentarily, almost knocking him from his feet. He staggered backward but managed to stay upright.

Barber said something to the other two, and the three

came forward, pointing at him and firing charms, one
after another. Seph struggled to keep up, knowing that if
he lost focus for a moment, it would be over. He fingered
the *dyrne sefa* and thought about disappearing, but it
would do no good if he couldn't keep up with the spell-
casting. He might end up immobile and unnoticeable, lost
in the Vermilion River Gorge forever.

Suddenly he saw movement just beyond the alumni in
the ravine, a flash of light off metal, and a familiar figure,
moving fast. The three wizards were so focused on their
intended victim that they didn't realize their peril until it
was too late.

Ellen Stephenson swung her blazing sword in a powerful two-handed sweep that sliced through Aaron
Hanlon's ribcage all the way to the spine, nearly cutting
him in half. Hanlon screamed and toppled facedown in
the river. He lay still, his blood clouding the water. She
swung again, metal singing, slicing through Warren
Barber's shoulder. A little different angle, and she'd have
taken his arm off. He spun away, cursing, clutching at the
wound with one hand.

Seph scrambled down the slope to join her, feet sliding in the loose shale. Ellen was breathing hard, but she
was grinning, triumphant. Now it was suddenly two
against two, and one wounded on the other side.

"You okay, Seph?" She kept her sword up, her eyes on
the two wizards.

"Ellen, I am so glad to see you," Seph said. He was
appreciating the benefits of having a warrior on his side.

Seph sent a volley of immobilization charms raining

down on the two remaining wizards. Ellen spiraled flames toward them, spinning off the tip of her sword and advancing on them with grim determination. Warren Barber staggered backward, feeling the effects of his wound. Now the alumni were the ones on the defensive.

Seph knew they'd better make the most of their temporary advantage. There might be more alumni waiting in the wings.

"Ellen!" He moved in close so he could speak quietly. "I'm going to make you invisible." He lifted the *dyrne sefa* from around his neck and hung it around hers. Then he gripped her arm and spoke the unnoticeable charm. "Don't let me lose hold of you. Now let's move!" he hissed, pulling her down off the slope and across the water to the other side.

The two remaining wizards swiveled about, splattering flames at random, muttering curses, scanning the sides of the canyon and the underbrush at the river edge. Frustrated, they closed in on the spot where Seph was last seen, raking it with wizard fire. Smoke filled the gorge as grass and brush began to smolder. Barber sent another hail of stones swirling down the gorge and Ellen hissed in pain as several hit home.

"McCauley!" Barber shouted, his face purple with rage. "We know where you live! We've been on fricking Jefferson Street. We'll find Linda Downey and her sister, Rebecca. We'll find your girl. We'll find your warrior friend. And in the end, we'll find you."

The alumni charged down the river at a dead run, convinced their quarry was getting away. Seph and Ellen splashed up the river in the opposite direction, toward the parking lot. They scrambled desperately through the gorge, slashed by briars and branches, water and mud sucking at Seph's flip-flops, Ellen's sword catching in the underbrush. He could hear no sounds of pursuit behind them, only their labored breathing and the racket they made as they forced their way through the trees.

They burst through the last of the brush into the parking lot. Madison was standing by the car, frantically punching numbers into a cell phone, when Seph and Ellen materialized out of the air, Ellen carrying her bloody sword.

Madison looked up and saw them. "You found him!" She shoved her cell phone into her purse. "Thank God! Are you okay?" She gripped Seph's elbows, peering anxiously into his face, touching his forehead where the rock had hit him. Then she looked over his shoulder at Ellen and said fiercely, "I hope you chopped them into little bits."

"Do you two know each other?" Seph asked, looking from Madison to Ellen.

Ellen was in a ready stance, facing the trailhead, watching for signs of pursuit. "Let's get out of here. We can chitchat later."

There were two more cars parked in the lot than when Seph and Madison had arrived. One was the old Jeep that Will and Ellen shared. The other one was unfamiliar, a black minivan with a rent-a-car sticker. It must belong to the alumni, Seph thought. At least he hoped so, because he melted all four tires.

Seph rode with Madison in the pickup. Ellen followed

behind in the Jeep. Madison seemed accustomed to nego-
tiating country roads; she drove fast, scarcely slowing for
the curves and corners.

What a disaster. He'd been a fool to take a chance with
Madison. If not for her odd resistance to wizards, she
would have been killed, hurt, or kidnapped.

If Ellen hadn't shown up, he might be on his way back
to the Havens by now. Which reminded him. "You didn't
seem surprised to see Ellen. And her sword."

Madison glanced at him, then back at the road. "Is that
her name? I was on my way to the parking lot when she
stepped out of the trees with that thing and demanded to
know where you were. *I* thought she was standing watch
for those creeps. *She* thought I'd led you into some kind
of trap. It took us a while to sort it out. Then she went
tearing down the trail after you and I went to the car to
call 911. Only, I couldn't get my cell phone to work. It's
like, fried."

She swerved around a slow-moving van. "What the
hell happened back there, anyway? Does this kind of thing
happen to you all the time?"

Seph was scratched and scraped and bruised and his
head was throbbing. He rested it back against the seat and
closed his eyes. "Not too often. Let's just say I made a mistake."

"Those men were all witches."

"Wizards."

"Whatever. So. Are you in some kind of magical
gang war?"

He eyed her glumly, wishing she were susceptible to

wizardry so he could just wipe her mind clean. "I used to go to school with them. Now they're after me. I don't know why." He hoped they hadn't noticed anything special about Maddie. He hoped they wouldn't think about her at all.

"You want to go straight to the police station? Or we could look for a pay phone . . ."

He shook his head, staring straight ahead. "The police can't help." She opened her mouth to speak, and he held up his hand. "What am I going to tell the cops? I was attacked by wizards who tried to snare me in a spider web? And then that nice Ellen Stephenson, who plays forward on the girls' soccer team, cut two of them to pieces with her magical sword?" He thought of Ross Childers and imagined his reaction. Not pretty. "Just take me home."

"Do you think they'll give up, after today?"

"No."

"Well, you can't just wait for them to try again."

"I don't intend to." He had no real choice. He'd known that all along. He could remain a prisoner in the Sanctuary, waiting for Leicester to target someone he cared about, or he could act.

She put her hand on his arm. "I'm worried about you."

"You should be worried about yourself. People who get involved with me tend to get hurt."

"Maybe I can help you."

He couldn't believe it. They'd only just met, and they'd just had the date from hell, and she was still on his side. "It's not up to you."

By now, they'd passed the city limits, the classy stone gateway for Trinity College and the sign that said TRINITY HIGH SCHOOL DIVISION III STATE SOCCER CHAMPIONS. Seph wondered if the soft barrier worked both ways, if the alumni knew he'd returned to the Sanctuary. Maybe they could track his movements all the time. The back of his neck prickled.

Madison swerved into Seph's driveway. Ellen pulled up behind them, but made no move to get out, giving them a moment of privacy.

Madison helped unload the picnic gear onto the sidewalk. "Here, I'll help you carry it inside."

"That's all right. I'll get it."

Madison leaned against her truck, twisting one of her tiny braids between her fingers. "I have to say, that was my most eventful picnic in a long time."

Seph looked away and swallowed. "No doubt."

She gripped his hands and looked up into his face. "But I had a good time before . . . ah . . . before the mayhem."

Seph shook his head, bewildered. "I don't get it. I had to practically bribe you to get you to go out with me in the first place."

"Who says we're going out?" She pulled back her hair, and the beads clattered softly together. "For one thing, my drawing's not done. I need you to sit some more." She touched his face gently, as if mapping the bone structure underneath. "Plus, I think we could maybe be friends. You're not nearly as arrogant as I thought you were at first." She grinned. "You better call me, Witch Boy, or I'll come find you, now that I know where you live." She climbed up into the seat.

Seph stood watching until the pickup disappeared around the corner at the end of the street.

Ellen vaulted over the side of the Jeep. "Need some help?" She shouldered one of the coolers and stuffed the quilt under her arm. They managed to carry everything into the kitchen in one trip. No one was around, but based on the debris left behind, Jack and his friends had passed through. Ellen drained two bottles of water while Seph put the food away.

Ellen was a mess. She was muddy and her clothes were torn. She had a nasty cut over one eye and her cheekbone was turning purple from the rockfall. She also looked positively elated. Seph was beginning to realize that Ellen liked nothing better than a good fight, well concluded. He brought the first-aid kit from the downstairs bathroom, and they sat at the table, methodically treating each other's wounds.

"You were really good today," Ellen said, lifting the *dyrne sefa* from around her neck and handing it to Seph. "I couldn't keep track of all the charms flying around. Those guys definitely got the worst of it. Too bad we had to split, because I think we could have taken them."

"Yeah." Seph swept back Ellen's chin-length brown hair and dabbed at her bloody ear. "Not that I'm not grateful, but . . . why were you at the park?" Seph asked.

"I was—you know—out hiking."

"I don't believe you."

Ellen opened the freezer, scooped up a handful of ice,

dropped it into a plastic bag, and handed it to Seph. "Put that on your head," she suggested.

He pressed it against the knot on his forehead. "So?"

Ellen licked her finger and rubbed at a splatter of blood on her arm. "It was my day to watch you, okay?"

"What?"

"We trade off. Jack and Nick and Linda and me. Today, Jack was playing soccer, Linda was out buying a house, Nick had just been on duty two days in a row and . . ." her voice trailed off.

"You're saying you've been following me around all summer?"

Ellen cleared her throat. "Linda was afraid something like this would happen, or they'd find a way to scare you enough to make you bolt. So . . ." She shrugged her shoulders.

"I don't believe this."

"Believe me, it hasn't been the most exciting duty, up until today. *Seph goes to church. Seph goes to the symphony. Seph gets hit on by girls at the beach.*" Ellen nibbled at a broken nail. "This afternoon, I felt like some kind of chaperone, following you and your girlfriend around. So I dropped way back. Guess I shouldn't have."

"Maybe they could've seen you if you'd been closer."

"Maybe. Look, I'm sorry about your . . . ah . . . date."

"You saved my life. Thank you." Seph was glad that it was Ellen and not Jack. "You've always treated me like I'm not, you know, the enemy."

Ellen finished tweezing bits of gravel from her skinned knees, and picked up the washcloth. "We have a lot in common, you know," she said, bending her head over her work. "I never knew my parents, either. I was raised for the tournaments by wizards of the Red Rose."

"Did they have some kind of warrior school?" he asked.

She snorted. "There aren't enough of us left to fill a school. I had a warriormaster—a wizard who specializes in training warriors. What you might call the coach from hell. We were constantly on the move, being hunted by the White Rose. So I've always been the stranger. New kid at school. Kind of like you." She shook back her shining helmet of hair, as likely to seek sympathy as any leopard.

"So how'd you meet Jack?"

"The Red Rose wizards learned that the White Rose had a warrior hidden away in Trinity. So I came here to kill him." She said this matter-of-factly. "Only, I didn't know who to kill, and he didn't know who I was. He sat behind me in homeroom, of all things. He was . . . you know . . . I saw him and I went, *whoa*! I guess I had this major crush. I'd never gone out with anyone, really. He'd just broken up with that . . . that Alicia Middleton." Her inflection gave the name another meaning. "I'm not—you know—good with people. And he was, like, Mr. Popular. But we kind of clicked, and one thing led to another. . . ." The color had come up into Ellen's cheeks.

"When did you figure it out?"

"Jack gave himself away in a street fight before we left Trinity. He didn't figure out who I was until we met on the field at Raven's Ghyll." She grinned. "I'll never forget the look on his face." She carried the basin of soapy water to the sink and dumped it out.

"Well, I don't think he likes me much."

"Oh, I wouldn't say that. Jack's just less open than he used to be, before Raven's Ghyll. It takes longer to win him over." She sat down across from Seph again.

"I mean, here he was, living this storybook life in Trinity. And then, in the space of a few months, he finds out that everyone he knows is someone else entirely. His surgeon is a wizard who turned him into a magical freak. His aunt is an enchanter with a past. The old caretaker who lives over the garage is his four-hundred-year-old wizard bodyguard. His former girlfriend is a treacherous, bottom-feeding, double-crossing trader who's had him under a spell."

Seph bit the insides of his cheeks to keep from laughing.

"Even his warriormaster, Hastings, has a secret plan—to play him in the Game and win dominion over the Wizard Houses. Jack goes to the tournament and finds out his opponent is the girl he's been going out with, who, by the way, came to Trinity to assassinate him."

Seph shook his head, rendered speechless.

"Yet despite all that, I've never met anyone who was so . . . so pure. I don't mean he's a saint or anything," she added quickly, rolling her eyes. "He just . . . knows who he is and what he believes in. He doesn't change his story day to day and week to week. He's the one you want to have next to you when the bad thing goes down."

Seph wished he had the same certainty, the same sense of trajectory. He'd lost something important at the river. Something he hadn't realized was his to lose: a growing sense of security.

He'd left the Havens with the intention of taking revenge on Gregory Leicester, but he'd allowed himself to be seduced by the magic of a midwestern college town. Leicester had warned him not to talk, and, for the most part, he hadn't.

Leicester wouldn't give up. It was only a matter of time before he tried again.

Unless Seph got to him first.

"So what did those guys want?" Ellen asked. "You never said."

"They said they came to take me back to school."

"I don't get it," Ellen admitted. "Do you think they've been stalking you all this time? Why?"

"I don't think even the alumni know," Seph said.

"The what?"

"The alumni. The ones who attacked us today. They used to go to school at the Havens; now they work for Dr. Leicester. I don't think they have a clue why he wants me." He took a breath. "But Aunt Linda does."

"What are you talking about?"

"I think Aunt Linda knows why they're after me. That's why she has you all watching me every day." He tossed the ice pack from hand to hand. "I don't suppose what happened today could be kept just between us?"

"No way. Are you crazy?" Ellen stretched out her long legs. "Come on, Seph. You're in danger, and you need help. Don't you think Linda deserves to know her instincts were right?" She looked sheepish. "For weeks, we've been trying to convince her that she was being paranoid and tailing you wasn't necessary."

"I already feel like a prisoner," Seph said. "It'll only get worse if she finds out what happened. Follow me around all you want. I promise I won't leave Trinity. I won't put you in danger again. You could've been killed today, too." He reached over and closed his hand over hers, looked her in the eyes. "Ellen. Please don't tell."

Her eyes widened and she tried to withdraw her hand. "Hey!"

He increased the gentle pressure, the flow of persuasion, feeling guilty as he did so. Finally she nodded. "Okay. Our secret." And Seph smiled, satisfied.

❦ CHAPTER FOURTEEN ❧
THE WIZARD COUNCIL

Linda Downey was in town only intermittently over the following two weeks. She seemed distracted, a bundle of nerves. Maybe it's the idea of being tied down, Seph thought. She'd closed on a house on Washington Street, one block north of Jefferson, overlooking the lake. It was a small Victorian, a former summer cottage that needed considerable work. She stayed in town long enough to hire a squadron of contractors, then put Seph in charge of supervising them. "You're good at this kind of thing," she said. "Pick out some paint and wallpaper, and keep them honest."

So he spent a lot of time at the new house and also working with Fitch and Harold. He avoided the beach in the early morning, and when Madison left messages on Seph's cell phone, he didn't call her back. When it came to keeping secrets, he had the experience of a lifetime to draw upon. He was determined not to allow her or anyone else to become entangled in his personal vendetta. He remembered Leicester's warnings.

But the girls at the pavilion were no longer appealing. The image of Madison always intruded: her floppy hat with the long ribbon, the long vintage skirts and lace blouses, her sprinkling of freckles and sun-painted hair. Even the way she looked down her nose at him when she thought he was being arrogant.

Leander Hastings returned to town the second week of August. The meeting of the Council of Wizards had finally been scheduled. It was to be held in Trinity.

He had spent an afternoon at the meadow with Jack and Ellen, coaching them through their routines. It was a hot day, and it had been a tough workout. Now the warriors were collapsed into the Adirondack chairs on the front porch, having put away about a gallon of iced tea. Hastings sat on the cool concrete of the porch steps with Seph next to him.

They were talking about the upcoming meeting. Jack disapproved of the location. "Create a sanctuary for the rest of us, then throw open the doors to wizards. That makes sense."

"It's actually a good thing," Hastings replied. "It must be, because Gregory Leicester and Claude D'Orsay are opposed." His glance rested on Seph a moment.

"Why is it a good thing?" Seph asked. Tiny, late-summer gnats rose up around him. He released a bit of power to keep them at bay.

"There's considerable pressure on the council right

now. Some members want to throw away the Rules of Engagement and put down the rebellion." He smiled at Jack and Ellen. "Go to war against the Anaweir. Put these warriors and enchanters in their places." He paused. "Others want to convene an Interguild Conference as the new rules direct, and come to a workable agreement. Here in Trinity, all voices are likely to be heard, with no trickery, sorcery, or black magic going on. Well, trickery perhaps." He smiled again.

"Where's it being held?" Ellen asked. She pushed her sweaty hair behind her ears.

"They'll have it at the Legends Inn."

"How many wizards are coming?" Seph asked.

"There will be twenty altogether. That's a lot of power and spark for a small town."

"Will the Dragon be there?" Seph couldn't help asking the question. He saw the Wizard Council meeting as the classic example of the mountain coming to Mohammad.

Hastings turned and faced Seph, resting his hands on his knees. "I don't know, Seph," he said. "Why do you ask?"

Seph shifted uncomfortably under the wizard's scrutiny. "Like I said. I'd like to meet him."

"I see." Hastings continued to gaze at Seph until he shifted his eyes away. "As I told you before, the Dragon is not on the Wizard Council. He prefers to work behind the scenes." He still had not answered Seph's question, and obviously didn't intend to.

Seph was determined to meet the Dragon if he came to Trinity. Surely, he would come. But then, he wouldn't know him if he saw him on the street. "I was hoping you could introduce me."

"If I see him, perhaps I'll tell him you're looking for him."

"Will Gregory Leicester be there?" Seph persisted.

"Dr. Leicester is on the council, yes. Despite his disapproval of the location, I'm sure he wouldn't miss it."

Maybe there would be an opportunity to take Leicester by surprise.

Hastings was watching him, green eyes intent under the dark brows. It was almost as if he could read Seph's mind. "I think you should all stay away from the inn during the meeting."

He spoke to all three of them, but the message was intended for Seph. Ellen and Jack nodded, but Seph merely leaned back against the steps, closing his eyes. He'd had a revelation. Leander Hastings doesn't trust me, Seph thought. That's what this is all about.

On the first day of the council meeting, Seph set his alarm and woke up early in his aerie of a bedroom. Since the ill-fated picnic, he'd seen Linda's bodyguards following him around and pretended not to notice. Today, he hoped to shake off his shadow by leaving the house before anyone was up.

He pulled on his shorts and T-shirt, then rooted in the back corner of his underwear drawer, retrieving a small ceramic bottle with a crystal stopper. He slid it into his pocket and padded downstairs. When he reached the second floor, he saw that Jack's door was open and his bed was made. Seph glanced up and down the hallway, stepped inside Jack's room, and closed the door. He crouched down next to the bed.

Jack's sword, Shadowslayer, was underneath, in its case. Seph knew better than to touch that. Will and Fitch had helped Jack dig it out of a warrior's grave. Fitch said he'd nearly been torched when he tried to open the case.

Seph slid his hand between the mattress and box spring and pulled out a short knife in a sheath. It was not Jack's weapon of choice, but he'd used it the day Seph arrived in Trinity. Seph shoved it under his T-shirt, into the waist of his jeans. He liked having it there. It made him feel as if he were finally going to take action, instead of sitting and waiting for another attack.

He'd been over to the Legends Inn the week before, familiarizing himself with the layout of the place. Today he planned to find out where the wizards were meeting, and in particular, where they were sleeping.

Seph crept down the back staircase, hoping to leave the house by the back door, but he ran right into Becka, who was on her way out, dressed for court.

"Good morning, Seph. You're up early," she said, smiling. "Linda's home. She and Jack are in the kitchen." She said it loudly, too, so Seph knew Linda would be waiting for him to come around the corner. Shaking his head, he went on into the kitchen.

Linda and Jack were just finishing breakfast. They abruptly stopped talking when Seph came into the room. Linda looked pale and tired. She wore the same black business suit she'd worn the day she'd rescued Seph at the

Havens. "I think you've grown," she said. "Every time I go away, you grow an inch!"

"Welcome home, Aunt Linda." Seph poured himself some coffee and brought it over to the table.

"How are my contractors doing, Seph? I'm meeting with them in a little while."

The contractors were absolutely dazzled by Linda Downey. Dave Martin, the general contractor, was always thinking of some enhancement that he wanted to run by Seph, to see if he thought Linda would approve. They never questioned the fact that they were working for a sixteen-year-old boy. It was another one of those strange Weir-Anaweir relationships.

"They seem to be on schedule," he said. "Dave has some changes he wants to go over with you. The revised drawings are on the dining room table." Seph was afraid she would suggest that he go along with her to the meeting, but she didn't. He thought it might be her day to watch him after her absence, but it wasn't, because she retrieved the plans from the dining room and picked up her briefcase.

"Have fun today, guys. Be good, Seph." And then she was gone.

Jack studied Seph as if he were a problem he might have to solve. Seph was very aware of the "borrowed" knife poking him in the thigh. I guess it's Jack's day to watch me, he thought.

"We're going sailing today," Jack said abruptly.

Seph's heart sank. The Swift-Downey family had a sailboat, a day sailer they kept in the water all season. Jack had been promising to take Seph out on the lake. But it had never worked out. Until today.

"Today?" Seph cast about for an excuse. "You know, today really isn't a very . . . I mean, I don't really . . ."

"We won't go very far out," Jack said, giving him that dead-on look. "We'll just run up and down the shoreline. Will and Fitch are coming. My mom packed a lunch. It's all set."

Seph was caught, and he knew it. Whose idea was this? he wondered. The plan was clearly designed to keep him away from the inn.

"Okay," Seph said, forcing enthusiasm. "Great!"

Will and Fitch were waiting on the pier, chatting with Harold Fry, when they arrived at the harbor.

Harold nodded to Jack and Seph. "Morning, boys." The old man watched as Jack leaped nimbly into the dinghy and stowed the gear. "When're you going to get yourself a real boat, Jack?"

"Thats okay, Harold, this is all I can handle for now." Jack braced the dinghy while Seph, Will, and Fitch climbed aboard.

"I'm psyched," Fitch said as they rowed out to where *Windego* was anchored in the harbor. "I've been dropping hints about going sailing all summer." It seemed everyone was happy about the excursion but Seph.

It *was* a beautiful day. The lake was a translucent bottle-green color, and only a few high clouds interrupted the endless blue of the sky as Jack fired up the motor to push the boat out of the harbor. Dozens of white sails pricked the horizon.

Once they were in open water, Seph resigned himself to the situation, working hard to crew under Jack's direction. He remembered a little about managing the sails from the times he'd been out with Warren Barber. Jack was a smart and aggressive skipper, if Seph was any judge. Eventually Jack turned the mainsail sheet over to Seph while he managed the jib. The wind was brisk out of the west, and when they got it right, the boat flew over the water, smashing through the great, lazy fair-weather swells. He and Jack traded off, but Will and Fitch seemed inclined to sit in the spray at the bow of the boat and do as little work as possible.

They anchored off one of the less-crowded beaches east of Trinity, and went swimming. Seph left Jack's knife carefully hidden in his clothes. The water was still cool, even in August, but it was a hot day, and after only a brief period on deck they were ready to go back in.

After a leisurely lunch and another swim, they dozed for a time on deck, the boat gently rocking in the swells, before heading back toward town. They were moving against the wind this time, and had to do some elaborate tacking. It took them much longer to return than it had to sail out.

"You're hired, Seph," Jack said, grinning as Seph nailed a complicated come-about. "Better than these two losers." He nodded at Will and Fitch.

Fitch lifted his can of pop in a toast. "To the crew."

It was late afternoon when Jack started up the motor and they threaded their way back into the harbor. A perfect day, but Seph couldn't help wondering if the meetings at the Legends might still be going on. He'd already wasted one day out of two.

The other three had remained in their swimming gear, but he had changed back into his clothes, sticking the knife back under his waistband.

When the dinghy had drifted close enough, Jack leaped out onto the pier and secured the line. He and Seph muscled the cooler out of the boat and carried their gear up the steps to the marina parking lot.

Jack turned back toward the marina office. "I'm going to go see what kind of bait Jerry's got," he explained. "Maybe we can go fishing tomorrow." He headed back down the steps.

And that will take care of tomorrow, Seph thought. Now might be his only chance to break away. As soon as Jack was out of sight, Seph said, as if he'd only just thought of it, "I just remembered, I was supposed to meet Aunt Linda over at the new house at four thirty. I'm already late. Tell Jack I had to go." Without waiting for a response, he sprinted through the parking lot and around the corner.

The Legends Inn was about a quarter mile west of the marina, on a point of land that formed one side of the harbor. Seph wondered if Jack would guess where he had gone and come after him. He would just have to move quickly enough to stay ahead of him.

The front door of the inn opened into the parlor, where he'd made his date with Madison Moss. From his previous visit, Seph knew that the meeting rooms and dining rooms lay immediately beyond. He stopped at the reception desk and smiled at the girl in the high-necked Victorian blouse.

"Can you tell me if the meeting is still going on?" he asked politely.

She looked Seph up and down skeptically, disapproving of his sailing clothes. "The meetings are over for the day. They just adjourned about a half hour ago."

"I have a message for one of the participants, name of Gregory Leicester. Can you tell me which room is his?"

"And you are?"

"Aaron Hanlon."

She extended her hand. "I'll give him the message."

"I need to deliver it in person."

"Shall I ring him for you?" She put her hand on the phone on the desk.

"That's okay," Seph said hastily. "If he's not there, I'll just slip it under his door."

She hesitated. There was obviously a policy. Seph was beginning to think he was going to have to use more overt persuasion. But it seemed she saw little threat in Seph. "He's in Room 210. Second floor. The elevator is over there." She pointed.

"Thank you."

He decided to take the stairs instead, reasoning that he was less likely to run into someone he knew. It also allowed him to delay things that much longer. He could think about murdering Gregory Leicester all the way up to coming face-to-face with the wizard. Then the image failed. Not a good omen. *"Vous devez envisager le success,"* Genevieve had often said to him. You must envision success.

He realized he was leaving a clear trail for anyone who wanted to track him down. More than that, he knew that murder was a mortal sin, the kind that took you straight to hell. But he had no choice. Leicester had already killed Trevor and Jason, and it seemed he still had plans for Seph. Painful plans, no doubt.

You've been a tough little bastard, Leicester had said. *Now we'll find out just how tough you are.* Fragments of nightmares came back to him, like jagged glass beneath his skin. They'd come close to taking him at the river; they might succeed the next time.

I know where you live, Barber had said. *We'll find Linda Downey and her sister, Rebecca. We'll find your girl. We'll find your warrior friend. And, in the end, we'll find you.*

Seph paused in the stairwell and readied his weapons.

His right hand found the knife under his T-shirt, and he slipped it out into his hand. He pulled the bottle from his pocket, yanked the stopper, and daubed the blade liberally with the contents. Mercedes Foster had warned him that it was more potent than the venom of any snake, and undetectable by Anaweir medicine. Carefully, he slid the knife back into its sheath. Returning the bottle to his pocket, he groped for the portal at his neck. He knew better than to engage Leicester directly. He would wait, unnoticed, like a viper in the grass, for the headmaster to come within reach of his sting.

Unnoticeable Seph emerged from the stairwell and walked quickly down the hall toward the end, where he knew 210 must be.

"Seph! Seph McCauley, is that you?"

He spun around, clutching for the knife, his breath catching in his throat. His first thought was that the always reliable unnoticeable charm hadn't worked.

But no. It was Madison Moss in a long skirt and sleeveless cotton sweater and little strappy sandals, her exuberant hair gathered into a net studded with rhinestones. His heart stuttered at the sight of her. She bore down on him, as beautiful and dangerous as a summer storm over the lake. It seemed that Madison was as impervious to unnoticeable charms as to other forms of wizardry.

"Where have you been?" she hissed. "I've left messages, I've stopped by your house . . ."

He raised his hands as if he could hold her off. "Madison, we can't. This isn't a good time."

"Well, I guess there *is* no good time. I thought we were friends. If this is about what happened at the river, I think I have the right to make my own choices."

She kept coming forward, and he backed away until she had him penned in a little alcove at the end of the hall. Desperate to stop the flow of words, he gripped her wrist and pulled her toward him, pressing his hand over her mouth. "Listen, some of those people we saw at the river are right here at the inn. They'd like nothing better than to finish what they started."

Madison broke away from him and looked up and down the hallway. Then she moved closer to him and lowered her voice. "Then why are you here?" Her voice tremored a bit.

A question that Seph could not answer. He gripped

her elbows. "They won't notice me. I'll be fine unless you give me away."

She blinked at him. "You expect me to believe you're invisible? Right." But she sounded a little unsure of her‐self.

Then he heard footsteps. He looked over Madison's shoulder and saw someone tall and angular striding toward them down the hall, like an avenging spirit.

It was Leander Hastings.

Seph nodded toward Hastings. "He's looking for me. Please don't say anything." And he faded back into the alcove.

Madison did not turn around. She advanced to the window and pretended to look out, resting her hands on the sill. Hastings came on, scanning the room numbers to either side. He paused when he came to 210, turned aside, put his ear to the door, and knocked. There was no response. He straightened and stood, watching Madison for a moment.

"Excuse me." She winced when he spoke, then turned toward him, gripping her skirts on either side. "Have you seen a young man about your age, tall and thin, dark curly hair?" Hastings lodged himself in the entrance to the alcove, effectively preventing escape.

"No, sir, I haven't." She looked up at him, eyes bright, color high. "If he's a guest at the inn, you could check at the front desk." Her eyes flicked quickly toward Seph, as if to verify that he was still there. Then back to Hastings.

"He's not a guest, though I have reason to believe he

might have come up here. He passed by the front desk not ten minutes ago." Hastings leaned against the doorframe, frowning.

Madison shrugged. "Haven't seen him. Now, if you'll excuse me, I have work to do."

Hasting didn't move. He searched the alcove with his eyes, then looked back at Madison. She glanced again at Seph. He shook his head, putting his finger to his lips. Hastings reached into his trouser pocket, drew out a small pouch, fumbled it open, then suddenly flung its contents toward Seph. It was a light, glittery powder, and it coalesced around Seph like a halo. Hastings groped into the middle of it, his fingers closing on the chain around Seph's neck. The links dissolved under the wizard's touch, and the *dyrne sefa* fell free.

Unnoticeable Seph was noticeable once again.

"So." Hastings retrieved the *dyrne sefa* and put it into his pocket. Then dropped a heavy hand onto Seph's shoulder, spun him around, and slammed him up against the wall. "I noticed at Becka's that you were wearing a heartstone. You've obviously learned how to use it." His eyes were cold and green as the ice that forms on the deepest lakes in Canada. "Who are you looking for, Seph?" the wizard said. "Perhaps I can help you."

It was hard to speak and hard not to, with all that wizard pressure on him.

"Tell me," Hastings said softly. "Are you still looking for the Dragon?" His hand pressed lightly against Seph's windpipe, vibrating with power. Even the slight pressure made it difficult to breathe.

"I'm . . . I'm looking for Gregory Leicester," Seph whispered faintly.

"You're looking for your master, then? Have something to tell him, do you?"

"You . . . leave . . . him . . . alone, do you hear me?"

In the heat of the moment, Seph had nearly forgotten Madison. Now Hastings and Seph both turned to look at her. Seph blinked to clear his vision and Hastings even loosened his grip slightly.

She grabbed Seph's arm. Power slid through Seph like hot metal through flesh, from Hastings to Madison, scouring Seph's brain of coherent thought. Seph fell, breaking the connection between them, landing awkwardly on his side.

Swearing softly, Maddie knelt next to Seph, cradling his head in her arms. Seph wanted to reassure her, but he could find no words. All he could do was gape at her.

She was angry. That was the first thing he noticed. But if the glitter powder revealed Seph's power like an aura, it layered her in shadow. It feathered her arms as she moved, shrouded her glittering hair, rendering her insubstantial as a spirit, a negative image to Seph's positive.

Hastings sat slumped against the wall, breathing hard, similarly incapacitated. He squinted at Madison and shook his head. "An elicitor," he whispered. "You must be. I didn't think they really existed."

"I don't know what you're talking about, but if you hurt him again, I'll . . ." She extended her hands toward Hasting, who drew back hastily, as if afraid of being burnt, still staring at Madison in wonder.

"Well, well. What am I interrupting, here?"

Like coconspirators, they looked up as one. Gregory Leicester stood in the entry to the alcove, holding an ice bucket that dripped condensation. He looked from Seph and Madison to Hastings, rubbing his chin thoughtfully.

"We were just talking about you, Gregory," Leander Hastings said, sounding somehow collected in spite of his position on the floor. He looked from Leicester to Seph as if trying to discern the links between them.

"Perhaps you would care to come in and have a drink, Leander," Leicester offered. "I was about to have one myself. You could celebrate your victory today."

"It wasn't my victory," Hastings said, rising to his feet. "There is considerable support for the new constitution on the council."

"But you spoke eloquently on its behalf. Though why you want to empower hedge prophets, enchanters, and warriors, I haven't a clue." He might have said slime, vermin, and scum of the earth.

"I don't know what you think you're giving up. Other than the ability to push people around."

"Then you won't join me for that drink?" Leicester seemed to notice Seph for the first time. "Hello, Joseph. Warren tells me he ran into you at the park the other day."

Seph extracted himself from Maddie's embrace and stood. "You stay away from me, and tell Barber and the others to do the same. Or no one walks away next time."

"And yet, here you are, lurking outside my door." Leicester glanced at Hastings, as if expecting him to intervene. "Perhaps you've finally realized that you belong with us."

"I'm never going back."

"We'll see." The wizard looked over Seph's shoulder at Madison. "Aren't you going to introduce me to your friend?"

Reverberating with anger, Madison tried to push forward, but Seph stuck out his arm to prevent her.

"You stay away from her," Seph said.

"Never mind. I know how to find her. Madison, isn't it? Such an unusual name." Leicester turned away, shifting the bucket into the crook of his arm and fitting his key into the lock.

Seph groped for his knife, slid it free, and lunged toward Leicester. Hastings reached around from behind and gripped his wrist, dragging him back, wrapping the other arm around his body, increasing the pressure and power until Seph's hand went numb and the knife thudded on the carpet. Hastings covered it with his foot.

Hastings held Seph immobile until the oblivious Leicester entered his room and shut the door. Hastings scooped up the knife and, gripping the back of Seph's neck, propelled him down the hall to Room 206. He unlocked the door and pushed him inside. Madison followed them in and pulled the door shut behind her.

The room seemed an odd setting for Hastings: fussy with fabrics and Victorian touches, furnished with antiques of mixed heritage. The window opened to a view of the lake. A suitcase lay open on one of the beds. A small table was drawn up by the window, littered with the debris of a meeting: cups, saucers, glasses, and papers.

Hastings looked at Madison, as if wishing he could make her disappear. Her expression and body language said she had no intention of leaving. Seph would have liked to have seen Hastings try and evict her after what she'd done to him in the hallway.

Instead, Hastings leaned against the door, his arms folded across his chest. "What shall we do with you, Seph?"

"This is none of your business. Why don't you just leave me alone?" Seph stood, feet braced apart, breathing hard. He jerked his head toward Madison. "You should go."

"I'm not leaving this time." Madison sat down on the bed, looking mulish.

Hastings ignored this exchange. "I told Linda it was too risky to let you stay here. It seems I was right. When Jack called me, I knew exactly where to look for you."

"If it's a problem, just drive me to the city limits. The alumni will be happy to take me off your hands."

Hastings's head came up. "The alumni?"

"Leicester's wizard slaves. I'm wanted back at school, it seems."

Hastings squinted at him as if puzzled. Then sat down in one of the chairs next to the table. "Tell me about school."

"The Havens? They have five hundred spectacular acres on the Atlantic Ocean. They win the sailing cup every year." Seph was being a smartass, and he knew it. "Do you have a specific question?"

"As it happens, I know something about the Havens,"

Hastings said. "Can you explain to me how you survived a year in that place? Can you tell me why you're not with them?"

Seph had a sudden strong desire to win the wizard over. He was tired of worrying about the alumni; tired of keeping secrets; tired of trying to solve his problems on his own; tired of sparring with a powerful wizard who should be his ally. If he couldn't find the Dragon, maybe Hastings would do. "I used the heartstone. The *dyrne sefa.*"

Hastings pulled the talisman out of his pocket and handed it back to Seph. "Where did you get it?"

"Another student gave it to me and taught me how to use it. His name was Jason Haley." Seph shoved the piece into the pocket of his shorts. "He was my friend. He was helping me. So they killed him." He began pacing back and forth. "A week ago, Leicester sent some of the alumni to kidnap me. I left the sanctuary, and they attacked me." He nodded at Madison. "If not for Madison, here, and Ellen, they would have taken me." He rubbed his temples. "I can't stand it anymore. They tortured me for months. They murdered my friends. Why won't they leave me alone?"

He walked to the window and rested his hands on the sill, looking out at the water. A chair scraped on the wood floor, and then Hastings was beside him. He grabbed Seph's chin and forced his face around so he could look him in the eyes. It reminded him of Jason, the night he'd explained to Seph about the Weir. After a moment, Hastings let him go and turned away.

Something had changed, but Seph wasn't sure what or

how. He went and sat down on the bed next to Madison and picked up her hand, enclosing it between his two. "I'm sorry, Madison. I've been a jerk. It's just . . . they threatened to . . . I don't want you to get hurt."

"There's more than one way to hurt a person, Witch Boy," she said, looking down at their joined hands. "And different kinds of risks." She looked up at Hastings. "What was that you called me in the hallway?"

The wizard turned and leaned against the window seat. "An elicitor."

She made a face. "What's that? It sounds, you know, like something you'd get arrested for."

"It's not nearly common enough to be illegal." Hastings studied her with frank interest. "In fact, although I've heard of elicitors, I've never encountered one before."

"Jason never mentioned elicitors when he described the guilds," Seph said.

Hastings nodded. "Elicitors are not Weir, since they have no Weirstones. But they have the ability to *elicit* magic, to draw it away from others. And, of course, they're resistant to charms. As you've probably guessed by now," he added.

"Are they just resistant to wizards, or to the Anawizard Weir?"

Hastings toyed with the ring on his right hand. "My understanding is that they draw magic of all kinds."

"What happens to the power?" Seph asked. "Does it just dissipate, or could an elicitor use it herself?"

Hastings shrugged. "I don't know."

Madison was looking from Seph to Hastings as if

they'd suddenly lapsed into French. "I have no idea what you two are talking about. Can someone help me out here?"

Seph traced the lines on her palm. "The Weir are people born with magical gifts. Wizards like us have the broadest range of powers. Others are specialists; for instance, they can see the future, or make magical tools and remedies. The witches you knew at home are probably either wizards or enchanters."

"How do you two know each other?" Hastings asked.

Madison kicked off her sandals and dug her bare toes into the rug. "Seph picked me up on the beach one morning."

"She works here at the inn," Seph added.

At that she looked at her watch, and groaned. "My supervisor's going to kill me. I'm on duty." She slipped her feet back into her shoes and stood. "I have to go."

"I'll call you," Seph said.

"Right." And she was out the door.

Hastings looked after her thoughtfully. "There's another term for elicitors," he said.

"What's that?"

"Eviscerators." He smiled wryly. "Coined by wizards, no doubt. Although they have no magic of their own, they're very dangerous creatures. Are you sure you can trust her? Unfortunately, there's no way to determine if she's telling the truth."

Meaning by a wizard's touch, no doubt. "So I guess we just have to rely on our judgment, don't we? Like the Anaweir," Seph retorted, looking Hastings in the eyes.

The wizard raised his hand. "All right. You're the best judge, I suppose." He paused, as if debating what to say next. "Look. It doesn't matter who you're after or how strong the justification. You cannot attack anyone at the conference. This wasn't a good day for Gregory Leicester. He would seize any excuse to undo what's been done."

"What happened?"

"The council agreed to convene an Interguild Conference to consider a new constitution based on the revised rules. If Leicester and D'Orsay can't get their own way within a council of their peers, it's even less likely where there are warriors and enchanters represented."

"Seph, you have to promise me you won't do anything to disrupt the conference. It would play right into Leicester's hands."

"Killing Leicester is the best thing that could happen, it seems to me." He looked up into Hastings's scowl. Reluctantly, he said, "Okay, I promise."

"You'll need to stick with Jack all day tomorrow, or I'll know about it. And you're not to come near the inn. If you violate either of those conditions, it doesn't matter what Linda says. I'll put you away where you can't cause any more mischief."

Seph nodded. He didn't have much choice. "Okay."

"I'll take you home, then," said Leander Hastings.

The next day, Jack and Seph left at four a.m. to go fishing in the western basin. Seph learned to bait hooks, cast a line, and clean fish. By the time they returned, the meetings at the Legends were over, and the council had dispersed. Most left the Sanctuary as quickly as possible.

That evening, Leander Hastings, Ellen Stephenson, and Madison Moss came to dinner. Becka was attending a concert at the Institute. It was one of the warm nights at the end of summer that make promises that won't be kept. Seph and Madison rolled lake perch in cracker crumbs and fried them while Linda and Jack made salads and roasted the corn. Although everyone was eager to hear what had transpired at the Legends, Linda would allow no discussion of events at the conference until dessert was served.

"So how'd it go?" Jack demanded, when the ban was finally lifted. They were eating ice cream on the screened porch. Seph and Madison had claimed the wicker swing and were pleasantly crowded in together.

"I'd say the outcome was mixed today," Hastings replied. "Leicester and D'Orsay introduced an alternative constitution and put it on the agenda for consideration at the joint meeting." He shook his head. "I don't know how it could possibly pass. It's a nasty document. Worse than the original rules." He looked over at Linda, as if to get her reaction, but she seemed to be deep in thought.

"One concern is the location of the conference. They were unable to change the composition of the Interguild Council, but they argued against holding the next meeting in the Sanctuary. They say that this is a hostile environment, that the whole concept was forced on the Wizard Council at the tournament last summer. Which it was."

Hastings shrugged. "Leicester and his group had

already lost on many of the important issues. I think there was some desire on the part of the Wizard Council to appease them somehow."

"Where will the meeting be held?" Seph asked.

"Second Sister. It's an island in Lake Erie, in the western basin, actually Canadian." Hastings explained. "Privately owned."

"Second Sister?" Jack raised an eyebrow. "I didn't think there was anything there."

"There's an old winery, rather like a great stone castle. It's been renovated into a guesthouse. The feeling was that this would be a good compromise. Close to the Sanctuary, convenient for everyone."

"They didn't want to have it in Raven's Ghyll?" Jack asked. That had been the site of the tournament the summer before, in England. It was Claude D'Orsay's ancestral home, a stronghold of wizards. D'Orsay was the hereditary Gamemaster for the tournaments. Seph knew all this from Jack and Ellen.

Hastings shook his head. "Frankly, none of the other Weir would set foot in the Ghyll. It will be hard enough to convince them to sit down in the same room with members of the Wizard Council.

"They also insisted that members of the Wizard Council be present as observers. That notion was popular with wizards, of course, those on both sides of the issue who want to keep an eye on the process. I just hope we haven't given up something important. The location was suggested by Adam Sedgwick. He's an ally of D'Orsay's. And D'Orsay and Leicester seconded it right away."

"Have you found out who owns it?" Linda asked.

"A group of investors from Detroit. Friends of Sedgwick's." He shrugged.

"When will the meeting be?" Seph asked.

"In two weeks," said Hastings. "Invitations will go out in a week. A subcommittee is going to decide who gets invited. That's me, Ravenstock, Leicester, and D'Orsay."

Seph became alert at the name Ravenstock. "I hope Ravenstock is on our side," he said.

"He's with us now. So the subcommittee is evenly divided. It won't be easy coming to an agreement on the membership."

"I don't think wizards should pick the attendees," Linda said, as if coming out of her trance. "Seems like the other guilds should choose their own representatives."

"Seems like," Hastings agreed. "Only, they're not well organized. Until this year, they were either hiding out or in service to wizards." He turned to Jack and Ellen. "Don't be surprised if you are named to the Interguild Council."

Ellen sat up straighter, looking dismayed. "Can't you find someone else? How am I supposed to negotiate with a bunch of wizards?"

"Don't worry." Hastings smiled at her. "There will be a whole team there. Besides, I think you underestimate yourself."

Seph heard this exchange as if from a distance, distracted by Madison's hip pressing against his and her long hair brushing his arm, her bare back with its scattering of freckles. He knew he didn't have to worry about being invited to the council meeting. He was small change in the wizard world.

He wondered if the results of the proceedings would make any difference in his own personal situation. Perhaps a new constitution would get Leicester off his back, give him something else to keep him occupied, since the current rules had done nothing to discourage him. It was something to hope for, but Seph was not optimistic.

There was one other card to play. He looked across at Linda Downey. Every day his wizardry skills were growing. One day soon, he would ask his questions, and she would answer him.

ᝦ Chapter Fifteen ᝦ
The Storm

The day after the conference, Hastings left for New York, where the subcommittee was convening. Matters were moving fast. The invitees would not have much time to make their decisions. Perhaps that was part of the strategy.

School was scheduled to start in a few weeks, but it was hard to focus on that with so much going on in the parallel universe of the Weir. Seph had already registered at the high school and signed up for his classes. He had never gone to a public school, but he was looking forward to it, especially now that he might actually stay and graduate.

Linda's house was scheduled to be finished by Halloween. She and Seph visited daily to monitor its progress. His room had its own bathroom and a turret with a winding staircase, another special touch the contractor had suggested.

Madison worked a heavy schedule at the Legends, but Seph often met her for breakfast before she started her shift. They sometimes walked on the beach early in the morning or on muggy summer nights after her shift ended. They attended openings at Trinity's Chapel Gallery. When she worked a double shift, they would go to afternoon matinees in the air-conditioned downtown theater, blinking like nocturnal animals when they emerged into the brilliant sunshine.

She set limits that suggested that she just wanted to be friends. Seph was hoping for something more. She seemed to look on Seph as a window into another world.

There was a wistful urgency to summer pastimes in the last days before school started. Jack made plans to take the sailboat out of the water, since it was unlikely there would be time to go sailing once school was in session. So a week after the end of the Wizard Council, Jack invited Ellen, Seph, and Madison to go sailing one last time.

It was a beautiful late-summer day, not too hot, with high clouds and a brisk breeze coming out of the west. There were whitecaps out beyond the cut from the harbor. The spray hit their faces as they headed into the wind, toward Sandusky. Madison had never been sailing; she couldn't swim, in fact. Seph had strapped her into a bright orange life jacket before they left the dock. She'd been pale and snappish, but determined to go.

Now her apprehension seemed to have faded. She sat in the right rear corner of the boat, one hand trailing in the water, her face turned up to catch the spray. She'd pulled her hair back into a ponytail, anchoring a Cincinnati Reds baseball cap.

Ellen's sailing skills were on par with Seph's. She'd never sailed before coming to Trinity, having spent all her time training to kill people. But she was strong and willing, and soon Seph and Ellen were making the boat fly over the waves, while Jack supervised from a seat on the side of the boat.

Seph loved this business of capturing the wind, of having his way with it. The breeze made him feel like he was flying. He suddenly realized that he was very much at home on the water after a summer in Trinity. The contrast with his season at the Havens was breathtaking.

It was after two when they started out, and by four, they were already several miles west of Trinity. The weather seemed to be turning. Great towers of clouds had piled up off to the west, and the sky that had been blue was rapidly darkening.

"I don't remember hearing anything about thunderstorms," Jack said, puzzled. "We'd better head back." Seph and Ellen brought the boat about, expecting the sails to fill with the freshening wind, but it died away suddenly, then changed direction, now blowing strongly from the east. They continued to have to tack back and forth, finding it just as hard to head back as it had been to head out, against the wind.

"That's weird," Jack said. "Especially with what's coming out of the west." He looked apprehensively over his shoulder. The ragged edges of the cloud bank were overtaking them. The surface winds were blowing one way, and the winds aloft another. "We'd better use the engine or we'll never outrun it. I'll bring her in a little closer to shore." He sat down in the captain's chair and tried to start up the engine. There was no response—no sound, save the slap of water against the hull of the boat.

Jack lifted the cowling, peered into the tangle of metal, made a few adjustments, and tried again. Still nothing. He shook his head. "This thing worked fine two hours ago when we left the harbor." He stood carefully and looked about, scanning the horizon. The few boats that were left were far ahead of them, scurrying for shore.

The strange easterly was blowing stronger than ever, and the boat began to wobble in the heavy seas. Madison crouched in the corner, holding on to her hat with one hand, gripping the toe rail with the other. Jack helped Seph and Ellen put up the storm jib and took over the management of the sails. Despite all their efforts and Jack's expertise, the boat seemed to be standing still in the water as the storm overtook them. Jack strapped on his life jacket and made sure everyone else did, too.

The light had fled, and the lake had turned from a deep blue to a slate gray color, flecked with white-and-yellow foam. The boat pitched and rolled as the seas grew heavier. Lightning strobed across the sky and thunder boomed from not far off.

"Try the radio," Jack directed Ellen. She played with it for a few minutes. There was no static. Nothing. "Either I'm not doing it right, or it's not working." she reported. Leaving the sails in Seph's hands for a moment, Jack tried it himself. The radio was dead.

By now the wind was a gale, the noise of the wind and the water so loud they couldn't hear each other, even when they shouted. Jack moved quickly from one side of the boat to the other, ducking under the boom, directing them with hand gestures. A few large drops of rain splattered on the deck, although by now there was so much water aboard it was hard to tell.

Seph realized the boat was actually being driven backward in the water, stern first, pushed by the wind toward the west. He looked at Jack, who had stopped fussing with the sails and was staring, one hand on the tiller, at the rear of the boat. Slipping and sliding on the wet decking, they lowered the sails with the downhaul sheets and snugged the sails to the poles. Water slopped over the stern as the boat plowed on, threatening to founder them. Jack used the rudder to bring the boat about. They picked up speed, cutting through the tops of waves as if they were under full canvas. Heading northwest.

And then it came to Seph, a revelation. *You're no longer in the Sanctuary. You're nowhere, but you're going somewhere, and you're taking three people with you.*

The rain was sheeting down in torrents, icy needles against the skin. Their clothes and hair were plastered to their bodies, and the noise of the storm was a constant clamor. Madison hung on grimly, shifting her weight on command to keep the boat righted. Jack was still maneuvering the rudder, while Seph and Ellen released a little reefed canvas. The boat flew on toward an unknown destination. Away from Trinity.

Seph had an idea, a desperate one. Being careful to

keep a firm hold on the rail, he worked his way to the stern, where there was a storage compartment under the seat. He forced the door open and pulled out a bright yellow, rubbery cylindrical object. Seph staggered back to the rail, clutching his prize against his chest.

"What are you doing with the raft?" Jack demanded.

Seph hooked both arms over the rail and then lifted his leg over.

"Seph, don't!" Madison released her death hold on the rail and slip-slid toward him. Then the boat bucked and she lost her footing and fell, sliding across the wet deck. She grabbed on to the rail and pulled herself into a sitting position. A cut above her right eye welled up, the blood sluicing away in the rain as quickly as it appeared.

"Stay where you are!" he shouted, lifting his other leg over the rail. He clung to the outside, great swells crashing over him, trying to maneuver the raft into the right position.

"Seph!" Madison was inching toward him again. "What's the matter with you?"

"Don't you see? The storm's for me," Seph said.

Jack struggled with the tiller, trying to keep the boat from turning crosswise to the wind. "If you think this is wizardry, you're wrong! Not even a wizard can control the weather."

"Explain this, then!" Seph would have waved his arm had he dared to let go. "I'm going to bail. Maybe you'll be all right."

"Come on, man!" Jack said desperately. "Get back in the boat. We've done okay so far."

"It's not just the journey, it's the destination you should worry about." The boat was still flying west, as if pushed by an invisible engine.

The next part would be tricky. Somehow he needed to land in the raft. Turning his back to the rail, he grabbed the cord on the CO_2 cartridge in his teeth and gave it a fierce yank. The raft inflated like a yellow bomb going off and Seph let go of the rail just as a body slammed into him.

He fell through space in a tangle of arms and legs. The raft smacked into the water, and Seph and his attacker smacked into the raft a moment later. Water washed over them, and the raft bobbed to the surface like a cork. Seph thrashed free, rolled over, and pushed himself into a sitting position, spitting out saltwater.

Madison lay next to him, coughing and sputtering. He slid his hands under her arms and hauled her upright, slapping her back to clear the water from her lungs. Her hair hung in tangles, her teeth were chattering, and she looked scared to death.

"Why would you do that?" he said, genuinely bewildered.

She just shook her head. He pulled her in close, trying to warm her with his body. The sailboat was nowhere to be seen. He and Madison and the raft were still flying before the wind.

Jack saw the raft momentarily, a yellow spot on the dark water, before it was swallowed up by the storm. He stood at the railing where he'd tried to grab Seph at the last minute. Ellen was kneeling, stunned, in the bottom of the boat.

The boat pitched and shuddered as the swells crashed into it. Jack lunged and seized the rudder, turning the boat into the wind, while Ellen pulled to her feet and scanned the water around them for the raft.

The storm seemed to be abating. The wind dwindled, the rain slowed and stopped. The sickening pitching of the boat receded. Ellen released her grip on the rail, regaining a little color. Jack looked to the west, where a dark curtain receded across the sullen waves. To the east, the sky was brightening.

There was no sign of Seph McCauley or Madison Moss.

Seph soon realized that what he did or did not do had absolutely no influence on the trajectory or speed of the raft. He lay back, holding tightly to the rubber handles on the sides, with Madison tucked in next to him, her head resting on his shoulder. When they hit a particularly fierce wave, water cascaded over them, but they could not be any wetter than they were already. The storm raged around them, despite the fact that Seph was cooperating in the only way he knew how.

Wherever they were going, he was sure it was bad news; although, if they were going to the Havens, they were heading in the wrong direction.

He looked down at Madison. She was lying still, eyes wide open, her left hand still gripping his life jacket. Eventually, like an animal retreating from too much stimulus, he slept.

When he awoke, it was dark and still storming, lightning harsh against his eyes, and thunder grumbling like the sound of a battle moving away from him. But it wasn't thunder or lightning that had woken him, but the grating crunch as the floor of the raft hit bottom.

Looking over the side, he saw that it had been driven up in the shallows next to a beach. It was a typical lake beach, a mixture of sand and rocks. The surface of the water surrounding the boat was littered with seaweed and debris, driven there by the storm.

He shook Madison awake. She blinked at him, then floundered a bit, trying to sit up. Gripping her wrist, he pulled her upright. "We've run aground somewhere. They probably know I'm here, but I doubt they know about you."

Seph slid out of the raft into knee-deep water and helped Madison out after him. They waded toward shore, pushing the raft ahead of them. Seph was covered in bruises, cuts, and scrapes.

They shoved the raft high on the beach, so it was out of the water and they were satisfied it wouldn't float away. He put a large rock in its center to anchor it. It would have made a good shelter, but a bright yellow raft was just too conspicuous.

Dense forest crowded the beach on three sides. The sand was spattered with flotsam from the storm, pockmarked from the rain, empty of footprints. Seph shivered. The air was chilly, and he was soaked through. It had nearly stopped raining.

"Come on." Seph was anxious to get off the open beach.

The late-summer woods were dark and clogged with underbrush. Water cascaded down on them from above as they fought their way through it. Seph plowed forward, squinting into the gloom on either side. He finally found a place where two trees had sagged together, forming a sort of cave that was reasonably dry and half filled with leaves. Not the best, but just then he couldn't be choosy.

"Why don't you stay here," he said to Madison. "If you burrow down into the leaves it might be warmer."

She swiped her hair back. "I think it's better if we stay together. I could help you."

"If they're looking for me it's better if we split up. I'm going to try to find out where we are and what's going on, and then I'll come back for you. If I don't come by sunup, try to find a house or a police station." Hopefully, someone other than Leicester or the alumni. It was the only plan he could come up with.

Frowning, she reached up and picked leaves from the tangle of his hair. "If you don't come back, Witch Boy, I'm coming after you." Then she crawled back into the shadows between the great trees.

Reasoning that those hunting him would most likely target the beach where they'd landed, Seph walked east, away from the beach. An overgrown path followed the shoreline. It was easier going on the trail than through the tangle of trees and briars and poison ivy. The humid air had cleared in the wake of the storm, and it had cooled considerably. Clouds sailed east, driven by a brisk wind, and a few stars pricked the western sky. The birds were beginning their predawn chorus.

He had walked nearly a mile when he came upon a ramshackle dock and padlocked, boarded-up cottage. He judged that it would make a better shelter for a cold, wet person than a hollow between two trees. Not only that, the padlock looked flimsy. Seph stooped and pried up a stone from the walkway.

A slight sound behind him alerted him to danger. Then a nervous voice, mangling the language of magic. He turned, still in a crouch, so as to make a smaller target, and threw. The stone struck Peter Conroy in the forehead, shattering his glasses and putting an immediate end to the charm. Seph tackled him around the knees, and they rolled down the slope into the water. They wrestled in the shallows, spouting charms and counters until Seph got Peter in a headlock and held his head under water long enough to lay an immobilization charm on him. Then he gripped Peter by the shoulders and dragged him up onto the beach, not an easy task since Peter probably outweighed him by half.

Peter was agitated, wheezing, red in the face. "Inhaler!" he gasped. Seph dug in Peter's jacket pocket, found the inhaler and gave him a puff. The wheezing subsided and Peter no longer looked as if he were asphyxiating, though he still looked terrified.

"Please don't tell Dr. Leicester," he begged. Despite the chilly air, sweat pebbled his forehead and ran down his face.

"I won't say anything if you tell me what's going on," Seph said. "Where are we?"

"I . . . I . . . S-s-Second Sister. We're on Second Sister."

Seph sat back on his heels. "Second Sister? Isn't that the island where the Interguild Conference is being held?"

Peter nodded miserably. "Dr. Leicester wanted us to bring you before they all got here."

"*You* brought me? How'd you do that? I thought wizards can't control the weather."

"Usually, they can't. But Dr. Leicester, he uses us, he *links* us, and with all of us together, he can do whatever he wants."

"What do you mean, he links you?" Jason had used that term, but Seph wasn't sure what it meant. "You mean, like what he wanted to do to me at the chapel?"

"It's a charm. Back at school, I . . . I didn't even know about wizardry, and I was having these terrible nightmares, and Dr. Leicester said if I would agree to link to him, the nightmares would stop. And they did, only . . . he just takes over, and makes you do terrible things. It's like being p-possessed." He swallowed hard. "I'm sorry about Trevor. At Christmas, you came to dinner, and we'd just k-killed him, and there you were, and you didn't know."

Seph recalled the bizarre Christmas dinner, the relentless drinking. Warren Barber accusing him of being too good to join the rest of them. Martin Hall holding Barber off with his knife, tears running down his face, saying, *Hasn't there been enough bloodshed already?*

"Can't you leave? Or gang up on him?" Seph said.

Peter's pale eyes swam in tears. "He's linked to us. All the time, he's linked to our stones. If we try to resist, it's like he sets fire to our insides." Tears spilled over. "I used to think the dreams were bad."

Seph shuddered, thinking of what might have been. What could still happen. "What's Leicester planning to do? What does he want with me?"

"I don't know. But we're all out looking for you."

Seph couldn't help looking over his shoulder, scanning the dark shoreline. "Who's here?"

"Dr. Leicester. The fourteen of us who are left. Aaron Hanlon died, you know, after . . . uh . . . after he and Warren and Bruce tried to bring you back."

An image of Hanlon lying on his face in the Vermilion River surfaced. "What else is here on the island?"

Peter blinked in surprise. "The winery, of course. And some abandoned cottages and fishing camps. He owns the whole thing."

So much for finding help. "How did you get here? Is there a boat?"

"Dr. Leicester has a boat," Peter said. "There's a dock at the winery. And some of us flew in."

"How do I get to the winery from here?"

"You could keep following the shore path. But they're waiting for you. There's also a path across the island. They're probably watching that, too."

"Any suggestions?"

"Turn yourself in?"

Seph thought of Madison hiding near the beach where they'd landed. He should go back and find her, get her to someplace safe. Wherever that was.

There was the problem of Peter. Leicester might

suspect Seph was on the island, but he didn't know for sure. Seph preferred to keep it that way.

Peter stirred, reading something in Seph's expression. "Don't leave me like this. If Dr. Leicester finds me, he'll know I screwed up."

"What am I supposed to do with you?" Seph asked.

"Well." Peter cast about for an idea. "You could kill me."

In the end, Seph left Peter alive, tied up and hidden in the boarded-up cottage. He knew Leicester and the alumni might search the place, but he couldn't think what else to do. Eventually, he reasoned, Peter would work himself free.

Seph loped back down the trail toward Madison's hiding place. They'd find a less-traveled sanctuary closer to the inn, and then maybe they would find a way to steal the boat or call off-island or something.

He found the place where the two trees leaned together, the cavelike hollow between. But the hideout was empty. Madison was gone, leaving only a trampled-down place where her body had lain. He just had time to register that fact when the immobilization charm smashed into him.

He went down in the leaves, and a dozen hands grabbed him. They propped him up, and he saw a kaleidoscope of familiar faces: Bruce Hays, Kenyon King, Martin Hall, Wayne Eggars. Then Warren Barber loomed up in his field of vision. He gripped Seph's shirtfront and jerked him to his feet. Bracing Seph against a tree, he punched him, once, twice, three times. Face, stomach, face again.

Finally Barber released him. Seph hit the ground hard and lay there, his leg bent at an uncomfortable angle, the world spinning. Someone kicked him.

He heard sounds of a struggle, Barber swearing, saying something about Hanlon, and King saying, "Warren! Hey, Warren! Are you crazy? You know Dr. Leicester wants him alive."

Why did Leicester want him alive? And where was Madison?

He had little time to speculate. They flipped him face down and tied his hands securely behind his back. Many hands hauled him to his feet. Then they were moving down the path in the direction of the inn. They carried him, hands under his arms, holding on to the waist of his jeans. He dangled like a poorly put together puppet in their grip.

Lights bled through the dripping trees. A hundred yards farther, and he could see a great, hulking mass of stone. It was a huge house, a castle that resembled a large outcropping of the rock itself. Elaborate walkways and gardens surrounded it, illuminated by tiny lights that glittered like stars through the wet foliage.

They brought him in a side entrance, which led into a long corridor paved in stone and lined with elaborate metal wall sconces and slitted windows. The interior was layered in velvets and hand-loomed tapestries depicting hunting scenes. They turned some corners and pushed open a door, ending in a large study lined with bookshelves, a stone fireplace at one end. Oriental rugs covered the floors. A desk and credenza anchored one side of the room, loaded with computer and communications equipment.

"Dr. Leicester?" Hays cleared his throat. "We found him."

Leicester materialized from the shadows at the perimeter of the room like a predator with perfect camouflage.

He surveyed Seph dispassionately. Seph hung between Hays and Eggars, soaked and slimed with blood, sand, and mud, an anomaly in the elegant room.

"Release the charm and step away."

Hays disabled the charm and propped Seph up on his feet.

Leicester opened a drawer in the desk and brought out a digital camera. He took several photographs of Seph from different angles, then set the camera down next to the computer. Retrieving a knife from the drawer, he extended it to Eggars, along with a small plastic bag.

"Get me some of his hair. Then cut him free and remove his shirt."

Eggars carefully lifted a lock of Seph's hair, sliced it away, and dropped it into the plastic bag. Then he cut Seph's hands free.

Seph rotated his shoulders and rubbed his chafed wrists.

"I'm sorry, Joseph," Eggars whispered, not moving his lips.

He and Hays stripped off Seph's filthy, blood-smeared T-shirt. Leicester held out a larger plastic bag, and they stuffed it in.

"Get him something else to put on," Leicester said, and Martin Hall left the room.

Seph stood shivering while Leicester opened a small cabinet at one side of the fireplace, chose from the bottles clustered on a sideboard, and poured several inches of amber liquor into a glass.

"Would you like something, Joseph?" he asked, without turning around.

Seph said nothing.

Leicester laughed. "Will you relax? Believe me, I plan on keeping you reasonably intact. For at least a few more days."

Martin returned with a worn navy sweatshirt and handed it to Seph. He pulled it on.

"Wait outside," Leicester said. The alumni obediently filed out.

"So," said the headmaster, in a way that suggested that matters were just as they should be, "welcome to Second Sister." He paused, anticipating a reaction, and looking disappointed when it didn't come. "Yes. The site of the Interguild Conference. We're quite anxious to show it off."

"Why did you bring me here? I have nothing to do with this."

"You'll be staying here a few days, at least until your father comes."

Father. A percussion began inside Seph's chest, reverberating into his throat.

Leicester misread his expression. "Really. How long did you expect to keep it a secret?"

"My father is dead." The old lie came back to him. *Software engineer. Died in a fire. . . .*

"He sent you to the Havens to spy on me, yes? And then sent Linda Downey to extricate you when you were about to be exposed."

"What?" It was just like when he was back in school and he was being accused of things. Except in those days he was always guilty.

"Though I'm surprised the Dragon would put his own son in harm's way. He must have considerable confidence in your abilities." Leicester swirled the liquid in his glass. "I often wondered why you were so resistant to persuasion. You and Jason Haley were the only recruits who refused my offer. I should have known you were getting help."

"You think the Dragon is my father."

Leicester smiled, returned to the sideboard, refilled his glass.

"Why? What makes you think so?" Seth said.

"We launched an operation against the Dragon's hideout in London. He escaped, unfortunately, but we found a file on you. Joseph McCauley. Correspondence to and from a law firm, admissions papers from a school in Scotland. Dunham's Field, I believe it was."

Dunham's Field. He'd lasted six months at Dunham's Field.

"When we looked into your background, we discovered certain . . . discrepancies." Leicester sipped at his drink. "You see, we've developed considerable scientific capabilities that will make it easier to track the lesser guilds, to ferret them out of their burrows. We'll come to power in a different world. You left a large quantity of blood behind in my office. We've made a DNA match."

The tempo of Seph's pulse quickened. "A match with who?"

"Now I suppose we'll see whether your father feels any sort of obligation toward you."

"A match with who?"

"Since you and the Dragon have been working together, perhaps you can tell us where to find the others involved in your organization. Those who won't be attending the conference."

"Right. Well, you know, I don't think the Dragon really exists. I think you all use him as an excuse. Someone to blame things on."

"I had hoped that by now you understood the price of resistance. That you would want to cooperate." Leicester didn't look disappointed, though. His expression was that of a man sitting down to a feast.

Leicester set his empty glass on the table and came toward him. Seph took one step back, another, then held his ground, his body tensing with remembered pain. He searched his memory of the lessons with Snowbeard. Countercharms. *Focus.*

Leicester gripped his shoulders. His lips were moving, speaking the charm, but Seph wasn't listening. He was shaping the counter. Flames coalesced on Leicester's fingertips, but when he launched them, Seph gathered them up and sent them roaring back.

Leicester screamed and released him as though he'd been scalded. He managed to throw up a shield—a hardened wall of air—in time to turn Seph's following volley of flame. Seph assembled his shield, hardened it, pressed against Leicester's barrier, forced the headmaster back; back to the wall, flat against the wall; pressed harder. They stood face-to-face, the clear shields between them. Leicester's eyes stretched open in surprise, the white visible around the ball-bearing centers. Sweat rolled down the headmaster's face, his jaw clenched with effort. His hands came up, palms pressing against the shield, trying to force Seph back. Flame ran in rivulets on both sides, like rainwater down a window, eagerly seeking a way through.

Jason, Seph thought. Jason, Trevor, Jason's father, and me. How many tortured, how many lives destroyed? The alumni, once students like him, made into monsters. He pushed harder, trying to squeeze the life out of Leicester, to press him like a grape.

The alumni poured into the room and dragged him back, beating him to the floor with their charms until he lay helpless on the cold stones. They gripped him by the hair, raised his head, and poured a thick, sweet liquid down his throat. It must be Weirsbane, he thought, recognizing it from Mercedes's array of potions. Disables the Weirstone. He coughed, spat, and rolled his head from side to side, but they managed to get most of it down.

"Why won't you let me kill him?" he whispered. "What's wrong with you?"

He heard Leicester's voice issuing orders. They lifted him, carried him out of the study. Down a narrow stairway, around turns, with scarcely room to manipulate his uncooperative body. The air cooled, smelling of damp stone. Lights flared ahead of them, driving away the dark. They passed through an arched doorway into a small, rough chamber. Now the air smelled of damp and yeast and fermentation. Barrels lined the wall.

It was an old winery. That was it.

They laid him on a table, immobilized him, and disappeared. He lay flat on his back, squinting into the glare of a bare lightbulb in a metal cage. The Weirsbane was taking effect. His thoughts moped about, colliding randomly, to little purpose.

Madison. Where was Madison Moss? No one had mentioned her. Was she dead? Held captive? Or had she escaped? If she'd escaped, where could she go? How big was Second Sister? Would there be places to hide?

Come back to me, Witch Boy. Or I'll come after you.

He willed her to stay away.

Leicester said the Dragon was his father. And said there was proof. If it was true, why had he never claimed him?

He heard a sound, the door opening and closing, footsteps. Leicester appeared within his field of vision and leaned over him. The headmaster's left hand was wrapped in gauze midway up to his forearm. Above the wrapping, the skin was angry red and blistered. Seph's work.

The gray eyes had changed, too. They were no longer flat, opaque, metallic. Now they burned with hate.

He set a leather bag on the table next to Seph. Brushed Seph's hair back from his forehead, an intimate gesture that made Seph's skin crawl.

"Now," the headmaster said. "We'll talk."

CHAPTER SIXTEEN
OLD STORIES

Being at home was unbearable, Jack thought. The house on Jefferson Street had turned into a dismal place, where people snapped at each other and blame hung in the air, unassigned.

It had been three days since Seph and Madison disappeared. That first day, Coast Guard helicopters had searched until dark, but could find no sign of the raft. The search resumed on subsequent days, in wider and wider circles from the point at which they'd disappeared. It was hard to remain optimistic as the hours dragged by.

After the storm passed, Jack tried the engine again, and it worked fine, the radio too. When he radioed the Coast Guard, he'd had to tell them that Seph and Madison had gone over the side during the storm, a few miles offshore. He and Ellen had been interrogated and tested for drugs and alcohol by law enforcement staff, who seemed to suspect that the accident had a more mundane explanation than the one they offered.

The Coast Guard referred to the storm itself as a "squall line." At least it had shown up on radar. Everyone agreed that Lake Erie in autumn could be treacherous. But no other boats had been trapped by the storm. Only theirs.

If the Coast Guard and the police were bad, Linda and Hastings questioned them even more relentlessly. They used Snowbeard's apartment over the garage as a command post. Linda sat, still and focused, her face pale as porcelain. Hastings paced back and forth like a tiger in a cage.

"It's Leicester. You know it is," Linda said. Jack had never seen his aunt so desolate. She looked . . . extinguished.

Hastings shook his head. "No wizard is strong enough to control the weather." He turned to Jack. "Is it possible that it was a natural storm and Seph just panicked, thinking it was wizardry?"

Jack looked at Ellen, raised his eyebrows. She shrugged and looked away. "Anything's possible on Lake Erie," he said. "But I've been sailing for years, and I've never seen anything like this. We were literally flying backward through the water under no canvas at all. As soon as Seph and Madison jumped, it stopped."

Ellen leaned against the counter. "What I'm wondering is, if it's Leicester, why did he want Seph back so much? I mean, first, the thing at the park, and then . . ." Her voice trailed off and she looked a little confused.

"What thing at the park?" Jack asked.

Ellen frowned. "I don't know. There was something that had to do with Seph and Leicester and the park . . . and I kind of forgot it." She pressed her fingertips to her forehead as if she could rearrange thoughts from the outside. "Wizards attacked Seph at the Vermilion River," she said haltingly. "They said they were going to take him back to the Havens." She looked up, wide-eyed. "I killed one."

"And you *forgot*?" Linda demanded.

Ellen looked totally lost. "I don't know, I . . ."

Hastings swore softly, pounding his fist into his open palm. "Seph. He must have used mind magic on you. Leicester said something to him at the Legends about the park. Seph told Leicester to stay away from him. Leicester blew him off and Seph tried to jump him."

Ellen shook her head, muttering to herself. Jack took her hand and pressed it between his two.

"If we find Leicester, we'll find Seph," Linda said.

"Where else should we look?" Hastings said, crackling with power and impatience. "We know they're not in Maine. Leicester and his apprentices are gone and the school is locked up. He's not at his place in Cornwall and they're not at Raven's Ghyll. That's three places they're not."

"We'll see him at the conference in ten days," Jack said dryly.

The subcommittee had met and the selections had been made. Ellen Stephenson and Jack Swift would represent the Warrior Guild; Linda Downey, the enchanters;

Blaise Highbourne, the seers; and Mercedes Foster, the sorcerers. There were others Jack didn't know. The meetings would be held over a weekend at Second Sister.

"Something bothers me," Jack continued. "Leicester and D'Orsay approved each and every one of us to come. You said as much."

"So it seems." Hastings said.

"Why would they do that?" Jack demanded as though it was somehow Hastings's fault. "They hate us. Ellen and I started this whole thing, when we refused to kill each other in the tournament."

"Well, in your case, they probably didn't have much choice."

Jack snorted. "What about Aunt Linda?" He gestured toward her with his chin. "She's caused them a lot of trouble already. You think they couldn't find another enchanter to nominate? Someone easier to handle?"

"So what are you thinking?"

"They let us choose our own representatives to the meeting because they're bringing all their enemies together in one place," Jack said. "It's a trap."

Linda nodded. "Probably. But either way, they have us. If we stay away, they win. If we go . . ."

"If we go, we'll find out what they're planning," Hastings said bluntly. "The trick will be to do that and survive."

Jack tried again. "If each guild has one vote, then we really only need one representative from a guild. I could go, and Ellen could stay here."

"What?" Ellen sat up straight, bracing her hands on

her knees. "Why? Don't you think I can handle it?"

"You said you didn't want to sit down and negotiate with a bunch of wizards," Jack pointed out. "At least if there's an attack of some kind, I can use wizardry. Maybe that would be some protection."

Ellen rose gracefully to her full height. Her T-shirt and jeans didn't show it off, but Jack knew she was in fighting condition. They'd fought a match three days ago, and he was still feeling it.

Ellen's cheeks were flaming. "If you think I'm going to stay here in Trinity while you go off to put your neck in a noose, you're crazy. Who was flat on his back at the point of my sword last summer, tell me that?" Ellen almost never brought that up. Except once or twice a week.

Jack turned to his aunt, hoping for an ally. "Do you have to be the one to go, Aunt Linda? Aren't there lots of enchanters to choose from?"

"I have to go, Jack, trust me." She looked as if she would say more, but then caught herself, and said quietly, "We're the ones who started this, and we have to finish it. Besides, would you have me send someone else into a trap?"

Ellen rolled her eyes. "You notice he always wants to leave the women at home?"

Now Jack stood up and faced her. "I would like to keep two people I care about out of danger," he said bluntly. "It's not my fault that they both happen to be women."

Jack and Ellen stood, toe to toe and eye to eye, power spiraling around them. Then Jack reached out and put a hand on the back of Ellen's head and pulled her into his arms. They stood holding each other for a long time.

The following evening, Linda went to the new house after the contractors had gone. They'd finished most of the exterior work and had shifted to the inside. Rolls of paper and cans of paint were stacked in the utility room. Seph had selected most of it.

She climbed the stairs to the second floor and went into Seph's room. It already had a hollow, abandoned feeling. All the dreams she'd had were ending in this nightmare. She had been a fool to think she could protect him, sanctuary or no. She'd been greedy, and this was the result.

If only Seph had never gone to the Havens. If only she'd allowed him to leave the Sanctuary, to hide somewhere else. She pictured him and Madison huddled in the raft, flying through the darkness.

Linda sat on the floor in a corner of the room, wrapped her arms around her knees, and wept as the light faded.

After a time, she looked up, suddenly aware that she was no longer alone. Leander Hastings stood in the doorway, his face shrouded in shadow.

"So here you are," he said.

He crossed the room until he stood over her. He put out his hand and dropped something into her lap. It was a plastic bag containing two pictures, some wadded up cloth, and a lock of hair, dark, with a little curl to it. Hair that could have belonged to Leander Hastings, but didn't.

She looked at the pictures first. They had come off a computer printer. It was Seph in a filthy green shirt and blue jeans, looking warily at the camera. In one view she could see that his hands were tied behind his back. She pulled the cloth from the bag. It was the shirt he was wearing in the photograph, smeared with blood and dirt.

She looked up at Hastings, waited for him to explain.

"Gregory Leicester contacted me. He's holding Seph. He wants to meet and make a deal." His voice. Something in his voice. But Linda's thoughts were already swirling madly.

Seph was alive! Panic and hope and fear flooded through her by turns. And then, *Why did Leicester contact Hastings?*

Hastings squatted so that his face was almost on a level with hers. Close. She pressed herself back against the wall, but could put no more distance between them.

"Now here's the strange part. He told me he was holding my son." He paused. "And I was confused, because I don't have a son."

Linda looked away.

He already knows the truth. As soon as he'd heard it, he must have known. All the man had ever needed was a clue. She was cornered, literally, in every way, her back against the wall. She knew it was no use dissembling. "I'm sorry, Lee."

"You disappeared. I searched for you for more than a year. I nearly went crazy. Then all of a sudden, last year, as from the grave, you call me. All business, as if the past never happened. Could I help your warrior nephew Jack and save him from the wizards." He made an irritated sound. "I guess you knew where I was all the time."

She spoke hesitantly. "Well, you have to admit, you cut a rather wide path."

The wizard sat down on the floor and leaned against the wall next to Linda. He looked sideways at her. "You never told your family about the baby? Not even Becka?"

She shook her head. "No one knows. Except Nick. Genevieve LeClerc helped me. I knew her from some of the networks. I stayed with her until I delivered. She was a godsend," Linda said. "She was great with Seph."

"So you just went off and left him with this woman?" He intended it to be cruel, and it was.

"Seph needed the kind of stability I couldn't provide. I couldn't risk anyone connecting him with us. It was the right thing to do," she added defensively.

"He should have been with his parents. You made that choice for both of us. That wasn't fair. And it wasn't fair to Seph."

"Can't you see that this is the proof that I was right? Someone's discovered his parentage, and now he's paying for it." Tears slid down her face. "I gave up everything to keep him safe. First you. Then him." She was unable to speak for a moment.

Finally, fiercely scrubbing the tears away with the back of her hand, Linda asked, "What does Leicester want?"

"He wants me to travel to New York tomorrow, and come alone. He'll contact me there, and tell me the terms." He massaged his forehead as if it hurt. "You know he thinks I'm the Dragon. He has for a long time. I've let him think it."

"What if he finds out you're not?"

Hastings shrugged. "I don't know."

"Let me go meet Leicester," Linda said quickly. "Let me talk to him. You know it's a trap."

"What makes you think you would be an acceptable substitute?" He shook his head. "He doesn't see you as a political figure. Leicester just ends up with two hostages instead of one. The message was addressed to me, Linda. If I don't show tomorrow, Leicester says he'll mail me another piece of our son, something that won't grow back."

Linda buried her face in her hands.

Hastings stroked her back, soothing her. "Besides, I've done nothing for the boy in sixteen years. I want Seph to know who his father is."

❧ CHAPTER SEVENTEEN ❧
NEW THREATS

Each time Seph surfaced, the pain returned, so he dove deep and stayed there as long as he could. He felt oddly inverted. During his time at the Havens, he had come to fear the descent into the abyss of sleep. Now it was a refuge from what seemed like years of torture at Leicester's hands.

But hands plucked at him and voices nagged at him relentlessly. "Joseph." He gave up, opened his eyes, and looked into Martin Hall's worried face.

"What do you want?" he meant to say, but it emerged as a painful croak. He'd been screaming, as if in a nightmare. But it wasn't a dream. It was real.

The thought amused him, and he laughed. Unsuccessfully. More of a wheeze.

"Come on, Joseph," Martin said. "You have to eat something. You've been sleeping for three days." He picked up a sweet roll and waved it enticingly under Seph's nose. The mingled scents of yeast and sugar turned his stomach.

"Go away, Martin. I mean it." Seph tried to organize his face into a scowl, but his body wouldn't obey his commands. He felt as if his skin had been flayed off, his flesh exposed. Even the pressure of the sheet was almost too much to bear.

But Peter appeared on his other side, and together they hauled him into a half-sitting position. Peter gripped his jaw, forced his mouth open, and Martin poured in the Weirsbane. Seph offered only token resistance. It was an established routine by now.

But this time was different. They brought him a basin of warm water, soap, and a washcloth. Peter supported him while Martin carefully removed his sweatshirt and washed the blood from his body. They stripped off his jeans, stiff and stinking of lake water, sweat, and terror, and dressed him in fresh clothes, while he bit his lip to keep from groaning.

"So what's up, Peter?" he asked, feeling a little giddy. "Do I go to the gallows today, or has Leicester finally decided to surrender to me?"

It was a feeble joke, but Peter lit up anyway. "He's really p-pissed, you know, because he can't get anything out of you."

Seph rolled his eyes. The only part of him that didn't hurt. "I don't *know* anything. That's why he can't get anything out of me."

"But you haven't g-given in, either," Peter said,

admiration plain on his face. "You won't link with him. It makes him c-crazy."

"Yeah, well, I can't hold out forever." Seph took deep breaths, fighting down despair. He didn't need the alumni making him into a hero. Three things kept him going. First, the months of mental and emotional torture at the Havens had desensitized him somewhat. Second, he knew from Peter that surrender to Leicester was only the beginning of a lifetime of torment. And third, he knew that to give in was to betray Maddie's presence on Second Sister.

"He's scared of you," Martin confided. "That's why he keeps you doped up on Weirsbane."

"It was so c-cool," Peter said. "How we came in and you had him smashed up against the wall, and his eyes were b-bulging out. He was practically c-crapping himself."

Seph dragged his fingers through his resistant curls. "Oh? Then why didn't you let me finish him?"

"We're linked," Martin said. "If Leicester dies, so do we."

"There's got to be a way to break it." Seph looked from Peter to Martin, but they wouldn't meet his eyes.

Seph released a long, exasperated breath. "Are you guys holding anyone else down here?"

Martin and Peter glanced at each other, shook their heads. "Just you," Martin said.

So Maddie wasn't in Leicester's hands. Where was she then? *Stay hidden*, he said to himself. *Stay hidden until it's all over.*

He plucked at his clean shirt. "What's this all about?"

Peter looked about warily, as if someone might be eavesdropping. "I think you have a visitor."

Once he was more or less presentable, they led him back up the narrow stairway and down quiet corridors to the study where he'd met with Leicester the night of his arrival. A half dozen of the alumni milled about nervously. They took charge of him when he arrived, sitting him in a chair and binding his hands to its arms with cord. Seph submitted without protest. The Weirsbane was working, and he had no chance against those odds without magic.

Leicester entered, wearing jeans and a pristine white shirt. He spoke briefly to Bruce Hays and then stood behind Seph, resting his hands on his shoulders. By now, Seph could read the wizard's touch. Power and excitement and, yes, fear bled through Leicester's fingertips.

"What's up?" Seph asked, trying not to react.

"Your father's come. He's demanding proof that you're still alive."

Before Seph had time to process this, the door opened and Warren Barber entered, followed by another man. It was Leander Hastings.

Hastings advanced quickly toward them until Leicester put up a hand, stopping him several yards away. Hastings studied Seph from that distance, as if assuring himself that he was complete.

Leander Hastings his father. Could it be true? Seph sat pinned to the chair, feet on the floor, back straight, inhaling as if he could breathe in the image before him: the structure of the face, something like his own, but leaner, crisper in profile. The tumbled dark hair, unruly, familiar. The thick brows overshadowing deepset eyes. Seph wanted to fling himself forward. Leicester must have felt his muscles bunch under his hands, because his grip tightened and he said, "Don't."

"I've come as agreed," Hastings said. "That was the deal: a trade—me for the boy."

Seph found his voice. "Don't negotiate with him! You can't trust him!" Leicester tightened his grip and new pain laced into him, effectively stopping his speech and bringing tears to his eyes.

Hastings's expression didn't change, but rather crystallized, the green eyes like shadowed pools unruffled by any movement of air.

Leicester didn't seem to notice. "What will the rebels do without the Dragon? No one to pull the strings of the spy network. No one to set traps for the unwary."

"They'll manage, no doubt," Hastings said, seeming to choose his words carefully. "Let Seph go now." He took a step forward, and Leicester raised his hand again.

"I'll need to restrain you first." Leicester nodded to the alumni. They converged on the wizard, but stopped about four feet away, as if hitting a wall, unable to approach.

Leicester sighed and flattened Seph's right hand against the table next to the chair. He isolated the little finger, pulling it away from the others, then picked up a knife from the table, the same as he had used before. Seph watched in horrified fascination, his breathing quick and shallow, his hand pink and vulnerable against the bleached wood of the tabletop.

Hastings saw what Leicester had in mind. "I give," he said quickly.

"That's better," said Leicester.

The alumni shackled Hastings's hands with a heavy chain.

"The torc." Leicester nodded to Martin Hall.

Martin opened a jeweled box on the table and brought out a glittering gold band, etched with runes and studded with jewels. He encircled Hastings's neck with it, being careful not to touch the wizard. Martin's hands were shaking, and it took him several tries to close it. Once fastened, the metal immediately tarnished and the jewels darkened, like stars blinking out.

Hastings ran a finger under the collar. "Now this is a rare piece, Gregory. Who did you steal it from?"

Leicester smiled. "It came from the Hoard, of course. I'll actually miss having the Dragon at large. He always gets the blame for everything that goes missing. The curator assured me it would keep you quite docile for the time you have left."

Leicester's weight shifted, his grip tightening on the hand on the table. Seph had time to close his eyes before the blade came down. There was a terrible pain in his right hand, and he had to work on it a while, convince himself it was somebody else's hand and somebody else's pain, lose his affection for what had been taken from him.

It took a minute, and several deep breaths, but when he opened his eyes he could look at his hand with some detachment. It was not his little finger, but the tips of his middle and ring finger that had been clipped off, across the nail, even with his forefinger. They were bleeding heavily, blood staining the unfinished wood of the table.

Seph took another deep breath, lifted his chin, and looked straight across the room at Hastings. The wizard held his gaze for a moment. His face was impassive, but Seph could feel his anger, like a beast crouching in the room.

Hastings shifted his eyes to Leicester. "I won't forget this," he said softly.

"That's the idea," Leicester said, smiling. "I needed to verify that the restraints are working. You see, I can't release the boy after all. I have plans for him."

Hastings's eyes flicked from the alumni to Seph, and back to Leicester. "Plans?"

"I've offered Joseph a place in my collaborative. I can be very persuasive." He wiped the bloody knife on Seph's shirt and carelessly dropped it back onto the table beside him. "Once we come to an agreement, he'll play a special role in the upcoming conference."

"What do you have in mind?"

"I'm going to use him to destroy the conference participants. Beginning with you."

By the time they reached the cellar, Seph was close to fainting. He remained upright only through the efforts of Martin and Peter, who gripped his elbows. Peter wrapped Seph's shirttail around the bleeding hand, surreptitiously applying pressure.

Hastings surveyed the cellar chamber, frowning like a guest in a substandard hotel: Seph's mattress in one corner, his pile of clothes next to it, Leicester's awful worktable as the centerpiece. The room was cavelike, roughly square, perhaps twenty by twenty feet, with a damp stone floor and a moist, organic odor. One corner of it had been dry-walled into a crude enclosure containing a shower and toilet. Electrical conduits had been run across the ceiling to a light fixture in the center sprouting four bare bulbs that shed a harsh light over the center of the room. The corners were shrouded in darkness.

"Let's hope the rest of the inn is a bit more comfortable." Hastings turned to the half dozen alumni who had escorted them down. "We'll need dressings, bandages, and antiseptic. Bring down some bedding, towels and soap, and a change of clothes for him." He issued orders as easily as if he were master of the house, welcoming a guest, rather than a prisoner. He turned to Seph. "What would you like to eat?"

Seph shook his head and slid down against the wall until he was sitting against it. He closed his eyes, resting his injured hand over his heart.

"Bring us something anyway," Hastings directed the alumni. "I'll see if I can persuade him to eat something."

"Yes, sir." The alumni practically bowed their way out. Seph heard a bolt sliding into place on the other side of the door.

"Dr. Leicester's students are not used to thinking for themselves," Hastings said. He knelt next to Seph. "Now let me see the hand."

Seph kept his hand folded tightly against his chest, ignoring the blood soaking into his shirt. "Is it true?"

Hastings sat back on his heels. "I am your father, yes. I'm sorry our first meeting as father and son has to take place under these circumstances."

"How long have you known about me?"

"I found out about you three days ago. Unfortunately, from Gregory Leicester."

"Somebody knew about me." Seph kept his eyes on Hastings's face, drinking in the detail.

"Yes. Somebody did." The wizard took Seph's hand and unfolded the bleeding fingers, wrapped them in the shirttail, applied gentle pressure.

"Who?"

"Your mother." The wizard spoke matter-of-factly, with none of the drama warranted by this revelation.

"My mother." And then, afraid he would die in the instant before he asked the question, he plunged on. "Who?"

"Perhaps it's best to discuss that when you're out of Leicester's hands." Hastings said it as if rescue was just hours away. "He doesn't appear to know who your mother is, and I would prefer to keep it that way."

Seph wrenched his hand free. "No. I've waited long enough. Gregory Leicester had to introduce me to my father, but you're going to tell me who my mother is."

Hastings inclined his head slightly. "All right." He spun out a gossamer thread from his fingertips, fine as a spider-web, casting it into a large circle around them on the floor until it enclosed half the room. At Seph's puzzled look, he said only, "Discourages eavesdropping."

The wizard massaged his forehead with his thumb and

forefinger, as if he were a man who found it hard to give up secrets. "It's Linda Downey."

Linda Downey. Who seemed to know him so well, his habits, his favorite foods. Who'd pretended to be his guardian. Who was building a house for them in Trinity.

Nick Snowbeard's words came back to him. *Linda and Hastings were involved, years ago.*

Seph scarcely noticed when Hastings picked up his hand again. He felt a slight tingling now, replacing the pain. Hastings pulled a small bottle from a pouch at his belt, uncorked it, and handed it to Seph. Seph took a cautious sip. "Finish it," Hastings ordered, and Seph drained the bottle. It spread through him, warming him.

Hastings sat down next to Seph, shoulder to shoulder, against the wall, still keeping hold of his hand. The wizard's strength flowed into him, the pain fleeing before it.

Hastings smiled. "I guess I still have a little power in me, despite the torc."

"What do you mean? What does it do?"

Hastings shrugged. "It drains power."

"Oh. They gave me Weirsbane."

"It seems we are a dangerous pair."

Seph liked the notion of being dangerous, in league with his father.

Hastings returned to the topic of relationships. "Your mother cares for you very much. She's been beside herself these last few days."

"If you say so."

"She was only trying to protect you, Seph."

"Right. It was for my own good. Now I understand

why I've been an orphan my whole life." They'd lied to him. They'd all lied to him. Genevieve. His own mother.

Hastings closed his eyes, as if trying to summon the right words. "She wasn't much older than you when we met. But she'd been through a lot, at the hands of wizards. Have you ever heard of the Trade?"

Seph shook his head.

"It's an underground slave market, run by wizards, dealing in the gifted. Warriors and enchanters, mostly. Linda was ensnared in it, for a time. That's how we met. I was already fighting the Trade. She joined me.

"It was a dangerous business. We were always on the move, working our network of spies, living under assumed names. Linda was especially good at it, because wizards tend to underestimate enchanters

"It's likely we would have been caught, eventually. But when you're young, you think you're immortal. And in wartime, you don't really think about the future.

"Then she disappeared. I was sure she'd been taken back to the Trade. But in fact, she'd discovered she was expecting you."

Seph tried to imagine a very young Linda Downey, what it must have been like.

"She knew you'd be a target if our enemies ever discovered your existence. So she gave you up."

"Why didn't she tell you?"

Hastings shrugged. "She didn't trust me to support that decision, and she was right. My family—your family —my father and brother and sister were all murdered by the Roses. No one's left. I would have refused to give up the only family I have. My son.

"She couldn't entirely give you up, either. She watched over you, arranged for your schooling, received progress reports. That's how Leicester and D'Orsay found out about you."

Seph leaned his head back against the wall. "All my life, I've dreamed of this. I've finally found my parents, and now . . . Leicester is going to torture me until I agree to link to him. When I do, he'll force me to murder you, and everyone else I care about."

Hastings touched his arm. "Courage, Seph."

Seph looked up, startled. It was the same phrase Linda Downey had used, the day she'd rescued him from the Havens.

"He should never have brought me here," Hastings went on. "He should have killed me as soon as he had the chance. His need to show off, his desire to bully and intimidate people will be his downfall."

"But he has what he wants," Seph said. "Everyone's heading right into his trap, and there's nothing we can do."

"I will not let Gregory Leicester lay a hand on you again," Hastings said, looking him in the eyes. And despite all the evidence to the contrary, Seph believed him.

"There's something else," Seph said. "Madison is here. The girl from the Legends. The—ah—elicitor."

Hastings sat up straighter. "Where is she?"

Seph shook his head. "I don't know. I haven't seen her since the night we landed. I don't think they know she's here."

"We can't let Leicester get hold of her. For several reasons." Hastings pondered this.

Then they heard the *snick* of the bolt sliding back. Martin and Peter entered, bringing bedding materials, first-aid supplies, and two small folding cots. They also brought a change of clothes for Seph and a tray of leftovers from dinner. They set up the cots side by side in a corner, and spread out the blankets on top. They carried in a small wooden table and two chairs, and laid out the food. There was even a bottle of wine for Hastings, which Martin uncorked. "It's last year's Zin from Second Sister," Martin explained. "Let me know what you think."

And then they were gone, the bolt replaced. Hastings looked over at Seph. The corners of his mouth twitched. "I've stayed in better accommodations, but things are improving."

Using his bound hands together, Hastings dressed Seph's wounded hand with gauze, tying it off securely. Then Hastings unbuttoned Seph's bloody shirt, and between the two of them, they pulled it off his shoulders. Seph put his hands carefully through the sleeves of the new shirt and managed to get it on and buttoned.

"Do you want to sit up at the table?" Hastings rose, a little awkwardly, to his feet. There was about three inches of play in the chain between his hands.

Seph shook his head. "I'm not hungry." He felt entirely filled up with what he'd already learned. And consumed with what he stood to lose.

"I insist that you eat something," Hastings said. "In a situation like this, it's wise to eat when you can."

Seph wondered how often his father had been in a situation like this. His parents were assassins, spies, operatives, in the thick of the rebellion. What would Jason say?

Hastings prepared a plate, pulling apart a piece of chicken so Seph could eat it easily with one hand, adding cheese, grapes, a slice of bread. He brought it over to where Seph was sitting against the wall. Then he brought him a glass of wine. Seph looked up at him, startled. "Go ahead and drink it, Seph. It might improve things if it's any good."

Despite his desperate situation, Seph felt cared for.

Hastings sat down next to him, balancing his own plate on his knees, the bottle of wine by his side.

"Where did the name 'the Dragon' come from?" Seph asked.

"Do you know the legend of how the magical guilds were founded?"

Seph shook his head. It hadn't come up.

"Supposedly the guilds were sired by five cousins, who wandered into a magical valley in northern Britain centuries ago. There they found a powerful dragon guarding a hoard of fabulous treasure. Much of it consisted of precious stones mined in the valley itself, magical artifacts, and such. The dragon welcomed them to the valley and treated them as honored guests. However, the cousins were greedy and wanted to take the dragon's hoard for themselves. One night they slipped into the treasure room beneath the sleeping dragon. When the dragon awoke, they swallowed the jewels they had stolen. Those became the first Weirstones, and conferred unique magical gifts on the cousins."

The wine was having its effect. Seph leaned his head against Hastings's shoulder. If anyone had told him he would be sitting in a dungeon on Second Sister listening to his father tell fairy tales, he would never have believed it.

Hastings drained his glass of wine, poured another. His hand shook a little, splashing wine onto the stone floor. For the first time Seph noticed that the wizard looked drawn and tired, with deep lines of weariness etched into his face.

"Are you all right?" Seph asked, feeling uneasy.

"It's been a long day," Hastings said. Then continued with his story. He was a surprisingly skilled storyteller.

"One of the cousins had swallowed the stone that delivered the gift of the spoken charm. That was the wizard, of course.

"So the wizard conjured a plan to overcome the dragon and take control of the magical valley. He charmed the others into submitting to him, because he needed the talents of the other cousins. The sorcerer prepared a powerful poison, the enchanter sang the dragon to sleep, the warrior poured the brew into his mouth, and so on. There are several versions of the story. Some say the dragon was killed outright. Others that he sleeps in the mountain to this day.

"Some say the story is just a fable. Some claim that one day the dragon will awake and right the wrong that was done by the magical guilds and kill us all. Others that the dragon will awake and free the underguilds from the autocracy of wizards. Hence the name."

They ate in silence for a few minutes. Then Hastings leaned his head back against the wall, looking up at the ceiling. When he spoke, it was almost as if he were talking to himself. "One wonders what a father should tell his son at a time like this." He put his hands on his knees, the chains on his hands clanking softly. "I've spent my life in the pursuit of greatness. Great feats of courage, daring acts of revenge, great demonstrations of hatred. Even great acts of love, when the opportunity presented itself." He smiled.

"Your mother has accused me of being obsessed with taking revenge on the Roses for the loss of my family. And it's true. The wrongs done to me have been an excuse for everything I've done: murder, betrayal, seduction, larceny. All for the cause. Very convenient.

"I was willing to sacrifice anything and anybody. It wasn't until recently that I realized what I'd given up. Relationships are a series of small, daily sacrifices. Negotiations, compromises, and gray areas. You become enmeshed. It's not well suited to someone on a mission."

Seph shifted on the hard floor. Was Hastings trying to apologize for not being a better father? But he hadn't even known Seph existed. "Why are you telling me this?"

"I see myself in you. I don't want you to make the same mistakes I've made. I have to think it's possible to suffer a great wrong and walk away from it. To build a life of small, exquisitely important moments."

"But I still don't . . ."

"Just promise me you'll consider what I've said."

Hastings lapsed into silence. Seph looked over a few

minutes later and realized the wizard was asleep, leaning against the wall. Perhaps weariness and wine had prompted the speech.

Setting his plate aside, Seph stretched out on the cot closest to the wall. Hastings's potion, whatever it was, was working. Between that and the wine, Seph could scarcely keep his eyes open.

It has been an awful and a tremendous day. It was tremendous, because he had found his father and learned about his mother. He tried not to think of the awful part, but it was there just the same, and it appeared that more awful things lay before him. But his father's words came back to him, warming him.

I would have refused to give up the only family I have. My son.

And so he slept.

❧ CHAPTER EIGHTEEN ❧
REUNIONS

First he noticed the harsh glare of the bare bulbs against his eyelids. Then he became aware of the sound of voices in quiet conversation nearby. For some reason, his right hand was bothering him, his fingers feeling fat like sausages, exceedingly tender. For a few blessed minutes, Seph forgot where he was. And then he remembered, and everything made sense but the voices, so he opened his eyes.

Two people were sitting at the table, which had been pulled into the shadows in one of the corners. The one closest to Seph was Hastings. He couldn't tell who the other person was, so he propped up on his elbows, peering through the gloom. Somehow it still seemed awkward to claim the relationship with Hastings, to call him anything other than his name, so he said, "Hastings?" out loud.

"He lives," the other one said, laughing softly. The voice and the laugh were familiar, and Seph knew he was either dead or dreaming, because he was never going to hear that voice again. The owner of the voice rose and crossed the room to him and stood silhouetted against the light, looking down at him.

"Hey, Clueless," he whispered, the light catching the gold at his right ear. "You been working out or what? I think you've grown."

Impossible. It was impossible. "Jason?" Seph said it louder than he intended, and Jason Haley put his finger to his lips.

"Careful. Don't want to draw the alumni to this reunion. They'd spoil it for sure." He grinned crookedly. Jason's hair had grown out somewhat, still ragged where it had been spiked. There was just a suggestion of bleach at the tips. Wherever he'd been since leaving the Havens, he'd been unable to maintain his usual style. He was wearing faded jeans and a sweatshirt. He seemed thinner than Seph remembered, although somehow more alive, as if the flesh had been pared away to let the spirit burn brighter.

"Leicester said you were dead," Seph whispered, as seemed appropriate in speaking to a ghost.

"As far as he knows, I am." Jason sat down on the edge of the cot. Seph pushed himself into a sitting position and embraced Jason.

Jason patted his back awkwardly. "Hey, anybody ever tell you that you look like your old man?"

"What happened? How did you get away?" Seph released Jason and leaned back against the wall, waiting for an explanation that would convince him it was true.

Jason gazed out into space. "To say I got away would be stretching a bit. They got me at the Weirweb. They'd changed the configuration of the barrier, so my counter-charms didn't work." He paused, apparently editing, picking and choosing what he shared with Seph. "Leicester must've decided that a drowning was easiest to explain. So when they were done . . . ah . . . *talking* to me, they took me to the cove."

Seph shuddered. Ever since his dream about the boathouse, the experience of drowning was never far away.

Jason went on, speaking in short, economical phrases. "Fortunately, Leicester didn't disable me. Guess he wanted to see me kick and struggle. They held me under water. I fought them for a while, and then I used the *dyrne sefa* to step away. I looked good and dead, but didn't even suck in any seawater. They 'found' the body, called my stepmother with the bad news, and shipped me out the next day in a body bag."

"We never heard anything," Seph said quietly. "You just disappeared. I thought you got away, until Leicester told me."

"I split at the airport, scared a few people when I unzipped." He grinned. "Had to wipe a few minds clean on that one. Then I went home to square things there, keep the family from calling the Havens when my body didn't show up." He shook his head. "Thank God for the Anaweir. You never have to explain anything to them if you don't want to.

"I called Sloane's, but they said you'd left school,

that you were with your guardian. I thought they'd killed you.

"Then I looked up this hacker friend of mine from high school. The Dragon was posting messages on the Web at the time—secrets, coded messages, that kind of thing. I asked my friend to track it down, get a location on the machine the stuff was coming from."

Jason grinned. The next thing I know, your father here tracked *me* down. He put his wizard hands around my throat, wanting to know who I'm working for, and why I'm so damned interested in the Dragon."

Hastings shrugged, a slight smile on his face. Even after a night's sleep, he still looked pale and tired. The torc around his neck was nearly black, like a piece of silver exposed to the elements.

"Of course, I'd heard of Leander Hastings. Everyone has. It wasn't easy convincing him not to kill me. I told him all about the Havens, what Gregory and the gang were up to, showed him the portal and how it worked. Naturally, he was real interested once he was persuaded I wasn't on the other side."

"That's why you knew about the alumni," Seph said, looking at Hastings. "And you weren't surprised when I showed you the portal stone at the Legends."

Hastings nodded. "I assumed you were working for Leicester until I found out Jason had been helping you. After our conversation at the Legends, I asked Jason about you and confirmed that you were telling the truth."

"And you let me keep thinking Jason was dead?" Seph shook his head in disbelief.

Hastings hesitated. "It's important that Leicester and the alumni not find out that Jason is alive."

"Now, let's see what the old bastard did to you," Jason said, changing the subject. Reluctantly, Seph extended his right hand. Jason examined it gently, turning it over, being careful of the injured fingers. "He gave you a witch's hand, Seph," he said softly.

"Witch's hand? What are you talking about?" Seph pulled his hand back.

"Three middle fingers, all the same length. Old Magic. Witch's hand," Jason said solemnly.

Just then, they heard the rattle of the bolt on the door sliding back, and Jason went unnoticeable as it opened. It was Martin Hall and Bruce Hays.

Martin was carrying a breakfast tray. He set it down on the table. "How was the wine?" he asked Hastings.

"Perfect," the wizard replied, indicating the empty bottle by the door. "My compliments."

Martin looked pleased. He took off his glasses, polished them on his shirt, returned them to his face. "Not too much berry?"

"Perfect," Hastings said again.

"Enjoy your breakfast," Martin said. "I'll bring another bottle tonight. The other guests will be arriving tomorrow night, so I'll be pretty busy after that," he said, almost apologetically. The alumni left, and they heard the bolt slide back into place. They sat quietly for a moment, to be sure they were gone, and then Jason reappeared.

Seph and Hastings ate at the table, while Jason sat on one of the cots. Jason didn't eat much before he set his plate on the floor. He rose, pacing back and forth like a tiger in a cage.

"So what are you doing here?" Seph asked, pushing his plate away. He was finding that eating with his left hand was awkward. He had eaten his muffin without butter because he didn't think he could handle the knife, and he didn't want to ask for help. "How did you get in here? Are you just visiting the prisoners, or what?"

Jason stopped pacing. There was another exchange of glances with Hastings.

"Your father and I have been working together," Jason said. Seph felt a twinge of jealousy that Jason had this shared experience with his father. "When they brought him here, I hitched a ride." He hesitated, looking at Hastings again, as if for permission to go on.

Hastings nodded. "Although we don't know exactly what the plan is, Jason and I are going to do what we can to ruin it. The first thing we're going to do is get you out of here." He gestured, indicating their surroundings.

"What do you mean?" Seph looked from one to the other.

"We don't want them searching the island for you. It's just too small," Jason said. "So the thing is, we'll have to kill you."

Martin noticed something different as soon as he entered the cellar. It was emptier, somehow, and deadly quiet. Before he stepped farther into the room, he waited until his eyes adjusted to the dim light along the borders of the chamber. He finally made out two recumbent forms on the cots. No one rose to greet him, however.

He carried the lunch tray to the table and set it on the floor so he could remove the breakfast dishes. Bruce Hays remained by the door. He didn't like playing waiter, but Martin didn't mind. In fact, he considered it a privilege to serve the Dragon. He transferred lunch to the table and the breakfast dishes to the tray.

"It's lunchtime!" he cried. He'd brought soup and he didn't want it to get cold.

Hastings spoke without moving. "I don't care for any," he said quietly.

"What about Seph?" Martin gestured at the other cot.

"He won't need any, either." Hastings paused. "Not anymore. The boy is dead."

Martin stood frozen for a moment. "What are you talking about?" he demanded. Bruce Hays warily took a step into the room, as if anticipating an attack. Martin crossed to Seph's cot. Seph lay on his back, his face waxy and pale against the sheets, hair tumbled dark against the pillow, his bandaged hands folded, a still life. Martin shoved his fingers under Seph's chin, feeling for a pulse. There was none, and he was cold to the touch. Even in the dim light, Martin could see the bruising at the base of his neck.

Martin could scarcely speak. He'd liked Seph, he'd always liked him. And he'd enjoyed Leander Hastings, someone with power and a knowledge of and appreciation for good wine. Now all was ruined.

He sat back on his heels. "Go get Dr. Leicester," he said to Bruce Hays, who was still hovering by the door.

Hays hesitated. "You shouldn't stay in here alone with . . ." He didn't finish.

Martin shook his head impatiently. "Just get him."

Bruce shrugged and left, bolting the door behind him.

"How could you?" Martin asked, staring down at Seph's face. "He was your son."

Hastings said nothing.

They heard a fumbling at the door, someone in a hurry. It swung open and Gregory Leicester stalked in, followed by Bruce Hays, Warren Barber, and Peter Conroy. Hastings sat up and waited, hands on his knees.

Without looking at Hastings, Leicester knelt next to Seph's cot and ran his fingers over him, felt for a pulse, lifted his eyelids, touched the blueblack fingerprints at the base of his neck. He shook his head, his face a mask of anger.

"Not so tender after all, are we, Hastings?" The wizard spat the words out, and stood.

"I thought he was restrained," Warren Barber said, his voice rising. "I thought he couldn't do anything."

"It's not that hard to kill a boy," Hastings said, as if from experience. "Restrained or not."

"I would have expected you would find it hard to kill *this* boy," Leicester said. "I guess I was wrong." There was a grudging admiration in the flat gray eyes. "Now your Achilles heel is gone, much good it will do you now. But why come all this way to kill your son, when we would have done it for you?"

Hastings shook his head. "No. I came to ransom him, remember? And you reneged on the deal. He was frightened of what lay ahead of him. He asked me to save him from it and I did." He met Leicester's eyes without remorse. "I spoke a few words over him, but could we get him a priest?"

Leicester shook his head. "His immortal soul is your problem, Hastings, since you saw fit to free it."

"Then let me take care of the body, at least," Hastings countered.

Leicester hesitated, shaken by the loss of his hostage. Martin wondered if the headmaster would decide that now was the time to kill Hastings, before the conference started. No matter how powerful Hastings was, he knew they could do it, all of them together, the way Leicester used them before.

But no. Dr. Leicester had other plans. He looked at Hastings, but spoke to the others in the room. "Hastings has proven himself to be dangerous, despite his restraints. Now that the boy is dead, I think we'd better chain him to the wall. Bruce and I will see to it. Warren, you and Martin and Peter take the body, weight it down, and throw it in the lake. We don't want it resurfacing while our guests are here."

❧ CHAPTER NINETEEN ❧
SECOND SISTER

Warren Barber wished Leicester had assigned someone else to the task of disposing of Joseph's body. Perhaps Leicester didn't trust Hall or Conroy not to do something foolish and sentimental. Like what? Saying a Rosary over the corpse? The kid was dead, after all.

They'd carried the body down the path, through the woods past the grove to the far side of the island, where a low cliff descended directly into deep water. It was as far as possible from the dock and winery complex. Although the body wasn't heavy, it made a long and awkward package, difficult to maneuver through the undergrowth and over the uneven terrain. They were hot, sweaty, and exhausted when they finally set their burden down at the edge of the cliff.

Now what to use for weight. They'd brought a coil of rope along but couldn't find anything suitable at the top of the cliff. Then Warren remembered the concrete blocks that had been used in the restoration work. "Go get a couple of those cinder blocks from the back of the winery," he ordered the other two. "One for his head and one for his feet. I'll keep an eye on Joseph, here."

"Why do *we* have to go?" Conroy whined, smacking at a mosquito.

Hall stood over the corpse like he was ready to pick a fight. "We'll stay with Seph. You go." He'd been sullen and uncooperative all the way across the island. Warren hadn't forgotten that Hall had pulled a knife on him at Christmas when Warren had gotten into it with McCauley.

Warren sighed and rolled his eyes. "Look, *idiots*, he's not going anywhere. We'll all go. We can get something cold to drink while we're down there." They dragged Seph's body into the underbrush next to the cliff face, and headed back toward the winery building.

They returned forty-five minutes later, each carrying a block. Cutting two lengths of rope, they threaded them through the concrete and tied them securely. But when they went to retrieve the body, it was gone. Warren searched the underbrush in all directions, just to make sure.

"D-do you think some kind of animal dragged him away?" Peter asked. Sweat rolled down his fat face, and he took a puff from his inhaler.

"How the hell should I know?" Warren said peevishly. "Do I look like Tarzan?"

"I don't think there's anything that big around here." Martin had this earnest look on his face, like they were discussing some remotely interesting topic. "Coyotes and eagles and ospreys, maybe."

For a moment, the only sound was the wind in the trees and Peter's wheezing. Then Warren said, "Look, not a word about any of this to Leicester. I'm not catching hell for losing a corpse. The story is, we threw McCauley in the lake. Understand?"

Hall and Conroy nodded, wide-eyed.

Seph came awake with a start, aware only of someone hovering over him. He swung out awkwardly with his fist, and his wrist was captured in a tight grip. "You'll be sorry if you punch me with that hand," Jason told him. When Seph relaxed, he released him. "About time you rejoined the living."

Seph lay in a muddle of blankets on a dirt floor. At first he thought he was still in the cellar, since the walls and ceiling of the room were made of stone. But light trickled in from an unseen source around a corner, and cool, moist air brushed his face. He sat up.

He was in a cave that had been made over into living quarters. Cans and boxes of food were stacked against the wall, and a Coleman stove stood in one corner. Clothing was piled on top of a wooden crate, out of the dirt. Three large kerosene lamps lined the perimeter. Books and more boxes were heaped to the rear.

"Nearly as posh as your old room at the Havens," Seph said.

Next to him, in contrast with the rest of the mess, was a neatly rolled bedroll, with a Cincinnati baseball cap on top.

"Good morning, Witch Boy."

He turned so quickly, he slammed his elbow against the wall of the cave.

"Madison!"

She was dressed in a man's shirt and blue jeans rolled at the bottoms. Her hair was caught back in a rubber band, and a red bandana was knotted at her neck. That was all he had time to see, and then she threw her arms around him. "Don't you ever scare me like that again, or I'll have your hide off in little bits," she said.

"Scare you?" He gripped her shoulders, holding her out for inspection. "Scare *you*? You disappeared. What happened to you? Where've you been?"

"What happened to your hand?" She pulled his gauze-wrapped hand closer for inspection. "You treat *me* like *I'm* helpless, but *you* . . ."

He heard Jason's voice from behind him. "Will you two stop flirting? You're making me feel like three's a crowd. Not that I don't approve. If you're going to wash ashore on an island, best to bring a woman along."

Maddie gave him the eye. "For . . . ?"

Seph rubbed his elbow. "I'm serious. How did you and Jason find each other?"

Maddie sat back and wrapped her arms around her knees. "After you left me in that hiding place, a half dozen witch men started poking around, so I had to sneak away. I saw them grab you, but there was nothing I could do against all of them.

Jason sprawled onto a pile of blankets. "I found your friend here creeping up on the castle after I left you last night. And wasn't I surprised to find out she could see unnoticeable me. I figured out who she was, based on Hastings's description. So I invited her to be my guest in the villa, here." He rolled his eyes. "It wasn't easy to convince her. What were you thinking, Seph, taking up with a vampire who sucks magic from innocent wizards?"

"I don't trouble the innocent," Madison drawled. "Keep your magic to yourself and we'll get along."

"Where are we?" Seph whispered. He felt stiff and sore all over, and he was all scraped up, as if he'd been dragged through brambles. "What happened?"

Jason grinned. "The portal stone worked like, well, like a charm. Just like back in the cove. Cold blooded, really, a father killing his own son. If I didn't know better, I'd've been crying, myself. Leicester was so pissed. You keep slipping out of his hands, one way and another. Dying and such. Leicester sent the guys to throw your body in the lake. I intercepted them."

Seph looked up, alarmed. "You what?"

"I thought I might have to fish you out of the water, but they left you alone while they went to get drinks."

"When Leicester hears about it, he'll know something's up."

"Trust me. He won't hear about it. Leicester ain't that forgiving of screwups." Jason grinned, stretching out his thin body. "I don't know why I can't be the kind of hero who gets to live in the castle. It's always the basement or the cave for me."

"But where *are* we?" Seph asked again.

"We're on the north side of the island, in a cave on the cliff face. Before the Civil War, they hid slaves here who were escaping to Canada. Then bootleg liquor during Prohibition. Now us. Take a look if you want." Jason gestured toward the doorway.

Seph rose shakily to his feet, hobbled to the entrance, and peered out. The opening looked straight out over the lake, toward Canada, he supposed. Far below, waves crashed against the rocks. There was a sheer cliff on either side. It was a dull, gray day, and the air was full of the smell of rain.

"How'd you get down here?"

"There's sort of a path," Jason said. He and Maddie had joined him at the entrance.

"If it's such a historical spot, aren't you afraid someone else will find it?" Seph asked.

Jason shook his head. "It was described in an old manuscript at the Great Lakes Museum. I stole it." He leaned against the rock face. "Listen. There's a boat coming from Trinity bringing reps to the conference today. That means it's going back later this afternoon."

Seph shrugged. "So?"

"We're going to make you unnoticeable and put you on it, and then you're out of here."

"Why me?"

"I promised Hastings."

"What about Maddie?"

"Well." Jason scratched his head. "We can't make Maddie unnoticeable. So I don't know how we could sneak her on board, right in front of the winery."

Seph looked from Jason to Maddie. "You think I'm going to go and leave her here? It's my fault she's here in the first place."

"I jumped in the raft after you." Maddie touched his arm. "I made a choice."

"Drowning in the lake is one thing. Gregory Leicester is another. You didn't sign on for that."

"And you did?" Tendrils of hair had been ripped free by the wind and were spiraling about her face.

Jason held up both hands. "Seph. In my book, saving somebody is better than saving nobody. They all think you're dead. Just like me. Believe me, it's very freeing. You can go wherever you want. No worries about Leicester and the others hunting you down."

"No."

"This could be a massacre. If you leave now, you can avoid it. Later, you can take your revenge. They won't be expecting it. They won't know what hit them."

Seph scowled. "I don't want to take revenge for a massacre. I want to stop one."

Jason stared out at the horizon. "Easier said than done."

"Couldn't we meet the boat when it arrives and warn them?" Maddie suggested. "Then we all leave together."

"What's to keep Leicester from conjuring up another little storm?" Jason said. "He could bring the boat back here, or torch it, or send it to the bottom of the lake. Very tidy."

"Well." Maddie thought a moment. "Then let's call them and tell them to stay away."

"My cell phone doesn't work. I haven't seen any land lines on the island, not even in the winery." Jason fumbled in his pocket for a cigarette, and sent a stream of smoke into the wind. "Tell you true, I don't know if we can stop him. We have to split him from the alumni somehow. As long as he's linked up with them, he'll win any contest involving magic. We'd have to outsmart him."

"So we outsmart him. I'm not leaving," Seph said.

"Hastings is going to be pissed."

"Then let him." The man finds out he's my father and begins ordering me around, Seph thought. He fingered the *dyrne sefa* around his neck. "We can at least get Hastings . . . get my father out, can't we?"

Jason shook his head. "If we try and bust him out, they'll know we're here for sure. If they start looking, they'll find us."

Maddie removed the elastic from her hair, combed her hair with her hands, and reapplied it. "You mean to tell me you and Mr. Hastings showed up here without any kind of a plan?"

Jason stubbed his cigarette out on the wall of the cave and flicked the butt into a coffee can. "This *is* the plan, I'm sorry to say." He turned to Seph. "Your father made a conscious decision to come after you. Knowing he was unlikely to make it out alive."

Seph recalled Hastings's speech in the cellar. It definitely had elements of deathbed advice. "You mean he's just giving *up*?"

"I think he sees you as a kind of legacy. So even if he goes, well . . ." Jason cleared his throat and looked away.

"You saw that thing they put around his neck. It's called a *gefyllan de sefa*, created during the wizard wars as a counter to High Magic."

"What is it?" Seph asked. "Hastings said it drains magic."

"It means *heart killer*—it disables a wizard's stone. Once it's on, only the wizard who placed it can take it off. It will kill a wizard in about five days."

It does look like a castle, Linda thought, looking up at the building. The walk from the dock to the winery was lined with chrysanthemums and asters in containers. Someone had gone to considerable trouble to make the place attractive, even though it was the end of the season.

Just inside the front door was a massive foyer. A young wizard stationed at a desk had keys for everyone. He introduced himself as Martin Hall, explaining that he was the viniculturist for the winery. In fact, the place was full of polite young wizards: the small, nervous man who played the grand piano in the foyer, the one who showed her to her room. She had the feeling Seph would have recognized them all.

She asked Martin Hall if Dr. Leicester had arrived. After a moment of polite confusion, he said yes, indeed he had. So Leicester had been there for some time. That might mean Seph was somewhere on the property. If he was still alive.

But where was Hastings? She'd not heard a word since he'd left to meet Leicester.

"Could you tell Dr. Leicester I would like to meet

with him this evening, before the conference begins?"
She handed Martin a business card. "He'll know the
name."

Her room was furnished with antiques and reproduc-
tions, a four-poster bed with velvet curtains all around.
The window overlooked the lake, although given the
weather and the late hour, she couldn't see much. But
when she opened the window, she could hear the sound
of water breaking on the rocks somewhere far below.

She set up the laptop and spread the papers from her
briefcase over the desk, including the two constitutions
that had been put forward at the council meeting at the
Legends: their own and the one introduced by Leicester
and D'Orsay.

Her thoughts spiraled away from the task at hand.
Leicester probably wouldn't make a deal. Why should he?
He held all the cards.

There was a tap on the door. It was Martin Hall. "Dr.
Leicester wonders if now would be a convenient time to
meet."

Well. Leicester was certainly eager. "Now is fine,"
Linda said. She picked up her portfolio and followed
Martin down the stairs and into the back hallway. They
took a couple of turns and then Martin ushered her into
a walnut-paneled library.

"Dr. Leicester will join you shortly." Martin bowed
himself out.

Linda looked around the room. Bookshelves lined the
walls, and there was a desk with computer equipment to
one side. Someone had built a fire in the stone fireplace,

and expensive rugs lay scattered on the floors. The scene looked familiar.

She dug in the portfolio and pulled out the photographs of Seph that Leicester had sent to Hastings. Yes. They'd been taken here, in the library. So Seph had been here recently, perhaps just a day or two ago. She studied the pictures. He stood near the door, looking vulnerable and cold, his hair wet and plastered against his head.

"Welcome to Second Sister." Linda jumped when she heard the voice behind her. She swung around to see Gregory Leicester framed in the doorway, wearing a sweater and jeans, deck shoes and no socks. He made no attempt to hide the fact that he was very much at home. Instinctively, she moved out toward the center of the room, where there was more room to maneuver, less chance of being trapped against the wall. He moved to the sideboard, chose a bottle, uncorked it with a practiced hand, and poured two glasses. He handed one to Linda.

"Try this. It's a Sauvignon blanc. Something new for us."

She sipped at it. "A little sweet for me." This is your son's kidnapper, she thought. This is the torturer of children.

"I'll have Martin pour something drier tomorrow night," Leicester said. He paused. "I was glad to hear you were coming."

"I expect you would be, since you engineered it," she said. She turned the wineglass in her hands. "Where is Seph?"

There was a flicker in the flat-gray eyes, but he said

nothing, and waited for her to go on. It was meant to intimidate, but in fact it had the opposite effect. If she'd had a gun, she would have shot him. Instead, she drained her glass and set it down.

"You kidnapped him. You asked Hastings to meet you, said you wanted to make a deal. I want to know where he is."

Another flicker in the eyes. Amusement. Anticipation. And suddenly she knew what he was about to say. She didn't want to hear it, couldn't look him in the face to hear it, so she turned away.

He stood just behind her, very close. She could feel his breath on her neck. "Joseph is dead," he said softly. "Hastings killed him."

She spun away from him, turned to face him again.

"You're a liar."

"Not this time." A pause. "Don't you want to know how he did it?"

"No."

"He strangled him."

An image arose of those strong hands around Seph's throat, knuckles white, squeezing.

"Where's Hastings? Let him tell me himself."

Leicester looked steadily at her, saying nothing.

"Show me Seph's body," she said. "Then I'll believe you."

"It's in the lake."

"Then we have nothing to talk about." And she pushed past him into the hallway.

★ ★ ★

Back in her room, Linda threw herself onto her bed and lay on her back in the dark, staring up at the thicker darkness that was the canopy over her head. She felt hollow and cold, like a vessel that had been emptied too many times. She had been crying all week. And now, when the truth was worse than she had ever anticipated, her eyes were dry.

Could she believe Leicester when he said that Seph was dead at Hastings's hands? There was no question that Hastings was capable of killing. But could he take the life of his own son? Perhaps. To save him from Leicester.

She didn't want to think about the second possibility. The possibility that Hastings wanted to make sure that Linda didn't make a deal of her own.

Either way, Leicester was a fool. He had played right into Hastings's hands. He should have kept her guessing and hoping, right through the conference. Because now she had nothing left to lose.

Madison came up on her knees when Seph entered the cave, but slumped back against the wall when she saw who it was. "Oh, it's you. I didn't expect you back so soon." Shivering, she wrapped her blanket more closely around her shoulders. It was cold in the cave, and she didn't have a jacket. "What did your father say?"

"I didn't see him." He dropped onto the floor of the cave, sliding his hips backward until he was leaning against the wall opposite Madison. It was pouring down rain. He was soaked through, water draining off his hair and down his neck.

Jason emerged from the shadows at the back of the cave and handed Seph a towel. "What happened?"

"I couldn't get in. They've spun a web clear around the winery, enclosing the grounds. If we breach it, they'll know we're here."

Jason swore softly. "If they find out we're here, there won't be a hole deep enough to hide in on this rock."

Seph pushed wet hair out of his face. "But why would they put up a wall? Who are they keeping out, if they don't know we're here?"

"They must be trying to keep everybody *in*," Madison suggested, digging glumly through Jason's sparse food supplies.

"Meanwhile, we don't have a clue what's going on inside. And my father will be dead in four days."

Jason sat down in the doorway to the cave and lit a cigarette. "Hastings thinks Leicester will wait and see what happens at the conference sessions tomorrow. They may first try to get their way through their usual tactics: bullying and subtle mind magic. The entire Wizard Council will be here, supposedly to make sure everything's on the up and up. So they may be in on the plot. Whatever it is."

"Did you and Hastings have a plan for the conference?"

Jason gazed out at the lake. "My plan was to lurk in the conference hall. When the badness goes down, I'll distract everyone with a glamour and kill Leicester and D'Orsay."

"That sounds more like suicide than a plan. You told me yourself there was no way to beat him as long as he's linked up with the alumni."

"Well, it's the best I can do, all right?" Jason took a

drag on the cigarette, released a stream of smoke. "I'll scare the hell out of them, anyway."

Seph realized that, all along he'd been counting on Jason or Hastings to come up with a plan, a way out of this mess. Some way that he could help without assuming responsibility for its success or failure.

But Hastings was chained in the winery, his power dwindling away. Since Seph's summer with Snowbeard, he'd surpassed Jason's skills in wizardry, both in native power and the learned use of charms. Jason's glamours were more than convincing, but it was just smoke and mirrors. They posed no physical threat. All Leicester had to do was identify the source and destroy him.

More and more, it looked like Leicester would win, unless Seph could come up with a way to stop him. Their only hope was to take them by surprise, and now, that wasn't going to happen.

"We're not going to be able to sneak into the conference unnoticed," Seph said. "We can't get through Barber's Weirweb without their knowing."

"I can."

Seph and Jason both swiveled to look at Madison. She had opened a box of canned goods and was rooting through the contents.

"What are you talking about?" Seph said.

"I can go through the Weirweb. I can help you." She came up with a can of soup, popped the top, and handed it to Seph. "Here, Witch Boy. Heat this up."

Seph heated the soup between his hands and handed it back to her.

"I don't like it," Jason said. "It's not just a matter of magical power. If they get hold of you . . ."

"Then I won't let them get hold of me." She sipped the hot soup. "It's better than your plan."

"She has a point," Seph said.

"What?" Jason demanded. "Do you really want her to walk in there alone?"

Seph shook his head. "Look. Everyone I care about is here on this island. I'm guessing there's going to be a bloodbath if we don't do something. If the worst happens, we can't hide out in this cave forever. Sooner or later we'll be caught. We have talent here and the element of surprise. We've got to think of a way to make it work against them."

❦ CHAPTER TWENTY ❧
THE INTERGUILD COUNCIL

Jack surveyed the conference room critically. It was a large, three-storied hall with a gallery that ran along three sides on the second level. A long, polished table stood in the center of the room, surrounded by chairs. Other chairs lined the walls. The table had flat monitors set into the surface at each seat, with pullout keyboards underneath. At one end of the room was a fireplace so massive, a tall man could walk straight into it. At the other end, someone had laid out coffee, juices, and pastry.

Jack hadn't had the chance to talk to Aunt Linda since their arrival. He'd tried her room, but either she wasn't in, or wasn't answering her door. She'd been closeted up with Nick all morning.

Jack glanced down at the nearest monitor. It said, "Jackson Swift, Warrior Guild." He circled the table, noting names and guilds, verifying what he'd learned the night before. The subcommittee had chosen two representatives from each guild. The Soothsayers were represented by Blaise Highbourne of Trinity and Aaron Bryan, of Staffordshire, England. The sorcerers were Mercedes Foster of Trinity and Kip McKenzie, from Scotland. The warriors, of course, were Jack and Ellen. In addition to Linda, the other enchanter was a tall, black woman—Akana Moon—whom Jack had met the night before.

Two representatives for each of the five guilds, except wizards. There were four of those: Leicester, D'Orsay, Ravenstock, and Nick. Plus the entire Wizard Council, present as observers. Members of the other guilds were invited as well, but none had dared show. Memories of the Trade still lingered among the members of the so-called "servant" guilds.

Wizards, Jack thought sourly. Just what we need less of. And only one that he knew could be trusted.

Ellen laid a hand on his arm. "They still only get one vote, Jack."

He wished Hastings were there. He wished he knew where Hastings was. And Seph and Madison. He wanted to be optimistic, for Ellen's sake if nothing else. She was still beating herself up about the attack at the park.

"Do you think they're here somewhere?" Ellen said, as if she could read his mind. "Seph and Madison?"

"Who knows?" Jack took the loss of his passengers very personally. He'd take the place apart if he thought he could find them.

A tall, bald man in a bulky gray sweater and black jeans emerged from a side door and took his place at the head of the table. Jack studied him with interest, knowing this must be the infamous Gregory Leicester. Seph's former headmaster. The wizard looked around the table, smiling, lingering for a long moment on Linda. She lifted her head and met his gaze directly. He flinched a little at whatever was in her eyes.

"If we can all take our seats, we had best get under-way," Leicester said. "We are already running a little late." The low murmur of voices ceased.

Jack and Ellen moved reluctantly to their seats. Linda ignored the video display and sat next to Nick. She was pale, and there were purple shadows under her eyes. Still, she looked grim and determined, and rather corporate in a pinstripe suit. Jack and Ellen sat next to Nick, and Akana Moon next to Linda.

The seats against the wall were filling up with members of the Wizard Council. Jack noticed some familiar faces. Geoffrey Wylie, the wizard who had played Ellen in the tournament, and had tried to kidnap him in Trinity the summer before. Jessamine Longbranch, the wizard surgeon who had implanted Jack's stone, saving his life in order to sacrifice him in the Game. Others he didn't know.

Ellen's hand crept over and covered his under the table. She had insisted on coming, though she had good reason to be wary of wizards. She'd spent most of her life under their control. If she could deal with it, he could, too. And, to be honest, he was glad to have her strength at his right hand.

The joint council participants were each introduced,

and Leicester read out the agenda. There were only two items, the two different constitutional proposals: one that Hastings had pushed through the Wizard Council, and one that Leicester and D'Orsay had favored. Leicester asked for approval of the agenda and Nick raised his hand.

"First, I move that we select a chairperson and a scribe," the old wizard suggested. The bear's head mounted on his staff gleamed softly.

They'd tried to take his staff away from him at the door of the conference room. He'd said he would have to sit in the hallway, then, because he was an old man of 465 years and needed its support. The alumnus at the door was no match for him, and Nick retained his staff.

Leicester shrugged. He had automatically assumed the role of chair. "Perhaps one of our council observers would be willing?" He looked at the wizards in the gallery.

"I move that the chair be a non-wizard," Nick said quickly. "I think it would help reassure some of our Anawizard participants that this is a fair process."

"I second the motion," said Aaron Bryan, the seer, without waiting for an invitation. Nick had done considerable networking the night before.

"Which motion?" Leicester looked confused.

"It's one motion," Nick explained, "In several parts."

Immediately, Jack could sense an almost physical pressure from the wizards in the spectator seats. The Anawizard Weir looked around uneasily. Wizards were not accustomed to democracy. It made them edgy.

"There is a motion on the floor," Leicester said. "Is there discussion?"

"It's a good idea," said Jeremy Ravenstock, one of the wizard representatives. "And it might make all of us more comfortable." He frowned at Leicester and scanned the gallery. So far, Jack noticed, wizards were doing most of the talking.

There was no further discussion. The Interguild Council took a vote, and the motion carried. Even the wizards voted for it.

Leicester sighed. "Are there any nominations or volunteers for chairperson?"

Blaise Highbourne rose to his feet, his trademark silver cuffs and neckpiece glittering in the light from the wall sconces. "I nominate Linda Downey."

"An *enchanter*?" Leicester raised an eyebrow. "Are you serious?"

"I second the nomination." The enchanter Akana Moon didn't rise from her chair. She looked nervous, and her voice shook, but she said it just the same.

"We don't even know if the girl is willing to serve," Leicester said. "After all, it's a lot to ask of a . . ."

"I'll do it," Linda said. "As long as the ground rules are understood. I promise to be impartial as chair of the meeting. But I want to make it clear that I will participate as an advocate on those issues I feel strongly about."

"Of course," said Leicester, amused. "All in favor?" The motion carried. "It's settled then. The enchanter is chair."

"My name is Linda Downey," Linda said in a clear voice. "Make a note of it, Dr. Leicester."

Leicester looked up, startled, his smile fading. Linda

turned to the rest of the participants. "Are there any volunteers for scribe?" There was another long pause during which no one volunteered. None of the wizards wanted to be secretary, and none of the Anawizard representatives dared to. "Jack, you're good at keyboarding. Help me out here."

"Okay." Jack slid the tray out from under the table, glad to be doing something he had some skill at.

Linda nodded. "Thanks, Jack. Now, let's take another look at our agenda. Are there any changes in the items?" There were none. "Well, I have something to add," she said "Before we vote on the constitutions that are before us, I suggest that we discuss the issue that drove this constitutional effort in the first place: that of wizard aggression against the Anawizard Weir."

There was a shocked silence. Then Claude D'Orsay rose to his feet. "I don't think that would be constructive, *Linda Downey*," he said pointedly. "Our time is limited, and, after all, we have come together here as peacemakers. Why bring up old issues that are bound to cause hard feelings?"

"Some of the issues are very new," Linda said evenly. "Some of them are downright *current*." She spat out the word. "Those of us who are not students of history are condemned to repeat it."

The magical pressure from the sidelines was increasing. Linda staggered a bit, as if from a physical blow. She inclined her head and said something to Nick. He stood and put his arm around her, steadying her, and his staff flared up brightly.

After a moment, Linda was able to speak. "If the council observers cannot resist intruding on the proceedings, we will have to clear the room."

"This is a joke," the wizard Geoffrey Wylie snarled from his seat against the wall.

"I did not recognize you, Mr. Wylie," Linda said coldly. "You are an observer and not a participant in this process. Speak again, and you're out of here. *Think* again, and you're out of here."

The Anawizard Weir stared at Linda with a mixture of admiration and astonishment. Jack suspected the wizards in the room were already regretting their choice of the enchanter as chair.

The observers settled, still fuming, but the pressure dissipated a little.

"Is there a motion to add this issue to the agenda?" Linda asked, looking around the room.

"I so move," said Akana Moon, who seemed to have found her courage. She defiantly turned her eyes toward the Wizard Council.

"I second," said Jack. Ah, well, he thought. We may all end up dead, but we're sticking it to them in the meantime. He was worried about his aunt, though. It almost seemed as if she were trying to pick a fight.

The motion carried.

Gregory Leicester spoke up. "In the interest of time, I suggest that we table this truth-finding enterprise until after we consider the constitutional issues."

"Is that a motion, Dr. Leicester?" Linda asked.

Leicester sizzled with irritation. He put the suggestion

forward in the form of a motion, seconded by D'Orsay. It was voted down.

"If you'd like to make a motion, Dr. Leicester, we can also allocate time for a discussion of attacks by members of the other guilds against wizards," Linda offered sweetly.

"That will take two minutes," Jack muttered to Ellen.

Leicester shook his head, drumming his fingers on the tabletop.

"The issue is, wizard aggression against the other Weir. Is there anyone who has something to share on this topic?" Linda gazed around the table.

Jack rose to his feet. "I'm Jackson Swift, a warrior. Actually, I should have been a wizard, but Dr. Longbranch here fraudulently planted a warrior stone in me." He pointed toward Jessamine Longbranch, then Geoffrey Wylie. "Mr. Wylie tried to kidnap me, to keep me from playing in the Game. And then Dr. Longbranch tried to kill me when I wouldn't play for her."

"You ungrateful mixed-blood mongrel! You wouldn't even be alive today if it weren't for me." Longbranch combed crimson-painted nails through her mane of pitch-black hair. She looked like she would have said more, but stopped herself, sliding a look at Linda Downey.

"Warriors are bred for the tournaments," D'Orsay said coldly. "That is their purpose. It makes good use of their natural talents. I don't know what all this whining is about."

"Precisely why we need to have this dialogue," said Linda Downey. "Anyone else?"

Almost everyone had a story, and grew more and more

confident in the telling as the morning wore on. Jack was amazed at how Aunt Linda worked the group, without seeming to. She encouraged a little more detail here, asked a question there, headed off a challenge by the wizards in the room.

She's done this before, Jack thought. It comes naturally to her. The group was coalescing into a righteously angry body with a common grievance. One that might take a chance on a new beginning.

Finally, Ellen Stephenson stood and cleared her throat. "I have something to say." Her hand crept to her side, groping for a weapon that wasn't there.

"Go on, Ellen," Linda said.

Ellen lifted her chin, drew herself up, and faced Geoffrey Wylie, who did not look happy at this development. "I am Ellen Stephenson, a warrior. Wizards kidnapped me from my parents when I was a baby so I could be trained for the tournaments. They stole my childhood and turned me into a killer." She looked at Jack, and he nodded encouragingly.

"When I refused to kill my friend Jack, they attacked me on the tournament field and tried to murder me." She looked over at D'Orsay. "Some of you know all about it, because some of you were directly involved," she said softly. She sat down. The other Weir nodded and whispered among themselves.

"Are there any questions for Ellen Stephenson?" Linda asked.

"I have a question," Claude D'Orsay said. "Why doesn't this girl hire a therapist instead of wasting the committee's time complaining about her difficult child-hood?"

The conference participants rumbled with anger.

"I have a story, too," Linda said, ignoring D'Orsay. She gazed around the room, pausing until she had everyone's attention. "There are actually many stories I could tell, but I would like to tell you about my son."

Madison hesitated at the edge of the trees, scanning the grounds of the winery. No one was around. Naturally, Leicester and the others would be focused on the proceedings in the conference room. Besides, it was a cold, dismal rainy day. A good day to be inside.

"Do you see it?" Seph whispered. "It goes all around the clearing." He extended a hand, then drew it back as if he were afraid of touching something.

"I'll take your word for it."

"You know who you're looking for?"

She nodded. "The blond guy from the picnic with the back-combed hair."

"Right. He'll be someplace quiet, watching the barrier. Now, remember, you don't want to let him get hold of you. You want a power release. Don't let him think he can get to you without it."

"We've been over all this," Maddie muttered. *You volunteered for this*, she reminded herself. But now, she just wanted to get it over with. She was scared she would let Seph and Jason down. Along with everyone else.

Seph gripped her arm as if he thought she might charge off before he'd had his say. His dark brows were drawn together in a frown, and his eyes changed in the light, from green to blue to gold. Yet not a trickle of power came through his fingers. She'd never met a witch with that much control.

But then, Seph McCauley didn't need any magic to slide the bones right out of her body. She took a deep breath and tried to focus on what he was saying.

"If he does get hold of you, fight like hell. Make him think he has to use power to keep you from getting away."

"Got it."

"He'll probably recognize you from the park. So you know what your story is?"

"Are you going to talk me to death or what? I'm freezing out here." Her teeth were chattering.

"Sorry." He let go of her arm, looking embarrassed. "I just don't want anything to happen to you, okay?"

"Okay."

She went to turn away, but he pulled her toward him and kissed her on the forehead. "For luck," he said.

She crossed the yard, hoping that she was the kind of girl whose luck could be improved by kisses. She entered the unlocked back door, shaking the excess water from her hair. She stood in the deserted kitchen, surrounded by the debris from meal preparation left for later cleanup. She scanned the room for weapons, pulled a large carving knife from a butcher block, and held it close to her side.

Where would Warren Barber be? Would he need to be someplace near the wall? She prayed he wouldn't be hanging out in the conference room where the meeting was taking place.

She ghosted through the rooms on the ground floor, skirting the great hall. No Barber. Her breath came faster, and her pulse quickened. Time was wasting. She decided to try the garden. Maybe he didn't know enough to come in out of the rain.

As soon as she stepped onto the stone patio, she heard someone talking. Crooning, as one might to a small child or a pet. She walked toward the sound, down a crushed-stone pathway, between clipped boxwood hedges and beds crammed with ragged mums, through an arbor intertwined with wisteria.

And there was Warren Barber, like some kind of grotesque gardener mime, tending to his invisible wizard wall. Making little adjustments and repairs, straightening tangles, twining new additions into place. He must be powerful, Madison thought. It was still raining, a cold drizzle, but he lit up the entire corner of the garden. His clothes were dry, even steaming a little. He was using some kind of charm to keep the wet away.

He was concentrating so hard that she'd almost reached him when he looked up and noticed her. "Well, well," he said. "What's this?"

"What have you done with Seph?" Madison tried to look scared and determined at the same time. Which wasn't difficult, since that was how she was feeling anyway.

Barber looked her up and down and smiled, revealing crooked teeth. His blue eyes were so pale as to be almost colorless, the lashes invisible. "I remember you. You were at the river with McCauley."

"Where is he?" she demanded, her voice tremoring a little.

"How the hell did you get here?" Barber asked.

"I . . . I came in the raft with him."

"Well, now," Barber said, advancing toward her, hands extended. "Here's how it works. You be nice to me, and maybe I'll tell you where he is."

Madison brought the butcher knife from behind her back. "You tell me where he is and I won't use this."

Barber's eyes widened at the sight of the blade. Then he grinned. "Not the way to win me over, sweetheart." He extended his hands toward her and spoke a charm.

Seph and Jason crouched in the trees, their eyes focused on the wizard wall.

"I hope she's okay," Jason muttered, for perhaps the third time. "Maybe one of us should have gone with her. I mean, Barber's a nasty son of a . . ."

"She knows what she's doing." Seph checked his watch. Almost noon. Madison had been gone half an hour, and the wall was still up. But then, it would take time for her to find Barber and get the plan underway. But what if she'd run into someone else along the way, or several someones?

"What could be taking so long?" Jason swiped rainwater from his face. "What if she can't find him?"

"If she can't find him, she'll keep looking." Seph looked at his watch again. Noon. Where could she be? Maybe they should go after her.

Seph looked back at the winery building. Blinked and

looked again. The Weirweb was wavering, fading, dissolving into wisps of mist that broke and swirled against the building. For a moment it lingered like a vapor on the stones. And then it was gone.

Seph and Jason grinned at each other like idiots.

"I knew she could do it," Jason said happily.

"Let's go." They pushed to their feet and loped across the grounds, squelching in the wet leaves. They ducked into the entrance that Madison had used.

Madison met them in the kitchen, effervescent with relief. "He's out in the garden." She pointed with a large knife, slicing the air with it like a scimitar.

Barber lay flat on his back on the crushed stone path, totally drained, soaking wet and furious. He would have been steaming had he been able to muster the power to do so. When he saw Seph and Jason, his eyes widened in amazement and alarm.

"Back from the dead," Jason said, grinning. "Boo!"

"How long will this last, d'you think?" Seph asked, looking down at Barber dispassionately.

Madison shrugged. "You're the witch. I have no idea."

"We'd better make sure he stays quiet," Seph said.

Seph knelt beside Barber, placed his hands on his collarbone, and spilled the immobilization charm into him. Barber twitched once, and was still.

Seph looked up to find Madison staring at him, blue eyes standing out against her paler face. "What did you . . . ?"

"Don't worry. He's just in for a long sleep." Seph and Jason dragged Barber's unresisting body into the bushes, where it was less likely to be found at an inopportune moment.

Seph turned to Madison. "Now. Jason and I are going to make ourselves unnoticeable, sneak into the hall, and see what's going on. There's a little corridor that leads from the butler's pantry to the hall. Hide in there until we come get you."

Madison frowned and fingered her hair, which was beginning to dry into long waves. "I don't like it. I think we should stay together."

Seph touched her arm reassuringly. "Unfortunately, there's no way to sneak you in there. Please, Madison."

She finally nodded, still scowling.

Bruce Hays and Kenyon King were stationed at the doors into the great hall. Occasionally one of the other alumni came or went to replenish the refreshments for the attendees or deliver a message to Leicester. At one of those times, unnoticeable Seph and Jason slipped through the doors after them and into the conference room. They drifted the length of the room and stood on the great hearth, from which they could command a good view of the proceedings.

The Weir representatives were ranged around a polished oak table. Members of the Wizard Council were seated in chairs around the periphery. To Seph's surprise, Linda Downey stood at the head of the table, running the meeting. She looked angry, pale, and drawn.

"Which one is your mother?" Jason's voice came eerily out of the air.

"She's the one talking." It was the first time Seth had seen her since learning she was his mother. He studied her, seeking something of himself in her. He guessed he favored his father, though maybe something about the eyes . . .

"Hey," Jason whispered. "She's talking about you."

"I had a son named Joseph Downey McCauley," Linda was saying. "Leander Hastings was his father."

She was using the past tense.

And then Seph finally understood. *She thinks I'm dead. That's why she's so angry.*

"I hid my son to keep him out of harm's way, to keep him away from wizards who might use him as a weapon against his father. I gave him up to protect him." She paused. "Last year he ended up at Gregory Leicester's private school. Dr. Leicester tortured him for almost a year."

"McCauley was a wizard," Leicester protested. More past tense. "Whatever happened, this is a matter between wizards."

"An attack on my son is an attack on me," Linda Downey said. "I was able to rescue him from the Havens, but then last week, Dr. Leicester kidnapped him again."

"Don't be ridiculous!" Leicester snapped. "The boy was lost in a storm on the lake. I didn't have anything to do with that. It's impossible, in fact."

Linda ignored him. "Dr. Leicester did it to keep Leander Hastings away from the conference."

"You have no proof I was behind any of this," Leicester objected.

Linda handed a jump drive to Jack. "Can you bring

these pictures up on the display?" Jack put it into his port. He struck a few keys, and in a few moments, a picture materialized on their screens, replacing the agenda. It was Seph, hands tied behind his back. Seph in the library.

"Dr. Leicester sent these photographs to Hastings. They were taken here in the winery. If you like, I can show you the very spot."

Leicester sat back in his chair and placed his hands flat on the table. "I don't understand the purpose of this," he said. "After all, I didn't kill the boy. Hastings did." And in saying it, he confirmed everything.

Once again, the room fell silent. Jack was pale, his knuckles white where he gripped the arms of his chair. Ellen scrubbed away tears and glared at Leicester. Blaise and Mercedes stared down at the table.

"What is my purpose?" There were spots of color on Linda's cheeks, and the gold was back in her eyes. "We are going to consider two possible Weir constitutions to replace the one that was set aside at Raven's Ghyll a year ago. One more or less resurrects the old system. The other introduces a new order.

"You've been told the current system does not need fixing. I want to make sure that all of the guild representatives remember our history, and the price we've paid over the years for the dominance of wizards. I also want them to understand just exactly who these people are."

"I'm liking your mother more and more," Jason said. Seph just nodded wordlessly.

Linda returned to the agenda. "Now. We'll allow the sponsors of each of the constitutions ten minutes in which to present the merits and rationale of their proposals. Dr. Leicester, Mr. D'Orsay?"

Still looking a little shell-shocked, D'Orsay stood and addressed the representatives. The essence of the argument was that, despite some flaws, the old hierarchy was a good system that met everyone's needs. The role of the various guilds was clear and consistent with their talents. The Rules of Engagement had created a kind of *Pax Romana* over the centuries, keeping bloodshed and conflict to a minimum. Although there had been some regrettable excesses now and then, on the whole, the wizards had served as benevolent rulers.

In the end, Leicester put forward a motion to accept the new constitution. D'Orsay seconded it. It was brought up for a vote, and was soundly defeated, four to zero, with the wizards abstaining since they were split on the vote, two to two.

Jeremy Ravenstock introduced the second constitution, as he was the only one present who had supported it on the Wizard Council. He was a blunt, straightforward speaker, and no poet. Nick said a few words in support of it as well, and then Linda took over.

She looked around the table, making eye contact with each of the participants. "I know this has been difficult. You all took a risk in agreeing to serve. The fact that you are here proves that you know what the stakes are. I realize you are not used to saying no to wizards.

"But I want you to think about how your lives have been under the old hierarchy. I want you to think about everything you heard here this morning. This is our

opportunity to make sure that it will be different for our
. . . children." Her voice broke a little. "Shame on us if we
squander it."

Seph stared at his mother. She was a small woman, and
not a wizard, yet she held the entire joint conference in
thrall, wizards as well as Anawizard Weir. Somehow, she
made freedom seem possible to the Anawizard Weir, who
had been oppressed for years.

The Hastings/Downey constitution was passed by the
Interguild Council, again by a vote of four to zero.

Leicester gestured, and Bruce Hays left the hall.

Seph looked up at the gallery windows, trying to
judge the time. It was only mid afternoon, but it seemed
much later. No light was coming through the windows,
and the fitful rain had somehow turned into a gale.

Still, Linda wasn't finished. She looked over the heads
of those at the table and spoke to the Wizard Council representatives ranged against the wall.

"Dr. Leicester claims that the murder of my son is a
wizard issue. Fair enough. The Rules of Engagement have
long forbidden warfare among wizards. If Dr. Leicester
witnessed the murder of my son at Hastings's hands, then
what has he done about it? Where is Hastings? Hastings is
your colleague, a member of the Wizard Council. Perhaps
he should be allowed to speak on his own behalf."

The wizards in the gallery stirred. Whispers rolled
through them like wind through marsh grass. "Where *is*
Hastings?" Longbranch demanded. "I'm surprised he'd
miss this event, since he was one of the architects."

"I'm surprised you would allow yourself to be

directed and interrogated by an enchanter," Leicester said acidly. "This is wizard business, as I said."

"But Hastings *is* a member of the Wizard Council," Ravenstock pointed out. "And deserves as much protection under the rules as any of the rest of us."

"Leander Hastings is a murderer, a schemer, and a traitor to his kind," Adam Sedgwick said.

"Like any other wizard," Jason muttered.

Seph recalled that Sedgwick was an ally of Leicester's, who had supported him at the Legends meeting. He was a tall, aristocratic-looking man, probably the youngest wizard on the council.

"He's encouraged this rebellion of the servant guilds by serving as their spokesperson and instigator," Sedgwick went on. "Do you think they would have succeeded to this degree on their own, without the support of wizards?"

"Then where is he?" Geoffrey Wylie asked, looking about pointedly. "If this is his scheme, where is the schemer?"

"If this is his triumph, then why isn't he here to enjoy it?" Ravenstock added, warming to the subject. "As council member or participant, he should be here."

"Perhaps we should search the premises," Linda suggested. "Perhaps the Council of Wizards would like to ask Dr. Leicester why he has recruited, tortured, and enslaved more than a dozen young wizards at the school he calls the Havens. Perhaps the council would like to know what Leicester and D'Orsay plan to do with that kind of power. Do you really believe he plans to use it against enchanters, warriors, sorcerers, and seers?"

The low buzz from the sidelines increased to a rumble. Seph stirred. "I'm going to tell them where Hastings is," he said.

Jason gripped his arm. "Something's coming down. Let them show their hand, first."

Bruce Hays returned and handed Gregory Leicester a rolled parchment. Leicester cleared his throat. "We'll address these issues in a moment. But before we hare off on a tangent, why don't we finish what we started? We have a new constitution to sign."

"That doesn't make sense.," Jason said. "He can't be anxious to sign off on the new constitution."

In answer, Seph looked up toward the gallery. Unnoticed by the rest of the conference participants, the alumni were lining up along the rail, looking down at them, everyone but Warren Barber, who lay immobile in the garden.

Leicester was speaking again. "We'll need one representative from each guild to sign it. You can decide among yourselves who will have that honor." He paused. "We'll start with the Seers Guild."

Blaise Highbourne and Aaron Bryan were seated together on one side of the table. Hays brought the parchment around to their side and put it before them. Bryan picked up the pen, but Blaise was reading it. He put his finger to the page, reread a passage.

Seph was watching his face, saw it change. Blaise looked up at Leicester. "This is not the document we voted on."

Leicester shrugged. "The document *is* different than the ones we considered previously." His voice hardened. "But you will all sign it, nevertheless."

Jeremy Ravenstock stood. "We have already chosen a constitution," he said coldly. "We are not signing any other."

Leicester looked up at the alumni in the gallery, then back at Ravenstock. He extended his hand, and a bolt of blue flame erupted from his fingertips. For a moment, Ravenstock was a silhouette, spinning from the force of the blow, outlined in flames. And the next moment he lay, unmoving, on the floor, the stone scorched under him. A wisp of smoke spiraled upward, and the air was filled with the stench of burning flesh. There was a shocked silence.

"I only need one wizard," said Leicester. "And I will sign. Everyone else is expendable. Our experiment in representative government has come to its conclusion."

At a gesture from D'Orsay, every door into the hall slammed shut.

Several members of the council came to their feet. "What do you think you're doing?" Wylie demanded furiously.

"This." Drawing on the strength of the alumni in the gallery, Leicester cast an immobilization charm that smashed down on everyone in the room, paralyzing them and pinning them to their seats. Save Claude D'Orsay and Adam Sedgwick and a woman Seph didn't know, who had thrown up shields prior to the launch of the charm. And Seph and Jason, who had retreated deep into the fireplace.

D'Orsay took his place next to Leicester. Sedgwick and the woman wizard joined them, smiling.

"Who's the woman next to Sedgwick?" Seph asked Jason.

"Nora Whitehead. Bad news," Jason replied.

D'Orsay spoke. "Esteemed colleagues, members of the Council of Wizards, I would like to thank you all for attending this little gathering. It has made our task that much easier."

He smiled. "Did you really think I would go to such lengths to appease the servant class?" He shook his head. "However, it was a perfect excuse to assemble the most powerful members of the Wizard Guild in one place.

"We wizards can no longer afford to debate endlessly and fight among ourselves. You see, we've grown weak over the years. Toothless. How else to explain this rebellion of the underguilds? It should have been put down immediately and ruthlessly. We believe it's time to unite under a new and simpler covenant with clear rules of succession."

Leicester unrolled the parchment, flattened it against the walnut surface of the podium, cleared his throat, and began to read to his captive audience.

It was all there. Reinstatement of the guild hierarchy. Codification of the subservient status of what Leicester called the lesser guilds. Abolition of the Sanctuary. Implementation of a warrior-breeding program with eventual resumption of the tournaments.

However, under the new regime, the tournaments would be held for tradition's sake, for entertainment purposes only. Their role in allocating power would no longer be necessary. Gregory Leicester and Claude D'Orsay would be established guildmasters for life with control over the magical artifacts of both wizard houses and lineal descent to their male children. The alumni would form the core of a disciplinary force bound to Leicester and D'Orsay. They would adjudicate any wizard disputes and mete out discipline to other wizards as they saw fit.

When Leicester finished reading, he looked around the room. "Are there any questions?"

One of the council wizards spoke, an older man wearing a coat embroidered with red roses, someone Seph didn't know. "Yes. I have a question. Are you two out of your minds?"

D'Orsay nodded to Leicester, and Leicester incinerated the old man on the spot. There were no more questions.

"So," Leicester said. "Let's proceed with the signing." He returned his attention to the seers, Aaron Bryan and Blaise Highbourne. "Mr. . . . Bryan, is it? I see you have the pen in your hand. Mr. Hays?" Bruce Hays shoved the parchment in front of him.

Bryan dropped the pen on the table and shook his head stubbornly, looking around at the others at the table for support. Hays gripped his shoulder, pushed power through his hand. The soothsayer gasped with pain, the blood leaving his face. Hays leaned down and spoke softly into his ear. It only took a few minutes. The seer signed.

Leicester smiled. "That wasn't difficult, and it doesn't have to be painful. It's up to you."

They moved on to the Sorcerers' Guild, and Hays focused his powers of persuasion on Kip McKenzie rather than Mercedes. Trinity had been a focus of rebellion for a long time. Leicester and D'Orsay apparently hoped the other representatives would be easier to intimidate.

Kip didn't hold out for much longer than Aaron Bryan. Anyone could see it was a hopeless cause. The illusion of power that they had all enjoyed so briefly was dissipating like the soft breath of the lake. It was just wizards, once again, making all the rules, pushing people around.

Hays carried the parchment to Akana Moon. But Leicester shook his head. He walked back along the table until he stood behind Linda Downey. He rested his hands lightly on her shoulders, as if formally taking possession.

"Perhaps *Linda Downey* would like the honor," Leicester suggested, emphasizing the name. "Since she's played such an important role in today's proceedings."

Linda stared straight ahead, her face a mask of indifference.

She'll die before she signs Leicester's document, Seph thought. He glanced around the room. All the doors were magically welded shut. There was no way to put their plan into motion.

"We've got to reach Madison," he said to Jason.

"We can't walk through walls."

Seth peered up into the chimney and shook his head. Not even Jason's slender body would fit through.

At the table, Akana Moon looked from Leicester to Linda. She pulled the parchment toward her. "I'll sign," she said quickly. And did.

And then there was just Jack and Ellen, the two warriors, both of the Trinity faction.

"Who'll it be?" Hays asked, grinning. Ellen and Jack looked at each other, as if establishing a pact of resistance between them.

Hays looked from Jack to Ellen, debating. After a moment's indecision, he chose Ellen and put his hands on her shoulders. Power crackled into her. She went rigid, gasping a little, eyes wide, but saying nothing. He leaned down and whispered in her ear. Jack, watching, looked like he might jump out of his own skin, but Ellen stubbornly shook her head.

"Ellen," Linda said tonelessly. "Please. There's no point. You might as well sign."

Ellen shook her head, and Hays sent the flame in again. All the blood drained from Ellen's face. She bit her lip until it bled, still saying nothing. It seemed to go on forever, and then he released her, and her head drooped forward, sweat dripping from her face onto the table. Jack let out his breath in a long hiss.

Hays looked at Leicester, shrugging helplessly. "I'm afraid . . . if I do more, it might kill her."

Leicester sighed. "You're handling it all wrong. Give the pen to the boy. Kill the girl if he won't sign." Hays seemed intrigued by the idea, but didn't go very far with it, because Jack scribbled his name on the document and shoved it back to Hays. Ellen glared at him but he wouldn't meet her eyes. And it was done.

By now, Seph and Jason had walked the length of the hall, trying all the doors, just to be sure. All were secured.

Leicester and D'Orsay meant to make sure no one slipped away from the party early. But when Seph looked up at the alumni in the gallery, he noticed that some of them were missing.

After the constitution was "approved," there was a brief pause while Leicester looked it over and then signed it with a flourish on behalf of the wizards.

"Now, all that remains is to carry this new constitution to Raven's Ghyll and have it consecrated," Leicester said. "But first we have a matter of discipline to attend to."

CHAPTER TWENTY-ONE
WIZARD DISCIPLINE

Time passed slowly in the cellar room behind the fermentation chamber. There was no clear evidence of its progress, no clues as to weather, or events in the world outside. Martin had brought breakfast to Hastings the day before, but hadn't appeared since. So Jason hadn't been able to get to him.

Hastings wasn't hungry anyway. He was sleeping more and more, his body conserving its resources, resisting the draining of power from his stone.

It took some getting used to, walking into traps. He'd spent a lifetime avoiding them. Still, Seph was safely out of harm's way, for the time being at least. By now he would be back in Trinity. Hastings consoled himself with that. His was an ancient line, and it would continue through Seph. Throughout more than a hundred years of risk and intrigue, that had never seemed important. Until now.

A slight sound at the door alerted him that someone was coming. The bolt slid back, and then he was blinded as the switch was thrown and the bare bulb kindled. Someone came and stood over him, backlit by the fixture.

"Mr. Hastings."

"Martin? What a pleasant surprise." Those few words seemed to claim all his breath.

Martin dropped to his knees beside him. "They're coming for you. We only have a few minutes."

"They're coming for me?" Hastings tried to show a spark of interest. "What for?"

"To kill you. There's two wizards dead already. And I think we're going to kill some more people after you." Martin stared at the floor.

"Who's dead?"

"Ravenstock. And Hadrian Brennan, from the Wizard Council."

"From the Wizard Council?" Hastings's sluggish mind tried to fit that into some scheme. "Why are you attacking them? What's going on?"

Martin's eyes slid away. "Dr. Leicester wrote up a new constitution. Everybody just signed it. He and D'Orsay are kings for life. Something like that."

"I see. So, Martin. Why are you here?"

"I wanted to tell you that I'm sorry for everything that's happened."

Hastings sighed. "If you've come to make confession, I can scarcely offer absolution."

But Martin rolled on. "I understand why you killed Joseph. It was a brave thing to do. Dr. Leicester was . . . was torturing him. Leicester is a coward. He was afraid of Joseph. Even . . . even with our help. That's why he kept him doped up on Weirsbane. And he's afraid of you. That's why he had me place the torc."

And then, unexpectedly he smiled, the brown eyes lighting behind his glasses. "Only the wizard who places a *gefyllan de sefa* can remove it," he said. He reached for the collar.

Hastings held up a hand. "Are you sure you want to do this? It probably won't make any difference in the end."

"It does to me."

"Leicester will kill you."

"I don't really care." Again, Martin reached toward Hastings, took hold of the collar around his neck, and manipulated the catch. The torc fell away, landing with a clang on the stone floor. It was sooty black, tarnished, and unrecognizable as the jeweled collar Martin had placed three days before.

The immediate effect was anything but pleasant. The little power that was left in Hastings slammed back into his stone, protecting the source over everything else. For a moment, Hastings thought he might vomit all over Martin Hall. He leaned his head back against the wall, taking deep breaths.

"It's not that I'm not grateful, but it's a pity you couldn't have managed this a day or two ago."

Martin picked up the collar. "Now I'll reverse the charm. But I'm afraid it will take some time to restore your stone fully. And . . ." He glanced toward the door. Hastings could hear it, too. Someone coming.

Martin refastened the collar around Hastings's neck, fumbling in his haste. It was all Hastings could do to submit. He would prefer dying unencumbered. Martin muttered the countercharm as the door opened.

Leicester had sent only three of the alumni to fetch him, a reflection of Hastings's presumed diminished powers and the need to keep watch on those council in the chamber. The one in the lead, Bruce Hays, skidded to a halt when he saw Martin. "What are you doing here?"

"I've asked Mr. Hastings to forgive us for everything we've done," Martin said, without hesitation. "I wanted him to understand we had no choice."

"Oh, please." Hays rolled his eyes. "Do you realize how powerful we'll be under the new constitution? We'll be the enforcers. We'll have all the toys at our disposal. Unlimited access to the servant guilds."

Hastings could feel the power returning, a faint trickle, like good brandy into his gut. So slowly.

Hays unfastened the chains from the wall. They hauled him to his feet and propelled him toward the door, Martin Hall following behind. They half lifted him up the stairs, out of the cellar, and into the fresher air above.

Hastings looked quickly about him when they entered the hall. The Weir representatives were seated around a large table at the center of the room, bodies locked in place. Thirty-odd members of the Wizard Council were ranged along the wall, similarly incapacitated.

Linda was seated at the head of the table. Leicester was standing just behind her, his hands resting on her shoulders. She had her enchanter mask on, the carefully blank expression that could mean anything at all. Hastings could tell that it frustrated Leicester, and he smothered a smile.

But then Linda saw Hastings, and the mask slipped a little. Her expression was complex: surprise, pain, a question. She thinks I killed our son, Hastings reminded himself. And realized that she might never learn the truth.

The end of the room opposite the door was anchored by a huge fireplace. What looked like an executioner's block had been placed just in front of the hearth. Leicester's young wizards were milling around it. This, then, was their destination.

Hays directed Hastings to stand just behind the block. The alumni arranged themselves in two arcs on either side of the fireplace with the stone at their center and the open end toward the conference table. The wizards along the perimeter and the other Weir at the table shifted and whispered like a class at dismissal time.

Leicester faced his audience. "Under the new constitution, punishment for traitorous activity will be quick and direct, as it was in centuries past. This serves all of us.

"For years, a traitorous wizard who styles himself as the Dragon has interfered with the administration of the Rules of Engagement and incited the servant guilds to rebellion against their lawful lords and masters. The fact that he has survived this long speaks to our lack of an organized enforcement entity.

"Through our efforts, we have captured the Dragon and disabled the gift that he has dishonored and misused. We will now mete out justice before your eyes."

A rumble of excitement and dismay rolled through the crowd: muted excitement from the wizards on the perimeter and dismay around the table.

Two of the alumni advanced, bearing an elaborate velvet robe that they settled about Leicester's shoulders. Two more came forward carrying a long, jeweled case. They knelt before Leicester and opened the case. He lifted from it an elaborate staff that he held aloft in his two hands.

"Leander Hastings, known as the Dragon, you have been convicted of treason and inciting of rebellion among the servant guilds. Do you have anything to say before your sentencing?"

Hastings raised his brows. "I've been convicted? Somehow that got by me. By what court?"

"You're a traitor, Hastings. You don't deserve due process."

Hastings looked him up and down. "You always did like to play dress-up, Gregory. Get on with it, then."

"And so for these crimes you are sentenced to death. Sentence to be carried out immediately."

"Leicester! May I speak?" It was Linda.

Hastings swore under his breath. "Linda, no. Leave it be."

Linda ignored him. "I have something to say relative to this man's crimes."

"Just get on with it, will you?" Hastings said to Leicester. "Don't you have other murders to commit yet tonight?" He looked over at the wizards against the wall, and they shifted uneasily.

Leicester smiled. "No, Hastings, I think she deserves to

be heard. After all, you murdered her son." He walked back to where Linda was sitting, yanked her to her feet, and led her to the front of the room, pointing her at the defendant. "Speak!"

But Linda did not speak to Hastings. Instead, she turned and addressed the assembly. "Leicester and D'Orsay are to be commended. God knows, they are efficient. Risking life and limb, they kidnapped an adolescent boy so they could lure the Dragon here to Second Sister. They captured the notorious Leander Hastings, locked him in a wine cellar, and within hours, convicted him of a capital crime. Now they propose to summarily execute him.

"What are the Dragon's crimes? He is known to be in the habit of asking difficult questions. He is a spymaster who turns over stones and exposes what's underneath. He reveals secrets. On occasion, his followers have stolen magical objects and blown things up. Yet it seems to me the Dragon's greatest crime has been revealing the truth about the guild hierarchy."

You could have heard the beat of a butterfly's wing in the hall. The whisper of snow sifting into the treetops.

D'Orsay shook his head as if he couldn't believe what he was hearing.

Linda went on. "Tyranny is the most efficient form of government. But I would suggest that due process has a purpose. That there is a difference between efficiency and justice. You see, Leander Hastings is not the Dragon. I am."

As soon as she said it, Seph knew it was true. From the elegant way she'd gutted Leicester and D'Orsay. From the look on Leander Hastings's face. From so many mysteries finally explained.

The solution to a puzzle seems obvious, once you know what it is.

Jason nudged him. "So, Seph. Guess you're the son of the Dragon after all," he said dryly.

Leicester and D'Orsay were staring at Linda as if they'd never really seen her before. And might never underestimate her again.

"So," Leicester said, attempting to regain his equilibrium. "We have here the brains and body of the rebellion. We are most thankful that you spoke up, Ms. Downey, in time to prevent a serious miscarriage of justice. It appears that two executions are called for, instead of one."

"Come, Gregory," D'Orsay said hastily. "Surely not. Such a waste, I mean, an *enchanter*? Surely she can be rehabilitated."

"We've got to do *something*," Seph muttered. "Even if we can't do what we originally planned."

"Let's split up and take our stations," Jason whispered. "I'm going up to the gallery."

Seph concealed himself in the alcove just outside the butler's pantry. He turned and tapped gently on the warded door, hoping Madison might hear him and Leicester and D'Orsay would not.

"Madison!"

No answer. Seph turned back to the hall and peered out from his hiding place next to the fireplace.

Leicester had prevailed, because Seph's parents were being escorted to the front of the room by a crowd of nervous alumni as Leicester stood by with the staff. It appeared to be the same one he'd used the night at the outdoor chapel, when he'd tried to "recruit" Seph. It seemed a decade ago.

"Perhaps, just this once, we'll forgo 'ladies first,'" Leicester said, smiling. "So you can watch the execution of the man who murdered your son."

They shoved Hastings to his knees. Leicester gripped the staff with both hands, raised it high.

Then Martin Hall said, "Look!" He was focused on something over Leicester's shoulder. Leicester swung around to see the shimmer in the air behind them coalesce rapidly into a terrifying presence.

It stretched from the floor nearly to the ceiling in the great hall. Flames bled off in all directions, writhed against the ceiling and licked the stone floor. Showers of sparks cascaded over the assembly and exploded into the galleries. The image continually shifted shape, but it was too bright to look at for very long, anyway. Although it was midday, the light coming from the windows in the galleries seemed to have been extinguished. The room was illuminated only by the fireplace, and by a Dragon whose glittering wings reached from wall to wall.

The alumni backed away, leaving the prisoners alone at the block. Hastings pushed to his feet and faced the dragon, shoving Linda behind him. He was frowning, as if puzzled, but he didn't look particularly frightened.

Leicester stared fixedly at the image before him, the color bleached from his face by its brilliance. Seph sensed the headmaster's mind questing out, trying to discover and destroy the wizard behind the image, but finding nothing, no trail of magic, no stone, no flesh and blood to focus on.

Jason Haley, the puppeteer, was safely ensconced in the gallery above.

The dragon's voice reverberated through the hall. "Who dares to tamper with the constitution consecrated at Raven's Ghyll last Midsummer's Day?"

The alumni stirred and muttered, backstepping yet again.

"Quite the pet you have there, Hastings," Leicester said. "Does he have a name?"

Hastings looked from the dragon to Leicester and shook his head. "It isn't mine."

"It takes very little power to conjure a phantom. Apparently we haven't wrung you dry as yet. We'll see if it disappears when you're dead." He turned to the alumni. "It's just a construct. It can't hurt us. Proceed." The alumni shuffled forward unenthusiastically.

Now to give the dragon some bite. Seph disabled the unnoticeable charm and stepped back into the partial concealment of the pantry. He focused on Leicester, drew power in from all his extremities, collecting it in his arms and fingers, then gave it everything he had as the dragon breathed out. Flame slammed into Leicester, ran in hungry rivulets over his skin, charred his elegant clothes, and scorched the floor all around him before being drawn into the head of the staff, leaving Leicester still standing, astonished, but unhurt. Linked as he was with the alumni, he was just too strong.

Seph had made an impression, just the same. As far as the alumni were concerned, Leicester's harmless "construct" had just spewed flame clear across the hall. Pushing and shoving, they fled toward the back of the room.

If wizard fire made no impression, perhaps something else would. An enormous candelabra hung from the ceiling at the front of the room. Seph flamed the cable, focusing white-hot heat on the metal fittings. It finally parted, sending the fixture crashing to the floor. Leicester just managed to sidestep out of the way.

The flames in the sconces along the walls flared up and ran across the ceiling, charring the ceiling beams. Next, Seph collected armloads of air, hardened it, and smashed through the gallery windows. Shards of glass pinged on the stone floor. The roar of the storm was suddenly amplified, and rain poured down on them.

The Dragon spoke again. "Leicester's wizard slaves! It is time to reclaim what has been stolen from you. You are more powerful than any wizard, if you work together, as you have been taught. You believe you are owned by another, but you belong to me, before all else!"

Seph wasn't so sure that was true, but it was enough to enrage Leicester. He screamed at the cowering alumni. "This is wizardry, you idiots! It's a wizard behind all of this! I'll show you." Spinning, he thrust forward the staff. Flame gouted from the crystalline tip and slammed into Hastings, throwing him backward onto the stone floor, where he lay still, his clothes smoldering.

There was a dead silence, save the shriek of the wind and clatter of the rain.

Linda knelt next to Hastings and cradled his head in her lap.

Leicester turned to look at the dragon. It hung over them mournfully for a long moment, wingtips drooping a little, then reared up, drawing its lips back to reveal stalactite-size teeth.

Flame gushed forth, enveloping Leicester. The hot breath of the dragon extended to the far end of the hall, blackening the walnut paneling around the doorway and setting the papers on the conference table aflame. Smoke and confusion filled the chamber. People were screaming, shouting orders, demanding to be released.

But when the flames died away, Leicester was still on his feet, though noticeably singed and unsettled.

"Cut us loose before we're incinerated where we sit!" Wylie demanded from the sidelines. "This is obviously not Hastings's work unless the man can conjure from the grave."

Now Leicester focused his attention on the dragon, extending the staff, sending bolt after bolt of wizard fire into the beast. The dragon remained unharmed, but the wall of the conference room began to disintegrate under the assault. Seph ducked back into the butler's pantry to avoid falling masonry. The huge stone fireplace was reduced to heaps of rubble and he could see into the corridors beyond the conference room.

Seph looked for other targets. Claude D'Orsay had taken cover when the fireworks started. Sedgwick and Whitehead were nowhere to be seen.

Seph slammed his fist against the wall in frustration and pain. His father lay dead on the conference room floor. He and Jason were taking the winery apart, but it would do no good if they couldn't take down Leicester. Sooner or later, the headmaster would figure out what was going on and nail them. The only thing he could think of was to go after the alumni, try and pick them off one by one, diminishing Leicester's power.

But he knew that at least some, if not all, of the alumni were unwilling participants in Leicester's schemes. He thought of nervous Peter Conroy with his inhaler and Martin Hall, the principled viniculturist. Wayne Eggars, the physician, and little Ashton Rice, the music teacher. He forced himself to make a list in his mind, putting them in priority order. Barber would be first, of course, but he was out in the garden. Then Bruce Hays, who'd seemed to enjoy torturing Ellen and the others.

All the while, he maintained a constant assault on Gregory Leicester, keeping him and the others occupied, directing his fire to make it appear it was coming from Jason's dragon. Cautiously, he leaned out from his hiding place, looking for Bruce Hays, and was met with a blast of wizard fire that he only just turned by throwing up a shield and ducking back into hiding.

"Ah," said Leicester, sounding relieved. "I think we've discovered the guilty party."

Seph retreated into the butler's pantry, desperately trying to conceive of a plan. And backed into somebody who grabbed him around the waist.

"Witch Boy! Sounds like all hell's broken loose. Why didn't you come get me?"

It was Madison.

Seph didn't waste words. "Doors were blocked. And now I've been spotted."

Leicester continued his assault on his hiding place. Seph shoved Madison up against the wall and covered her body with his as masonry pelted him on the head and shoulders. A large chunk smashed into his right elbow with stunning force, and his arm went numb. "Look, you'd better get out of here. You might be resistant to wizardry, but if a wall falls on you, you're dead."

She shook her head. Bits of debris were caught in her hair, and her face was powdered with plaster dust. "No. We have to work the plan."

"Right. Like that's possible."

Seph moved cautiously forward with Madison just behind him. Just as he reached the entrance into the hall, Leicester called out to him.

"Joseph! Stop this foolishness and come out. Your mother wishes to speak with you."

Throwing up a shield, Seph stepped into the doorway and looked out into the conference room.

Leicester stood amid the ruins, one arm around Linda Downey, the other gripping her by the throat. "Surrender and I'll let her live."

Seph hesitated, glancing back at Madison. "You'll set her free?"

Leicester smiled, showing his teeth. "Of course. I have no quarrel with enchanters."

Linda screamed, "Seph! Don't you dare!" before Leicester silenced her.

"What about her?" Seph pointed over his shoulder at

Madison, who was shaking her head. "You'll leave my friend alone, too?"

If Leicester was surprised to see Madison, he didn't show it. "You have my word on it."

"All right." Seph stepped from the pantry, and taking a deep breath, he dropped his shield.

Leicester waited until he was clear of the doorway. Still using Linda as a shield, he raised the staff. A cataract of flame streaked toward Seph, an attack that should have reduced him to cinders. In what was one of the most difficult things he'd ever done, Seph stepped behind Madison Moss, allowing her to take the full brunt of the assault.

Seph watched Leicester. At first, the wizard smiled, eyes glittering, smug and triumphant. Then his face changed as doubt and then horror crept in. He staggered backward, hands still extended, bound to Madison by the force of the charm. He struggled to free himself, to let go of the staff, twisting and turning as power flowed from the alumni into him, then out of his body and into Madison.

All around the room, the alumni staggered and fell as they were drained, much the way Seph had collapsed that day on the beach. Then Leicester went down on his back, shaking violently, eyes wide, throwing off sparks like a broken power line. The link with the alumni was broken. Seph circled Madison and charged toward him.

But Jason was quicker. He vaulted over the railing of the gallery, hung a moment, then dropped to the floor next to Leicester. Kneeling next to the wizard's thrashing body, he reached for him, but Seph yanked him back.

"Don't touch him directly unless you want to be wrung out yourself."

Glancing around for a weapon, Jason bent and gripped a huge chunk of stone that had fallen from the fireplace. Between the two of them, Jason and Seph managed to lift it.

They smashed the stone down on Leicester's head. His heels drummed on the pavement for a long minute, and then he went still.

"That's for my father, John Haley," Jason gasped.

"And for *my* father, Leander Hastings, and for Trevor Hill, and for every alumnus of the Havens, gifted or not," Seph added. He turned his face away and shuddered. Jason sank to the floor amid the rubble and put his face in his hands.

Seph knew he should finish what he'd started, that he should determine the intentions of the alumni, find Claude D'Orsay, and do something about Warren Barber in the garden. But he did none of those things.

He felt too weary to take another step, but he forced himself to stagger across the room to where Madison stood braced against the wall, eyes wide, fists clenched, as if in shock. He was covered with blood, his elbow was swollen and misshapen where it had been hit by falling debris. He pulled her close. He could feel her heart pounding against his chest, her quick, shallow breaths.

He kept saying, "It's all right," and "I'm sorry," over and over. Then she was sobbing into his shoulder and he was patting her back, making little circles with his hand.

Finally, he pulled away and took her hand, leading her

over to where his mother cradled his father in her arms. He knelt next to her, full of regret, but empty of words to express it.

She greeted him with a brilliant smile, though tears ran down her face. "You're alive!" she said, shifting Hastings so she could grip Seph's hand.

Seph blinked back his own tears. "Mother," he said, the word large and awkward in his mouth. Then his voice broke. "I'm sorry," he said huskily.

But she was still smiling, rather damply. "When I said you were alive, I meant *both* of you."

It was impossible. Leaning forward, Seph looked down at his father and reached out and touched his cheek. It was warm, suffused with blood. Hastings frowned and shifted away, groaning. His eyelids fluttered, then opened, focused on his face.

Seph shook his head, still unable to believe it. "I don't get it. Leicester blasted you. No one could have survived that." He reached out and touched the collar around his father's neck. "Not in the shape you were in."

"It was Martin Hall." Hastings's voice was a hoarse whisper. "He removed the collar and reversed the charm before we came into the hall." He paused, took a breath. "I was still weak, but I'd managed to throw up a shield. I expected he might attack your mother or me."

The corners of his mouth twitched in amusement. "I must say, I was surprised when the dragon came to call. I had no idea where Jason was going with that." He struggled to sit upright, with Linda's help. "Aren't you supposed to be in Trinity?"

Jason spoke from behind him. "Dude ain't so easy to bully anymore. Some fool's been training him in wizardry."

Seph turned to look at him, and Jason managed a creditable courtly bow. "It's been my dream to meet the Dragon," he said, grinning at Linda. "But somehow, I always pictured him as a wizard with a long, gray beard. I think I like this better."

With the death of Leicester, a number of spells were broken. The immobilization charms dissolved, and the Interguild representatives and the Wizard Council collected into two distinct groups that eyed each other warily. Some organized themselves into an impromptu fire brigade and began putting out the fires that still smoldered throughout the room.

Ellen retrieved Leicester's staff and held it close by her side. Jack produced a wicked-looking knife from somewhere and was very obviously honing it against a stone pillar.

Nick Snowbeard came to look after Hastings, and Seph immediately felt more confident.

Madison still seemed to be in shock, a ghost with watercolor eyes, shivering and teeth chattering. Seph sat her down in one of the chairs by the conference table, wishing he knew what to do for her.

Wylie and Longbranch broke away from the rest of the Council and came toward them. "Where is D'Orsay?" they demanded, glaring at Seph.

Good question. "How should I know?" Seph replied. "I've been kind of busy."

"The constitution is missing, too. If he manages to get it to Raven's Ghyll, it will be a disaster." Wylie looked as if this were somehow Seph's fault.

"Then you'd better go after him, don't you think?" Seph said. "Maybe you can catch him at the dock."

"First we'll deal with his associates," Longbranch said.

The council conspirators were nowhere to be seen, but the alumni still lay where they'd fallen, as helpless as Seph had been on the beach. But they were alive, at least. Their link with Leicester had been broken when Maddie drained his power away.

Before Seph knew what she was about, Longbranch strode over to Ashton Rice, knelt, and shoved her fingers under his chin.

"Hey!" Seph gripped the wizard's wrist with his good hand and wrenched it away. "What do you think you're doing?"

She looked up at him in surprise and annoyance. "These young men are collaborators. Allies of D'Orsay and Leicester. Best to destroy them while we can."

"I wouldn't call them allies, exactly," Seph said. "More like victims, most of them."

"Don't you understand what's happening?" Longbranch spoke as one might to the mentally impaired. "This is war. The truce between wizards is over. Which side are you on?"

Suddenly Jack and Ellen flanked him. Jason and Madison drifted in from behind.

"I'm not on your side. Or D'Orsay's. You're going to have to have your war without me," Seph said.

"We'll see," Longbranch said. She extended her hand, and he took a step back, out of range of those long, red nails. "You're powerful, I'll give you that. You take after your father in that regard. You're going to have to decide whether to follow after him in other ways."

She looked over at Madison, studying her as if she were an especially interesting specimen. "What's your girl's name?" she asked, toying with a large emerald that hung from a chain around her neck.

Seph didn't honor that question with an answer.

Longbranch tch'ed. "Are you going to waste your life as a nursemaid to the servant guilds or learn to navigate the world of wizards, where the real power lies? Think about it."

"I don't have to think about it," Seph said, but Longbranch had already turned away.

Jack and Ellen were looking curiously at Jason. With the death of Gregory Leicester, some of Jason's intensity and spirit seemed to have drained away. He leaned against a stone pillar, looking tired and thin, almost ill. It reminded Seph of his first day in Trinity, when he was the outsider.

"Jack Swift and Ellen Stephenson, this is Jason Haley," Seph said. "He's a friend from the Havens. He saved my life."

Leicester still lay on the floor where he had fallen. Seph felt no joy at the way he had died, only intense relief and the conviction that the death of the wizard was a matter of survival for him and the people he cared about.

Up in the gallery, the newly freed Warren Barber looked down on the survivors of the battle in the conference room. He felt an incredible joy. He was on his own again, no longer answerable to any authority. Up until a short while ago, Leicester had seemed like the horse to back. But he'd died like anyone else. The rest of the alumni lay on the floor like so many carcasses. They deserved to be ruled, he thought. But not Warren Barber. He would not let that happen, ever again.

He thought of McCauley's girl, and his breath came quicker. First, there was the episode at the river, when she'd put King down on his back. Then Warren had tried to spell her in the garden, and had gone down like a rock. Leicester and the alumni had done no better. Was she a wizard with a powerful stone, or was she carrying an amulet of some kind? Warren was no scholar, but he figured he could find out.

He couldn't resist sliding his hand inside his shirt, feeling the parchment that lay next to his skin. It had been easy enough to nick it from the desk where Hanlon had hidden it. He knew all the hiding places at Second Sister.

He hadn't decided what he would do with it, but he knew it represented power. D'Orsay would give anything to get his hands on it. So would anyone on the council. Then again, why shouldn't Warren Barber be king?

❦ CHAPTER TWENTY-TWO ❧
TRINITY AND CUMBRIA

"As you can see, we have a large family in Britain, Seph." Hastings gestured, taking in the tumbled grave-stones that broke through the wind-blasted heather. "Unfortunately, they're all underground."

Seph stooped and picked up a broken piece of granite. He scraped away at the moss that obscured the inscription on the nearest marker until it was revealed. HASTYNGS. He traced the letters with his fingers and looked back toward the great stone house. It brooded in boreal grandeur amid the frowning fells, set in a valley stitched over with stone walls. The light was decaying, although it was only late afternoon. Dusk came early this far north. Cumbria. Home of his ancestors. Hastings—his father—said the house had been in the family for gener-ations.

As he watched, Jason emerged from the house, waved

to get their attention, and disappeared back inside. "I guess dinner is ready," Seph said. He stuffed his gloved hands into his pockets.

"I feel like I've found a family and a home, and Jason lost his," he said.

Hastings stared off toward Scotland, his face bleak and still as the weathered hills. "I promised Jason that if he stayed in Trinity and finished school, I would get him involved in wizard politics." Without shifting his gaze, he answered Seph's unspoken objection. "Believe me, I know all about the cost of holding on to anger, yet I can't talk him out of it. He still wants to go after D'Orsay."

The political future of the Weirguilds was still cloudy. The council that had met at Second Sister had signed off on the Hastings-Downey constitution before they disbanded, but it was unclear how to get the document consecrated. The whereabouts of the Leicester-D'Orsay constitution was unknown. And, for the first time in more than five hundred years, the wizards were officially at war.

Linda and Hastings often held strategy sessions at the house that lasted late into the night. Sometimes Hastings was still there in the morning.

The role of family man did not come easily to Hastings. Much of Hastings and Seph's time together was spent in training: reviews of charms and countercharms, tutorials on the Old Magic. Seph realized his father was doing his best to hone his skills in wizardry for his own protection. That was love, delivered in Hastings's relentless fashion.

Madison was still working at the Legends and attending classes at Trinity. Despite her apprehension, she melded well with the upscale, grunge, art-student culture. Her work was even featured by one of the galleries close to campus.

She'd been wary of Seph since the episode at Second Sister. She held back, kept secrets as if she saw a new risk in their relationship that hadn't been there before. She was friendly enough, but he almost had the sense she was avoiding being alone with him. Linda had offered to fly her to Britain for Christmas, but she'd gone home to Coalton County instead.

Seph had chosen a present for her, four framed sketches of cathedrals he'd found in a gallery in London.

Hastings broke into his reverie. "We'd better go back. It won't do to be late to dinner on Christmas Eve."

Dinner was served by candlelight in the great hall, roast beef and vegetables and Yorkshire puddings: a feast for three people, and they'd all had a hand in it. Afterward, they ate Stilton and pears and drank wine by the fire while the snow came down outside. Later, they would brave the weather to attend midnight mass at the Catholic church down in the village. Seph hoped it would keep snowing. Hastings had promised to bring out the sleigh.

Brightly wrapped packages of intriguing possibility waited under the towering Douglas fir in the hearth corner.

Hastings went first. For Seph, there were two books of spellcraft from Hastings's private collection. For Jason, a pair of English climbing boots, suitable for winter hikes in the fells. For Linda, a pendant with the flat-gray color of a sorcerer's piece, set with garnet.

Linda had a barn coat for Hastings, a heavy Scots-wool sweater for Jason. And a mysterious package for Seph. When she put it into his hands and he felt the weight of it, he knew what it was before he tore the paper away. It was his Weirbook, his history between his hands.

When Seph looked back at the events of the summer and fall, he realized his personal philosophy had changed. "Don't expect much, and you won't be disappointed," he'd always said, a kind of charm of self-protection.

He had never planned on or expected parents, let alone a complicated pair like Linda Downey and Leander Hastings. As a family, they were still just a collection of strangers. *Who knows what will happen?* But he couldn't help but be optimistic.

Madison was still a mystery to him, but a mystery he hoped to solve. He would find a way to make it work, because he finally understood that sometimes you have to raise your expectations. And sometimes you need to make a claim on the world and the people you love to get what you most desire.